S0-EPP-443

ALPHONSE DAUDET

INTERNATIONAL
SHORT STORIES

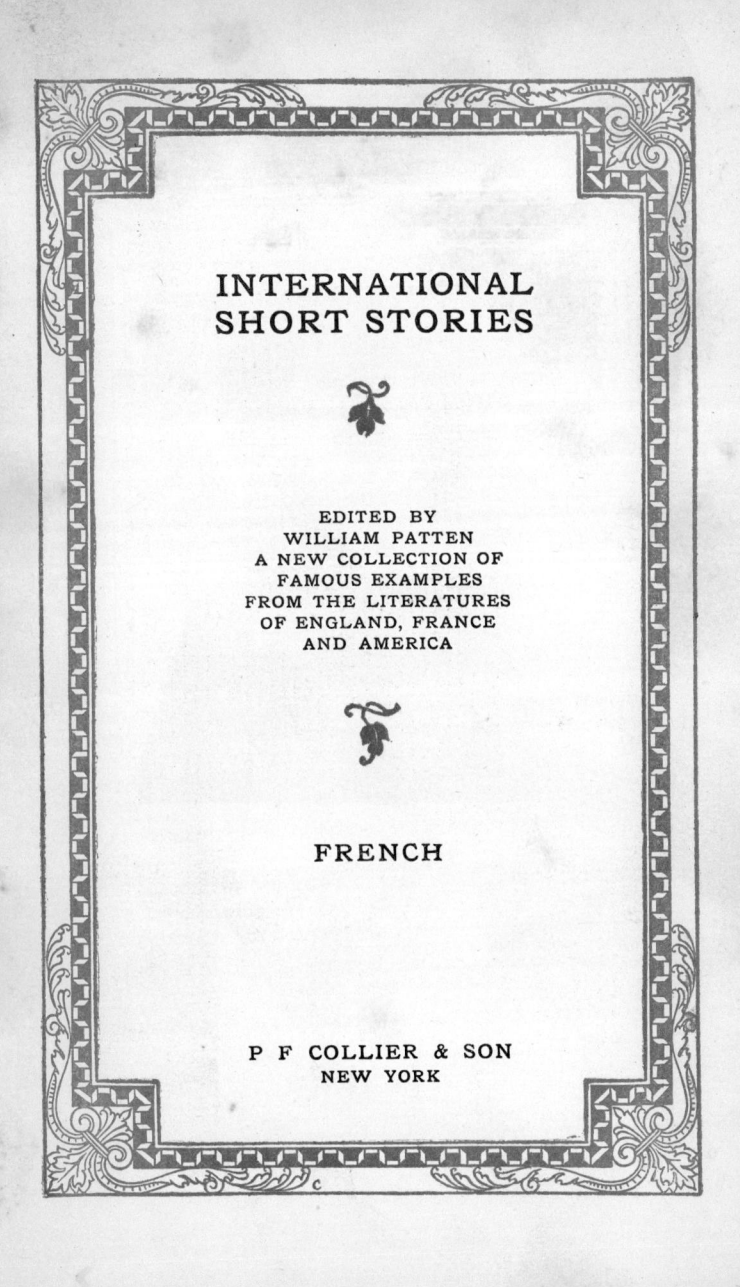

EDITED BY
WILLIAM PATTEN
A NEW COLLECTION OF
FAMOUS EXAMPLES
FROM THE LITERATURES
OF ENGLAND, FRANCE
AND AMERICA

FRENCH

P F COLLIER & SON
NEW YORK

Copyright, 1910
BY P. F. COLLIER & SON

The use of the copyrighted stories in this collection has been authorized in each case by their authors or by their representatives.

FRENCH STORIES

A PIECE OF BREAD	By Francois Coppee	2
THE ELIXIR OF LIFE	By Honore de Balzac	13
THE AGE FOR LOVE	By Paul Bourget	37
MATEO FALCONE	By Prosper Merimee	53
THE MIRROR	By Catulle Mendes	69
MY NEPHEW JOSEPH	By Ludovic Halevy	77
A FOREST BETROTHAL	By Erckmann-Chatrian	89
ZADIG THE BABYLONIAN	By Francois Marie Arouet de Voltaire	103
ABANDONED	By Guy de Maupassant	161
THE GUILTY SECRET	By Paul de Kock	171
JEAN MONETTE	By Eugene Francois Vidocq	181
SOLANGE: DR. LEDRU'S STORY OF THE REIGN OF TERROR	By Alexandre Dumas	191
THE BIRDS IN THE LETTER-BOX	By Rene Bazin	209
JEAN GOURDON'S FOUR DAYS	By Emile Zola	217
BARON DE TRENCK	By Clemence Robert	263
THE PASSAGE OF THE RED SEA	By Henry Murger	283
THE WOMAN AND THE CAT	By Marcel Prevost	291
GIL BLAS AND DR. SANGRADO	By Alain Rene Le Sage	303
A FIGHT WITH A CANNON	By Victor Hugo	315
TONTON	By A. Cheneviere	329
THE LAST LESSON	By Alphonse Daudet	337
CROISILLES	By Alfred de Musset	345
THE VASE OF CLAY	By Jean Aicard	375

A PIECE OF BREAD[1]

By FRANCOIS COPPEE

THE young Duc de Hardimont happened to be at Aix in Savoy, whose waters he hoped would benefit his famous mare, Perichole, who had become wind-broken since the cold she had caught at the last Derby,—and was finishing his breakfast while glancing over the morning paper, when he read the news of the disastrous engagement at Reichshoffen.

He emptied his glass of chartreuse, laid his napkin upon the restaurant table, ordered his valet to pack his trunks, and two hours later took the express to Paris; arriving there, he hastened to the recruiting office and enlisted in a regiment of the line.

In vain had he led the enervating life of a fashionable swell —that was the word of the time—and had knocked about race-course stables from the age of nineteen to twenty-five. In circumstances like these, he could not forget that Enguerrand de Hardimont died of the plague at Tunis the same day as Saint Louis, that Jean de Hardimont commanded the Free Companies under Du Guesclin, and that François-Henri de Hardimont was killed at Fontenoy with "Red" Maison. Upon learning that France had lost a battle on French soil, the young duke felt the blood mount to his face, giving him a horrible feeling of suffocation.

And so, early in November, 1870, Henri de Hardimont returned to Paris with his regiment, forming part of Vinoy's corps, and his company being the advance guard before the redoubt of Hautes Bruyères, a position fortified in haste, and which protected the cannon of Fort Bicêtre.

It was a gloomy place; a road planted with clusters of broom, and broken up into muddy ruts, traversing the leprous

[1] Copyrighted 1896 Current Literature Publishing Company.

fields of the neighborhood; on the border stood an abandoned tavern, a tavern with arbors, where the soldiers had established their post. They had fallen back here a few days before; the grape-shot had broken down some of the young trees, and all of them bore upon their bark the white scars of bullet wounds. As for the house, its appearance made one shudder; the roof had been torn by a shell, and the walls seemed whitewashed with blood. The torn and shattered arbors under their network of twigs, the rolling of an upset cask, the high swing whose wet rope groaned in the damp wind, and the inscriptions over the door, furrowed by bullets; "Cabinets de societé—Absinthe—Vermouth—Vin à 60 cent. le litre"—encircling a dead rabbit painted over two billiard cues tied in a cross by a ribbon,—all this recalled with cruel irony the popular entertainment of former days. And over all, a wretched winter sky, across which rolled heavy leaden clouds, an odious sky, angry and hateful.

At the door of the tavern stood the young duke, motionless, with his gun in his shoulder-belt, his cap over his eyes, his benumbed hands in the pockets of his red trousers, and shivering in his sheepskin coat. He gave himself up to his sombre thoughts, this defeated soldier, and looked with sorrowful eyes toward a line of hills, lost in the fog, where could be seen each moment, the flash and smoke of a Krupp gun, followed by a report.

Suddenly he felt hungry.

Stooping, he drew from his knapsack, which stood near him leaning against the wall, a piece of ammunition bread, and as he had lost his knife, he bit off a morsel and slowly ate it.

But after a few mouthfuls, he had enough of it; the bread was hard and had a bitter taste. No fresh would be given until the next morning's distribution, so the commissary officer had willed it. This was certainly a very hard life sometimes. The remembrance of former breakfasts came to him, such as he had called "hygienic," when, the day after too over-heating a supper, he would seat himself by a window on the ground floor of the Café-Anglais, and be served with a cutlet, or buttered eggs with asparagus tips, and the butler, knowing his tastes, would bring him a fine bottle of old

A PIECE OF BREAD

Léoville, lying in its basket, and which he would pour out with the greatest care. The deuce take it! That was a good time, all the same, and he would never become accustomed to this life of wretchedness.

And, in a moment of impatience, the young man threw the rest of his bread into the mud.

At the same moment a soldier of the line came from the tavern, stooped and picked up the bread, drew back a few steps, wiped it with his sleeve and began to devour it eagerly.

Henri de Hardimont was already ashamed of his action, and now with a feeling of pity, watched the poor devil who gave proof of such a good appetite. He was a tall, large young fellow, but badly made; with feverish eyes and a hospital beard, and so thin that his shoulder-blades stood out beneath his well-worn cape.

"You are very hungry?" he said, approaching the soldier.

"As you see," replied the other with his mouth full.

"Excuse me then. For if I had known that you would like the bread, I would not have thrown it away."

"It does not harm it," replied the soldier, "I am not dainty."

"No matter," said the gentleman, "it was wrong to do so, and I reproach myself. But I do not wish you to have a bad opinion of me, and as I have some old cognac in my can, let us drink a drop together."

The man had finished eating. The duke and he drank a mouthful of brandy; the acquaintance was made.

"What is your name?" asked the soldier of the line.

"Hardimont," replied the duke, omitting his title. "And yours?"

"Jean-Victor—I have just entered this company—I am just out of the ambulance—I was wounded at Châtillon—oh! but it was good in the ambulance, and in the infirmary they gave me horse bouillon. But I had only a scratch, and the major signed my dismissal. So much the worse for me! Now I am going to commence to be devoured by hunger again—for, believe me, if you will, comrade, but, such as you see me, I have been hungry all my life."

The words were startling, especially to a Sybarite who had just been longing for the kitchen of the Café-Anglais, and the

FRANCOIS COPPEE

Duc de Hardimont looked at his companion in almost terrified amazement. The soldier smiled sadly, showing his hungry, wolf-like teeth, as white as his sickly face, and, as if understanding that the other expected something further in the way of explanation or confidence:

"Come," said he, suddenly ceasing his familiar way of speaking, doubtless divining that his companion belonged to the rich and happy; "let us walk along the road to warm our feet, and I will tell you things, which probably you have never heard of—I am called Jean-Victor, that is all, for I am a foundling, and my only happy remembrance is of my earliest childhood, at the Asylum. The sheets were white on our little beds in the dormitory; we played in a garden under large trees, and a kind Sister took care of us, quite young and as pale as a wax-taper—she died afterwards of lung trouble— I was her favorite, and would rather walk by her than play with the other children, because she used to draw me to her side and lay her warm thin hand on my forehead. But when I was twelve years old, after my first communion, there was nothing but poverty. The managers put me as apprentice with a chair mender in Faubourg Saint-Jacques. That is not a trade, you know, it is impossible to earn one's living at it, and as proof of it, the greater part of the time the master was only able to engage the poor little blind boys from the Blind Asylum. It was there that I began to suffer with hunger. The master and mistress, two old Limousins—afterwards murdered, were terrible misers, and the bread, cut in tiny pieces for each meal, was kept under lock and key the rest of the time. You should have seen the mistress at supper time serving the soup, sighing at each ladleful she dished out. The other apprentices, two blind boys, were less unhappy; they were not given more than I, but they could not see the reproachful look the wicked woman used to give me as she handed me my plate. And then, unfortunately, I was always so terribly hungry. Was it my fault, do you think? I served there for three years, in a continual fit of hunger. Three years! And one can learn the work in one month. But the managers could not know everything, and had no suspicion that the children were abused. Ah! you were astonished just now when you saw me take the bread out of

A PIECE OF BREAD

the mud? I am used to that for I have picked up enough of it; and crusts from the dust, and when they were too hard and dry, I would soak them all night in my basin. I had windfalls sometimes, such as pieces of bread nibbled at the ends, which the children would take out of their baskets and throw on the sidewalks as they came from school. I used to try to prowl around there when I went on errands. At last my time was ended at this trade by which no man can support himself. Well, I did many other things, for I was willing enough to work. I served the masons; I have been shop-boy, floor-polisher, I don't know what all! But, pshaw; to-day, work is lacking, another time I lose my place. Briefly, I never have had enough to eat. Heavens! how often have I been crazy with hunger as I have passed the bakeries! Fortunately for me, at these times I have always remembered the good Sister at the Asylum, who so often told me to be honest, and I seemed to feel her warm little hand upon my forehead. At last, when I was eighteen I enlisted; you know as well as I do, that the trooper has only just enough. Now,—I could almost laugh—here is the siege and famine! You see, I did not lie, when I told you just now that I have always, always, been hungry!"

The young duke had a kind heart, and was profoundly moved by this terrible story, told him by a man like himself, by a soldier whose uniform made him his equal. It was even fortunate for the phlegm of this dandy, that the night wind dried the tears which dimmed his eyes.

"Jean-Victor," said he, ceasing in his turn, by a delicate tact, to speak familiarly to the foundling, "if we survive this dreadful war, we will meet again, and I hope that I may be useful to you. But, in the meantime, as there is no bakery but the commissary, and as my ration of bread is twice too large for my delicate appetite,—it is understood, is it not?— we will share it like good comrades."

It was strong and hearty, the hand-clasp which followed: then, harassed and worn by their frequent watches and alarms, as night fell, they returned to the tavern, where twelve soldiers were sleeping on the straw; and throwing themselves down side by side, they were soon sleeping soundly.

FRANCOIS COPPEE

Toward midnight Jean-Victor awoke, being hungry probably. The wind had scattered the clouds, and a ray of moonlight made its way into the room through a hole in the roof, lighting up the handsome blonde head of the young duke, who was sleeping like an Endymion.

Still touched by the kindness of his comrade, Jean-Victor was gazing at him with admiration, when the sergeant of the platoon opened the door and called the five men who were to relieve the sentinels of the out-posts. The duke was of the number, but he did not waken when his name was called.

"Hardimont, stand up!" repeated the non-commissioned officer.

"If you are willing, sergeant," said Jean-Victor rising, "I will take his duty, he is sleeping so soundly—and he is my comrade."

"As you please."

The five men left, and the snoring recommenced.

But half an hour later the noise of near and rapid firing burst upon the night. In an instant every man was on his feet, and each with his hand on the chamber of his gun, stepped cautiously out, looking earnestly along the road, lying white in the moonlight.

"What time is it?" asked the duke. "I was to go on duty to-night."

"Jean-Victor went in your place."

At that moment a soldier was seen running toward them along the road.

"What is it?" they cried as he stopped, out of breath.

"The Prussians have attacked us, let us fall back to the redoubt."

"And your comrades?"

"They are coming—all but poor Jean-Victor."

"Where is he?" cried the duke.

"Shot through the head with a bullet—died without a word!—ough!"

*   *   *   *   *

One night last winter, the Duc de Hardimont left his club about two o'clock in the morning, with his neighbor, Count de Saulnes; the duke had lost some hundred louis, and had a slight headache.

A PIECE OF BREAD

"If you are willing, André," he said to his companion, "we will go home on foot—I need the air."

"Just as you please, I am willing, although the walking may be bad."

They dismissed their coupés, turned up the collars of their overcoats, and set off toward the Madeleine. Suddenly an object rolled before the duke which he had struck with the toe of his boot; it was a large piece of bread spattered with mud.

Then to his amazement, Monsieur de Saulnes saw the Duc de Hardimont pick up the piece of bread, wipe it carefully with his handkerchief embroidered with his armorial bearings, and place it on a bench, in full view under the gaslight.

"What did you do that for?" asked the count, laughing heartily, "are you crazy?"

"It is in memory of a poor fellow who died for me," replied the duke in a voice which trembled slightly, "do not laugh, my friend, it offends me."

THE ELIXIR OF LIFE
BY HONORE DE BALZAC

THE ELIXIR OF LIFE

By HONORE DE BALZAC

IN a sumptuous palace of Ferrara, one winter evening, Don Juan Belvidéro was entertaining a prince of the house of Este. In those days a banquet was a marvelous affair, which demanded princely riches or the power of a nobleman. Seven pleasure-loving women chatted gaily around a table lighted by perfumed candles, surrounded by admirable works of art whose white marble stood out against the walls of red stucco and contrasted with the rich Turkey carpets. Clad in satin, glittering with gold and laden with gems which sparkled only less brilliantly than their eyes, they all told of passions, intense, but of various styles, like their beauty. They differed neither in their words nor their ideas; but an expression, a look, a motion or an emphasis served as a commentary, unrestrained, licentious, melancholy or bantering, to their words.

One seemed to say: "My beauty has power to rekindle the frozen heart of age." Another: "I love to repose on soft cushions and think with rapture of my adorers." A third, a novice at these fêtes, was inclined to blush. "At the bottom of my heart I feel compunction," she seemed to say. "I am a Catholic and I fear hell; but I love you so—ah, so dearly—that I would sacrifice eternity to you!" The fourth, emptying a cup of Chian wine, cried: "Hurrah, for pleasure! I begin a new existence with each dawn. Forgetful of the past, still intoxicated with the violence of yesterday's pleasures, I embrace a new life of happiness, a life filled with love."

The woman sitting next to Belvidèro looked at him with flashing eyes. She was silent. "I should have no need to call on a bravo to kill my lover if he abandoned me." Then she had laughed; but a comfit dish of marvelous workmanship was shattered between her nervous fingers.

Copyrighted 1899 Current Literature Publishing Company.

"When are you to be grand duke?" asked the sixth of the prince, with an expression of murderous glee on her lips and a look of Bacchanalian frenzy in her eyes.

"And when is your father going to die?" said the seventh, laughing and throwing her bouquet to Don Juan with maddening coquetry. She was an innocent young girl who was accustomed to play with sacred things.

"Oh, don't speak of it!" cried the young and handsome Don Juan. "There is only one immortal father in the world, and unfortunately he is mine!"

The seven women of Ferrara, the friends of Don Juan, and the prince himself gave an exclamation of horror. Two hundred years later, under Louis XV., well-bred persons would have laughed at this sally. But perhaps at the beginning of an orgy the mind had still an unusual degree of lucidity. Despite the heat of the candles, the intensity of the emotions, the gold and silver vases, the fumes of wine, despite the vision of ravishing women, perhaps there still lurked in the depths of the heart a little of that respect for things human and divine which struggles until the revel has drowned it in floods of sparkling wine. Nevertheless, the flowers were already crushed, the eyes were steeped with drink, and intoxication, to quote Rabelais, had reached even to the sandals. In the pause that followed a door opened, and, as at the feast of Balthazar, God manifested himself, He seemed to command recognition now in the person of an old, white-haired servant with unsteady gait and drawn brows; he entered with gloomy mien and his look seemed to blight the garlands, the ruby cups, the pyramids of fruits, the brightness of the feast, the glow of the astonished faces and the colors of the cushions dented by the white arms of the women; then he cast a pall over this folly by saying, in a hollow voice, the solemn words: "Sir, your father is dying!"

Don Juan rose, making a gesture to his guests, which might be translated: "Excuse me, this does not happen every day."

Does not the death of a parent often overtake young people thus in the fulness of life, in the wild enjoyment of an orgy? Death is as unexpected in her caprices as a woman in

THE ELIXIR OF LIFE

her fancies, but more faithful—Death has never duped any one.

When Don Juan had closed the door of the banquet hall and walked down the long corridor, which was both cold and dark, he compelled himself to assume a mask, for, in thinking of his rôle of son, he had cast off his merriment as he threw down his napkin. The night was black. The silent servant who conducted the young man to the death chamber, lighted the way so insufficiently that Death, aided by the cold, the silence, the gloom, perhaps by a reaction of intoxication, was able to force some reflections into the soul of the spendthrift; he examined his life, and became thoughtful, like a man involved in a lawsuit when he sets out for the court of justice.

Bartholomeo Belvidéro, the father of Don Juan, was an old man of ninety, who had devoted the greater part of his life to business. Having traveled much in Oriental countries he had acquired there great wealth and learning more precious, he said, than gold or diamonds, to which he no longer gave more than a passing thought. "I value a tooth more than a ruby," he used to say, smiling, "and power more than knowledge." This good father loved to hear Don Juan relate his youthful adventures, and would say, banteringly, as he lavished money upon him: "Only amuse yourself, my dear child!" Never did an old man find such pleasure in watching a young man. Paternal love robbed age of its terrors in the delight of contemplating so brilliant a life.

At the age of sixty, Belvidéro had become enamored of an angel of peace and beauty. Don Juan was the sole fruit of this late love. For fifteen years the good man had mourned the loss of his dear Juana. His many servants and his son attributed the strange habits he had contracted to this grief. Bartholomeo lodged himself in the most uncomfortable wing of his palace and rarely went out, and even Don Juan could not intrude into his father's apartment without first obtaining permission. If this voluntary recluse came or went in the palace or in the streets of Ferrara he seemed to be searching for something which he could not find. He walked dreamily, undecidedly, preoccupied like a man battling with an idea or with a memory. While the young man gave magnificent entertainments and the palace re-echoed his mirth, while the horses pawed the ground in the courtyard and the pages quarreled at their game of dice on the stairs, Bartholomeo ate seven ounces of bread a day and drank water. If he asked for a little poultry it was merely that he might give the bones to a black spaniel, his faithful companion. He never complained of the noise. During his illness if the blast of horns or the barking of dogs interrupted his sleep, he only said: "Ah, Don Juan has come home." Never before was so untroublesome and indulgent a father to be found on this earth; consequently young Belvidéro, accustomed to treat him without ceremony, had all the faults of a spoiled child. His attitude toward Bartholomeo was like that of a capricious woman toward an elderly lover, passing off an impertinence with a smile, selling his good humor and submitting to be loved. In calling up the picture of his youth, Don Juan recognized that it would be difficult to find an instance in which his father's goodness had failed him. He felt a newborn remorse while he traversed the corridor, and he very nearly forgave his father for having lived so long. He reverted to feelings of filial piety, as a thief returns to honesty in the prospect of enjoying a well-stolen million.

Soon the young man passed into the high, chill rooms of his father's apartment. After feeling a moist atmosphere and breathing the heavy air and the musty odor which is given forth by old tapestries and furniture covered with dust, he found himself in the antique room of the old man, in front of a sick bed and near a dying fire. A lamp standing on a table of Gothic shape shed its streams of uneven light sometimes more, sometimes less strongly upon the bed and showed the form of the old man in ever-varying aspects. The cold air whistled through the insecure windows, and the snow beat with a dull sound against the panes.

This scene formed so striking a contrast to the one which Don Juan had just left that he could not help shuddering. He felt cold when, on approaching the bed, a sudden flare of light, caused by a gust of wind, illumined his father's face. The features were distorted; the skin, clinging tightly to the bones, had a greenish tint, which was made the more horrible by the whiteness of the pillows on which the old man rested; drawn with pain, the mouth, gaping and toothless, gave

FRANÇOIS COPPÉE

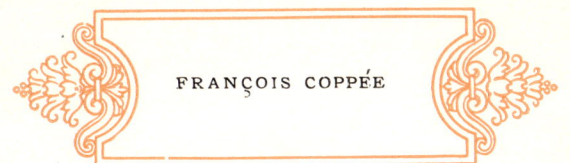

THE ELIXIR OF LIFE

breath to sighs which the howling of the tempest took up and drew out into a dismal wail. In spite of these signs of dissolution an incredible expression of power shone in the face. The eyes, hollowed by disease, retained a singular steadiness. A superior spirit was fighting there with death. It seemed as if Bartholomeo sought to kill with his dying look some enemy seated at the foot of his bed. This gaze, fixed and cold, was made the more appalling by the immobility of the head, which was like a skull standing on a doctor's table. The body, clearly outlined by the coverlet, showed that the dying man's limbs preserved the same rigidity. All was dead, except the eyes. There was something mechanical in the sounds which came from the mouth. Don Juan felt a certain shame at having come to the deathbed of his father with a courtesan's bouquet on his breast, bringing with him the odors of a banquet and the fumes of wine.

"You were enjoying yourself!" cried the old man, on seeing his son.

At the same moment the pure, high voice of a singer who entertained the guests, strengthened by the chords of the viol by which she was accompanied, rose above the roar of the storm and penetrated the chamber of death. Don Juan would gladly have shut out this barbarous confirmation of his father's words.

Bartholomeo said: "I do not grudge you your pleasure, my child."

These words, full of tenderness, pained Don Juan, who could not forgive his father for such goodness.

"What, sorrow for me, father!" he cried.

"Poor Juanino," answered the dying man, "I have always been so gentle toward you that you could not wish for my death?"

"Oh!" cried Don Juan, "if it were possible to preserve your life by giving you a part of mine!" ("One can always say such things," thought the spendthrift; "it is as if I offered the world to my mistress.")

The thought had scarcely passed through his mind when the old spaniel whined. This intelligent voice made Don Juan tremble. He believed that the dog understood him.

"I knew that I could count on you, my son," said the

dying man. "There, you shall be satisfied. I shall live, but without depriving you of a single day of your life."

"He raves," said Don Juan to himself.

Then he said, aloud: "Yes, my dearest father, you will indeed live as long as I do, for your image will be always in my heart."

"It is not a question of that sort of life," said the old nobleman, gathering all his strength to raise himself to a sitting posture, for he was stirred by one of those suspicions which are only born at the bedside of the dying. "Listen, my son," he continued in a voice weakened by this last effort. "I have no more desire to die than you have to give up your lady loves, wine, horses, falcons, hounds and money——"

"I can well believe it," thought his son, kneeling beside the pillow and kissing one of Bartholomeo's cadaverous hands. "But, father," he said aloud, "my dear father, we must submit to the will of God!"

"God! I am also God!" growled the old man.

"Do not blaspheme!" cried the young man, seeing the menacing expression which was overspreading his father's features. "Be careful what you say, for you have received extreme unction and I should never be consoled if you were to die in a state of sin."

"Are you going to listen to me?" cried the dying man, gnashing his toothless jaws.

Don Juan held his peace. A horrible silence reigned. Through the dull wail of the snowstorm came again the melody of the viol and the heavenly voice, faint as the dawning day.

The dying man smiled.

"I thank you for having brought singers and music! A banquet, young and beautiful women, with dark locks, all the pleasures of life. Let them remain. I am about to be born again."

"The delirium is at its height," said Don Juan to himself.

"I have discovered a means of resuscitation. There, look in the drawer of the table—you open it by pressing a hidden spring near the griffin."

"I have it, father."

"Good! Now take out a little flask of rock crystal."

THE ELIXIR OF LIFE

"Here it is."

"I have spent twenty years in——"

At this point the old man felt his end approaching, and collected all his energy to say:

"As soon as I have drawn my last breath rub me with this water and I shall come to life again."

"There is very little of it," replied the young man.

Bartholomeo was no longer able to speak, but he could still hear and see. At these words he turned his head toward Don Juan with a violent wrench. His neck remained twisted like that of a marble statue doomed by the sculptor's whim to look forever sideways, his staring eyes assumed a hideous fixity. He was dead, dead in the act of losing his only, his last illusion. In seeking a shelter in his son's heart he had found a tomb more hollow than those which men dig for their dead. His hair, too, had risen with horror and his tense gaze seemed still to speak. It was a father rising in wrath from his sepulchre to demand vengeance of God.

"There, the good man is done for!" exclaimed Don Juan.

Intent upon taking the magic crystal to the light of the lamp, as a drinker examines his bottle at the end of a repast, he had not seen his father's eye pale. The cowering dog looked alternately at his dead master and at the elixir, as Don Juan regarded by turns his father and the phial. The lamp threw out fitful waves of light. The silence was profound, the viol was mute. Belvidéro thought he saw his father move, and he trembled. Frightened by the tense expression of the accusing eyes, he closed them, just as he would have pushed down a window-blind on an autumn night. He stood motionless, lost in a world of thought.

Suddenly a sharp creak, like that of a rusty spring, broke the silence. Don Juan, in his surprise, almost dropped the flask. A perspiration, colder than the steel of a dagger, oozed out from his pores. A cock of painted wood came forth from a clock and crowed three times. It was one of those ingenious inventions by which the savants of that time were awakened at the hour fixed for their work. Already the daybreak reddened the casement. The old timepiece was more faithful in its master's service than Don Juan had been in his duty to Bartholomeo. This instrument was composed of wood, pulleys, cords and wheels, while he had that mechanism peculiar to man, called a heart.

In order to run no further risk of losing the mysterious liquid the skeptical Don Juan replaced it in the drawer of the little Gothic table. At this solemn moment he heard a tumult in the corridor. There were confused voices, stifled laughter, light footsteps, the rustle of silk, in short, the noise of a merry troop trying to collect itself in some sort of order. The door opened and the prince, the seven women, the friends of Don Juan and the singers, appeared, in the fantastic disorder of dancers overtaken by the morning, when the sun disputes the paling light of the candles. They came to offer the young heir the conventional condolences.

"Oh, oh, is poor Don Juan really taking this death seriously?" said the prince in la Brambilla's ear.

"Well, his father was a very good man," she replied.

Nevertheless, Don Juan's nocturnal meditations had printed so striking an expression upon his face that it commanded silence. The men stopped, motionless. The women, whose lips had been parched with wine, threw themselves on their knees and began to pray. Don Juan could not help shuddering as he saw this splendor, this joy, laughter, song, beauty, life personified, doing homage thus to Death. But in this adorable Italy religion and revelry were on such good terms that religion was a sort of debauch and debauch religion. The prince pressed Don Juan's hand affectionately, then all the figures having given expression to the same look, half-sympathy, half-indifference, the phantasmagoria disappeared, leaving the chamber empty. It was, indeed, a faithful image of life! Going down the stairs the prince said to la Rivabarella:

"Heigho! who would have thought Don Juan a mere boaster of impiety? He loved his father, after all!"

"Did you notice the black dog?" asked la Brambilla.

"He is immensely rich now," sighed Bianca Cavatolini.

"What is that to me?" cried the proud Veronese, who had broken the comfit dish.

"What is that to you?" exclaimed the duke. With his ducats he is as much a prince as I am!"

At first Don Juan, swayed by a thousand thoughts, wav-

THE ELIXIR OF LIFE

ered toward many different resolutions. After having ascertained the amount of the wealth amassed by his father, he returned in the evening to the death chamber, his soul puffed up with a horrible egoism. In the apartment he found all the servants of the household busied in collecting the ornaments for the bed of state on which "feu monseigneur" would lie to-morrow—a curious spectacle which all Ferrara would come to admire. Don Juan made a sign and the servants stopped at once, speechless and trembling.

"Leave me alone," he said in an altered voice, "and do not return until I go out again."

When the steps of the old servant, who was the last to leave, had died away on the stone flooring, Don Juan locked the door hastily, and, sure that he was alone, exclaimed:

"Now, let us try!"

The body of Bartholomeo lay on a long table. To hide the revolting spectacle of a corpse whose extreme decrepitude and thinness made it look like a skeleton, the embalmers had drawn a sheet over the body, which covered all but the head. This mummy-like figure was laid out in the middle of the room, and the linen, naturally clinging, outlined the form vaguely, but showing its stiff, bony thinness. The face already had large purple spots, which showed the urgency of completing the embalming. Despite the skepticism with which Don Juan was armed, he trembled as he uncorked the magic phial of crystal. When he stood close to the head he shook so that he was obliged to pause for a moment. But this young man had allowed himself to be corrupted by the customs of a dissolute court. An idea worthy of the Duke of Urbino came to him, and gave him a courage which was spurred on by lively curiosity. It seemed as if the demon had whispered the words which resounded in his heart: "Bathe an eye!" He took a piece of linen and, after having moistened it sparingly with the precious liquid, he passed it gently over the right eyelid of the corpse. The eye opened!

"Ah!" said Don Juan, gripping the flask in his hand as we clutch in our dreams the branch by which we are suspended over a precipice.

He saw an eye full of life, a child's eye in a death's head, the liquid eye of youth, in which the light trembled. Protected by beautiful black lashes, it scintillated like one of those solitary lights which travelers see in lonely places on winter evenings. It seemed as if the glowing eye would pierce Don Juan. It thought, accused, condemned, threatened, judged, spoke—it cried, it snapped at him! There was the most tender supplication, a royal anger, then the love of a young girl imploring mercy of her executioners. Finally, the awful look that a man casts upon his fellowmen on his way to the scaffold. So much life shone in this fragment of life that Don Juan recoiled in terror. He walked up and down the room, not daring to look at the eye, which stared back at him from the ceiling and from the hangings. The room was sown with points full of fire, of life, of intelligence. Everywhere gleamed eyes which shrieked at him.

"He might have lived a hundred years longer!" he cried involuntarily when, led in front of his father by some diabolical influence, he contemplated the luminous spark.

Suddenly the intelligent eye closed, and then opened again abruptly, as if assenting. If a voice had cried, "Yes," Don Juan could not have been more startled.

"What is to be done?" he thought.

He had the courage to try to close this white eyelid, but his efforts were in vain.

"Shall I crush it out? Perhaps that would be parricide?" he asked himself.

"Yes," said the eye, by means of an ironical wink.

"Ah!" cried Don Juan, "there is sorcery in it!"

He approached the eye to crush it. A large tear rolled down the hollow cheek of the corpse and fell on Belvidéro's hand.

"It is scalding!" he cried, sitting down.

This struggle had exhausted him, as if, like Jacob, he had battled with an angel.

At last he arose, saying: "So long as there is no blood—"

Then, collecting all the courage needed for the cowardly act, he crushed out the eye, pressing it in with the linen without looking at it. A deep moan, startling and terrible, was heard. It was the poor spaniel, who died with a howl.

THE ELIXIR OF LIFE

"Could he have been in the secret?" Don Juan wondered, surveying the faithful animal.

Don Juan was considered a dutiful son. He raised a monument of white marble over his father's tomb, and employed the most prominent artists of the time to carve the figures. He was not altogether at ease until the statue of his father, kneeling before Religion, imposed its enormous weight on the grave, in which he had buried the only regret that had ever touched his heart, and that only in moments of physical depression.

On making an inventory of the immense wealth amassed by the old Orientalist, Don Juan became avaricious. Had he not two human lives in which he should need money? His deep, searching gaze penetrated the principles of social life, and he understood the world all the better because he viewed it across a tomb. He analyzed men and things that he might have done at once with the past, represented by history, with the present, expressed by the law, and with the future revealed by religion. He took soul and matter, threw them into a crucible, and found nothing there, and from that time forth he became Don Juan.

Master of the illusions of life he threw himself—young and beautiful—into life; despising the world, but seizing the world. His happiness could never be of that bourgeois type which is satisfied by boiled beef, by a welcome warming-pan in winter, a lamp at night and new slippers at each quarter. He grasped existence as a monkey seizes a nut, peeling off the coarse shell to enjoy the savory kernel. The poetry and sublime transports of human passion touched no higher than his instep. He never made the mistake of those strong men who, imagining that little souls believe in the great, venture to exchange noble thoughts of the future for the small coin of our ideas of life. He might, like them, have walked with his feet on earth and his head among the clouds, but he preferred to sit at his ease and sear with his kisses the lips of more than one tender, fresh and sweet woman. Like Death, wherever he passed, he devoured all without scruple, demanding a passionate, Oriental love and easily won pleasure. Loving only woman in women, his soul found its natural trend in irony. When his inamoratas mounted to the skies in an ecstasy of bliss, Don Juan followed, serious, unreserved, sincere as a German student. But he said "I" while his lady love, in her folly, said "we." He knew admirably how to yield himself to a woman's influence. He was always clever enough to make her believe that he trembled like a college youth who asks his first partner at a ball: "Do you like dancing?" But he could also be terrible when necessary; he could draw his sword and destroy skilled soldiers. There was banter in his simplicity and laughter in his tears, for he could weep as well as any woman who says to her husband: "Give me a carriage or I shall pine to death."

For merchants the world means a bale of goods or a quantity of circulating notes; for most young men it is a woman; for some women it is a man; for certain natures it is society, a set of people, a position, a city; for Don Juan the universe was himself! Noble, fascinating and a model of grace, he fastened his bark to every bank; but he allowed himself to be carried only where he wished to go. The more he saw the more skeptical he became. Probing human nature he soon guessed that courage was rashness; prudence, cowardice; generosity, shrewd calculation; justice, a crime; delicacy, pusillanimity; honesty, policy; and by a singular fatality he perceived that the persons who were really honest, delicate, just, generous, prudent and courageous received no consideration at the hands of their fellows.

"What a cheerless jest!" he cried. "It does not come from a god!"

And then, renouncing a better world, he showed no mark of respect to holy things and regarded the marble saints in the churches merely as works of art. He understood the mechanism of human society, and never offended too much against the current prejudices, for the executioners had more power than he; but he bent the social laws to his will with the grace and wit that are so well displayed in his scene with M. Dimanche. He was, in short, the embodiment of Molière's Don Juan, Goethe's Faust, Byron's Manfred, and Maturin's Melmoth—grand pictures drawn by the greatest geniuses of Europe, and to which neither the harmonies of Mozart nor the lyric strains of Rossini are lacking. Terrible pictures in

THE ELIXIR OF LIFE

which the power of evil existing in man is immortalized, and which are repeated from one century to another, whether the type come to parley with mankind by incarnating itself in Mirabeau, or be content to work in silence, like Bonaparte; or to goad on the universe by sarcasm, like the divine Rabelais; or again, to laugh at men instead of insulting things, like Maréchal de Richelieu; or, still better, perhaps, if it mock both men and things, like our most celebrated ambassador.

But the deep genius of Don Juan incorporated in advance all these. He played with everything. His life was a mockery, which embraced men, things, institutions, ideas. As for eternity, he had chatted for half an hour with Pope Julius II., and at the end of the conversation he said, laughing:

"If it were absolutely necessary to choose, I should rather believe in God than in the devil; power combined with goodness has always more possibilities than the spirit of evil."

"Yes; but God wants one to do penance in this world."

"Are you always thinking of your indulgences?" replied Belvidéro. "Well, I have a whole existence in reserve to repent the faults of my first life."

"Oh, if that is your idea of old age," cried the Pope, "you are in danger of being canonized."

"After your elevation to the papacy, one may expect anything."

And then they went to watch the workmen engaged in building the huge basilica consecrated to St. Peter.

"St. Peter is the genius who gave us our double power," said the Pope to Don Juan, "and he deserves this monument. But sometimes at night I fancy that a deluge will pass a sponge over all this, and it will need to be begun over again."

Don Juan and the Pope laughed. They understood each other. A fool would have gone next day to amuse himself with Julius II. at Raphael's house or in the delightful Villa Madama; but Belvidéro went to see him officiate in his pontifical capacity, in order to convince himself of his suspicions. Under the influence of wine della Rovere would have been capable of forgetting himself and criticising the Apocalypse.

When Don Juan reached the age of sixty he went to live

in Spain. There, in his old age, he married a young and charming Andalusian. But he was intentionally neither a good father nor a good husband. He had observed that we are never so tenderly loved as by the women to whom we scarcely give a thought. Doña Elvira, piously reared by an old aunt in the heart of Andalusia in a castle several leagues from San Lucas, was all devotion and meekness. Don Juan saw that this young girl was a woman to make a long fight with a passion before yielding to it, so he hoped to keep from her any love but his until after his death. It was a serious jest, a game of chess which he had reserved for his old age.

Warned by his father's mistakes, he determined to make the most trifling acts of his old age contribute to the success of the drama which was to take place at his deathbed. Therefore, the greater part of his wealth lay buried in the cellars of his palace at Ferrara, whither he seldom went. The rest of his fortune was invested in a life annuity, so that his wife and children might be interested in keeping him alive. This was a species of cleverness which his father should have practiced; but this Machiavelian scheme was unnecessary in his case. Young Philippe Belvidéro, his son, grew up a Spaniard as conscientiously religious as his father was impious, on the principle of the proverb: "A miserly father, a spendthrift son."

The Abbot of San Lucas was selected by Don Juan to direct the consciences of the Duchess of Belvidéro and of Philippe. This ecclesiastic was a holy man, of fine carriage, well proportioned, with beautiful black eyes and a head like Tiberius. He was wearied with fasting, pale and worn, and continually battling with temptation, like all recluses. The old nobleman still hoped perhaps to be able to kill a monk before finishing his first lease of life. But, whether the Abbot was as clever as Don Juan, or whether Doña Elvira had more prudence or virtue than Spain usually accords to women, Don Juan was obliged to pass his last days like a country parson, without scandal. Sometimes he took pleasure in finding his wife and son remiss in their religious duties, and insisted imperiously that they should fulfil all the obligations imposed upon the faithful by the court of

THE ELIXIR OF LIFE

Rome. He was never so happy as when listening to the gallant Abbot of San Lucas, Doña Elvira and Philippe engaged in arguing a case of conscience.

Nevertheless, despite the great care which the lord of Belvidéro bestowed upon his person, the days of decrepitude arrived. With this age of pain came cries of helplessness, cries made the more piteous by the remembrance of his impetuous youth and his ripe maturity. This man, for whom the last jest in the farce was to make others believe in the laws and principles at which he scoffed, was compelled to close his eyes at night upon an uncertainty. This model of good breeding, this duke spirited in an orgy, this brilliant courtier, gracious toward women, whose hearts he had wrung as a peasant bends a willow wand, this man of genius, had an obstinate cough, a troublesome sciatica and a cruel gout. He saw his teeth leave him, as, at the end of an evening, the fairest, best dressed women depart one by one, leaving the ballroom deserted and empty. His bold hands trembled, his graceful limbs tottered, and then one night apoplexy turned its hooked and icy fingers around his throat. From this fateful day he became morose and harsh. He accused his wife and son of being insincere in their devotion, charging that their touching and gentle care was showered upon him so tenderly only because his money was all invested. Elvira and Philippe shed bitter tears, and redoubled their caresses to this malicious old man, whose broken voice would become affectionate to say:

"My friends, my dear wife, you will forgive me, will you not? I torment you sometimes. Ah, great God, how canst Thou make use of me thus to prove these two angelic creatures! I, who should be their joy, am their bane!"

It was thus that he held them at his bedside, making them forget whole months of impatience and cruelty by one hour in which he displayed to them the new treasures of his favor and a false tenderness. It was a paternal system which succeeded infinitely better than that which his father had formerly employed toward him. Finally he reached such a state of illness that manœuvres like those of a small boat entering a dangerous canal were necessary in order to put him to bed.

Then the day of death came. This brilliant and skeptical man, whose intellect only was left unimpaired by the general decay, lived between a doctor and a confessor, his two antipathies. But he was jovial with them. Was there not a bright light burning for him behind the veil of the future? Over this veil, leaden and impenetrable to others, transparent to him, the delicate and bewitching delights of youth played like shadows.

It was on a beautiful summer evening that Don Juan felt the approach of death. The Spanish sky was gloriously clear, the orange trees perfumed the air and the stars cast a fresh glowing light. Nature seemed to give pledges of his resurrection. A pious and obedient son regarded him with love and respect. About eleven o'clock he signified his wish to be left alone with this sincere being.

"Philippe," he began, in a voice so tender and affectionate that the young man trembled and wept with happiness, for his father had never said "Philippe" like this before. "Listen to me, my son," continued the dying man. "I have been a great sinner, and all my life I have thought about death. Formerly I was the friend of the great Pope Julius II. This illustrious pontiff feared that the excessive excitability of my feelings would cause me to commit some deadly sin at the moment of my death, after I had received the blessed ointment. He made me a present of a flask of holy water that gushed forth from a rock in the desert. I kept the secret of the theft of the Church's treasure, but I am authorized to reveal the mystery to my son 'in articulo mortis.' You will find the flask in the drawer of the Gothic table which always stands at my bedside. The precious crystals may be of service to you also, my dearest Philippe. Will you swear to me by your eternal salvation that you will carry out my orders faithfully?"

Philippe looked at his father. Don Juan was too well versed in human expression not to know that he could die peacefully in perfect faith in such a look, as his father had died in despair at his own expression.

"You deserve a different father," continued Don Juan. "I must acknowledge that when the estimable Abbot of San Lucas was administering the 'viaticum' I was thinking of the incompatibility of two so wide-spreading powers as that of the devil and that of God."

"Oh, father!"

"And I said to myself that when Satan makes his peace he will be a great idiot if he does not bargain for the pardon of his followers. This thought haunted me. So, my child, I shall go to hell if you do not carry out my wishes."

"Oh, tell them to me at once, father!"

"As soon as I have closed my eyes," replied Don Juan, "and that may be in a few minutes, you must take my body, still warm, and lay it on a table in the middle of the room. Then put out the lamp—the light of the stars will be sufficient. You must take off my clothes, and while you recite 'Paters' and 'Aves' and uplift your soul to God, you must moisten my eyes, my lips, all my head first, and then my body, with this holy water. But, my dear son, the power of God is great. You must not be astonished at anything."

At this point Don Juan, feeling the approach of death, added in a terrible voice: "Be careful of the flask!"

Then he died gently in the arms of his son, whose tears fell upon his ironical and sallow face.

It was nearly midnight when Don Philippe Belvidéro placed his father's corpse on the table. After kissing the stern forehead and the gray hair he put out the lamp. The soft rays of the moonlight which cast fantastic reflections over the scenery allowed the pious Philippe to discern his father's body dimly, as something white in the midst of the darkness. The young man moistened a cloth in the liquid and then, deep in prayer, he faithfully anointed the revered head. The silence was intense. Then he heard indescribable rustlings, but he attributed them to the wind among the treetops. When he had bathed the right arm he felt himself rudely seized at the back of the neck by an arm, young and vigorous—the arm of his father! He gave a piercing cry, and dropped the phial, which fell on the floor and broke. The liquid flowed out.

The whole household rushed in, bearing torches. The cry had aroused and frightened them as if the trumpet of the last judgment had shaken the world. The room was crowded with people. The trembling throng saw Don

Philippe, fainting, but held up by the powerful arm of his father, which clutched his neck. Then they saw a supernatural sight, the head of Don Juan, young and beautiful as an Antinoüs, a head with black hair, brilliant eyes and crimson lips, a head that moved in a blood-curdling manner without being able to stir the skeleton to which it belonged.

An old servant cried: "A miracle!"

And all the Spaniards repeated: "A miracle!"

Too pious to admit the possibility of magic, Doña Elvira sent for the Abbot of San Lucas. When the priest saw the miracle with his own eyes he resolved to profit by it, like a man of sense, and like an abbot who asked nothing better than to increase his revenues. Declaring that Don Juan must inevitably be canonized, he appointed his monastery for the ceremony of the apotheosis. The monastery, he said, should henceforth be called "San Juan de Lucas." At these words the head made a facetious grimace.

The taste of the Spaniards for this sort of solemnities is so well known that it should not be difficult to imagine the religious spectacle with which the abbey of San Lucas celebrated the translation of "the blessed Don Juan Belvidéro" in its church. A few days after the death of this illustrious nobleman, the miracle of his partial resurrection had been so thoroughly spread from village to village throughout a circle of more than fifty leagues round San Lucas that it was as good as a play to see the curious people on the road. They came from all sides, drawn by the prospect of a "Te Deum" chanted by the light of burning torches. The ancient mosque of the monastery of San Lucas, a wonderful building, erected by the Moors, which for three hundred years had resounded with the name of Jesus Christ instead of Allah, could not hold the crowd which was gathered to view the ceremony. Packed together like ants, the hidalgos in velvet mantles and armed with their good swords stood round the pillars, unable to find room to bend their knees, which they never bent elsewhere. Charming peasant women, whose dresses set off the beautiful lines of their figures, gave their arms to white-haired old men. Youths with glowing eyes found themselves beside old

THE ELIXIR OF LIFE

women decked out in gala dress. There were couples trembling with pleasure, curious fiancées, led thither by their sweethearts, newly married couples and frightened children, holding one another by the hand. All this throng was there, rich in colors, brilliant in contrast, laden with flowers, making a soft tumult in the silence of the night. The great doors of the church opened.

Those who, having come too late, were obliged to stay outside, saw in the distance, through the three open doors, a scene of which the tawdry decorations of our modern operas can give but a faint idea. Devotees and sinners, intent upon winning the favor of a new saint, lighted thousands of candles in his honor inside the vast church, and these scintillating lights gave a magical aspect to the edifice. The black arcades, the columns with their capitals, the recessed chapels glittering with gold and silver, the galleries, the Moorish fretwork, the most delicate features of this delicate carving, were all revealed in the dazzling brightness like the fantastic figures which are formed in a glowing fire. It was a sea of light, surmounted at the end of the church by the gilded choir, where the high altar rose in glory, which rivaled the rising sun. But the magnificence of the golden lamps, the silver candlesticks, the banners, the tassels, the saints and the "ex voto" paled before the reliquary in which Don Juan lay. The body of the blasphemer was resplendent with gems, flowers, crystals, diamonds, gold, and plumes as white as the wings of a seraphim; it replaced a picture of Christ on the altar. Around him burned wax candles, which threw out waves of light. The good Abbot of San Lucas, clad in his pontifical robes, with his jeweled mitre, his surplice and his golden crozier reclined, king of the choir, in a large armchair, amid all his clergy, who were impassive men with silver hair, and who surrounded him like the confessing saints whom the painters group round the Lord. The percentor and the dignitaries of the order, decorated with the glittering insignia of their ecclesiastical vanities, came and went among the clouds of incense like planets revolving in the firmament.

When the hour of triumph was come the chimes awoke the echoes of the countryside, and this immense assembly raised its voice to God in the first cry of praise which begins the "Te Deum."

Sublime exultation! There were voices pure and high, ecstatic women's voices, blended with the deep sonorous tones of the men, thousands of voices so powerful that they drowned the organ in spite of the bellowing of its pipes. The shrill notes of the choir-boys and the powerful rhythm of the basses inspired pretty thoughts of the combination of childhood and strength in this delightful concert of human voices blended in an outpouring of love.

"Te Deum laudamus!"

In the midst of this cathedral, black with kneeling men and women, the chant burst forth like a light which gleams suddenly in the night, and the silence was broken as by a peal of thunder. The voices rose with the clouds of incense which threw diaphanous, bluish veils over the quaint marvels of the architecture. All was richness, perfume, light and melody.

At the moment at which this symphony of love and gratitude rolled toward the altar, Don Juan, too polite not to express his thanks and too witty not to appreciate a jest, responded by a frightful laugh, and straightened up in his reliquary. But, the devil having given him a hint of the danger he ran of being taken for an ordinary man, for a saint, a Boniface or a Pantaléon, he interrupted this harmony of love by a shriek in which the thousand voices of hell joined. Earth lauded, heaven condemned. The church trembled on its ancient foundations.

"Te Deum laudamus!" sang the crowd.

"Go to the devil, brute beasts that you are! 'Carajos demonios!' Beasts! what idiots you are with your God!"

And a torrent of curses rolled forth like a stream of burning lava at an eruption of Vesuvius.

"'Deus sabaoth! sabaoth'!" cried the Christians.

Then the living arm was thrust out of the reliquary and waved threateningly over the assembly with a gesture full of despair and irony.

"The saint is blessing us!" said the credulous old women, the children and the young maids.

It is thus that we are often deceived in our adorations.

THE ELIXIR OF LIFE

The superior man mocks those who compliment him, and compliments those whom he mocks in the depths of his heart.

When the Abbot, bowing low before the altar, chanted: "'Sancte Johannes, ora pro nobis'!" he heard distinctly: "'O coglione'!"

"What is happening up there?" cried the superior, seeing the reliquary move.

"The saint is playing devil!" replied the Abbot.

At this the living head tore itself violently away from the dead body and fell upon the yellow pate of the priest.

"Remember, Doña Elvira!" cried the head, fastening its teeth in the head of the Abbot.

The latter gave a terrible shriek, which threw the crowd into a panic. The priests rushed to the assistance of their chief.

"Imbecile! Now say that there is a God!" cried the voice, just as the Abbot expired.

THE AGE FOR LOVE
A REPORTER'S STORY
BY PAUL BOURGET

THE AGE FOR LOVE
By PAUL BOURGET

WHEN I submitted the plan of my Inquiry Upon the Age for Love to the editor-in-chief of the Boulevard, the highest type of French literary paper, he seemed astonished that an idea so journalistic —that was his word—should have been evolved from the brain of his most recent acquisition. I had been with him two weeks and it was my first contribution. "Give me some details, my dear Labarthe," he said, in a somewhat less insolent manner than was his wont. After listening to me for a few moments he continued: "That is good. You will go and interview certain men and women, first upon the age at which one loves the most, next upon the age when one is most loved? Is that your idea? And now to whom will you go first?"

"I have prepared a list," I replied, and took from my pocket a sheet of paper. I had jotted down the names of a number of celebrities whom I proposed to interview on this all-important question, and I began to read over my list. It contained two ex-government officials, a general, a Dominican father, four actresses, two café-concert singers, four actors, two financiers, two lawyers, a surgeon and a lot of literary celebrities. At some of the names my chief would nod his approval, at others he would say curtly, with an affectation of American manners, "Bad; strike it off," until I came to the name I had kept for the last, that of Pierre Fauchery, the famous novelist.

"Strike that off," he said, shrugging his shoulders. "He is not on good terms with us."

"And yet," I suggested, "is there any one whose opinion would be of greater interest to reading men as well as to women? I had even thought of beginning with him."

"The devil you had!" interrupted the editor-in-chief. "It is one of Fauchery's principles not to see any reporters. I have sent him ten if I have one, and he has shown them all the door. The Boulevard does not relish such treatment, so we have given him some pretty hard hits."

"Nevertheless, I will have an interview with Fauchery for the Boulevard," was my reply. "I am sure of it."

"If you succeed," he replied, "I'll raise your salary. That man makes me tired with his scorn of newspaper notoriety. He must take his share of it, like the rest. But you will not succeed. What makes you think you can?"

"Permit me to tell you my reason later. In forty-eight hours you will see whether I have succeeded or not."

"Go and do not spare the fellow."

Decidedly, I had made some progress as a journalist, even in my two weeks' apprenticeship, if I could permit Pascal to speak in this way of the man I most admired among living writers. Since that not far-distant time when, tired of being poor, I had made up my mind to cast my lot with the multitude in Paris, I had tried to lay aside my old self, as lizards do their skins, and I had almost succeeded. In a former time, a former time that was but yesterday, I knew—for in a drawer full of poems, dramas and half-finished tales I had proof of it—that there had once existed a certain Jules Labarthe who had come to Paris with the hope of becoming a great man. That person believed in Literature with a capital "L;" in the Ideal, another capital; in Glory, a third capital. He was now dead and buried. Would he some day, his position assured, begin to write once more from pure love of his art? Possibly, but for the moment I knew only the energetic, practical Labarthe, who had joined the procession with the idea of getting into the front rank, and of obtaining as soon as possible an income of thirty thousand francs a year. What would it matter to this second individual if that vile Pascal should boast of having stolen a march on the most delicate, the most powerful of the heirs of Balzac, since I, the new Labarthe, was capable of looking forward to an operation which required about as much delicacy as some of the performances of my editor-in-chief? I had, as a matter of fact, a sure means of obtaining the interview. It was this: When I was young and simple I had sent some verses and stories to Pierre Fauchery, the same verses and stories the refusal of which

THE AGE FOR LOVE

by four editors had finally made me decide to enter the field of journalism. The great writer was traveling at this time, but he had replied to me. I had responded by a letter to which he again replied, this time with an invitation to call upon him. I went. I did not find him. I went again. I did not find him that time. Then a sort of timidity prevented my returning to the charge. So I had never met him. He knew me only as the young Elia of my two epistles. This is what I counted upon to extort from him the favor of an interview which he certainly would refuse to a mere newspaper man. My plan was simple; to present myself at his house, to be received, to conceal my real occupation, to sketch vaguely a subject for a novel in which there should occur a discussion upon the Age for Love, to make him talk and then when he should discover his conversation in print —here I began to feel some remorse. But I stifled it with the terrible phrase, "the struggle for life," and also by the recollection of numerous examples culled from the firm with which I now had the honor of being connected.

The morning after I had had this very literary conversation with my honorable director, I rang at the door of the small house in the Rue Desbordes-Valmore where Pierre Fauchery lived, in a retired corner of Passy. Having taken up my pen to tell a plain unvarnished tale I do not see how I can conceal the wretched feeling of pleasure which, as I rang the bell, warmed my heart at the thought of the good joke I was about to play on the owner of this peaceful abode.

Even after making up one's mind to the sacrifices I had decided upon; there is always left a trace of envy for those who have triumphed in the melancholy struggle for literary supremacy. It was a real disappointment to see me when the servant replied, ill-humoredly, that M. Fauchery was not in Paris. I asked when he would return. The servant did not know. I asked for his address. The servant did not know that. Poor lion, who thought he had secured anonymity for his holiday! A half-hour later I had discovered that he was staying for the present at the Château de Proby, near Nemours. I had merely had to make inquiries of his publisher. Two hours later I bought my ticket at the Gare de

PAUL BOURGET

Lyon for the little town chosen by Balzac as the scene for his delicious story of Ursule Mirouet. I took a traveling bag and was prepared to spend the night there. In case I failed to see the master that afternoon I had decided to make sure of him the next morning. Exactly seven hours after the servant, faithful to his trust, had declared that he did not know where his master was staying, I was standing in the hall of the château waiting for my card to be sent up. I had taken care to write on it a reminder of our conversation of the year before, and this time, after a ten-minute wait in the hall, during which I noticed with singular curiosity and malice two very elegant and very pretty young women going out for a walk, I was admitted to his presence. "Aha," I said to myself, "this then is the secret of his exile; the interview promises well!"

The novelist received me in a cosy little room, with a window opening onto the park, already beginning to turn yellow with the advancing autumn. A wood fire burned in the fireplace and lighted up the walls which were hung with flowered cretonne and on which could be distinguished several colored English prints representing cross-country rides and the jumping of hedges. Here was the worldly environment with which Fauchery is so often reproached. But the books and papers that littered the table bore witness that the present occupant of this charming retreat remained a substantial man of letters. His habit of constant work was still further attested by his face, which I admit, gave me all at once a feeling of remorse for the trick I was about to play him. If I had found him the snobbish pretender whom the weekly newspapers were in the habit of ridiculing, it would have been a delight to outwit his diplomacy. But no! I saw, as he put down his pen to receive me, a man about fifty-seven years old, with a face that bore the marks of reflection, eyes tired from sleeplessness, a brow heavy with thought, who said as he pointed to an easy chair, "You will excuse me, my dear confrère, for keeping you waiting." I, his dear confrère. Ah! if he had known! "You see," and he pointed to the page still wet with ink, "that man cannot be free from the slavery of furnishing copy. One has less facility at my age than at yours. Now, let us speak of

THE AGE FOR LOVE

yourself. How do you happen to be at Nemours? What have you been doing since the story and the verses you were kind enough to send me?"

It is vain to try to sacrifice once for all one's youthful ideals. When a man has loved literature as I loved it at twenty, he cannot be satisfied at twenty-six to give up his early passion, even at the bidding of implacable necessity. So Pierre Fauchery remembered my poor verses! He had actually read my story! His allusion proved it. Could I tell him at such a moment that since the creation of those first works I had despaired of myself, and that I had changed my gun to the other shoulder? The image of the Boulevard office rose suddenly before me. I heard the voice of the editor-in-chief saying, "Interview Fauchery? You will never accomplish that;" so, faithful to my self-imposed rôle, I replied, "I have retired to Nemours to work upon a novel called The Age for Love, and it is on this subject that I wished to consult you, my dear master."

It seemed to me—it may possibly have been an illusion—that at the announcement of the so-called title of my so-called novel, a smile and a shadow flitted over Fauchery's eyes and mouth. A vision of the two young women I had met in the hall came back to me. Was the author of so many great masterpieces of analysis about to live a new book before writing it? I had no time to answer this question, for, with a glance at an onyx vase containing some cigarettes of Turkish tobacco, he offered me one, lighted one himself and began first to question, then to reply to me. I listened while he thought aloud and had almost forgotten my Machiavellian combination, so keen was my relish of the joyous intimacy of this communion with a mind I had passionately loved in his works. He was the first of the great writers of our day whom I had thus approached on something like terms of intimacy. As we talked I observed the strange similarity between his spoken and his written words. I admired the charming simplicity with which he abandoned himself to the pleasures of imagination, his superabundant intelligence, the liveliness of his impressions and his total absence of arrogance and of pose.

"There is no such thing as an age for love," he said in

substance, "because the man capable of loving—in the complex and modern sense of love as a sort of ideal exaltation—never ceases to love. I will go further; he never ceases to love the same person. You know the experiment that a contemporary physiologist tried with a series of portraits to determine in what the indefinable resemblances called family likeness consisted? He took photographs of twenty persons of the same blood, then he photographed these photographs on the same plate, one over the other. In this way he discovered the common features which determined the type. Well, I am convinced that if we could try a similar experiment and photograph one upon another the pictures of the different women whom the same man has loved or thought he had loved in the course of his life we should discover that all these women resembled one another. The most inconstant have cherished one and the same being through five or six or even twenty different embodiments. The main point is to find out at what age they have met the woman who approaches nearest to the one whose image they have constantly borne within themselves. For them that would be the age for love.

"The age for being loved?" he continued. "The deepest of all the passions I have ever known a man to inspire was in the case of one of my masters, a poet, and he was sixty years old at the time. It is true that he still held himself as erect as a young man, he came and went with a step as light as yours, he conversed like Rivarol, he composed verses as beautiful as De Vigny's. He was besides very poor, very lonely and very unhappy, having lost one after another, his wife and his children. You remember the words of Shakespeare's Moor: 'She loved me for the dangers I had passed, and I loved her that she did pity them.'

"So it was that this great artist inspired in a beautiful, noble and wealthy young Russian woman, a devotion so passionate that because of him she never married. She found a way to take care of him, day and night, in spite of his family, during his last illness, and at the present time, having bought from his heirs all of the poet's personal belongings, she keeps the apartment where he lived just as it was at the time of his death. That was years ago. In

THE AGE FOR LOVE

her case she found in a man three times her own age the person who corresponded to a certain ideal which she carried in her heart. Look at Goethe, at Lamartine and at many others! To depict feelings on this high plane, you must give up the process of minute and insignificant observation which is the bane of the artists of to-day. In order that a sixty-year-old lover should appear neither ridiculous nor odious you must apply to him what the elder Corneille so proudly said of himself in his lines to the marquise:

> " 'Cependant, j'ai quelques charmes
> Qui sont assez eclatants
> Pour n'avoir pas trop d' alarmes
> De ces ravages du temps.'

"Have the courage to analyze great emotions to create characters who shall be lofty and true. The whole art of the analytical novel lies there."

As he spoke the master had such a light of intellectual certainty in his eyes that to me he seemed the embodiment of one of those great characters he had been urging me to describe. It made me feel that the theory of this man, himself almost a sexagenarian, that at any age one may inspire love, was not unreasonable! The contrast between the world of ideas in which he moved and the atmosphere of the literary shop in which for the last few months I had been stifling was too strong. The dreams of my youth were realized in this man whose gifts remained unimpaired after the production of thirty volumes and whose face, growing old, was a living illustration of the beautiful saying: "Since we must wear out, let us wear out nobly." His slender figure bespoke the austerity of long hours of work; his firm mouth showed his decision of character; his brow, with its deep furrows, had the paleness of the paper over which he so often bent; and yet, the refinement of his hands, so well cared for, the sober elegance of his dress and an aristocratic air that was natural to him showed that the finer professional virtues had been cultivated in the midst of a life of frivolous temptations. These temptations had been no more of a disturbance to his ethical and spiritual nature than the academic honors, the financial successes, the numerous editions that had been his. Withal he was an awfully good fellow, for, after having talked at great length with me, he ended by saying, "Since you are staying in Nemours I hope to see you often, and to-day I cannot let you go without presenting you to my hostess."

What could I say? This was the way in which a mere reporter on the Boulevard found himself installed at a five-o'clock tea-table in the salon of a château, where surely no newspaper man had ever before set foot and was presented as a young poet and novelist of the future to the old Marquise de Proby, whose guest the master was. This amiable white-haired dowager questioned me upon my alleged work and I replied equivocally, with blushes, which the good lady must have attributed to bashful timidity. Then, as though some evil genius had conspired to multiply the witnesses of my bad conduct, the two young women whom I had seen going out, returned in the midst of my unlooked-for visit. Ah, my interview with this student of femininity upon the Age for Love was about to have a living commentary! How it would illumine his words to hear him conversing with these new arrivals! One was a young girl of possibly twenty—a Russian if I rightly understood the name. She was rather tall, with a long face lighted up by two very gentle black eyes, singular in their fire and intensity. She bore a striking resemblance to the portrait attributed to Francia in the Salon Carré, of the Louvre which goes by the name of the "Man in Black," because of the color of his clothes and his mantle. About her mouth and nostrils was that same subdued nervousness, that same restrained feverishness which gives to the portrait its striking qualities. I had not been there a quarter of an hour before I had guessed from the way she watched and listened to Fauchery what a passionate interest the old master inspired in her. When he spoke she paid rapt attention. When she spoke to him, I felt her voice shiver, if I may use the word, and he, the glorious writer, surfeited with triumphs, exhausted by his labors, seemed, as soon as he felt the radiance of her glance of ingenuous idolatry, to recover that vivacity, that elasticity of impression, which is the sovereign grace of youthful lovers.

"I understand now why he cited Goethe and the young girl of Marienbad," said I to myself with a laugh, as my hired carriage sped on toward Nemours. "He was thinking of himself. He is in love with that child, and she is in love with him. We shall hear of his marrying her. There's a wedding that will call forth copy, and when Pascal hears that I witnessed the courtship—but just now I must think of my interview. Won't Fauchery be surprised to read it day after to-morrow in his paper? But does he read the papers? It may not be right but what harm will it do him? Besides, it's a part of the struggle for life." It was by such reasoning, I remember, the reasoning of a man determined to arrive that I tried to lull to sleep the inward voice that cried, "You have no right to put on paper, to give to the public what this noble writer said to you, supposing that he was receiving a poet, not a reporter." But I heard also the voice of my chief saying, "You will never succeed." And this second voice, I am ashamed to confess, triumphed over the other with all the more ease because I was obliged to do something to kill time. I reached Nemours too late for the train which would have brought me back to Paris about dinner time. At the old inn they gave me a room which was clean and quiet, a good place to write, so I spent the evening until bedtime composing the first of the articles which were to form my inquiry. I scribbled away under the vivid impressions of the afternoon, my powers as well as my nerves spurred by a touch of remorse. Yes, I scribbled four pages which would have been no disgrace to the Journal des Goncourts, that exquisite manual of the perfect reporter. It was all there, my journey, my arrival at the château, a sketch of the quaint eighteenth century building, with its fringe of trees and its well-kept walks, the master's room, the master himself and his conversation; the tea at the end and the smile of the old novelist in the midst of a circle of admirers, old and young. It lacked only a few closing lines. "I will add these in the morning," I thought, and went to bed with a feeling of duty performed, such is the nature of a writer. Under the form of an interview I had done, and I knew it, the best work of my life.

What happens while we sleep? Is there, unknown to us, a secret and irresistible ferment of ideas while our senses are closed to the impressions of the outside world? Certain it is that on awakening I am apt to find myself in a state of mind very different from that in which I went to sleep. I had not been awake ten minutes before the image of Pierre Fauchery came up before me, and at the same time the thought that I had taken a base advantage of the kindness of his reception of me became quite unbearable. I felt a passionate longing to see him again, to ask his pardon for my deception. I wished to tell him who I was, with what purpose I had gone to him and that I regretted it. But there was no need of a confession. It would be enough to destroy the pages I had written the night before. With this idea I arose. Before tearing them up, I reread them. And then—any writer will understand me—and then they seemed to me so brilliant that I did not tear them up. Fauchery is so intelligent, so generous, was the thought that crossed my mind. What is there in this interview, after all, to offend him? Nothing, absolutely nothing. Even if I should go to him again this very morning, tell him my story and that upon the success of my little inquiry my whole future as a journalist might depend? When he found that I had had five years of poverty and hard work without accomplishing anything, and that I had had to go onto a paper in order to earn the very bread I ate, he would pardon me, he would pity me and he would say, "Publish your interview." Yes, but what if he should forbid my publishing it? But no, he would not do that.

I passed the morning in considering my latest plan. A certain shyness made it very painful to me. But it might at the same time conciliate my delicate scruples, my "amour-propre" as an ambitious chronicler, and the interests of my pocket-book. I knew that Pascal had the name of being very generous with an interview article if it pleased him. And besides, had he not promised me a reward if I succeeded with Fauchery? In short, I had decided to try my experiment, when, after a hasty breakfast, I saw, on stepping into the carriage I had had the night before, a victoria with coat-of-arms drive rapidly past and was stunned at recognizing Fauchery himself, apparently lost in a gloomy revery that was in singular contrast to his high spirits of the night before. A small trunk on the coachman's seat was a sufficient indication that he was going to the station. The train for Paris left in twelve minutes, time enough for me to pack my things pell-mell into my valise and hurriedly to pay my bill. The same carriage which was to have taken me to the Château de Proby carried me to the station at full speed, and when the train left I was seated in an empty compartment opposite the famous writer, who was saying to me, "You, too, deserting Nemours? Like me, you work best in Paris."

The conversation begun in this way, might easily have led to the confession I had resolved to make. But in the presence of my unexpected companion I was seized with an unconquerable shyness, moreover he inspired me with a curiosity which was quite equal to my shyness. Any number of circumstances, from a telegram from a sick relative to the most commonplace matter of business, might have explained his sudden departure from the château where I had left him so comfortably installed the night before. But that the expression of his face should have changed as it had, that in eighteen hours he should have become the careworn, discouraged being he now seemed, when I had left him so pleased with life, so happy, so assiduous in his attentions to that pretty girl, Mademoiselle de Russaie, who loved him and whom he seemed to love, was a mystery which took complete possession of me, this time without any underlying professional motive. He was to give me the key before we reached Paris. At any rate I shall always believe that part of his conversation was in an indirect way a confidence. He was still unstrung by the unexpected incident which had caused both his hasty departure and the sudden metamorphosis in what he himself, if he had been writing, would have called his "intimate heaven." The story he told me was "per sfogarsi," as Bayle loved to say; his idea was that I would not discover the real hero. I shall always believe that it was his own story under another name, and I love to believe it because it was so exactly his way of looking at things. It was àpropos of the supposed subject of my novel —oh, irony!—àpropos of the real subject of my interview that he began.

"I have been thinking about our conversation and about your book, and I am afraid that I expressed myself badly yesterday. When I said that one may love and be loved at any age I ought to have added that sometimes this love comes too late. It comes when one no longer has the right to prove to the loved one how much she is loved, except by love's sacrifice. I should like to share with you a human document, as they say to-day, which is in itself a drama with a dénouement. But I must ask you not to use it, for the secret is not my own." With the assurance of my discretion he went on: "I had a friend, a companion of my own age, who, when he was twenty, had loved a young girl. He was poor, she was rich. Her family separated them. The girl married some one else and almost immediately afterward she died. My friend lived. Some day you will know for yourself that it is almost as true to say that one recovers from all things as that there is nothing which does not leave its scar. I had been the confidant of his serious passion, and I became the confidant of the various affairs that followed that first ineffaceable disappointment. He felt, he inspired, other loves. He tasted other joys. He endured other sorrows and yet when we were alone and when we touched upon those confidences that come from the heart's depths, the girl who was the ideal of his twentieth year reappeared in his words. How many times he has said to me, 'In others I have always looked for her and as I have never found her, I have never truly loved any one but her.'

"And had she loved him?" I interrupted.

"He did not think so," replied Fauchery. "At least she had never told him so. Well, you must now imagine my friend at my age or almost there. You must picture him growing gray, tired of life and convinced that he had at last discovered the secret of peace. At this time he met, while visiting some relatives in a country house, a mere girl of twenty, who was the image, the haunting image of her whom he had hoped to marry thirty years before. It was one of those strange resemblances which extend from the color of the eyes to the 'timbre' of the voice, from the smile to the thought, from the gestures to the finest feelings of the heart. I could not, in a few disjointed phrases describe to you the

THE AGE FOR LOVE

strange emotions of my friend. It would take pages and pages to make you understand the tenderness, both present and at the same time retrospective, for the dead through the living; the hypnotic condition of the soul which does not know where dreams and memories end and present feeling begins; the daily commingling of the most unreal thing in the world, the phantom of a lost love, with the freshest, the most actual, the most irresistibly naïve and spontaneous thing in it, a young girl. She comes, she goes, she laughs, she sings, you go about with her in the intimacy of country life, and at her side walks one long dead. After two weeks of almost careless abandon to the dangerous delights of this inward agitation imagine my friend entering by chance one morning one of the less frequented rooms of the house, a gallery, where, among other pictures, hung a portrait of himself, painted when he was twenty-five. He approaches the portrait abstractedly. There had been a fire in the room, so that a slight moisture dimmed the glass which protected the pastel, and on this glass, because of this moisture, he sees distinctly the trace of two lips which had been placed upon the eyes of the portrait, two small delicate lips, the sight of which makes his heart beat. He leaves the gallery, questions a servant, who tells him that no one but the young woman he has in mind has been in the room that morning."

"What then?" I asked, as he paused.

"My friend returned to the gallery, looked once more at the adorable imprint of the most innocent, the most passionate of caresses. A mirror hung near by, where he could compare his present with his former face, the man he was with the man he had been. He never told me and I never asked what his feelings were at that moment. Did he feel that he was too culpable to have inspired a passion in a young girl whom he would have been a fool, almost a criminal, to marry? Did he comprehend that through his age which was so apparent, it was his youth which this child loved? Did he remember, with a keenness that was all too sad, that other, who had never given him a kiss like that at a time when he might have returned it? I only know that he left the same day, determined never again to see one whom he could no longer love as he had loved the other, with the hope, the purity, the soul of a man of twenty."

A few hours after this conversation, I found myself once more in the office of the Boulevard, seated in Pascal's den, and he was saying, "Already? Have you accomplished your interview with Pierre Fauchery?"

"He would not even receive me," I replied, boldly.

"What did I tell you?" he sneered, shrugging his big shoulders. "We'll get even with him on his next volume. But you know, Labarthe, as long as you continue to have that innocent look about you, you can't expect to succeed in newspaper work."

I bore with the ill-humor of my chief. What would he have said if he had known that I had in my pocket an interview and in my head an anecdote which were material for a most successful story? And he has never had either the interview or the story. Since then I have made my way in the line where he said I should fail. I have lost my innocent look and I earn my thirty thousand francs a year, and more. I have never had the same pleasure in the printing of the most profitable, the most brilliant article that I had in consigning to oblivion the sheets relating my visit to Nemours. I often think that I have not served the cause of letters as I wanted to, since, with all my laborious work I have never written a book. And yet when I recall the irresistible impulse of respect which prevented me from committing toward a dearly loved master a most profitable but infamous indiscretion, I say to myself, "If you have not served the cause of letters, you have not betrayed it." And this is the reason, now that Fauchery is no longer of this world, that it seems to me that the time has come for me to relate my first interview. There is none of which I am more proud.

MATEO FALCONE
BY PROSPER MERIMEE

MATEO FALCONE

By PROSPER MERIMEE

ON leaving Porto-Vecchio from the northwest and directing his steps towards the interior of the island, the traveller will notice that the land rises rapidly, and after three hours' walking over tortuous paths obstructed by great masses of rock and sometimes cut by ravines, he will find himself on the border of a great mâquis. The mâquis is the domain of the Corsican shepherds and of those who are at variance with justice. It must be known that, in order to save himself the trouble of manuring his field, the Corsican husbandman sets fire to a piece of woodland. If the flame spread farther than is necessary, so much the worse! In any case he is certain of a good crop from the land fertilized by the ashes of the trees which grow upon it. He gathers only the heads of his grain, leaving the straw, which it would be unnecessary labor to cut. In the following spring the roots that have remained in the earth without being destroyed send up their tufts of sprouts, which in a few years reach a height of seven or eight feet. It is this kind of tangled thicket that is called a mâquis. They are made up of different kinds of trees and shrubs, so crowded and mingled together at the caprice of nature that only with an axe in hand can a man open a passage through them, and mâquis are frequently seen so thick and bushy that the wild sheep themselves cannot penetrate them.

If you have killed a man, go into the mâquis of Porto-Vecchio. With a good gun and plenty of powder and balls, you can live there in safety. Do not forget a brown cloak furnished with a hood, which will serve you for both cover and mattress. The shepherds will ive you chestnuts, milk and cheese, and you will have nothing to fear from justice nor the relatives of the dead except when it is necessary for you to descend to the city to repleni h your ammunition.

When I was in Corsica in 18—, Mateo Falcone had his

Copyrighted 1895 Current Literature Publishing Company.

house half a league from this mâquis. He was rich enough for that country, living in noble style—that is to say, doing nothing—on the income from his flocks, which the shepherds, who are a kind of nomads, lead to pasture here and there on the mountains. When I saw him, two years after the event that I am about to relate, he appeared to me to be about fifty years old or more. Picture to yourself a man, small but robust, with curly hair, black as jet, an aquiline nose, thin lips, large, restless eyes, and a complexion the color of tanned leather. His skill as a marksman was considered extraordinary even in his country, where good shots are so common. For example, Mateo would never fire at a sheep with buckshot; but at a hundred and twenty paces, he would drop it with a ball in the head or shoulder, as he chose. He used his arms as easily at night as during the day. I was told this feat of his skill, which will, perhaps, seem impossible to those who have not travelled in Corsica. A lighted candle was placed at eighty paces, behind a paper transparency about the size of a plate. He would take aim, then the candle would be extinguished, and, at the end of a moment, in the most complete darkness, he would fire and hit the paper three times out of four.

With such a transcendent accomplishment, Mateo Falcone had acquired a great reputation. He was said to be as good a friend as he was a dangerous enemy; accommodating and charitable, he lived at peace with all the world in the district of Porto-Vecchio. But it is said of him that in Corte, where he had married his wife, he had disembarrassed himself very vigorously of a rival who was considered as redoubtable in war as in love: at least, a certain gun-shot which surprised this rival as he was shaving before a little mirror hung in his window was attributed to Mateo. The affair was smoothed over and Mateo was married. His wife Giuseppa had given him at first three daughters (which infuriated him), and finally a son, whom he named Fortunato, and who became the hope of his family, the inheritor of the name. The daughters were well married: their father could count at need on the poignards and carbines of his sons-in-law. The son was only ten years old, but he already gave promise of fine attributes.

MATEO FALCONE

On a certain day in autumn, Mateo set out at an early hour with his wife to visit one of his flocks in a clearing of the mâquis. The little Fortunato wanted to go with them, but the clearing was too far away; moreover, it was necessary some one should stay to watch the house; therefore the father refused: it will be seen whether or not he had reason to repent.

He had been gone some hours, and the little Fortunato was tranquilly stretched out in the sun, looking at the blue mountains, and thinking that the next Sunday he was going to dine in the city with his uncle, the Caporal,[1] when he was suddenly interrupted in his meditations by the firing of a musket. He got up and turned to that side of the plain whence the noise came. Other shots followed, fired at irregular intervals, and each time nearer; at last, in the path which led from the plain to Mateo's house, appeared a man wearing the pointed hat of the mountaineers, bearded, covered with rags, and dragging himself along with difficulty by the support of his gun. He had just received a wound in his thigh.

This man was an outlaw, who, having gone to the town by night to buy powder, had fallen on the way into an ambuscade of Corsican light-infantry. After a vigorous defense he was fortunate in making his retreat, closely followed and firing from rock to rock. But he was only a little in advance of the soldiers, and his wound prevented him from gaining the mâquis before being overtaken.

He approached Fortunato and said:

"You are the son of Mateo Falcone?"—"Yes."

"I am Gianetto Saupiero. I am followed by the yellow-collars.[2] Hide me, for I can go no farther."

"And what will my father say if I hide you without his permission?"

"He will say that you have done well."

"How do you know?"

"Hide me quickly; they are coming."

"Wait till my father gets back."

"How can I wait? Malediction! They will be here in five minutes. Come, hide me, or I will kill you."

---

[1] Civic Official. [2] Slang for Gendarmes.

Fortunato answered him with the utmost coolness:

"Your gun is empty, and there are no more cartridges in your belt."

"I have my stiletto."

"But can you run as fast as I can?"

He gave a leap and put himself out of reach.

"You are not the son of Mateo Falcone! Will you then let me be captured before your house?"

The child appeared moved.

"What will you give me if I hide you?" said he, coming nearer.

The outlaw felt in a leather pocket that hung from his belt, and took out a five-franc piece, which he had doubtless saved to buy ammunition with. Fortunato smiled at the sight of the silver piece; he snatched it, and said to Gianetto:

"Fear nothing."

Immediately he made a great hole in a pile of hay that was near the house. Gianetto crouched down in it and the child covered him in such a way that he could breathe without it being possible to suspect that the hay concealed a man. He bethought himself further, and, with the subtlety of a tolerably ingenious savage, placed a cat and her kittens on the pile, that it might not appear to have been recently disturbed. Then, noticing the traces of blood on the path near the house, he covered them carefully with dust, and, that done, he again stretched himself out in the sun with the greatest tranquillity.

A few moments afterwards, six men in brown uniforms with yellow collars, and commanded by an Adjutant, were before Mateo's door. This Adjutant was a distant relative of Falcone's. (In Corsica the degrees of relationship are followed much further than elsewhere.) His name was Tiodoro Gamba; he was an active man, much dreaded by the outlaws, several of whom he had already entrapped.

"Good day, little cousin," said he, approaching Fortunato; "how tall you have grown. Have you seen a man go past here just now?"

"Oh! I am not yet so tall as you, my cousin," replied the child with a simple air.

MATEO FALCONE

"You soon will be. But haven't you seen a man go by here, tell me?"

"If I have seen a man go by?"

"Yes, a man with a pointed hat of black velvet, and a vest embroidered with red and yellow."

"A man with a pointed hat, and a vest embroidered with red and yellow?"

"Yes, answer quickly, and don't repeat my questions?"

"This morning the curé passed before our door on his horse, Piero. He asked me how papa was, and I answered him——"

"Ah, you little scoundrel, you are playing sly! Tell me quickly which way Gianetto went? We are looking for him, and I am sure he took this path."

"Who knows?"

"Who knows? It is I know that you have seen him."

"Can any one see who passes when they are asleep?"

"You were not asleep, rascal; the shooting woke you up."

"Then you believe, cousin, that your guns make so much noise? My father's carbine has the advantage of them."

"The devil take you, you cursed little scapegrace! I am certain that you have seen Gianetto. Perhaps, even, you have hidden him. Come, comrades, go into the house and see if our man is there. He could only go on one foot, and the knave has too much good sense to try to reach the mâquis limping like that. Moreover, the bloody tracks stop here."

"And what will papa say?" asked Fortunato with a sneer; "what will he say if he knows that his house has been entered while he was away?"

"You rascal!" said the Adjutant, taking him by the ear, "do you know that it only remains for me to make you change your tone? Perhaps you will speak differently after I have given you twenty blows with the flat of my sword."

Fortunato continued to sneer.

"My father is Mateo Falcone," said he with emphasis.

"You little scamp, you know very well that I can carry you off to Corte or to Bastia. I will make you lie in a dungeon, on straw, with your feet in shackles, and I will have you guillotined if you don't tell me where Gianetto is."

The child burst out laughing at this ridiculous menace. He repeated:

"My father is Mateo Falcone."

"Adjutant," said one of the soldiers in a low voice, "let us have no quarrels with Mateo."

Gamba appeared evidently embarrassed. He spoke in an undertone with the soldiers who had already visited the house. This was not a very long operation, for the cabin of a Corsican consists only of a single square room, furnished with a table, some benches, chests, housekeeping utensils and those of the chase. In the meantime, little Fortunato petted his cat and seemed to take a wicked enjoyment in the confusion of the soldiers and of his cousin.

One of the men approached the pile of hay. He saw the cat, and gave the pile a careless thrust with his bayonet, shrugging his shoulders as if he felt that his precaution was ridiculous. Nothing moved; the boy's face betrayed not the slightest emotion.

The Adjutant and his troop were cursing their luck. Already they were looking in the direction of the plain, as if disposed to return by the way they had come, when their chief, convinced that menaces would produce no impression on Falcone's son, determined to make a last effort, and try the effect of caresses and presents.

"My little cousin," said he, "you are a very wide-awake little fellow. You will get along. But you are playing a naughty game with me; and if I wasn't afraid of making trouble for my cousin, Mateo, the devil take me! but I would carry you off with me."

"Bah!"

"But when my cousin comes back I shall tell him about this, and he will whip you till the blood comes for having told such lies."

"You don't say so!"

"You will see. But hold on!—be a good boy and I will give you something."

"Cousin, let me give you some advice: if you wait much longer Gianetto will be in the mâquis and it will take a smarter man than you to follow him."

The Adjutant took from his pocket a silver watch worth

MATEO FALCONE

about ten crowns, and noticing that Fortunato's eyes sparkled at the sight of it, said, holding the watch by the end of its steel chain:

"Rascal! you would like to have such a watch as that hung around your neck, wouldn't you, and to walk in the streets of Porto-Vecchio proud as a peacock? People would ask you what time it was, and you would say: 'Look at my watch.'"

"When I am grown up, my uncle, the Caporal, will give me a watch."

"Yes; but your uncle's little boy has one already; not so fine as this either. But then, he is younger than you."

The child sighed.

"Well! Would you like this watch, little cousin?"

Fortunato, casting sidelong glances at the watch, resembled a cat that has been given a whole chicken. It feels that it is being made sport of, and does not dare to use its claws; from time to time it turns its eyes away so as not to be tempted, licking its jaws all the while, and has the appearance of saying to its master, "How cruel your joke is!"

However, the Adjutant seemed in earnest in offering his watch. Fortunato did not reach out his hand for it, but said with a bitter smile:

"Why do you make fun of me?"

"Good God! I am not making fun of you. Only tell me where Gianetto is and the watch is yours."

Fortunato smiled incredulously, and fixing his black eyes on those of the Adjutant tried to read there the faith he ought to have had in his words.

"May I lose my epaulettes," cried the Adjutant, "if I do not give you the watch on this condition. These comrades are witnesses; I can not deny it."

While speaking he gradually held the watch nearer till it almost touched the child's pale face, which plainly showed the struggle that was going on in his soul between covetousness and respect for hospitality. His breast swelled with emotion; he seemed about to suffocate. Meanwhile the watch was slowly swaying and turning, sometimes brushing against his cheek. Finally, his right hand was gradually stretched toward it; the ends of his fingers touched it; then its whole weight was in his hand, the Adjutant still keeping hold of the chain. The face was light blue; the cases newly burnished. In the sunlight it seemed to be all on fire. The temptation was too great. Fortunato raised his left hand and pointed over his shoulder with his thumb at the hay against which he was reclining. The Adjutant understood him at once. He dropped the end of the chain and Fortunato felt himself the sole possessor of the watch. He sprang up with the agility of a deer and stood ten feet from the pile, which the soldiers began at once to overturn.

There was a movement in the hay, and a bloody man with a poignard in his hand appeared. He tried to rise to his feet, but his stiffened leg would not permit it and he fell. The Adjutant at once grappled with him and took away his stiletto. He was immediately secured, notwithstanding his resistance.

Gianetto, lying on the earth and bound like a fagot, turned his head towards Fortunato, who had approached.

"Son of—!" said he, with more contempt than anger.

The child threw him the silver-piece which he had received, feeling that he no longer deserved it; but the outlaw paid no attention to the movement, and with great coolness said to the Adjutant:

"My dear Gamba, I cannot walk; you will be obliged to carry me to the city."

"Just now you could run faster than a buck," answered the cruel captor; "but be at rest. I am so pleased to have you that I would carry you a league on my back without fatigue. Besides, comrade, we are going to make a litter for you with your cloak and some branches, and at the Crespoli farm we shall find horses."

"Good," said the prisoner. "You will also put a little straw on your litter that I may be more comfortable."

While some of the soldiers were occupied in making a kind of stretcher out of some chestnut boughs and the rest were dressing Gianetto's wound, Mateo Falcone and his wife suddenly appeared at a turn in the path that led to the mâquis. The woman was staggering under the weight of an enormous sack of chestnuts, while her husband was sauntering along, carrying one gun in his hands, while another was

MATEO FALCONE

slung across his shoulders, for it is unworthy of a man to carry other burdens than his arms.

At the sight of the soldiers Mateo's first thought was that they had come to arrest him. But why this thought? Had he then some quarrels with justice? No. He enjoyed a good reputation. He was said to have a particularly good name, but he was a Corsican and a highlander, and there are few Corsican highlanders who, in scrutinizing their memory, can not find some peccadillo, such as a gun-shot, dagger-thrust, or similar trifles. Mateo more than others had a clear conscience; for more than ten years he had not pointed his carbine at a man, but he was always prudent, and put himself into a position to make a good defense if necessary. "Wife," said he to Giuseppa, "put down the sack and hold yourself ready."

She obeyed at once. He gave her the gun that was slung across his shoulders, which would have bothered him, and, cocking the one he held in his hands, advanced slowly towards the house, walking among the trees that bordered the road, ready at the least hostile demonstration, to hide behind the largest, whence he could fire from under cover. His wife followed closely behind, holding his reserve weapon and his cartridge-box. The duty of a good housekeeper, in case of a fight, is to load her husband's carbines.

On the other side the Adjutant was greatly troubled to see Mateo advance in this manner, with cautious steps, his carbine raised, and his finger on the trigger.

"If by chance," thought he, "Mateo should be related to Gianetto, or if he should be his friend and wish to defend him, the contents of his two guns would arrive amongst us as certainly as a letter in the post; and if he should see me, notwithstanding the relationship!"

In this perplexity he took a bold step. It was to advance alone towards Mateo and tell him of the affair while accosting him as an old acquaintance, but the short space that separated him from Mateo seemed terribly long.

"Hello! old comrade," cried he. "How do you do, my good fellow? It is I, Gamba, your cousin."

Without answering a word, Mateo stopped, and in proportion as the other spoke, slowly raised the muzzle of his gun so that it was pointing upward when the Adjutant joined him.

"Good-day, brother," said the Adjutant, holding out his hand. "It is a long time since I have seen you."

"Good-day, brother."

"I stopped while passing, to say good-day to you and to cousin Pepa here. We have had a long journey to-day, but have no reason to complain, for we have captured a famous prize. We have just seized Gianetto Saupiero."

"God be praised!" cried Giuseppa. "He stole a milch goat from us last week."

These words reassured Gamba.

"Poor devil!" said Mateo, "he was hungry."

"The villain fought like a lion," continued the Adjutant, a little mortified. "He killed one of my soldiers, and not content with that, broke Caporal Chardon's arm; but that matters little, he is only a Frenchman. Then, too, he was so well hidden that the devil couldn't have found him. Without my little cousin, Fortunato, I should never have discovered him."

"Fortunato!" cried Mateo.

"Fortunato!" repeated Giuseppa.

"Yes, Gianetto was hidden under the hay-pile yonder, but my little cousin showed me the trick. I shall tell his uncle, the Caporal, that he may send him a fine present for his trouble. Both his name and yours will be in the report that I shall send to the Attorney-general."

"Malediction!" said Mateo in a low voice.

They had rejoined the detachment. Gianetto was already lying on the litter ready to set out. When he saw Mateo and Gamba in company he smiled a strange smile, then, turning his head towards the door of the house, he spat on the sill, saying:

"House of a traitor."

Only a man determined to die would dare pronounce the word traitor to Falcone. A good blow with the stiletto, which there would be no need of repeating, would have immediately paid the insult. However, Mateo made no other movement than to place his hand on his forehead like a man who is dazed.

MATEO FALCONE

Fortunato had gone into the house when his father arrived, but now he reappeared with a bowl of milk which he handed with downcast eyes to Gianetto.

"Get away from me!" cried the outlaw, in a loud voice. Then, turning to one of the soldiers, he said:

"Comrade, give me a drink."

The soldier placed his gourd in his hands, and the prisoner drank the water handed to him by a man with whom he had just exchanged bullets. He then asked them to tie his hands across his breast instead of behind his back.

"I like," said he, "to lie at my ease."

They hastened to satisfy him; then the Adjutant gave the signal to start, said adieu to Mateo, who did not respond, and descended with rapid steps towards the plain.

Nearly ten minutes elapsed before Mateo spoke. The child looked with restless eyes, now at his mother, now at his father, who was leaning on his gun and gazing at him with an expression of concentrated rage.

"You begin well," said Mateo at last with a calm voice, but frightful to one who knew the man.

"Oh, father!" cried the boy, bursting into tears, and making a forward movement as if to throw himself on his knees. But Mateo cried, "Away from me!"

The little fellow stopped and sobbed, immovable, a few feet from his father.

Giuseppa drew near. She had just discovered the watch-chain, the end of which was hanging out of Fortunato's jacket.

"Who gave you that watch?" demanded she in a severe tone.

"My cousin, the Adjutant."

Falcone seized the watch and smashed it in a thousand pieces against a rock.

"Wife," said he, "is this my child?"

Giuseppa's cheeks turned a brick-red.

"What are you saying, Mateo? Do you know to whom you speak?"

"Very well, this child is the first of his race to commit treason."

Fortunato's sobs and gasps redoubled as Falcone kept his

lynx-eyes upon him. Then he struck the earth with his gunstock, shouldered the weapon, and turned in the direction of the mâquis, calling to Fortunato to follow. The boy obeyed.

Giuseppa hastened after Mateo and seized his arm.

"He is your son," said she with a trembling voice, fastening her black eyes on those of her husband to read what was going on in his heart.

"Leave me alone," said Mateo, "I am his father."

Giuseppa embraced her son, and bursting into tears entered the house. She threw herself on her knees before an image of the Virgin and prayed ardently. In the meanwhile Falcone walked some two hundred paces along the path and only stopped when he reached a little ravine which he descended. He tried the earth with the butt-end of his carbine, and found it soft and easy to dig. The place seemed to be convenient for his design.

"Fortunato, go close to that big rock there."

The child did as he was commanded, then he kneeled.

"Say your prayers."

"Oh, father, father, do not kill me!"

"Say your prayers!" repeated Mateo in a terrible voice.

The boy, stammering and sobbing, recited the Pater and the Credo. At the end of each prayer the father loudly answered, "Amen!"

"Are those all the prayers you know?"

"Oh! father, I know the Ave Maria and the litany that my aunt taught me."

"It is very long, but no matter."

The child finished the litany in a scarcely audible tone.

"Are you finished?"

"Oh! my father, have mercy! Pardon me! I will never do so again. I will beg my cousin, the Caporal, to pardon Gianetto."

He was still speaking. Mateo raised his gun, and, taking aim, said:

"May God pardon you!"

The boy made a desperate effort to rise and grasp his father's knees, but there was not time. Mateo fired and Fortunato fell dead.

Without casting a glance on the body, Mateo returned to

the house for a spade with which to bury his son. He had gone but a few steps when he met Giuseppa, who, alarmed by the shot, was hastening hither.

"What have you done?" cried she.

"Justice."

"Where is he?"

"In the ravine. I am going to bury him. He died a Christian. I shall have a mass said for him. Have my son-in-law, Tiodoro Bianchi, sent for to come and live with us.

"THE MIRROR"
BY CATULLE MENDES

"THE MIRROR"

By CATULLE MENDES

THERE was once a kingdom where mirrors were unknown. They had all been broken and reduced to fragments by order of the queen, and if the tiniest bit of looking-glass had been found in any house, she would not have hesitated to put all the inmates to death with the most frightful tortures.

Now for the secret of this extraordinary caprice. The queen was dreadfully ugly, and she did not wish to be exposed to the risk of meeting her own image; and, knowing herself to be hideous, it was a consolation to know that other women at least could not see that they were pretty.

You may imagine that the young girls of the country were not at all satisfied. What was the use of being beautiful if you could not admire yourself?

They might have used the brooks and lakes for mirrors; but the queen had foreseen that, and had hidden all of them under closely joined flagstones. Water was drawn from wells so deep that it was impossible to see the liquid surface, and shallow basins must be used instead of buckets, because in the latter there might be reflections.

Such a dismal state of affairs, especially for the pretty coquettes, who were no more rare in this country than in others.

The queen had no compassion, being well content that her subjects should suffer as much annoyance from the lack of a mirror as she felt at the sight of one.

However, in a suburb of the city there lived a young girl called Jacinta, who was a little better off than the rest, thanks to her sweetheart, Valentin. For if someone thinks you are beautiful, and loses no chance to tell you so, he is almost as good as a mirror.

"Tell me the truth," she would say; "what is the color of my eyes?"

Copyrighted 1896 Current Literature Publishing Company.

"They are like dewy forget-me-nots."

"And my skin is not quite black?"

"You know that your forehead is whiter than freshly fallen snow, and your cheeks are like blush roses."

"How about my lips?"

"Cherries are pale beside them."

"And my teeth, if you please?"

"Grains of rice are not as white."

"But my ears, should I be ashamed of them?"

"Yes, if you would be ashamed of two little pink shells among your pretty curls."

And so on endlessly; she delighted, he still more charmed, for his words came from the depth of his heart and she had the pleasure of hearing herself praised, he the delight of seeing her. So their love grew more deep and tender every hour, and the day that he asked her to marry him she blushed certainly, but it was not with anger. But, unluckily, the news of their happiness reached the wicked queen, whose only pleasure was to torment others, and Jacinta more than anyone else, on account of her beauty.

A little while before the marriage Jacinta was walking in the orchard one evening, when an old crone approached, asking for alms, but suddenly jumped back with a shriek as if she had stepped on a toad, crying: "Heavens, what do I see?"

"What is the matter, my good woman? What is it you see? Tell me."

"The ugliest creature I ever beheld."

"Then you are not looking at me," said Jacinta, with innocent vanity.

"Alas! yes, my poor child, it is you. I have been a long time on this earth, but never have I met anyone so hideous as you!"

"What! am I ugly?"

"A hundred times uglier than I can tell you."

"But my eyes——"

"They are a sort of dirty gray; but that would be nothing if you had not such an outrageous squint!"

"My complexion——"

"THE MIRROR"

"It looks as if you had rubbed coal-dust on your forehead and cheeks."

"My mouth——"

"It is pale and withered, like a faded flower."

"My teeth——"

"If the beauty of teeth is to be large and yellow, I never saw any so beautiful as yours."

"But, at least, my ears——"

"They are so big, so red, and so misshapen, under your coarse elf-locks, that they are revolting. I am not pretty myself, but I should die of shame if mine were like them." After this last blow, the old witch, having repeated what the queen had taught her, hobbled off, with a harsh croak of laughter, leaving poor Jacinta dissolved in tears, prone on the ground beneath the apple-trees.

Nothing could divert her mind from her grief. "I am ugly—I am ugly," she repeated constantly. It was in vain that Valentin assured and reassured her with the most solemn oaths. "Let me alone; you are lying out of pity. I understand it all now; you never loved me; you are only sorry for me. The beggar woman had no interest in deceiving me. It is only too true—I am ugly. I do not see how you can endure the sight of me."

To undeceive her, he brought people from far and near; every man declared that Jacinta was created to delight the eyes; even the women said as much, though they were less enthusiastic. But the poor child persisted in her conviction that she was a repulsive object, and when Valentin pressed her to name their wedding-day—"I, your wife!" cried she. "Never! I love you too dearly to burden you with a being so hideous as I am." You can fancy the despair of the poor fellow so sincerely in love. He threw himself on his knees; he prayed; he supplicated; she answered still that she was too ugly to marry him.

What was he to do? The only way to give the lie to the old woman and prove the truth to Jacinta was to put a mirror before her. But there was no such thing in the kingdom, and so great was the terror inspired by the queen that no workman dared make one.

"Well, I shall go to Court," said the lover, in despair. "Harsh as our mistress is, she cannot fail to be moved by the tears and the beauty of Jacinta. She will retract, for a few hours at least, this cruel edict which has caused our trouble."

It was not without difficulty that he persuaded the young girl to let him take her to the palace. She did not like to show herself, and asked of what use would be a mirror, only to impress her more deeply with her misfortune; but when he wept, her heart was moved, and she consented, to please him.

"What is all this?" said the wicked queen. "Who are these people? and what do they want?"

"Your Majesty, you have before you the most unfortunate lover on the face of the earth."

"Do you consider that a good reason for coming here to annoy me?"

"Have pity on me."

"What have I to do with your love affairs?"

"If you would permit a mirror——"

The queen rose to her feet, trembling with rage. "Who dares to speak to me of a mirror?" she said, grinding her teeth.

"Do not be angry, your Majesty, I beg of you, and deign to hear me. This young girl whom you see before you, so fresh and pretty, is the victim of a strange delusion. She imagines that she is ugly."

"Well," said the queen, with a malicious grin, "she is right. I never saw a more hideous object."

Jacinta, at these cruel words, thought she would die of mortification. Doubt was no longer possible, she must be ugly. Her eyes closed, she fell on the steps of the throne in a deadly swoon.

But Valentin was affected very differently. He cried out loudly that her Majesty must be mad to tell such a lie. He had no time to say more. The guards seized him, and at a sign from the queen the headsman came forward. He was always beside the throne, for she might need his services at any moment

"THE MIRROR"

"Do your duty," said the queen, pointing out the man who had insulted her. The executioner raised his gleaming axe just as Jacinta came to herself and opened her eyes. Then two shrieks pierced the air. One was a cry of joy, for in the glittering steel Jacinta saw herself, so charmingly pretty —and the other a scream of anguish, as the wicked soul of the queen took flight, unable to bear the sight of her face in the impromptu mirror.

MY NEPHEW JOSEPH
BY LUDOVIC HALEVY

MY NEPHEW JOSEPH

By LUDOVIC HALEVY

(*Scene passes at Versailles; two old gentlemen are conversing, seated on a bench in the King's garden.*)

JOURNALISM, my dear Monsieur, is the evil of the times. I tell you what, if I had a son, I would hesitate a long while before giving him a literary education. I would have him learn chemistry, mathematics, fencing, cosmography, swimming, drawing, but not composition—no, not composition. Then, at least, he would be prevented from becoming a journalist. It is so easy, so tempting. They take pen and paper and write, it doesn't matter what, apropos to it doesn't matter what, and you have a newspaper article. In order to become a watchmaker, a lawyer, an upholsterer, in short, all the liberal arts, study, application, and a special kind of knowledge are necessary; but nothing like that is required for a journalist."

"You are perfectly right, my dear Monsieur, the profession of journalism should be restricted by examinations, the issuing of warrants, the granting of licenses——"

"And they could pay well for their licenses, these gentlemen. Do you know that journalism is become very profitable? There are some young men in it who, all at once, without a fixed salary, and no capital whatever, make from ten, twenty to thirty thousand francs a year."

"Now, that is strange! But how do they become journalists?"

"Ah! It appears they generally commence by being reporters. Reporters slip in everywhere, in official gatherings and theatres, never missing a first night, nor a fire, nor a great ball, nor a murder."

"How well acquainted you are with all this!"

"Yes, very well acquainted. Ah! Mon Dieu! You are my friend, you will keep my secret, and if you will not repeat this in Versailles—I will tell you how it is—we have one in the family."

"One what?"

"A reporter."

"A reporter in your family, which always seemed so united! How can that be?"

"One can almost say that the devil was at the bottom of it. You know my nephew Joseph——"

"Little Joseph! Is he a reporter?"

"Yes."

"Little Joseph, I can see him in the park now, rolling a hoop, bare-legged, with a broad white collar, not more than six or seven years ago—and now he writes for newspapers!"

"Yes, newspapers! You know my brother keeps a pharmacy in the Rue Montorgueil, an old and reliable firm, and naturally my brother said to himself, 'After me, my son.' Joseph worked hard at chemistry, followed the course of study, and had already passed an examination. The boy was steady and industrious, and had a taste for the business. On Sundays for recreation he made tinctures, prepared prescriptions, pasted the labels and rolled pills. When, as misfortune would have it, a murder was committed about twenty feet from my brother's pharmacy——"

"The murder of the Rue Montorgueil—that clerk who killed his sweetheart, a little brewery maid?"

"The very same. Joseph was attracted by the cries, saw the murderer arrested, and after the police were gone stayed there in the street, talking and jabbering. The Saturday before, Joseph had a game of billiards with the murderer."

"With the murderer!"

"Oh! accidentally—he knew him by sight, went to the same café, that's all, and they had played at pool together, Joseph and the murderer—a man named Nicot. Joseph told this to the crowd, and you may well imagine how important that made him, when suddenly a little blond man seized him. 'You know the murderer?' 'A little, not much; I played pool with him.' 'And do you know the motive of the crime?' 'It was love, Monsieur, love; Nicot had met a girl, named Eugénie——' 'You knew the victim, too?' 'Only by sight, she was there in the café the night we played.' 'Very well; but

MY NEPHEW JOSEPH

don't tell that to anybody; come, come, quick.' He took possession of Joseph and made him get into a cab, which went rolling off at great speed down the Boulevard des Italiens. Ten minutes after, Joseph found himself in a hall where there was a big table, around which five or six young men were writing. 'Here is a fine sensation,' said the little blond on entering. 'The best kind of a murder! a murder for love, in the Rue Montorgueil, and I have here the murderer's most intimate friend.' 'No, not at all,' cried Joseph, 'I scarcely know him.' 'Be still,' whispered the little blond to Joseph; then he continued, 'Yes, his most intimate friend. They were brought up together, and a quarter of an hour before the crime was committed were playing billiards. The murderer won, he was perfectly calm——' 'That's not it, it was last Saturday that I played with——' 'Be still, will you! A quarter of an hour, it is more to the point. Let's go. Come, come.' He took Joseph into a small room where they were alone, and said to him: 'That affair ought to make about a hundred lines—you talk—I'll write—there will be twenty francs for you.' 'Twenty francs!' 'Yes, and here they are in advance; but be quick, to business!' Joseph told all he knew to the gentleman—how an old and retired Colonel, who lived in the house where the murder was committed, was the first to hear the victim's cries; but he was paralyzed in both limbs, this old Colonel, and could only ring for the servant, an old cuirassier, who arrested the assassin. In short, with all the information concerning the game of billiards, Eugénie and the paralytic old Colonel, the man composed his little article, and sent Joseph away with twenty francs. Do you think it ended there?"

"I don't think anything—I am amazed! Little Joseph a reporter!"

"Hardly had Joseph stepped outside, when another man seized him—a tall, dark fellow. 'I've been watching for you,' he said to Joseph. 'You were present when the murder was committed in the Rue Montorgueil!' 'Why, no, I was not present——' 'That will do. I am well informed, come.' 'Where to?' 'To my newspaper office.' 'What for?' 'To tell me about the murder.' 'But I've already told all I know, there, in that house.' 'Come, you will still remember a few more little incidents—and I will give you twenty francs.' 'Twenty francs!' 'Come, come.' Another hall, another table, more young men writing, and again Joseph was interrogated. He recommenced the history of the old Colonel. 'Is that what you told them down there?' inquired the tall, dark man of Joseph. 'Yes, Monsieur.' 'That needs some revision, then.' And the tall, dark man made up a long story. How this old Colonel had been paralyzed for fourteen years, but on hearing the victim's heartrending screams, received such a shock that all at once, as if by a miracle, had recovered the use of his legs; and it was he who had started out in pursuit of the murderer and had him arrested.

"While dashing this off with one stroke of his pen, the man exclaimed: 'Good! this is perfect! a hundred times better than the other account.' 'Yes,' said Joseph, 'but it is not true.' 'Not true for you, because you are acquainted with the affair; but for our hundred thousand readers, who do not know about it, it will be true enough. They were not there, those hundred thousand readers. What do they want? A striking account—well! they shall have it!' And thereupon he discharged Joseph, who went home with his forty francs, and who naturally did not boast of his escapade. It is only of late that he has acknowledged it. However, from that day Joseph has shown less interest in the pharmacy. He bought a number of penny papers, and shut himself up in his room to write—no one knows what. At last he wore a business-like aspect, which was very funny. About six months ago I went to Paris to collect the dividends on my Northern stock."

"The Northern is doing very well; it went up this week——"

"Oh! it's good stock. Well, I had collected my dividends and had left the Northern Railway Station. It was beautiful weather, so I walked slowly down the Rue Lafayette. (I have a habit of strolling a little in Paris after I have collected my dividends.) When at the corner of the Faubourg Montmartre, whom should I see but my nephew, Joseph, all alone in a victoria, playing the fine gentleman. I saw very well that he turned his head away, the vagabond! But I overtook the carriage and stopped the driver. 'What are you

MY NEPHEW JOSEPH

doing there?' 'A little drive, uncle.' 'Wait, I will go with you,' and in I climbed. 'Hurry up,' said the driver, 'or I'll lose the trail.' 'What trail?' 'Why, the two cabs we are following.' The man drove at a furious rate, and I asked Joseph why he was there in that victoria, following two cabs. 'Mon Dieu, uncle,' he replied, 'there was a foreigner, a Spaniard, who came to our place in the Rue Montorgueil and bought a large amount of drugs, and has not paid us, so I am going after him to find out if he has not given us a wrong address.' 'And that Spaniard is in both the cabs?' 'No, uncle, he is only in one, the first.' 'And who is in the second?' 'I don't know, probably another creditor, like myself, in pursuit of the Spaniard.' 'Well, I am going to stay with you; I have two hours to myself before the train leaves at five o'clock and I adore this sort of thing, riding around Paris in an open carriage. Let's follow the Spaniard!' And then the chase commenced, down the boulevards, across the squares, through the streets, the three drivers cracking their whips and urging their horses on. This man-hunt began to get exciting. It recalled to my mind the romances in the Petit Journal. Finally, in a little street, belonging to the Temple Quarter, the first cab stopped."

"The Spaniard?"

"Yes. A man got out of it—he had a large hat drawn down over his eyes and a big muffler wrapped about his neck. Presently three gentlemen, who had jumped from the second cab, rushed upon that man. I wanted to do the same, but Joseph tried to prevent me. 'Don't stir, uncle!' 'Why not? But they are going to deprive us of the Spaniard!' And I dashed forward. 'Take care, uncle, don't be mixed up in that affair.' But I was already gone. When I arrived they were putting the handcuffs on the Spaniard. I broke through the crowd which had collected, and cried, 'Wait, Messieurs, wait; I also demand a settlement with this man.' They made way for me. 'You know this man?' asked one of the gentlemen from the second cab, a short, stout fellow. 'Perfectly; he is a Spaniard.' 'I a Spaniard!' 'Yes, a Spaniard.' 'Good,' said the short, stout man, 'Here's the witness!' and, addressing himself to one of the men, 'Take Monsieur to the Prefecture immediately." 'But I have not the time; I live in Versailles;

my wife expects me by the five o'clock train, and we have company to dinner, and I must take home a pie. I will come back to-morrow at any hour you wish.' 'No remarks,' said the short, stout man, 'but be off; I am the Police Commissioner.' 'But, Monsieur the Commissioner, I know nothing about it; it is my nephew Joseph who will tell you,' and I called 'Joseph! Joseph!' but no Joseph came."

"He had decamped?"

"With the victoria. They packed me in one of the two cabs with the detective, a charming man and very distinguished. Arriving at the Prefecture, they deposited me in a small apartment filled with vagabonds, criminals, and low, ignorant people. An hour after they came for me in order to bring me up for examination."

"You were brought up for examination?"

"Yes, my dear Monsieur, I was. A policeman conducted me through the Palais de Justice, before the magistrate, a lean man, who asked me my name and address. I replied that I lived in Versailles, and that I had company to dinner; he interrupted me, 'You know the prisoner?' pointing to the man with the muffler, 'Speak up.' But he questioned me so threateningly that I became disconcerted, for I felt that he was passing judgment upon me. Then in my embarrassment the words did not come quickly. I finished, moreover, by telling him that I knew the man without knowing him; then he became furious: 'What's that you say? You know a man without knowing him! At least explain yourself!' I was all of a tremble, and said that I knew he was a Spaniard, but the man replied that he was not a Spaniard. 'Well, well,' said the Judge. 'Denial, always denial; it is your way.' 'I tell you that my name is Rigaud, and that I was born in Josey, in Josas; they are not Spaniards that are born in Josey, in Josas.' 'Always contradiction; very good, very good!' And the Judge addressed himself to me. 'Then this man is a Spaniard?' 'Yes, Monsieur the Judge, so I have been told.' 'Do you know anything more about him?' 'I know he made purchases at my brother's pharmacy in the Rue Montorgueil.' 'At a pharmacy! and he bought, did he not, some chlorate of potash, azotite of potash, and sulphur powder; in a word, materials to manufacture explosives.' 'I

MY NEPHEW JOSEPH

don't know what he bought. I only know that he did not pay, that's all.' 'Parbleau! Anarchists never pay——' 'I did not need to pay. I never bought chlorate of potash in the Rue Montorgueil,' cried the man; but the Judge exclaimed, louder still, 'Yes, it is your audacious habit of lying, but I will sift this matter to the bottom; sift it, do you understand. And now why is that muffler on in the month of May?' 'I have a cold,' replied the other. 'Haven't I the right to have a cold?' 'That is very suspicious, very suspicious. I am going to send for the druggist in the Rue Montorgueil!'"

"Then they sent for your brother?"

"Yes; I wanted to leave, tried to explain to the Judge that my wife was expecting me in Versailles, that I had already missed the five o'clock train, that I had company to dinner, and must bring home a pie. 'You shall not go,' replied the Judge, 'and cease to annoy me with your dinner and your pie; I will need you for a second examination. The affair is of the gravest sort.' I tried to resist, but they led me away somewhat roughly, and thrust me again into the little apartment with the criminals. After waiting an hour I was brought up for another examination. My brother was there. But we could not exchange two words, for he entered the courtroom by one door and I by another. All this was arranged perfectly. The man with the muffler was again brought out. The Judge addressed my brother. "Do you recognize the prisoner?' 'No.' 'Ah! you see he does not know me!' 'Be silent!' said the Judge, and he continued talking excitedly: 'You know the man?' 'Certainly not.' 'Think well; you ought to know him.' 'I tell you, no.' 'I tell you, yes, and that he bought some chlorate of potash from you.' 'No!' 'Ah!' cried the Judge, in a passion. 'Take care, weigh well your words; you are treading on dangerous ground.' 'I!' exclaimed my brother. 'Yes, for there is your brother; you recognize him, I think.' 'Yes, I recognize him.' 'That is fortunate. Well, your brother there says that man owes you money for having bought at your establishment—I specify—materials to manufacture explosives.' 'But you did not say that.' 'No, I wish to re-establish the facts.' But that Judge would give no one a chance to speak. 'Don't interrupt me. Who is conducting this examination, you or I?' 'You, Monsieur the Judge?' 'Well, at all events, you said the prisoner owed your brother some money.' 'That I acknowledge.' 'But who told you all this?' asked my brother. 'Your son, Joseph!' 'Joseph!' 'He followed the man for the sake of the money, which he owed you for the drugs.' 'I understand nothing of all this,' said my brother; 'Neither do I,' said the man with the muffler; 'Neither do I,' I repeated in my turn; 'Neither do I any more,' cried the Judge; 'Or rather, yes, there is something that I understand very well; we have captured a gang, all these men understand one another, and side with one another; they are a band of Anarchists!' 'That is putting it too strong,' I protested to the Judge, 'I, a landowner, an Anarchist! Can a man be an Anarchist when he owns a house on the Boulevard de la Reine at Versailles and a cottage at Houlgate Calvados? These are facts.'"

"That was well answered."

"But this Judge would not listen to anything. He said to my brother, 'Where does your son live?' 'With me in the Rue Montorgueil.' 'Well, he must be sent for; and in the meanwhile, these two brothers are to be placed in separate cells.' Then, losing patience, I cried that this was infamy! But I felt myself seized and dragged through the corridors and locked in a little box four feet square. In there I passed three hours."

"Didn't they find your nephew Joseph?"

"No, it was not that. It was the Judge. He went off to his dinner, and took his time about it! Finally, at midnight, they had another examination. Behold all four of us before the Judge! The man with the muffler, myself, my brother and Joseph. The Judge began, addressing my nephew: 'This man is indeed your father?' 'Yes.' 'This man is indeed your uncle?' 'Yes.' 'And that man is indeed the Spaniard who purchased some chlorate of potash from you?' 'No.' 'What! No?' 'There,' exclaimed the fellow with the muffler. 'You can see now that these men do not know me.' 'Yes, yes,' answered the Judge, not at all disconcerted. 'Denial again! Let's see, young man, did you not say to your uncle——' 'Yes, Monsieur the Judge, that is true.' 'Ah! the truth! Here is the truth!' exclaimed the Judge, triumphantly. 'Yes,

MY NEPHEW JOSEPH

I told my uncle that the man purchased drugs from us, but that is not so.' 'Why isn't it?' 'Wait, I will tell you. Unknown to my family I am a journalist.' 'Journalist! My son a journalist! Don't believe that, Monsieur the Judge, my son is an apprentice in a pharmacy.' 'Yes, my nephew is an apprentice in a pharmacy,' I echoed. 'These men contradict themselves; this is a gang, decidedly a gang—are you a journalist, young man, or an apprentice in a pharmacy?' 'I am both.' 'That is a lie!' cried my brother, now thoroughly angry. 'And for what newspaper do you write?' 'For no paper at all,' replied my brother, 'I know that, for he is not capable.' 'I do not exactly write, Monsieur the Judge; I procure information; I am a reporter.' 'Reporter! My son a reporter? What's that he says?' 'Will you be still!' cried the Judge. 'For what newspaper are you a reporter?' Joseph told the name of the paper. 'Well,' resumed the Judge, 'we must send for the chief editor immediately—immediately, he must be awakened and brought here. I will pass the night at court. I've discovered a great conspiracy. Lead these men away and keep them apart.' The Judge beamed, for he already saw himself Court Counsellor. They brought us back, and I assure you I no longer knew where I was. I came and went up and down the staircases and through the corridors. If anyone had asked me at the time if I were an accomplice of Ravachol, I would have answered, 'Probably.' "

"When did all this take place?"

"One o'clock in the morning; and the fourth examination did not take place until two. But, thank Heaven! in five minutes it was all made clear. The editor of the newspaper arrived, and burst into a hearty laugh when he learned of the condition of affairs; and this is what he told the Judge. My nephew had given them the particulars of a murder, and had been recompensed for it, and then the young man had acquired a taste for that occupation, and had come to apply for the situation. They had found him clear-headed, bold, and intelligent, and had sent him to take notes at the executions, at fires, etc., and the morning after the editor had a good idea. 'The detectives were on the lookout for Anarchists, so I sent my reporters on the heels of each de-

MY NEPHEW JOSEPH

tective, and in this way I would be the first to hear of all the arrests. Now, you see, it all explains itself; the detective followed an Anarchist.'"

"And your nephew Joseph followed the detective?"

"Yes, but he dared not tell the truth, so he told me 'he was one of papa's debtors.' The man with the muffler was triumphant. 'Am I still a Spaniard?' 'No, well and good,' replied the Judge. 'But an Anarchist is another thing.' And in truth he was; but he only held one, that Judge, and was so vexed because he believed he had caught a whole gang, and was obliged to discharge us at four o'clock in the morning. I had to take a carriage to return to Versailles—got one for thirty francs. But found my poor wife in such a state!"

"And your nephew still clings to journalism?"

"Yes, and makes money for nothing but to ride about Paris that way in a cab, and to the country in the railway trains. The newspaper men are satisfied with him."

"What does your brother say to all this?"

"He began by turning him out of doors. But when he knew that some months he made two and three hundred francs, he softened; and then Joseph is as cute as a monkey. You know my brother invented a cough lozenge, 'Dervishes' lozenges?"

"Yes, you gave me a box of them."

"Ah! so I did. Well, Joseph found means to introduce into the account of a murderer's arrest an advertisement of his father's lozenges."—"How did he do it?"

"He told how the murderer was hidden in a panel, and that he could not be found. But having the influenza, had sneezed, and that had been the means of his capture. And Joseph added that this would not have happened to him had he taken the Dervishes Lozenges. You see that pleased my brother so much that he forgave him. Ah! there is my wife coming to look for me. Not a word of all this! It is not necessary to repeat that there is a reporter in the family, and there is another reason for not telling it. When I want to sell off to the people of Versailles, I go and find Joseph and tell him of my little plan. He arranges everything for me as it should be, puts it in the paper quietly, and they don't know how it comes there!"

A FOREST BETROTHAL
BY ERCKMANN-CHATRIAN

A FOREST BETROTHAL

By ERCKMANN-CHATRIAN

ONE day in the month of June, 1845, Master Zacharias' fishing-basket was so full of salmon-trout, about three o'clock in the afternoon, that the good man was loath to take any more; for, as Pathfinder says: "We must leave some for to-morrow!" After having washed his in a stream and carefully covered them with field-sorrel and rowell, to keep them fresh; after having wound up his line and bathed his hands and face; a sense of drowsiness tempted him to take a nap in the heather. The heat was so excessive that he preferred to wait until the shadows lengthened before re-climbing the steep ascent of Bigelberg.

Breaking his crust of bread and wetting his lips with a draught of Rikevir, he climbed down fifteen or twenty steps from the path and stretched himself on the moss-covered ground, under the shade of the pine-trees; his eyelids heavy with sleep.

A thousand animate creatures had lived their long life of an hour, when the judge was wakened by the whistle of a bird, which sounded strange to him. He sat up to look around, and judge his surprise; the so-called bird was a young girl of seventeen or eighteen years of age; fresh, with rosy cheeks and vermilion lips, brown hair, which hung in two long tresses behind her. A short poppy-colored skirt, with a tightly-laced bodice, completed her costume. She was a young peasant, who was rapidly descending the sandy path down the side of Bigelberg, a basket poised on her head, and her arms a little sunburned, but plump, were gracefully resting on her hips.

"Oh, what a charming bird; but she whistles well and her pretty chin, round like a peach, is sweet to look upon."

Mr. Zacharias was all emotion—a rush of hot blood, which

Copyrighted 1893 Current Literature Publishing Company.

made his heart beat, as it did at twenty, coursed through his veins. Blushing, he arose to his feet.

"Good-day, my pretty one!" he said.

The young girl stopped short—opened her big eyes and recognized him (for who did not know the dear old Judge Zacharias in that part of the country?).

"Ah!" she said, with a bright smile, "it is Mr. Zacharias Seiler!"

The old man approached her—he tried to speak—but all he could do was to stammer a few unintelligible words, just like a very young man—his embarrassment was so great that he completely disconcerted the young girl. At last he managed to say:

"Where are you going through the forest at this hour, my dear child?"

She stretched out her hand and showed him, way at the end of the valley, a forester's house.

"I am returning to my father's house, the Corporal Yeri Foerster. You know him, without doubt, Monsieur le Juge."

"What, are you our brave Yeri's daughter? Ah, do I know him? A very worthy man. Then you are little Charlotte of whom he has often spoken to me when he came with his official reports?"

"Yes, Monsieur; I have just come from the town and am returning home."

"That is a very pretty bunch of Alpine berries you have," exclaimed the old man.

She detached the bouquet from her belt and tendered it to him.

"If it would please you, Monsieur Seiler."

Zacharias was touched.

"Yes, indeed," he said, "I will accept it, and I will accompany you home. I am anxious to see this brave Foerster again. He must be getting old by now."

"He is about your age, Monsieur le Juge," said Charlotte innocently, "between fifty-five and sixty years of age."

This simple speech recalled the good man to his senses, and as he walked beside her he became pensive.

What was he thinking of? Nobody could tell; but how many times, how many times has it happened that a brave

A FOREST BETROTHAL

and worthy man, thinking that he had fulfilled all his duties, finds that he has neglected the greatest, the most sacred, the most beautiful of all—that of love. And what it costs him to think of it when it is too late.

Soon Mr. Zacharias and Charlotte came to the turn of the valley where the path spanned a little pond by means of a rustic bridge, and led straight to the corporal's house. They could now see Yeri Foerster, his large felt hat decorated with a twig of heather, his calm eyes, his brown cheeks and grayish hair, seated on the stone bench near his doorway; two beautiful hunting dogs, with reddish-brown coats, lay at his feet, and the high vine arbor behind him rose to the peak of the gable roof.

The shadows on Romelstein were lengthening and the setting sun spread its purple fringe behind the high fir-trees on Alpnach.

The old corporal, whose eyes were as piercing as an eagle's, recognized Monsieur Zacharias and his daughter from afar. He came toward them, lifting his felt hat respectfully.

"Welcome, Monsieur le Juge," he said in the frank and cordial voice of a mountaineer; "what happy circumstance has procured me the honor of a visit?"

"Master Yeri," replied the good man, "I am belated in your mountains. Have you a vacant corner at your table and a bed at the disposition of a friend?"

"Ah!" cried the Corporal, "if there were but one bed in the house, should it not be at the service of the best, the most honored of our ex-magistrates of Stantz? Monsieur Seiler, what an honor you confer on Yeri Foerster's humble home."

"Christine, Christine! Monsieur le Juge Zacharias Seiler wishes to sleep under our roof to-night."

Then a little old woman, her face wrinkled like a vine leaf, but still fresh and laughing, her head crowned by a cap with wide black ribbons, appeared on the threshold and disappeared again, murmuring:

"What? Is it possible? Monsieur le Juge!"

"My good people," said Mr. Zacharias, "truly you do me too much honor—I hope——."

"Monsieur le Juge, if you forget the favors you have done to others, they remember them."

Charlotte placed her basket on the table, feeling very proud at having been the means of bringing so distinguished a visitor to the house. She took out the sugar, the coffee and all the little odds and ends of household provisions which she had purchased in the town. And Zacharias, gazing at her pretty profile, felt himself agitated once more, his poor old heart beat more quickly in his bosom and seemed to say to him: "This is love, Zacharias! This is love! This is love!"

To tell you the truth, my dear friends, Mr. Seiler spent the evening with the Head Forester, Yeri Foerster, perfectly oblivious to the fact of Therèse's uneasiness, to his promise to return before seven o'clock, to all his old habits of order and submission.

Picture to yourself the large room, the time-browned rafters of the ceiling, the windows opened on the silent valley, the round table in the middle of the room, covered with a white cloth, with red stripes running through it; the light from the lamp, bringing out more clearly the grave faces of Zacharias and Yeri, the rosy, laughing features of Charlotte, and Dame Christine's little cap, with long fluttering streamers. Picture to yourself the soup-tureen, with gayly-flowered bowl, from which arose an appetising odor, the dish of trout garnished with parsley, the plates filled with fruits and little meal cakes as yellow as gold—; then worthy Father Zacharias, handing first one and then the other of the plates of fruit and cakes to Charlotte, who lowered her eyes, frightened at the old man's compliments and tender speeches.

Yeri was quite puffed up at his praise, but Dame Christine said: "Ah, Monsieur le Juge! You are too good. You do not know how much trouble this little girl gives us, or how headstrong she is when she wants anything. You will spoil her with so many compliments."

To which speech Mr. Zacharias made reply:

"Dame Christine, you possess a treasure! Mademoiselle Charlotte merits all the good I have said of her."

Then Master Yeri, raising his glass, cried out:

A FOREST BETROTHAL

"Let us drink to the health of our good and venerated Judge Zacharias Seiler!"

The toast was drunk with a will.

Just then the clock, in its hoarse voice, struck the hour of eleven. Out of doors there was the great silence of the forest, the grasshopper's last cry, the vague murmur of the river. As the hour sounded, they rose, preparatory to retiring. How fresh and agile he felt! With what ardor, had he dared, would he not have pressed a kiss upon Charlotte's little hand! Oh, but he must not think of that now! Later on, perhaps!

"Come, Master Yeri," he said, "it is bedtime. Goodnight, and many thanks for your hospitality."

"At what hour do you wish to rise, Monsieur?" asked Christine.

"Oh!" he replied gazing at Charlotte, "I am an early bird. I do not feel my age, though perhaps you might not think so. I rise at five o'clock."

"Like me, Monsieur Seiler," cried the Head Forester. I rise before daybreak; but I must confess it is tiresome all the same—we are no longer young. Ha! Ha!"

"Bah! I have never had anything ail me, Master Forester; I have never been more vigorous or more nimble."

And suiting his actions to his words, he ran briskly up the steep steps of the staircase. Really Mr. Zacharias was no more than twenty; but his twenty years lasted about twenty minutes, and once nestled in the large canopied bed, with the covers drawn up to his chin and his handkerchief tied around his head, in lieu of a nightcap, he said to himself:

"Sleep Zacharias! Sleep! You have great need of rest; you are very tired."

And the good man slept until nine o'clock. The forester returning from his rounds, uneasy at his non-appearance, went up to his room and wished him good morning. Then seeing the sun high in the heavens, hearing the birds warbling in the foliage, the Judge, ashamed of his boastfulness of the previous night, arose, alleging as an excuse for his prolonged slumbers, the fatigue of fishing and the length of the supper of the evening before.

"Ah, Monsieur Seiler," said the forester, "it is perfectly

natural; I would love dearly myself to sleep in the mornings, but I must always be on the go. What I want is a son-in-law, a strong youth to replace me; I would voluntarily give him my gun and my hunting pouch."

Zacharias could not restrain a feeling of great uneasiness at these words. Being dressed, he descended in silence. Christine was waiting with his breakfast; Charlotte had gone to the hay field.

The breakfast was short, and Mr. Seiler having thanked these good people for their hospitality, turned his face toward Stantz; he became pensive, as he thought of the worry to which Mademoiselle Therèse had been subjected; yet he was not able to tear his hopes from his heart, nor the thousand charming illusions, which came to him like a late-comer in a nest of warblers.

By Autumn he had fallen so into the habit of going to the forester's house that he was oftener there than at his own; and the Head Forester, not knowing to what love of fishing to attribute these visits, often found himself embarrassed at being obliged to refuse the multiplicity of presents which the worthy ex-magistrate (he himself being very much at home) begged of him to accept in compensation for his daily hospitality.

Besides, Mr. Seiler wished to share all his occupations, following him in his rounds in the Grinderwald and Entilbach.

Yeri Foerster often shook his head, saying: "I never knew a more honest or better judge than Mr. Zacharias Seiler. When I used to bring my reports to him, formerly, he always praised me, and it is to him that I owe my raise to the rank of Head Forester. "But," he added to his wife, "I am afraid the poor man is a little out of his head. Did he not help Charlotte in the hay field, to the infinite enjoyment of the peasants? Truly, Christine, it is not right; but then I dare not say so to him, he is so much above us. Now he wants me to accept a pension—and such a pension—one hundred florins a month. And that silk dress he gave Charlotte on her birthday. Do young girls wear silk dresses in our valley? Is a silk dress the thing for a forester's daughter?"

"Leave him alone," said the wife. "He is contented with

A FOREST BETROTHAL

a little milk and meal. He likes to be with us; it is a change from his lonesome city life, with no one to talk to but his old governess; whilst here the little one looks after him. He likes to talk to her. Who knows but he may end by adopting her and leave her something in his will?"

The Head Forester, not knowing what to say, shrugged his shoulders; his good judgment told him there was some mystery, but he never dreamed of suspecting the good man's whole folly.

One fine morning a wagon slowly wended its way down the sides of Bigelberg loaded with three casks of old Rikevir wine. Of all the presents that could be given to him this was the most acceptable, for Yeri Foerster loved, above everything else, a good glass of wine.

"That warms one up," he would say, laughing. And when he had tasted this wine he could not help saying:

"Mr. Zacharias is really the best man in the world. Has he not filled my cellar for me? Charlotte, go and gather the prettiest flowers in the garden; cut all the roses and the jasmine, make them into a bouquet, and when he comes you will present them to him yourself. Charlotte! Charlotte! Hurry up, here he comes with his long pole."

At this moment the old man appeared descending the hillside in the shade of the pines with a brisk step.

As far off as Yeri could make himself heard, he called out, his glass in his hand:

"Here is to the best man I know! Here is to our benefactor."

And Zacharias smiled. Dame Christine had already commenced preparations for dinner; a rabbit was turning at the spit and the savory odor of the soup whetted Mr. Seiler's appetite.

The old Judge's eyes brightened when he saw Charlotte in her short poppy-colored skirt, her arms bare to the elbow, running here and there in the garden paths gathering the flowers, and when he saw her approaching him with her huge bouquet, which she humbly presented to him with downcast eyes.

"Monsieur le Juge, will you deign to accept this bouquet from your little friend Charlotte?"

A sudden blush overspread his venerable cheeks, and as she stooped to kiss his hand, he said:

"No, no, my dear child; accept rather from your old friend, your best friend, a more tender embrace."

He kissed both her burning cheeks. The Head Forester laughing heartily, cried out:

"Monsieur Seiler, come and sit down under the acacia tree and drink some of your own wine. Ah, my wife is right when she calls you our benefactor."

Mr. Zacharias seated himself at the little round table, placing his pole behind him; Charlotte sat facing him, Yeri Foerster was on his right; then dinner was served and Mr. Seiler started to speak of his plans for the future.

He was wealthy and had inherited a fine fortune from his parents. He wished to buy some few hundred acres of forest land in the valley, and build in the midst a forester's lodge. "We would always be together," he said turning to Yeri Foerster, "sometimes you at my house, sometimes I at yours."

Christine gave her advice, and they chatted, planning now one thing, then another. Charlotte seemed perfectly contented, and Zacharias imagined that these simple people understood him.

Thus the time passed, and when night had fallen and they had had a surfeit of Rikevir, of rabbit and of Dame Christine's "koechten" sprinkled with cinnamon, Mr. Seiler, happy and contented, full of joyous hope, ascended to his room, putting off until to-morrow his declaration, not doubting for a moment but that it would be accepted.

About this time of the year the mountaineers from Harberg, Kusnacht and the surrounding hamlets descend from their mountains about one o'clock in the morning and commence to mow the high grass in the valleys. One can hear their monotonous songs in the middle of the night keeping time to the circular movement of the scythes, the jingle of the cattle bells, and the young men and girls' voices laughing afar in the silence of the night. It is a strange harmony, especially when the night is clear and there is a bright moon, and the heavy dew falling makes a pitter-patter on the leaves of the great forest trees.

A FOREST BETROTHAL

Mr. Zacharias heard nothing of all this, for he was sleeping soundly; but the noise of a handful of peas being thrown against the window waked him suddenly. He listened and heard outside at the bottom of the wall, a "scit! scit!" so softly whispered that you might almost think it the cry of some bird. Nevertheless, the good man's heart fluttered.

"What is that?" he cried.

After a few seconds' silence a soft voice replied:

"Charlotte, Charlotte—It is I!"

Zacharias trembled; and as he listened with ears on the alert for each sound, the foliage on the trellis struck against the window and a figure climbed up quietly—oh so quietly—then stopped and stared into the room.

The old man being indignant at this, rose and opened the window, upon which the stranger climbed through noiselessly.

"Do not be frightened, Charlotte," he said, "I have come to tell you some good news. My father will be here tomorrow."

He received no response, for the reason that Zacharias was trying to light the lamp.

"Where are you, Charlotte?"

"Here I am," cried the old man turning with a livid face and gazing fiercely at his rival.

The young man who stood before him was tall and slender, with large, frank, black eyes, brown cheeks, rosy lips, just covered with a little moustache, and a large brown, felt hat, tilted a little to one side.

The apparition of Zacharias stunned him to immovability. But as the Judge was about to cry out, he exclaimed:

"In the name of Heaven, do not call. I am no robber—I love Charlotte!"

"And—she—she?" stammered Zacharias.

"She loves me also! Oh, you need have no fear if you are one of her relations. We were betrothed at the Kusnacht feast. The fiancés of the Grinderwald and the Entilbach have the right to visit in the night. It is a custom of Unterwald. All the Swiss know that."

"Yeri Foerster—Yeri, Charlotte's father, never told me."

"No, he does not know of our betrothal yet," said the other, in a lower tone of voice; "when I asked his permission last year he told me to wait—that his daughter was too young yet—we were betrothed secretly. Only as I had not the Forester's consent, I did not come in the night-time. This is the first time. I saw Charlotte in the town; but the time seemed so long to us both that I ended by confessing all to my father, and he has promised to see Yeri to-morrow. Ah, Monsieur, I knew it would give such pleasure to Charlotte that I could not help coming to announce my good news."

The poor old man fell back in his chair and covered his face with his hands. Oh, how he suffered! What bitter thoughts passed through his brain; what a sad awakening after so many sweet and joyous dreams.

And the young mountaineer was not a whit more comfortable, as he stood leaning against a corner of the wall, his arms crossed over his breast, and the following thoughts running through his head:

"If old Foerster, who does not know of our betrothal, finds me here, he will kill me without listening to one word of explanation. That is certain."

And he gazed anxiously at the door, his ear on the alert for the least sound.

A few moments afterward, Zacharias lifting his head, as though awakening from a dream, asked him:

"What is your name?"

"Karl Imnant, Monsieur."

"What is your business?"

"My father hopes to obtain the position of a forester in the Grinderwald for me."

There was a long silence and Zacharias looked at the young man with an envious eye.

"And she loves you?" he asked in a broken voice.

"Oh, yes, Monsieur; we love each other devotedly."

And Zacharias, letting his eyes fall on his thin legs and his hands wrinkled and veined, murmured:

"Yes, she ought to love him; he is young and handsome."

And his head fell on his breast again. All at once he arose, trembling in every limb, and opened the window.

A FOREST BETROTHAL

"Young man, you have done very wrong; you will never know how much wrong you have really done. You must obtain Mr. Foerster's consent—but go—go—you will hear from me soon."

The young mountaineer did not wait for a second invitation; with one bound he jumped to the path below and disappeared behind the grand old trees.

"Poor, poor Zacharias," the old Judge murmured, "all your illusions are fled."

At seven o'clock, having regained his usual calmness of demeanor, he descended to the room below, where Charlotte, Dame Christine and Yeri were already waiting breakfast for him. The old man turning his eyes from the young girl, advanced to the Head Forester, saying:

"My friend, I have a favor to ask of you. You know the son of the forester of the Grinderwald, do you not?"

"Karl Imnant, why yes, sir!"

"He is a worthy young man, and well behaved, I believe."

"I think so, Monsieur."

"Is he capable of succeeding his father?"

"Yes, he is twenty-one years old; he knows all about tree-clipping, which is the most necessary thing of all—he knows how to read and how to write; but that is not all; he must have influence."

"Well, Master Yeri, I still have some influence in the Department of Forests and Rivers. This day fortnight, or three weeks at the latest, Karl Imnant shall be Assistant Forester of the Grinderwald, and I ask the hand of your daughter Charlotte for this brave young man."

At this request, Charlotte, who had blushed and trembled with fear, uttered a cry and fell back into her mother's arms.

Her father looking at her severely, said: "What is the matter, Charlotte? Do you refuse?"

"Oh, no, no, father—no!"

"That is as it should be! As for myself, I should never have refused any request of Mr. Zacharias Seiler's! Come here and embrace your benefactor."

Charlotte ran toward him and the old man pressed her to his heart, gazing long and earnestly at her, with eyes filled

A FOREST BETROTHAL

with tears. Then pleading business he started home, with only a crust of bread in his basket for breakfast.

Fifteen days afterward, Karl Imnant received the appointment of forester, taking his father's place. Eight days later, he and Charlotte were married.

The guests drank the rich Rikevir wine, so highly esteemed by Yeri Foerster, and which seemed to him to have arrived so opportunely for the feast.

Mr. Zacharias Seiler was not present that day at the wedding, being ill at home. Since then he rarely goes fishing—and then, always to the Brünnen—toward the lake—on the other side of the mountain.

ZADIG THE BABYLONIAN
BY FRANCOIS MARIE AROUET DE VOLTAIRE

ZADIG THE BABYLONIAN

By FRANCOIS MARIE AROUET DE VOLTAIRE

The Blind of One Eye

THERE lived at Babylon, in the reign of King Moabdar, a young man named Zadig, of a good natural disposition, strengthened and improved by education. Though rich and young, he had learned to moderate his passions; he had nothing stiff or affected in his behavior, he did not pretend to examine every action by the strict rules of reason, but was always ready to make proper allowances for the weakness of mankind.

It was matter of surprise that, notwithstanding his sprightly wit, he never exposed by his raillery those vague, incoherent, and noisy discourses, those rash censures, ignorant decisions, course jests, and all that empty jingle of words which at Babylon went by the name of conversation. He had learned, in the first book of Zoroaster, that self love is a football swelled with wind, from which, when pierced, the most terrible tempests issue forth.

Above all, Zadig never boasted of his conquests among the women, nor affected to entertain a contemptible opinion of the fair sex. He was generous, and was never afraid of obliging the ungrateful; remembering the grand precept of Zoroaster, "When thou eatest, give to the dogs, should they even bite thee." He was as wise as it is possible for man to be, for he sought to live with the wise.

Instructed in the sciences of the ancient Chaldeans, he understood the principles of natural philosophy, such as they were then supposed to be; and knew as much of metaphysics as hath ever been known in any age, that is, little or nothing at all. He was firmly persuaded, notwithstanding the new philosophy of the times, that the year consisted of three hundred and sixty-five days and six

FRANCOIS MARIE AROUET DE VOLTAIRE

hours, and that the sun was in the center of the world. But when the principal magi told him, with a haughty and contemptuous air, that his sentiments were of a dangerous tendency, and that it was to be an enemy to the state to believe that the sun revolved round its own axis, and that the year had twelve months, he held his tongue with great modesty and meekness.

Possessed as he was of great riches, and consequently of many friends, blessed with a good constitution, a handsome figure, a mind just and moderate, and a heart noble and sincere, he fondly imagined that he might easily be happy. He was going to be married to Semira, who, in point of beauty, birth, and fortune, was the first match in Babylon. He had a real and virtuous affection for this lady, and she loved him with the most passionate fondness.

The happy moment was almost arrived that was to unite them forever in the bands of wedlock, when happening to take a walk together toward one of the gates of Babylon, under the palm trees that adorn the banks of the Euphrates, they saw some men approaching, armed with sabers and arrows. These were the attendants of young Orcan, the minister's nephew, whom his uncle's creatures had flattered into an opinion that he might do everything with impunity. He had none of the graces nor virtues of Zadig; but thinking himself a much more accomplished man, he was enraged to find that the other was preferred before him. This jealousy, which was merely the effect of his vanity, made him imagine that he was desperately in love with Semira; and accordingly he resolved to carry her off. The ravishers seized her; in the violence of the outrage they wounded her, and made the blood flow from her person, the sight of which would have softened the tigers of Mount Imaus. She pierced the heavens with her complaints. She cried out, "My dear husband! they tear me from the man I adore." Regardless of her own danger, she was only concerned for the fate of her dear Zadig, who, in the meantime, defended himself with all the strength that courage and love could inspire. Assisted only by two slaves, he put the ravishers to flight and carried home Semira, insensible and bloody as she was.

ZADIG THE BABYLONIAN

On opening her eyes and beholding her deliverer, "O Zadig!" said she, "I loved thee formerly as my intended husband; I now love thee as the preserver of my honor and my life." Never was heart more deeply affected than that of Semira. Never did a more charming mouth express more moving sentiments, in those glowing words inspired by a sense of the greatest of all favors, and by the most tender transports of a lawful passion.

Her wound was slight and was soon cured. Zadig was more dangerously wounded; an arrow had pierced him near his eye, and penetrated to a considerable depth. Semira wearied Heaven with her prayers for the recovery of her lover. Her eyes were constantly bathed in tears; she anxiously awaited the happy moment when those of Zadig should be able to meet hers; but an abscess growing on the wounded eye gave everything to fear. A messenger was immediately dispatched to Memphis for the great physician Hermes, who came with a numerous retinue. He visited the patient and declared that he would lose his eye. He even foretold the day and hour when this fatal event would happen. "Had it been the right eye," said he, "I could easily have cured it; but the wounds of the left eye are incurable." All Babylon lamented the fate of Zadig, and admired the profound knowledge of Hermes.

In two days the abscess broke of its own accord and Zadig was perfectly cured. Hermes wrote a book to prove that it ought not to have been cured. Zadig did not read it; but, as soon as he was able to go abroad, he went to pay a visit to her in whom all his hopes of happiness were centered, and for whose sake alone he wished to have eyes. Semira had been in the country for three days past. He learned on the road that that fine lady, having openly declared that she had an unconquerable aversion to one-eyed men, had the night before given her hand to Orcan. At this news he fell speechless to the ground. His sorrow brought him almost to the brink of the grave. He was long indisposed; but reason at last got the better of his affliction, and the severity of his fate served to console him.

"Since," said he, "I have suffered so much from the cruel caprice of a woman educated at court, I must now think of marrying the daughter of a citizen." He pitched upon Azora, a lady of the greatest prudence, and of the best family in town. He married her and lived with her for three months in all the delights of the most tender union. He only observed that she had a little levity; and was too apt to find that those young men who had the most handsome persons were likewise possessed of most wit and virtue.

The Nose

One morning Azora returned from a walk in a terrible passion, and uttering the most violent exclamations. "What aileth thee," said he, "my dear spouse? What is it that can thus have discomposed thee?"

"Alas," said she, "thou wouldst be as much enraged as I am hadst thou seen what I have just beheld. I have been to comfort the young widow Cosrou, who, within these two days, hath raised a tomb to her young husband, near the rivulet that washes the skirts of this meadow. She vowed to heaven, in the bitterness of her grief, to remain at this tomb while the water of the rivulet should continue to run near it."—"Well," said Zadig, "she is an excellent woman, and loved her husband with the most sincere affection."

"Ah," replied Azora, "didst thou but know in what she was employed when I went to wait upon her!"

"In what, pray, beautiful Azora? Was she turning the course of the rivulet?"

Azora broke out into such long invectives and loaded the young widow with such bitter reproaches, that Zadig was far from being pleased with this ostentation of virtue.

Zadig had a friend named Cador, one of those young men in whom his wife discovered more probity and merit than in others. He made him his confidant, and secured his fidelity as much as possible by a considerable present. Azora, having passed two days with a friend in the country, returned home on the third. The servants told her, with tears in their eyes, that her husband died suddenly the night before; that they were afraid to send her an account of this mournful event; and that they had just been depositing his corpse in the tomb of his ancestors, at the end of the garden.

ZADIG THE BABYLONIAN

She wept, she tore her hair, and swore she would follow him to the grave.

In the evening Cador begged leave to wait upon her, and joined his tears with hers. Next day they wept less, and dined together. Cador told her that his friend had left him the greatest part of his estate; and that he should think himself extremely happy in sharing his fortune with her. The lady wept, fell into a passion, and at last became more mild and gentle. They sat longer at supper than at dinner. They now talked with greater confidence. Azora praised the deceased; but owned that he had many failings from which Cador was free.

During supper Cador complained of a violent pain in his side. The lady, greatly concerned, and eager to serve him, caused all kinds of essences to be brought, with which she anointed him, to try if some of them might not possibly ease him of his pain. She lamented that the great Hermes was not still in Babylon. She even condescended to touch the side in which Cador felt such exquisite pain.

"Art thou subject to this cruel disorder?" said she to him with a compassionate air.

"It sometimes brings me," replied Cador, "to the brink of the grave; and there is but one remedy that can give me relief, and that is to apply to my side the nose of a man who is lately dead."

"A strange remedy, indeed!" said Azora.

"Not more strange," replied he, "than the sachels of Arnon against the apoplexy." This reason, added to the great merit of the young man, at last determined the lady.

"After all," says she, "when my husband shall cross the bridge Tchinavar, in his journey to the other world, the angel Asrael will not refuse him a passage because his nose is a little shorter in the second life than it was in the first." She then took a razor, went to her husband's tomb, bedewed it with her tears, and drew near to cut off the nose of Zadig, whom she found extended at full length in the tomb. Zadig arose, holding his nose with one hand, and, putting back the razor with the other, "Madam," said he, "don't exclaim so violently against young Cosrou; the project of cutting off my nose is equal to that of turning the course of a rivulet."

FRANCOIS MARIE AROUET DE VOLTAIRE

The Dog and the Horse

Zadig found by experience that the first month of marriage, as it is written in the book of Zend, is the moon of honey, and that the second is the moon of wormwood. He was some time after obliged to repudiate Azora, who became too difficult to be pleased; and he then sought for happiness in the study of nature. "No man," said he, "can be happier than a philosopher who reads in this great book which God hath placed before our eyes. The truths he discovers are his own; he nourishes and exalts his soul; he lives in peace; he fears nothing from men; and his tender spouse will not come to cut off his nose."

Possessed of these ideas he retired to a country house on the banks of the Euphrates. There he did not employ himself in calculating how many inches of water flow in a second of time under the arches of a bridge, or whether there fell a cube line of rain in the month of the Mouse more than in the month of the Sheep. He never dreamed of making silk of cobwebs, or porcelain of broken bottles; but he chiefly studied the properties of plants and animals; and soon acquired a sagacity that made him discover a thousand differences where other men see nothing but uniformity.

One day, as he was walking near a little wood, he saw one of the queen's eunuchs running toward him, followed by several officers, who appeared to be in great perplexity, and who ran to and fro like men distracted, eagerly searching for something they had lost of great value. "Young man," said the first eunuch, "hast thou seen the queen's dog?" "It is a female," replied Zadig. "Thou art in the right," returned the first eunuch. "It is a very small she spaniel," added Zadig; "she has lately whelped; she limps on the left forefoot, and has very long ears." "Thou hast seen her," said the first eunuch, quite out of breath. "No," replied Zadig, "I have not seen her, nor did I so much as know that the queen had a dog."

Exactly at the same time, by one of the common freaks of fortune, the finest horse in the king's stable had escaped from the jockey in the plains of Babylon. The principal

ZADIG THE BABYLONIAN

huntsman and all the other officers ran after him with as much eagerness and anxiety as the first eunuch had done after the spaniel. The principal huntsman addressed himself to Zadig, and asked him if he had not seen the king's horse passing by. "He is the fleetest horse in the king's stable," replied Zadig; "he is five feet high, with very small hoofs, and a tail three feet and a half in length; the studs on his bit are gold of twenty-three carats, and his shoes are silver of eleven pennyweights." "What way did he take? where is he?" demanded the chief huntsman. "I have not seen him," replied Zadig, "and never heard talk of him before."

The principal huntsman and the first eunuch never doubted but that Zadig had stolen the king's horse and the queen's spaniel. They therefore had him conducted before the assembly of the grand desterham, who condemned him to the knout, and to spend the rest of his days in Siberia. Hardly was the sentence passed when the horse and the spaniel were both found. The judges were reduced to the disagreeable necessity of reversing their sentence; but they condemned Zadig to pay four hundred ounces of gold for having said that he had not seen what he had seen. This fine he was obliged to pay; after which he was permitted to plead his cause before the counsel of the grand desterham, when he spoke to the following effect:

"Ye stars of justice, abyss of sciences, mirrors of truth, who have the weight of lead, the hardness of iron, the splendor of the diamond, and many properties of gold: Since I am permitted to speak before this august assembly, I swear to you by Oramades that I have never seen the queen's respectable spaniel, nor the sacred horse of the king of kings. The truth of the matter was as follows: I was walking toward the little wood, where I afterwards met the venerable eunuch, and the most illustrious chief huntsman. I observed on the sand the traces of an animal, and could easily perceive them to be those of a little dog. The light and long furrows impressed on little eminences of sand between the marks of the paws plainly discovered that it was a female, whose dugs were hanging down, and that therefore she must have whelped a few days before. Other traces of a different

FRANCOIS MARIE AROUET DE VOLTAIRE

kind, that always appeared to have gently brushed the surface of the sand near the marks of the forefeet, showed me that she had very long ears; and as I remarked that there was always a slighter impression made on the sand by one foot than the other three, I found that the spaniel of our august queen was a little lame, if I may be allowed the expression.

"With regard to the horse of the king of kings, you will be pleased to know that, walking in the lanes of this wood, I observed the marks of a horse's shoes, all at equal distances. This must be a horse, said I to myself, that gallops excellently. The dust on the trees in the road that was but seven feet wide was a little brushed off, at the distance of three feet and a half from the middle of the road. This horse, said I, has a tail three feet and a half long, which being whisked to the right and left, has swept away the dust. I observed under the trees that formed an arbor five feet in height, that the leaves of the branches were newly fallen; from whence I inferred that the horse had touched them, and that he must therefore be five feet high. As to his bit, it must be gold of twenty-three carats, for he had rubbed its bosses against a stone which I knew to be a touchstone, and which I have tried. In a word, from the marks made by his shoes on flints of another kind, I concluded that he was shod with silver eleven deniers fine."

All the judges admired Zadig for his acute and profound discernment. The news of this speech was carried even to the king and queen. Nothing was talked of but Zadig in the antichambers, the chambers, and the cabinet; and though many of the magi were of opinion that he ought to be burned as a sorcerer, the king ordered his officers to restore him the four hundred ounces of gold which he had been obliged to pay. The register, the attorneys, and bailiffs, went to his house with great formality, to carry him back his four hundred ounces. They only retained three hundred and ninety-eight of them to defray the expenses of justice; and their servants demanded their fees.

Zadig saw how extremely dangerous it sometimes is to appear too knowing, and therefore resolved that on the next occasion of the like nature he would not tell what he had seen.

ZADIG THE BABYLONIAN

Such an opportunity soon offered. A prisoner of state made his escape, and passed under the window of Zadig's house. Zadig was examined and made no answer. But it was proved that he had looked at the prisoner from this window. For this crime he was condemned to pay five hundred ounces of gold; and, according to the polite custom of Babylon, he thanked his judges for their indulgence.

"Great God!" said he to himself, "what a misfortune it is to walk in a wood through which the queen's spaniel or the king's horse has passed! how dangerous to look out at a window! and how difficult to be happy in this life!"

The Envious Man

Zadig resolved to comfort himself by philosophy and friendship for the evils he had suffered from fortune. He had in the suburbs of Babylon a house elegantly furnished, in which he assembled all the arts and all the pleasures worthy the pursuit of a gentleman. In the morning his library was open to the learned. In the evening his table was surrounded by good company. But he soon found what very dangerous guests these men of letters are. A warm dispute arose on one of Zoroaster's laws, which forbids the eating of a griffin. "Why," said some of them, "prohibit the eating of a griffin, if there is no such an animal in nature?" "There must necessarily be such an animal," said the others, "since Zoroaster forbids us to eat it." Zadig would fain have reconciled them by saying, "If there are no griffins, we cannot possibly eat them; and thus either way we shall obey Zoroaster."

A learned man who had composed thirteen volumes on the properties of the griffin, and was besides the chief theurgite, hastened away to accuse Zadig before one of the principal magi, named Yebor, the greatest blockhead and therefore the greatest fanatic among the Chaldeans. This man would have impaled Zadig to do honors to the sun, and would then have recited the breviary of Zoroaster with greater satisfaction. The friend Cador (a friend is better than a hundred priests) went to Yebor, and said to him, "Long live the sun and the griffins; beware of punishing Zadig; he is a saint; he has griffins in his inner court and does not eat them; and his accuser is an heretic, who dares to maintain that rabbits have cloven feet and are not unclean."

"Well," said Yebor, shaking his bald pate, "we must impale Zadig for having thought contemptuously of griffins, and the other for having spoken disrespectfully of rabbits." Cador hushed up the affair by means of a maid of honor with whom he had a love affair, and who had great interest in the College of the Magi. Nobody was impaled.

This levity occasioned a great murmuring among some of the doctors, who from thence predicted the fall of Babylon. "Upon what does happiness depend?" said Zadig. "I am persecuted by everything in the world, even on account of beings that have no existence." He cursed those men of learning, and resolved for the future to live with none but good company.

He assembled at his house the most worthy men and the most beautiful ladies of Babylon. He gave them delicious suppers, often preceded by concerts of music, and always animated by polite conversation, from which he knew how to banish that affectation of wit which is the surest method of preventing it entirely, and of spoiling the pleasure of the most agreeable society. Neither the choice of his friends nor that of the dishes was made by vanity; for in everything he preferred the substance to the shadow; and by these means he procured that real respect to which he did not aspire.

Opposite to his house lived one Arimazes, a man whose deformed countenance was but a faint picture of his still more deformed mind. His heart was a mixture of malice, pride, and envy. Having never been able to succeed in any of his undertakings, he revenged himself on all around him by loading them with the blackest calumnies. Rich as he was, he found it difficult to procure a set of flatterers. The rattling of the chariots that entered Zadig's court in the evening filled him with uneasiness; the sound of his praises enraged him still more. He sometimes went to Zadig's house, and sat down at table without being desired; where he spoiled all the pleasure of the company, as the harpies are said to infect the viands they touch. It happened that one day he took it in his head to give an entertainment to a lady, who, instead of accepting it, went to sup with Zadig. At another time, as he was talking with Zadig at court, a minister of state came up to them, and invited Zadig to supper without inviting Arimazes. The most implacable hatred has seldom a more solid foundation. This man, who in Babylon was called the Envious, resolved to ruin Zadig because he was called the Happy. "The opportunity of doing mischief occurs a hundred times in a day, and that of doing good but once a year," as sayeth the wise Zoroaster.

The envious man went to see Zadig, who was walking in his garden with two friends and a lady, to whom he said many gallant things, without any other intention than that of saying them. The conversation turned upon a war which the king had just brought to a happy conclusion against the prince of Hircania, his vassal. Zadig, who had signalized his courage in this short war, bestowed great praises on the king, but greater still on the lady. He took out his pocketbook, and wrote four lines extempore, which he gave to this amiable person to read. His friends begged they might see them; but modesty, or rather a well-regulated self love, would not allow him to grant their request. He knew that extemporary verses are never approved of by any but by the person in whose honor they are written. He therefore tore in two the leaf on which he had wrote them, and threw both the pieces into a thicket of rose-bushes, where the rest of the company sought for them in vain. A slight shower falling soon after obliged them to return to the house. The envious man, who stayed in the garden, continued the search till at last he found a piece of the leaf. It had been torn in such a manner that each half of a line formed a complete sense, and even a verse of a shorter measure; but what was still more surprising, these short verses were found to contain the most injurious reflections on the king. They ran thus:

>   To flagrant crimes,
>   His crown he owes,
>   To peaceful times,
>   The worst of foes.

FRANCOIS MARIE AROUET DE VOLTAIRE

The envious man was now happy for the first time of his life. He had it in his power to ruin a person of virtue and merit. Filled with this fiendlike joy, he found means to convey to the king the satire written by the hand of Zadig, who, together with the lady and his two friends, was thrown into prison.

His trial was soon finished, without his being permitted to speak for himself. As he was going to receive his sentence, the envious man threw himself in his way and told him with a loud voice that his verses were good for nothing. Zadig did not value himself on being a good poet; but it filled him with inexpressible concern to find that he was condemned for high treason; and that the fair lady and his two friends were confined in prison for a crime of which they were not guilty. He was not allowed to speak because his writing spoke for him. Such was the law of Babylon. Accordingly he was conducted to the place of execution, through an immense crowd of spectators, who durst not venture to express their pity for him, but who carefully examined his countenance to see if he died with a good grace. His relations alone were inconsolable, for they could not succeed to his estate. Three-fourths of his wealth were confiscated into the king's treasury, and the other fourth was given to the envious man.

Just as he was preparing for death the king's parrot flew from its cage and alighted on a rosebush in Zadig's garden. A peach had been driven thither by the wind from a neighboring tree, and had fallen on a piece of the written leaf of the pocketbook to which it stuck. The bird carried off the peach and the paper and laid them on the king's knee. The king took up the paper with great eagerness and read the words, which formed no sense, and seemed to be the endings of verses. He loved poetry; and there is always some mercy to be expected from a prince of that disposition. The adventure of the parrot set him a-thinking.

The queen, who remembered what had been written on the piece of Zadig's pocketbook, caused it to be brought. They compared the two pieces together and found them to tally exactly; they then read the verses as Zadig had wrote them.

ZADIG THE BABYLONIAN

TYRANTS ARE PRONE	TO FLAGRANT CRIMES.
TO CLEMENCY	HIS CROWN HE OWES.
TO CONCORD AND	TO PEACEFUL TIMES.
LOVE ONLY IS	THE WORST OF FOES.

The king gave immediate orders that Zadig should be brought before him, and that his two friends and the lady should be set at liberty. Zadig fell prostrate on the ground before the king and queen; humbly begged their pardon for having made such bad verses and spoke with so much propriety, wit, and good sense, that their majesties desired they might see him again. He did himself that honor, and insinuated himself still farther into their good graces. They gave him all the wealth of the envious man; but Zadig restored him back the whole of it. And this instance of generosity gave no other pleasure to the envious man than that of having preserved his estate.

The king's esteem for Zadig increased every day. He admitted him into all his parties of pleasure, and consulted him in all affairs of state. From that time the queen began to regard him with an eye of tenderness that might one day prove dangerous to herself, to the king, her august comfort, to Zadig, and to the kingdom in general. Zadig now began to think that happiness was not so unattainable as he had formerly imagined.

The Generous

The time now arrived for celebrating a grand festival, which returned every five years. It was a custom in Babylon solemnly to declare at the end of every five years which of the citizens had performed the most generous action. The grandees and the magi were the judges. The first satrap, who was charged with the government of the city, published the most noble actions that had passed under his administration. The competition was decided by votes; and the king pronounced the sentence. People came to this solemnity from the extremities of the earth. The conqueror received from the monarch's hand a golden cup adorned with precious stones, his majesty at the same time making him this compliment:

FRANCOIS MARIE AROUET DE VOLTAIRE

"Receive this reward of thy generosity, and may the gods grant me many subjects like to thee."

This memorable day being come, the king appeared on his throne, surrounded by the grandees, the magi, and the deputies of all nations that came to these games, where glory was acquired not by the swiftness of horses, nor by strength of body, but by virtue. The first satrap recited, with an audible voice, such actions as might entitle the authors of them to this invaluable prize. He did not mention the greatness of soul with which Zadig had restored the envious man his fortune, because it was not judged to be an action worthy of disputing the prize.

He first presented a judge who, having made a citizen lose a considerable cause by a mistake, for which, after all, he was not accountable, had given him the whole of his own estate, which was just equal to what the other had lost.

He next produced a young man who, being desperately in love with a lady whom he was going to marry, had yielded her up to his friend, whose passion for her had almost brought him to the brink of the grave, and at the same time had given him the lady's fortune.

He afterwards produced a soldier who, in the wars of Hircania, had given a still more noble instance of generosity. A party of the enemy having seized his mistress, he fought in her defense with great intrepidity. At that very instant he was informed that another party, at the distance of a few paces, were carrying off his mother; he therefore left his mistress with tears in his eyes and flew to the assistance of his mother. At last he returned to the dear object of his love and found her expiring. He was just going to plunge his sword in his own bosom; but his mother remonstrating against such a desperate deed, and telling him that he was the only support of her life, he had the courage to endure to live.

The judges were inclined to give the prize to the soldier. But the king took up the discourse and said: "The action of the soldier, and those of the other two, are doubtless very great, but they have nothing in them surprising. Yesterday Zadig performed an action that filled me with wonder. I had a few days before disgraced Coreb, my minister and

ZADIG THE BABYLONIAN

favorite. I complained of him in the most violent and bitter terms; all my courtiers assured me that I was too gentle and seemed to vie with each other in speaking ill of Coreb. I asked Zadig what he thought of him, and he had the courage to commend him. I have read in our histories of many people who have atoned for an error by the surrender of their fortune; who have resigned a mistress; or preferred a mother to the object of their affection; but never before did I hear of a courtier who spoke favorably of a disgraced minister that labored under the displeasure of his sovereign. I give to each of those whose generous actions have been now recited twenty thousand pieces of gold; but the cup I give to Zadig."

"May it please your majesty," said Zadig, "thyself alone deservest the cup; thou hast performed an action of all others the most uncommon and meritorious, since, notwithstanding thy being a powerful king, thou wast not offended at thy slave when he presumed to oppose thy passion." The king and Zadig were equally the object of admiration. The judge, who had given his estate to his client; the lover, who had resigned his mistress to a friend; and the soldier, who had preferred the safety of his mother to that of his mistress, received the king's presents and saw their names enrolled in the catalogue of generous men. Zadig had the cup, and the king acquired the reputation of a good prince, which he did not long enjoy. The day was celebrated by feasts that lasted longer than the law enjoined; and the memory of it is still preserved in Asia. Zadig said, "Now I am happy at last;" but he found himself fatally deceived.

The Minister

The king had lost his first minister and chose Zadig to supply his place. All the ladies in Babylon applauded the choice; for since the foundation of the empire there had never been such a young minister. But all the courtiers were filled with jealousy and vexation. The envious man in particular was troubled with a spitting of blood and a prodigious inflammation in his nose. Zadig, having thanked the king and queen for their goodness, went likewise to thank the parrot. "Beautiful bird," said he, "'tis thou that hast saved my life and made me first minister. The queen's spaniel and the king's horse did me a great deal of mischief; but thou hast done me much good. Upon such slender threads as these do the fates of mortals hang! But," added he, "this happiness perhaps will vanish very soon."

"Soon," replied the parrot.

Zadig was somewhat startled at this word. But as he was a good natural philosopher and did not believe parrots to be prophets, he quickly recovered his spirits and resolved to execute his duty to the best of his power.

He made everyone feel the sacred authority of the laws, but no one felt the weight of his dignity. He never checked the deliberation of the diran; and every vizier might give his opinion without the fear of incurring the minister's displeasure. When he gave judgment, it was not he that gave it, it was the law; the rigor of which, however, whenever it was too severe, he always took care to soften; and when laws were wanting, the equity of his decisions was such as might easily have made them pass for those of Zoroaster. It is to him that the nations are indebted for this grand principle, to wit, that it is better to run the risk of sparing the guilty than to condemn the innocent. He imagined that laws were made as well to secure the people from the suffering of injuries as to restrain them from the commission of crimes. His chief talent consisted in discovering the truth, which all men seek to obscure.

This great talent he put in practice from the very beginning of his administration. A famous merchant of Babylon, who died in the Indies, divided his estate equally between his two sons, after having disposed of their sister in marriage, and left a present of thirty thousand pieces of gold to that son who should be found to have loved him best. The eldest raised a tomb to his memory; the youngest increased his sister's portion, by giving her part of his inheritance. Everyone said that the eldest son loved his father best, and the youngest his sister; and that the thirty thousand pieces belonged to the eldest.

Zadig sent for both of them, the one after the other. To

the eldest he said: "Thy father is not dead; he is recovered of his last illness, and is returning to Babylon." "God be praised," replied the young man; "but his tomb cost me a considerable sum." Zadig afterwards said the same to the youngest. "God be praised," said he, "I will go and restore to my father all that I have; but I could wish that he would leave my sister what I have given her." "Thou shalt restore nothing," replied Zadig, "and thou shalt have the thirty thousand pieces, for thou art the son who loves his father best."

The Disputes and the Audiences

In this manner he daily discovered the subtilty of his genius and the goodness of his heart. The people at once admired and loved him. He passed for the happiest man in the world. The whole empire resounded with his name. All the ladies ogled him. All the men praised him for his justice. The learned regarded him as an oracle; and even the priests confessed that he knew more than the old archmagi Yebor. They were now so far from prosecuting him on account of the griffin, that they believed nothing but what he thought credible.

There had reigned in Babylon, for the space of fifteen hundred years, a violent contest that had divided the empire into two sects. The one pretended that they ought to enter the temple of Mitra with the left foot foremost; the other held this custom in detestation and always entered with the right foot first. The people waited with great impatience for the day on which the solemn feast of the sacred fire was to be celebrated, to see which sect Zadig would favor. All the world had their eyes fixed on his two feet, and the whole city was in the utmost suspense and perturbation. Zadig jumped into the temple with his feet joined together, and afterwards proved, in an eloquent discourse, that the Sovereign of heaven and earth, who accepted not the persons of men, makes no distinction between the right and left foot. The envious man and his wife alleged that his discourse was not figurative enough, and that he did not make the rocks and mountains to dance with sufficient agility.

"He is dry," said they, "and void of genius; he does not

make the flea to fly, and stars to fall, nor the sun to melt wax; he has not the true Oriental style." Zadig contented himself with having the style of reason. All the world favored him, not because he was in the right road or followed the dictates of reason, or was a man of real merit, but because he was prime vizier.

He terminated with the same happy address the grand difference between the white and the black magi. The former maintained that it was the height of impiety to pray to God with the face turned toward the east in winter; the latter asserted that God abhorred the prayers of those who turned toward the west in summer. Zadig decreed that every man should be allowed to turn as he pleased.

Thus he found out the happy secret of finishing all affairs, whether of a private or public nature, in the morning. The rest of the day he employed in superintending and promoting the embellishments of Babylon. He exhibited tragedies that drew tears from the eyes of the spectators, and comedies that shook their sides with laughter; a custom which had long been disused, and which his good taste now induced him to revive. He never affected to be more knowing in the polite arts than the artists themselves; he encouraged them by rewards and honors, and was never jealous of their talents. In the evening the king was highly entertained with his conversation, and the queen still more. "Great minister!" said the king. "Amiable minister!" said the queen; and both of them added, "It would have been a great loss to the state had such a man been hanged."

Never was a man in power obliged to give so many audiences to the ladies. Most of them came to consult him about no business at all, that so they might have some business with him. But none of them won his attention.

Meanwhile Zadig perceived that his thoughts were always distracted, as well when he gave audience as when he sat in judgment. He did not know to what to attribute this absence of mind; and that was his only sorrow.

He had a dream in which he imagined that he laid himself down upon a heap of dry herbs, among which there were many prickly ones that gave him great uneasiness, and that he afterwards reposed himself on a soft bed of roses from which there sprung a serpent that wounded him to the heart with its sharp and venomed tongue. "Alas," said he, "I have long lain on these dry and prickly herbs, I am now on the bed of roses; but what shall be the serpent?"

Jealousy

Zadig's calamities sprung even from his happiness and especially from his merit. He every day conversed with the king and Astarte, his august comfort. The charms of his conversation were greatly heightened by that desire of pleasing, which is to the mind what dress is to beauty. His youth and graceful appearance insensibly made an impression on Astarte, which she did not at first perceive. Her passion grew and flourished in the bosom of innocence. Without fear or scruple, she indulged the pleasing satisfaction of seeing and hearing a man who was so dear to her husband and to the empire in general. She was continually praising him to the king. She talked of him to her women, who were always sure to improve on her praises. And thus everything contributed to pierce her heart with a dart, of which she did not seem to be sensible. She made several presents to Zadig, which discovered a greater spirit of gallantry than she imagined. She intended to speak to him only as a queen satisfied with his services and her expressions were sometimes those of a woman in love.

Astarte was much more beautiful than that Semira who had such a strong aversion to one-eyed men, or that other woman who had resolved to cut off her husband's nose. Her unreserved familiarity, her tender expressions, at which she began to blush; and her eyes, which, though she endeavored to divert them to other objects, were always fixed upon his, inspired Zadig with a passion that filled him with astonishment. He struggled hard to get the better of it. He called to his aid the precepts of philosophy, which had always stood him in stead; but from thence, though he could derive the light of knowledge, he could procure no remedy to cure the disorders of his lovesick heart. Duty, gratitude, and violated majesty presented themselves to his mind as so many avenging gods. He struggled; he conquered; but this victory, which he was obliged to purchase afresh every moment, cost him many sighs and tears. He no longer dared to speak to the queen with that sweet and charming familiarity which had been so agreeable to them both. His countenance was covered with a cloud. His conversation was constrained and incoherent. His eyes were fixed on the ground; and when, in spite of all his endeavors to the contrary, they encountered those of the queen, they found them bathed in tears and darting arrows of flame. They seemed to say, We adore each other and yet are afraid to love; we both burn with a fire which we both condemn.

Zadig left the royal presence full of perplexity and despair, and having his heart oppressed with a burden which he was no longer able to bear. In the violence of his perturbation he involuntarily betrayed the secret to his friend Cador, in the same manner as a man who, having long supported the fits of a cruel disease, discovers his pain by a cry extorted from him by a more severe fit and by the cold sweat that covers his brow.

"I have already discovered," said Cador, "the sentiments which thou wouldst fain conceal from thyself. The symptoms by which the passions show themselves are certain and infallible. Judge, my dear Zadig, since I have read thy heart, whether the king will not discover something in it that may give him offense. He has no other fault but that of being the most jealous man in the world. Thou canst resist the violence of thy passion with greater fortitude than the queen because thou art a philosopher, and because thou art Zadig. Astarte is a woman: she suffers her eyes to speak with so much the more imprudence, as she does not as yet think herself guilty. Conscious of her innocence, she unhappily neglects those external appearances which are so necessary. I shall tremble for her so long as she has nothing wherewithal to reproach herself. Were ye both of one mind, ye might easily deceive the whole world. A growing passion, which we endeavor to suppress, discovers itself in spite of all our efforts to the contrary; but love, when gratified, is easily concealed."

Zadig trembled at the proposal of betraying the king, his

ZADIG THE BABYLONIAN

benefactor; and never was he more faithful to his prince than when guilty of an involuntary crime against him.

Meanwhile the queen mentioned the name of Zadig so frequently and with such a blushing and downcast look; she was sometimes so lively and sometimes so perplexed when she spoke to him in the king's presence, and was seized with such deep thoughtfulness at his going away, that the king began to be troubled. He believed all that he saw and imagined all that he did not see. He particularly remarked that his wife's shoes were blue and that Zadig's shoes were blue; that his wife's ribbons were yellow and that Zadig's bonnet was yellow; and these were terrible symptoms to a prince of so much delicacy. In his jealous mind suspicions were turned into certainty.

All the slaves of kings and queens are so many spies over their hearts. They soon observed that Astarte was tender and that Moabdar was jealous. The envious man brought false reports to the king. The monarch now thought of nothing but in what manner he might best execute his vengeance. He one night resolved to poison the queen and in the morning to put Zadig to death by the bowstring. The orders were given to a merciless eunuch, who commonly executed his acts of vengeance. There happened at that time to be in the king's chamber a little dwarf, who, though dumb, was not deaf. He was allowed, on account of his insignificance, to go wherever he pleased, and, as a domestic animal, was a witness of what passed in the most profound secrecy. This little mute was strongly attached to the queen and Zadig. With equal horror and surprise he heard the cruel orders given. But how to prevent the fatal sentence that in a few hours was to be carried into execution! He could not write, but he could paint; and excelled particularly in drawing a striking resemblance. He employed a part of the night in sketching out with his pencil what he meant to impart to the queen. The piece represented the king in one corner, boiling with rage, and giving orders to the eunuch; a bowstring, and a bowl on a table; the queen in the middle of the picture, expiring in the arms of her woman, and Zadig strangled at her feet. The horizon represented a rising sun, to express that this shocking execution was to be performed in the morning. As soon as he had finished the picture he ran to one of Astarte's women, awakened her, and made her understand that she must immediately carry it to the queen.

At midnight a messenger knocks at Zadig's door, awakes him, and gives him a note from the queen. He doubts whether it is a dream; and opens the letter with a trembling hand. But how great was his surprise! and who can express the consternation and despair into which he was thrown upon reading these words: "Fly this instant, or thou art a dead man. Fly, Zadig, I conjure thee by our mutual love and my yellow ribbons. I have not been guilty, but I find I must die like a criminal."

Zadig was hardly able to speak. He sent for Cador, and, without uttering a word, gave him the note. Cador forced him to obey, and forthwith to take the road to Memphis. "Shouldst thou dare," said he, "to go in search of the queen, thou wilt hasten her death. Shouldst thou speak to the king, thou wilt infallibly ruin her. I will take upon me the charge of her destiny; follow thy own. I will spread a report that thou hast taken the road to India. I will soon follow thee, and inform thee of all that shall have passed in Babylon." At that instant, Cador caused two of the swiftest dromedaries to be brought to a private gate of the palace. Upon one of these he mounted Zadig, whom he was obliged to carry to the door, and who was ready to expire with grief. He was accompanied by a single domestic; and Cador, plunged in sorrow and astonishment, soon lost sight of his friend.

This illustrious fugitive arriving on the side of a hill, from whence he could take a view of Babylon, turned his eyes toward the queen's palace, and fainted away at the sight; nor did he recover his senses but to shed a torrent of tears and to wish for death. At length, after his thoughts had been long engrossed in lamenting the unhappy fate of the loveliest woman and the greatest queen in the world, he for a moment turned his views on himself and cried: "What then is human life? O virtue, how hast thou served me! Two women have basely deceived me, and now a third, who is innocent, and more beautiful than both the others, is going to be put to death! Whatever good I have done hath been to me a continual source of calamity and affliction; and I have only been raised to the height of grandeur, to be tumbled down the most horrid precipice of misfortune." Filled with these gloomy reflections, his eyes overspread with the veil of grief, his countenance covered with the paleness of death, and his soul plunged in an abyss of the blackest despair, he continued his journey toward Egypt.

The Woman Beaten

Zadig directed his course by the stars. The constellation of Orion and the splendid Dog Star guided his steps toward the pole of Cassiopeia. He admired those vast globes of light, which appear to our eyes but as so many little sparks, while the earth, which in reality is only an imperceptible point in nature, appears to our fond imaginations as something so grand and noble.

He then represented to himself the human species as it really is, as a parcel of insects devouring one another on a little atom of clay. This true image seemed to annihilate his misfortunes, by making him sensible of the nothingness of his own being, and of that of Babylon. His soul launched out into infinity, and, detached from the senses, contemplated the immutable order of the universe. But when afterwards, returning to himself, and entering into his own heart, he considered that Astarte had perhaps died for him, the universe vanished from his sight, and he beheld nothing in the whole compass of nature but Astarte expiring and Zadig unhappy. While he thus alternately gave up his mind to this flux and reflux of sublime philosophy and intolerable grief, he advanced toward the frontiers of Egypt; and his faithful domestic was already in the first village, in search of a lodging.

Upon reaching the village Zadig generously took the part of a woman attacked by her jealous lover. The combat grew so fierce that Zadig slew the lover. The Egyptians were then just and humane. The people conducted Zadig to the town house. They first of all ordered his wounds to be dressed, and then examined him and his servant apart, in order to discover the truth. They found that Zadig was not an assassin; but as he was guilty of having killed a man, the law condemned him to be a slave. His two camels were sold for the benefit of the town; all the gold he had brought with him was distributed among the inhabitants; and his person, as well as that of the companion of his journey, was exposed to sale in the marketplace.

An Arabian merchant, named Setoc, made the purchase; but as the servant was fitter for labor than the master, he was sold at a higher price. There was no comparison between the two men. Thus Zadig became a slave subordinate to his own servant. They were linked together by a chain fastened to their feet, and in this condition they followed the Arabian merchant to his house.

By the way Zadig comforted his servant, and exhorted him to patience; but he could not help making, according to his usual custom, some reflections on human life. "I see," said he, "that the unhappiness of my fate hath an influence on thine. Hitherto everything has turned out to me in a most unaccountable manner. I have been condemned to pay a fine for having seen the marks of a spaniel's feet. I thought that I should once have been impaled on account of a griffin. I have been sent to execution for having made some verses in praise of the king. I have been upon the point of being strangled because the queen had yellow ribbons; and now I am a slave with thee, because a brutal wretch beat his mistress. Come, let us keep a good heart; all this perhaps will have an end. The Arabian merchants must necessarily have slaves; and why not me as well as another, since, as well as another, I am a man? This merchant will not be cruel; he must treat his slaves well, if he expects any advantage from them." But while he spoke thus, his heart was entirely engrossed by the fate of the Queen of Babylon.

Two days after, the merchant Setoc set out for Arabia Deserta, with his slaves and his camels. His tribe dwelt near the Desert of Oreb. The journey was long and painful. Setoc set a much greater value on the servant than the master, because the former was more expert in loading the camels; and all the little marks of distinction were shown to him. A camel having died within two days' journey of Oreb, his burden was divided and laid on the backs of the servants; and Zadig had his share among the rest.

Setoc laughed to see all his slaves walking with their bodies inclined. Zadig took the liberty to explain to him the cause, and inform him of the laws of the balance. The merchant was astonished, and began to regard him with other eyes. Zadig, finding he had raised his curiosity, increased it still further by acquainting him with many things that related to commerce, the specific gravity of metals, and commodities under an equal bulk; the properties of several useful animals; and the means of rendering those useful that are not naturally so. At last Setoc began to consider Zadig as a sage, and preferred him to his companion, whom he had formerly so much esteemed. He treated him well and had no cause to repent of his kindness.

The Stone

As soon as Setoc arrived among his own tribe he demanded the payment of five hundred ounces of silver, which he had lent to a Jew in presence of two witnesses; but as the witnesses were dead, and the debt could not be proved, the Hebrew appropriated the merchant's money to himself, and piously thanked God for putting it in his power to cheat an Arabian. Setoc imparted this troublesome affair to Zadig, who was now become his counsel.

"In what place," said Zadig, "didst thou lend the five hundred ounces to this infidel?"

"Upon a large stone," replied the merchant, "that lies near Mount Oreb."

"What is the character of thy debtor?" said Zadig.

"That of a knave," returned Setoc.

"But I ask thee whether he is lively or phlegmatic, cautious or imprudent?"

"He is, of all bad payers," said Setoc, "the most lively fellow I ever knew."

"Well," resumed Zadig, "allow me to plead thy cause."
In effect Zadig, having summoned the Jew to the tribunal,

addressed the judge in the following terms: "Pillow of the throne of equity, I come to demand of this man, in the name of my master, five hundred ounces of silver, which he refuses to pay."

"Hast thou any witnesses?" said the judge.

"No, they are dead; but there remains a large stone upon which the money was counted; and if it please thy grandeur to order the stone to be sought for, I hope that it will bear witness. The Hebrew and I will tarry here till the stone arrives; I will send for it at my master's expense."

"With all my heart," replied the judge, and immediately applied himself to the discussion of other affairs.

When the court was going to break up, the judge said to Zadig, "Well, friend, is not thy stone come yet?"

The Hebrew replied with a smile, "Thy grandeur may stay here till the morrow, and after all not see the stone. It is more than six miles from hence; and it would require fifteen men to move it."

"Well," cried Zadig, "did not I say that the stone would bear witness? Since this man knows where it is, he thereby confesses that it was upon it that the money was counted." The Hebrew was disconcerted, and was soon after obliged to confess the truth. The judge ordered him to be fastened to the stone, without meat or drink, till he should restore the five hundred ounces, which were soon after paid.

The slave Zadig and the stone were held in great repute in Arabia.

The Funeral Pile

Setoc, charmed with the happy issue of this affair, made his slave his intimate friend. He had now conceived as great esteem for him as ever the King of Babylon had done; and Zadig was glad that Setoc had no wife. He discovered in his master a good natural disposition, much probity of heart, and a great share of good sense; but he was sorry to see that, according to the ancient custom of Arabia, he adored the host of heaven; that is, the sun, moon, and stars. He sometimes spoke to him on this subject with great

ZADIG THE BABYLONIAN

prudence and discretion. At last he told him that these bodies were like all other bodies in the universe, and no more deserving of our homage than a tree or a rock.

"But," said Setoc, "they are eternal beings; and it is from them we derive all we enjoy. They animate nature; they regulate the seasons; and, besides, are removed at such an immense distance from us that we cannot help revering them."

"Thou receivest more advantage," replied Zadig, "from the waters of the Red Sea, which carry thy merchandise to the Indies. Why may not it be as ancient as the stars? and if thou adorest what is placed at a distance from thee, thou oughtest to adore the land of the Gangarides, which lies at the extremity of the earth."

"No," said Setoc, "the brightness of the stars command my adoration."

At night Zadig lighted up a great number of candles in the tent where he was to sup with Setoc; and the moment his patron appeared, he fell on his knees before these lighted tapers, and said, "Eternal and shining luminaries! be ye always propitious to me." Having thus said, he sat down at table, without taking the least notice of Setoc.

"What art thou doing?" said Setoc to him in amaze.

"I act like thee," replied Zadig, "I adore these candles, and neglect their master and mine." Setoc comprehended the profound sense of this apologue. The wisdom of his slave sunk deep into his soul; he no longer offered incense to the creatures, but adored the eternal Being who made them.

There prevailed at that time in Arabia a shocking custom, sprung originally from Leythia, and which, being established in the Indies by the credit of the Brahmans, threatened to overrun all the East. When a married man died, and his beloved wife aspired to the character of a saint, she burned herself publicly on the body of her husband. This was a solemn feast and was called the Funeral Pile of Widowhood, and that tribe in which most women had been burned was the most respected.

An Arabian of Setoc's tribe being dead, his widow, whose name was Almona, and who was very devout, pub-

FRANCOIS MARIE AROUET DE VOLTAIRE

lished the day and hour when she intended to throw herself into the fire, amidst the sound of drums and trumpets. Zadig remonstrated against this horrible custom; he showed Setoc how inconsistent it was with the happiness of mankind to suffer young widows to burn themselves every other day, widows who were capable of giving children to the state, or at least of educating those they already had; and he convinced him that it was his duty to do all that lay in his power to abolish such a barbarous practice.

"The women," said Setoc, "have possessed the right of burning themselves for more than a thousand years; and who shall dare to abrogate a law which time hath rendered sacred? Is there anything more respectable than ancient abuses?"

"Reason is more ancient," replied Zadig; "meanwhile, speak thou to the chiefs of the tribes and I will go to wait on the young widow."

Accordingly he was introduced to her; and, after having insinuated himself into her good graces by some compliments on her beauty and told her what a pity it was to commit so many charms to the flames, he at last praised her for her constancy and courage. "Thou must surely have loved thy husband," said he to her, "with the most passionate fondness."

"Who, I?" replied the lady. "I loved him not at all. He was a brutal, jealous, insupportable wretch; but I am firmly resolved to throw myself on his funeral pile."

"It would appear then," said Zadig, "that there must be a very delicious pleasure in being burned alive."

"Oh! it makes nature shudder," replied the lady, "but that must be overlooked. I am a devotee, and I should lose my reputation and all the world would despise me if I did not burn myself."

Zadig having made her acknowledge that she burned herself to gain the good opinion of others and to gratify her own vanity, entertained her with a long discourse, calculated to make her a little in love with life, and even went so far as to inspire her with some degree of good will for the person who spoke to her.

ZADIG THE BABYLONIAN

"Alas!" said the lady, "I believe I should desire thee to marry me."

Zadig's mind was too much engrossed with the idea of Astarte not to elude this declaration; but he instantly went to the chiefs of the tribes, told them what had passed, and advised them to make a law, by which a widow should not be permitted to burn herself till she had conversed privately with a young man for the space of an hour. Since that time not a single woman hath burned herself in Arabia. They were indebted to Zadig alone for destroying in one day a cruel custom that had lasted for so many ages and thus he became the benefactor of Arabia.

The Supper

Setoc, who could not separate himself from this man, in whom dwelt wisdom, carried him to the great fair of Balzora, whither the richest merchants in the earth resorted. Zadig was highly pleased to see so many men of different countries united in the same place. He considered the whole universe as one large family assembled at Balzora.

Setoc, after having sold his commodities at a very high price, returned to his own tribe with his friend Zadig; who learned, upon his arrival, that he had been tried in his absence, and was now going to be burned by a slow fire. Only the friendship of Almona saved his life. Like so many pretty women, she possessed great influence with the priesthood. Zadig thought it best to leave Arabia.

Setoc was so charmed with the ingenuity and address of Almona that he made her his wife. Zadig departed, after having thrown himself at the feet of his fair deliverer. Setoc and he took leave of each other with tears in their eyes, swearing an eternal friendship, and promising that the first of them that should acquire a large fortune should share it with the other.

Zadig directed his course along the frontiers of Assyria, still musing on the unhappy Astarte, and reflecting on the severity of fortune which seemed determined to make him the sport of her cruelty and the object of her persecution.

"What," said he to himself, "four hundred ounces of gold for having seen a spaniel! condemned to lose my head for four bad verses in praise of the king! ready to be strangled because the queen had shoes of the color of my bonnet! reduced to slavery for having succored a woman who was beat! and on the point of being burned for having saved the lives of all the young widows of Arabia!"

The Robber

Arriving on the frontiers which divide Arabia Petræa from Syria, he passed by a pretty strong castle, from which a party of armed Arabians sallied forth. They instantly surrounded him and cried, "All thou hast belongs to us, and thy person is the property of our master." Zadig replied by drawing his sword; his servant, who was a man of courage, did the same. They killed the first Arabians that presumed to lay hands on them; and, though the number was redoubled, they were not dismayed, but resolved to perish in the conflict. Two men defended themselves against a multitude; and such a combat could not last long.

The master of the castle, whose name was Arbogad, having observed from a window the prodigies of valor performed by Zadig, conceived a high esteem for this heroic stranger. He descended in haste and went in person to call off his men and deliver the two travelers.

"All that passes over my lands," said he, "belongs to me, as well as what I find upon the lands of others; but thou seemest to be a man of such undaunted courage that I will exempt thee from the common law." He then conducted him to his castle, ordering his men to treat him well; and in the evening Arbogad supped with Zadig.

The lord of the castle was one of those Arabians who are commonly called robbers; but he now and then performed some good actions amid a multitude of bad ones. He robbed with a furious rapacity, and granted favors with great generosity; he was intrepid in action; affable in company; a debauchee at table, but gay in debauchery; and particularly remarkable for his frank and open behavior.

ZADIG THE BABYLONIAN

He was highly pleased with Zadig, whose lively conversation lengthened the repast.

At last Arbogad said to him: "I advise thee to enroll thy name in my catalogue; thou canst not do better; this is not a bad trade; and thou mayest one day become what I am at present."

"May I take the liberty of asking thee," said Zadig, "how long thou hast followed this noble profession?"

"From my most tender youth," replied the lord. "I was a servant to a pretty good-natured Arabian, but could not endure the hardships of my situation. I was vexed to find that fate had given me no share of the earth, which equally belongs to all men. I imparted the cause of my uneasiness to an old Arabian, who said to me: 'My son, do not despair; there was once a grain of sand that lamented that it was no more than a neglected atom in the desert; at the end of a few years it became a diamond; and is now the brightest ornament in the crown of the king of the Indies.' This discourse made a deep impression on my mind. I was the grain of sand, and I resolved to become the diamond. I began by stealing two horses; I soon got a party of companions; I put myself in a condition to rob small caravans; and thus, by degrees, I destroyed the difference which had formerly subsisted between me and other men. I had my share of the good things of this world; and was even recompensed with usury for the hardships I had suffered. I was greatly respected, and became the captain of a band of robbers. I seized this castle by force. The Satrap of Syria had a mind to dispossess me of it; but I was too rich to have anything to fear. I gave the satrap a handsome present, by which means I preserved my castle and increased my possessions. He even appointed me treasurer of the tributes which Arabia Petræa pays to the king of kings. I perform my office of receiver with great punctuality; but take the freedom to dispense with that of paymaster.

"The grand Desterham of Babylon sent hither a pretty satrap in the name of King Moabdar, to have me strangled. This man arrived with his orders: I was apprised of all; I caused to be strangled in his presence the four persons he had brought with him to draw the noose; after which I asked him how much his commission of strangling me might be worth. He replied, that his fees would amount to about three hundred pieces of gold. I then convinced him that he might gain more by staying with me. I made him an inferior robber; and he is now one of my best and richest officers. If thou wilt take my advice thy success may be equal to his; never was there a better season for plunder, since King Moabdar is killed, and all Babylon thrown into confusion."

"Moabdar killed!" said Zadig, "and what is become of Queen Astarte?"

"I know not," replied Arbogad. "All I know is, that Moabdar lost his senses and was killed; that Babylon is a scene of disorder and bloodshed; that all the empire is desolated; that there are some fine strokes to be struck yet; and that, for my own part, I have struck some that are admirable."

"But the queen," said Zadig; "for heaven's sake, knowest thou nothing of the queen's fate?"

"Yes," replied he, "I have heard something of a prince of Hircania; if she was not killed in the tumult, she is probably one of his concubines; but I am much fonder of booty than news. I have taken several women in my excursions; but I keep none of them. I sell them at a high price, when they are beautiful, without inquiring who they are. In commodities of this kind rank makes no difference, and a queen that is ugly will never find a merchant. Perhaps I may have sold Queen Astarte; perhaps she is dead; but, be it as it will, it is of little consequence to me, and I should imagine of as little to thee." So saying he drank a large draught which threw all his ideas into such confusion that Zadig could obtain no further information.

Zadig remained for some time without speech, sense, or motion. Arbogad continued drinking; told stories; constantly repeated that he was the happiest man in the world; and exhorted Zadig to put himself in the same condition. At last the soporiferous fumes of the wine lulled him into a gentle repose.

Zadig passed the night in the most violent perturbation.

ZADIG THE BABYLONIAN

Meanwhile, Zadig continued to make fresh inquiries, and to shed tears. "What, my lord!" cried the fisherman, "art thou then so unhappy, thou who bestowest favors?"

"An hundred times more unhappy than thou art," replied Zadig.

"But how is it possible," said the good man, "that the giver can be more wretched than the receiver?"

"Because," replied Zadig, "thy greatest misery arose from poverty, and mine is seated in the heart."

"Did Orcan take thy wife from thee?" said the fisherman.

This word recalled to Zadig's mind the whole of his adventures.

He repeated the catalogue of his misfortunes, beginning with the queen's spaniel, and ending with his arrival at the castle of the robber Arbogad. "Ah!" said he to the fisherman, "Orcan deserves to be punished; but it is commonly such men as those that are the favorites of fortune. However, go thou to the house of Lord Cador, and there wait my arrival." They then parted, the fisherman walked, thanking Heaven for the happiness of his condition; and Zadig rode, accusing fortune for the hardness of his lot.

The Basilisk

Arriving in a beautiful meadow, he there saw several women, who were searching for something with great application. He took the liberty to approach one of them, and to ask if he might have the honor to assist them in their search. "Take care that thou dost not," replied the Syrian; "what we are searching for can be touched only by women."

"Strange," said Zadig, "may I presume to ask thee what it is that women only are permitted to touch?"

"It is a basilisk," said she.

"A basilisk, madam! and for what purpose, pray, dost thou seek for a basilisk?"

"It is for our lord and master Ogul, whose cattle thou seest on the bank of that river at the end of the meadow. We are his most humble slaves. The lord Ogul is sick.

FRANCOIS MARIE AROUET DE VOLTAIRE

His physician hath ordered him to eat a basilisk, stewed in rose water; and as it is a very rare animal, and can only be taken by women, the lord Ogul hath promised to choose for his well-beloved wife the woman that shall bring him a basilisk; let me go on in my search; for thou seest what I shall lose if I am prevented by my companions."

Zadig left her and the other Assyrians to search for their basilisk, and continued to walk in the meadow; when coming to the brink of a small rivulet, he found another lady lying on the grass, and who was not searching for anything. Her person seemed to be majestic; but her face was covered with a veil. She was inclined toward the rivulet, and profound sighs proceeded from her mouth. In her hand she held a small rod with which she was tracing characters on the fine sand that lay between the turf and the brook. Zadig had the curiosity to examine what this woman was writing. He drew near; he saw the letter Z, then an A; he was astonished; then appeared a D; he started. But never was surprise equal to his when he saw the two last letters of his name.

He stood for some time immovable. At last, breaking silence with a faltering voice: "O generous lady! pardon a stranger, an unfortunate man, for presuming to ask thee by what surprising adventure I here find the name of Zadig traced out by thy divine hand!"

At this voice, and these words, the lady lifted up the veil with a trembling hand, looked at Zadig, sent forth a cry of tenderness, surprise and joy, and sinking under the various emotions which at once assaulted her soul, fell speechless into his arms. It was Astarte herself; it was the Queen of Babylon; it was she whom Zadig adored, and whom he had reproached himself for adoring; it was she whose misfortunes he had so deeply lamented, and for whose fate he had been so anxiously concerned.

He was for a moment deprived of the use of his senses, when he had fixed his eyes on those of Astarte, which now began to open again with a languor mixed with confusion and tenderness: "O ye immortal powers!" cried he, "who preside over the fates of weak mortals, do ye indeed restore Astarte to me! at what a time, in what a place, and in what

ZADIG THE BABYLONIAN

a condition do I again behold her!" He fell on his knees before Astarte, and laid his face in the dust at her feet. The Queen of Babylon raised him up, and made him sit by her side on the brink of the rivulet. She frequently wiped her eyes, from which the tears continued to flow afresh. She twenty times resumed her discourse, which her sighs as often interrupted; she asked by what strange accident they were brought together, and suddenly prevented his answers by other questions; she waived the account of her own misfortunes, and desired to be informed of those of Zadig.

At last, both of them having a little composed the tumult of their souls, Zadig acquainted her in a few words by what adventure he was brought into that meadow. "But, O unhappy and respectable queen! by what means do I find thee in this lonely place, clothed in the habit of a slave, and accompanied by other female slaves, who are searching for a basilisk, which, by order of the physician, is to be stewed in rose water?"

"While they are searching for their basilisk," said the fair Astarte, "I will inform thee of all I have suffered, for which Heaven has sufficiently recompensed me by restoring thee to my sight. Thou knowest that the king, my husband, was vexed to see thee the most amiable of mankind; and that for this reason he one night resolved to strangle thee and poison me. Thou knowest how Heaven permitted my little mute to inform me of the orders of his sublime majesty. Hardly had the faithful Cador advised thee to depart, in obedience to my command, when he ventured to enter my apartment at midnight by a secret passage. He carried me off and conducted me to the temple of Oromazes, where the magi his brother shut me up in that huge statue whose base reaches to the foundation of the temple and whose top rises to the summit of the dome. I was there buried in a manner; but was saved by the magi; and supplied with all the necessaries of life. At break of day his majesty's apothecary entered my chamber with a potion composed of a mixture of henbane, opium, hemlock, black hellebore, and aconite; and another officer went to thine with a bowstring of blue silk. Neither of us was to be found. Cador, the better to deceive the king, pretended to come and accuse us both. He said that thou hadst taken the road to the Indies, and I that to Memphis, on which the king's guards were immediately dispatched in pursuit of us both.

"The couriers who pursued me did not know me. I had hardly ever shown my face to any but thee, and to thee only in the presence and by the order of my husband. They conducted themselves in the pursuit by the description that had been given them of my person. On the frontiers of Egypt they met with a woman of the same stature with me, and possessed perhaps of greater charms. She was weeping and wandering. They made no doubt but that this woman was the Queen of Babylon and accordingly brought her to Moabdar. Their mistake at first threw the king into a violent passion; but having viewed this woman more attentively, he found her extremely handsome and was comforted. She was called Missouf. I have since been informed that this name in the Egyptian language signifies the capricious fair one. She was so in reality; but she had as much cunning as caprice. She pleased Moabdar and gained such an ascendancy over him as to make him choose her for his wife. Her character then began to appear in its true colors. She gave herself up, without scruple, to all the freaks of a wanton imagination. She would have obliged the chief of the magi, who was old and gouty, to dance before her; and on his refusal, she persecuted him with the most unrelenting cruelty. She ordered her master of the horse to make her a pie of sweetmeats. In vain did he represent that he was not a pastry-cook; he was obliged to make it, and lost his place, because it was baked a little too hard. The post of master of the horse she gave to her dwarf, and that of chancellor to her page. In this manner did she govern Babylon. Everybody regretted the loss of me. The king, who till the moment of his resolving to poison me and strangle thee, had been a tolerably good kind of man, seemed now to have drowned all his virtues in his immoderate fondness for this capricious fair one. He came to the temple on the great day of the feast held in honor of the sacred fire. I saw him implore the gods in behalf of Missouf, at the feet of the statue in which I was inclosed. I raised my voice, I cried out, 'The gods reject the prayers of a king who is now be-

ZADIG THE BABYLONIAN

come a tyrant, and who attempted to murder a reasonable wife, in order to marry a woman remarkable for nothing but her folly and extravagance.' At these words Moabdar was confounded and his head became disordered. The oracle I had pronounced, and the tyranny of Missouf, conspired to deprive him of his judgment, and in a few days his reason entirely forsook him.

"Moabdar's madness, which seemed to be the judgment of Heaven, was the signal to a revolt. The people rose and ran to arms; and Babylon, which had been so long immersed in idleness and effeminacy, became the theater of a bloody civil war. I was taken from the heart of my statue and placed at the head of a party. Cador flew to Memphis to bring thee back to Babylon. The Prince of Hircania, informed of these fatal events, returned with his army and made a third party in Chaldea. He attacked the king, who fled before him with his capricious Egyptian. Moabdar died pierced with wounds. I myself had the misfortune to be taken by a party of Hircanians, who conducted me to their prince's tent, at the very moment that Missouf was brought before him. Thou wilt doubtless be pleased to hear that the prince thought me beautiful; but thou wilt be sorry to be informed that he designed me for his seraglio. He told me, with a blunt and resolute air, that as soon as he had finished a military expedition, which he was just going to undertake, he would come to me. Judge how great must have been my grief. My ties with Moabdar were already dissolved; I might have been the wife of Zadig; and I was fallen into the hands of a barbarian. I answered him with all the pride which my high rank and noble sentiment could inspire. I had always heard it affirmed that Heaven stamped on persons of my condition a mark of grandeur, which, with a single word or glance, could reduce to the lowliness of the most profound respect those rash and forward persons who presume to deviate from the rules of politeness. I spoke like a queen, but was treated like a maidservant. The Hircanian, without even deigning to speak to me, told his black eunuch that I was impertinent, but that he thought me handsome. He ordered him to take care of me, and to put me under the regimen of favorites, that so my complexion being improved, I might be the more worthy of his favors when he should be at leisure to honor me with them. I told him that rather than submit to his desires I would put an end to my life. He replied, with a smile, that women, he believed, were not so bloodthirsty, and that he was accustomed to such violent expressions; and then left me with the air of a man who had just put another parrot into his aviary. What a state for the first queen of the universe, and, what is more, for a heart devoted to Zadig!"

At these words Zadig threw himself at her feet and bathed them with his tears. Astarte raised him with great tenderness and thus continued her story: "I now saw myself in the power of a barbarian and rival to the foolish woman with whom I was confined. She gave me an account of her adventures in Egypt. From the description she gave me of your person, from the time, from the dromedary on which you were mounted, and from every other circumstance, I inferred that Zadig was the man who had fought for her. I doubted not but that you were at Memphis, and, therefore, resolved to repair thither. Beautiful Missouf, said I, thou art more handsome than I, and will please the Prince of Hircania much better. Assist me in contriving the means of my escape; thou wilt then reign alone; thou wilt at once make me happy and rid thyself of a rival. Missouf concerted with me the means of my flight; and I departed secretly with a female Egyptian slave.

"As I approached the frontiers of Arabia, a famous robber, named Arbogad, seized me and sold me to some merchants, who brought me to this castle, where Lord Ogul resides. He bought me without knowing who I was. He is a voluptuary, ambitious of nothing but good living, and thinks that God sent him into the world for no other purpose than to sit at table. He is so extremely corpulent that he is always in danger of suffocation. His physician, who has but little credit with him when he has a good digestion, governs him with a despotic sway when he has eaten too much. He has persuaded him that a basilisk stewed in rose water will effect a complete cure. The Lord Ogul hath promised his hand to the female slave that brings him a basilisk. Thou seest that I leave them to vie with each other in meriting this honor; and never was I less desirous of finding the basilisk than since Heaven hath restored thee to my sight."

This account was succeeded by a long conversation between Astarte and Zadig, consisting of everything that their long-suppressed sentiments, their great sufferings, and their mutual love could inspire into hearts the most noble and tender; and the genii who preside over love carried their words to the sphere of Venus.

The woman returned to Ogul without having found the basilisk. Zadig was introduced to this mighty lord and spoke to him in the following terms: "May immortal health descend from heaven to bless all thy days! I am a physician; at the first report of thy indisposition I flew to thy castle and have now brought thee a basilisk stewed in rose water. Not that I pretend to marry thee. All I ask is the liberty of a Babylonian slave, who hath been in thy possession for a few days; and, if I should not be so happy as to cure thee, magnificent Lord Ogul, I consent to remain a slave in her place."

The proposal was accepted. Astarte set out for Babylon with Zadig's servant, promising, immediately upon her arrival, to send a courier to inform him of all that had happened. Their parting was as tender as their meeting. The moment of meeting and that of parting are the two greatest epochs of life, as sayeth the great book of Zend. Zadig loved the queen with as much ardor as he professed; and the queen loved him more than she thought proper to acknowledge.

Meanwhile Zadig spoke thus to Ogul: "My lord, my basilisk is not to be eaten; all its virtues must enter through thy pores. I have inclosed it in a little ball, blown up and covered with a fine skin. Thou must strike this ball with all thy might and I must strike it back for a considerable time; and by observing this regimen for a few days thou wilt see the effects of my art." The first day Ogul was out of breath and thought he should have died with fatigue. The second he was less fatigued, slept better. In eight days he recovered all the strength, all the health, all the agility and cheerfulness of his most agreeable years.

"Thou hast played at ball, and thou hast been temperate," said Zadig; "know that there is no such thing in nature as a basilisk; that temperance and exercise are the two great preservatives of health; and that the art of reconciling intemperance and health is as chimerical as the philosopher's stone, judicial astrology, or the theology of the magi."

Ogul's first physician, observing how dangerous this man might prove to the medical art, formed a design, in conjunction with the apothecary, to send Zadig to search for a basilisk in the other world. Thus, having suffered such a long train of calamities on account of his good actions, he was now upon the point of losing his life for curing a gluttonous lord. He was invited to an excellent dinner and was to have been poisoned in the second course, but, during the first, he happily received a courier from the fair Astarte. "When one is beloved by a beautiful woman," says the great Zoroaster, "he hath always the good fortune to extricate himself out of every kind of difficulty and danger."

The Combats

The queen was received at Babylon with all those transports of joy which are ever felt on the return of a beautiful princess who hath been involved in calamities. Babylon was now in greater tranquillity. The Prince of Hircania had been killed in battle. The victorious Babylonians declared that the queen should marry the man whom they should choose for their sovereign. They were resolved that the first place in the world, that of being husband to Astarte and King of Babylon, should not depend on cabals and intrigues. They swore to acknowledge for king the man who, upon trial, should be found to be possessed of the greatest valor and the greatest wisdom. Accordingly, at the distance of a few leagues from the city, a spacious place was marked out for the list, surrounded with magnificent amphitheaters. Thither the combatants were to repair in complete armor. Each of them had a separate apartment behind the amphitheaters, where they were neither to be seen nor known by anyone. Each was to encounter four knights, and those that were so happy as to conquer four were then to engage with

ZADIG THE BABYLONIAN

one another; so that he who remained the last master of the field would be proclaimed conqueror at the games.

Four days after he was to return with the same arms and to explain the enigmas proposed by the magi. If he did not explain the enigmas he was not king; and the running at the lances was to be begun afresh till a man would be found who was conqueror in both these combats; for they were absolutely determined to have a king possessed of the greatest wisdom and the most invincible courage. The queen was all the while to be strictly guarded: she was only allowed to be present at the games, and even there she was to be covered with a veil; but was not permitted to speak to any of the competitors, that so they might neither receive favor, nor suffer injustice.

These particulars Astarte communicated to her lover, hoping that in order to obtain her he would show himself possessed of greater courage and wisdom than any other person. Zadig set out on his journey, beseeching Venus to fortify his courage and enlighten his understanding. He arrived on the banks of the Euphrates on the eve of this great day. He caused his device to be inscribed among those of the combatants, concealing his face and his name, as the law ordained; and then went to repose himself in the apartment that fell to him by lot. His friend Cador, who, after the fruitless search he had made for him in Egypt, was now returned to Babylon, sent to his tent a complete suit of armor, which was a present from the queen; as also, from himself, one of the finest horses in Persia. Zadig presently perceived that these presents were sent by Astarte; and from thence his courage derived fresh strength, and his love the most animating hopes.

Next day, the queen being seated under a canopy of jewels, and the amphitheaters filled with all the gentlemen and ladies of rank in Babylon, the combatants appeared in the circus. Each of them came and laid his device at the feet of the grand magi. They drew their devices by lot; and that of Zadig was the last. The first who advanced was a certain lord, named Itobad, very rich and very vain, but possessed of little courage, of less address, and hardly of any judgment at all. His servants had persuaded him that such a man as he ought to be king; he had said in reply, "Such a man as I ought to reign"; and thus they had armed him for a cap-a-pie. He wore an armor of gold enameled with green, a plume of green feathers, and a lance adorned with green ribbons. It was instantly perceived by the manner in which Itobad managed his horse, that it was not for such a man as he that Heaven reserved the scepter of Babylon. The first knight that ran against him threw him out of his saddle; the second laid him flat on his horse's buttocks, with his legs in the air, and his arms extended. Itobad recovered himself, but with so bad a grace that the whole amphitheater burst out a-laughing. The third knight disdained to make use of his lance; but, making a pass at him, took him by the right leg and, wheeling him half round, laid him prostrate on the sand. The squires of the game ran to him laughing, and replaced him in his saddle. The fourth combatant took him by the left leg, and tumbled him down on the other side. He was conducted back with scornful shouts to his tent, where, according to the law, he was to pass the night; and as he climbed along with great difficulty he said, "What an adventure for such a man as I!"

The other knights acquitted themselves with greater ability and success. Some of them conquered two combatants; a few of them vanquished three; but none but Prince Otamus conquered four. At last Zadig fought him in his turn. He successively threw four knights off their saddles with all the grace imaginable. It then remained to be seen who should be conqueror, Otamus or Zadig. The arms of the first were gold and blue, with a plume of the same color; those of the last were white. The wishes of all the spectators were divided between the knight in blue and the knight in white. The queen, whose heart was in a violent palpitation, offered prayers to Heaven for the success of the white color.

The two champions made their passes and vaults with so much agility, they mutually gave and received such dexterous blows with their lances, and sat so firmly in their saddles, that everybody but the queen wished there might be two kings in Babylon. At length, their horses being tired and their lances broken, Zadig had recourse to this stratagem: He passes behind the blue prince; springs upon

ZADIG THE BABYLONIAN

the buttocks of his horse; seizes him by the middle; throws him on the earth; places himself in the saddle; and wheels around Otamus as he lay extended on the ground. All the amphitheater cried out, "Victory to the white knight!"

Otamus rises in a violent passion, and draws his sword; Zadig leaps from his horse with his saber in his hand. Both of them are now on the ground, engaged in a new combat, where strength and agility triumph by turns. The plumes of their helmets, the studs of their bracelets, the rings of their armor, are driven to a great distance by the violence of a thousand furious blows. They strike with the point and the edge; to the right, to the left, on the head, on the breast; they retreat; they advance; they measure swords; they close; they seize each other; they bend like serpents; they attack like lions; and the fire every moment flashes from their blows.

At last Zadig, having recovered his spirits, stops; makes a feint; leaps upon Otamus; throws him on the ground and disarms him; and Otamus cries out, "It is thou alone, O white knight, that oughtest to reign over Babylon!" The queen was now at the height of her joy. The knight in blue armor and the knight in white were conducted each to his own apartment, as well as all the others, according to the intention of the law. Mutes came to wait upon them and to serve them at table. It may be easily supposed that the queen's little mute waited upon Zadig. They were then left to themselves to enjoy the sweets of repose till next morning, at which time the conqueror was to bring his device to the grand magi, to compare it with that which he had left, and make himself known.

Zadig, though deeply in love, was so much fatigued that he could not help sleeping. Itobad, who lay near him, never closed his eyes. He arose in the night, entered his apartment, took the white arms and the device of Zadig, and put his green armor in their place. At break of day he went boldly to the grand magi to declare that so great a man as he was conqueror. This was little expected; however, he was proclaimed while Zadig was still asleep. Astarte, surprised and filled with despair, returned to Babylon. The amphitheater was almost empty when Zadig awoke; he sought for his arms, but could find none but the green armor. With this he was obliged to cover himself, having nothing else near him. Astonished and enraged, he put it on in a furious passion, and advanced in this equipage.

The people that still remained in the amphitheater and the circus received him with hoots and hisses. They surrounded him and insulted him to his face. Never did man suffer such cruel mortifications. He lost his patience; with his saber he dispersed such of the populace as dared to affront him; but he knew not what course to take. He could not see the queen; he could not claim the white armor she had sent him without exposing her; and thus, while she was plunged in grief, he was filled with fury and distraction. He walked on the banks of the Euphrates, fully persuaded that his star had destined him to inevitable misery, and resolving in his own mind all his misfortunes, from the adventure of the woman who hated one-eyed men to that of his armor. "This," said he, "is the consequence of my having slept too long. Had I slept less, I should now have been King of Babylon and in possession of Astarte. Knowledge, virtue, and courage have hitherto served only to make me miserable." He then let fall some secret murmurings against Providence, and was tempted to believe that the world was governed by a cruel destiny, which oppressed the good and prospered knights in green armor. One of his greatest mortifications was his being obliged to wear that green armor which had exposed him to such contumelious treatment. A merchant happening to pass by, he sold it to him for a trifle and bought a gown and a long bonnet. In this garb he proceeded along the banks of the Euphrates, filled with despair, and secretly accusing Providence, which thus continued to persecute him with unremitting severity.

The Hermit

While he was thus sauntering he met a hermit, whose white and venerable beard hung down to his girdle. He held a book in his hand, which he read with great attention. Zadig stopped, and made him a profound obeisance. The hermit returned the compliment with such a noble and

ZADIG THE BABYLONIAN

engaging air, that Zadig had the curiosity to enter into conversation with him. He asked him what book it was that he had been reading? "It is the Book of Destinies," said the hermit; "wouldst thou choose to look into it?" He put the book into the hands of Zadig, who, thoroughly versed as he was in several languages, could not decipher a single character of it. This only redoubled his curiosity.

"Thou seemest," said this good father, "to be in great distress."

"Alas," replied Zadig, "I have but too much reason."

"If thou wilt permit me to accompany thee," resumed the old man, "perhaps I may be of some service to thee. I have often poured the balm of consolation into the bleeding heart of the unhappy."

Zadig felt himself inspired with respect for the air, the beard, and the book of the hermit. He found, in the course of the conversation, that he was possessed of superior degrees of knowledge. The hermit talked of fate, of justice, of morals, of the chief good, of human weakness, and of virtue and vice, with such a spirited and moving eloquence, that Zadig felt himself drawn toward him by an irresistible charm. He earnestly entreated the favor of his company till their return to Babylon.

"I ask the same favor of thee," said the old man; "swear to me by Oromazes, that whatever I do, thou wilt not leave me for some days." Zadig swore, and they set out together.

In the evening the two travelers arrived in a superb castle. The hermit entreated a hospitable reception for himself and the young man who accompanied him. The porter, whom one might have easily mistaken for a great lord, introduced them with a kind of disdainful civility. He presented them to a principal domestic, who showed them his master's magnificent apartments. They were admitted to the lower end of the table, without being honored with the least mark of regard by the lord of the castle; but they were served, like the rest, with delicacy and profusion. They were then presented with water to wash their hands, in a golden basin adorned with emeralds and rubies. At last they were conducted to bed in a beautiful apartment; and in the morning a domestic brought each of them a piece of gold, after which they took their leave and departed.

"The master of the house," said Zadig, as they were proceeding on the journey, "appears to be a generous man, though somewhat too proud; he nobly performs the duties of hospitality." At that instant he observed that a kind of large pocket, which the hermit had, was filled and distended; and upon looking more narrowly he found that it contained the golden basin adorned with precious stones, which the hermit had stolen. He durst not take any notice of it, but he was filled with a strange surprise.

About noon, the hermit came to the door of a paltry house inhabited by a rich miser, and begged the favor of an hospitable reception for a few hours. An old servant, in a tattered garb, received them with a blunt and rude air, and led them into the stable, where he gave them some rotten olives, moldy bread, and sour beer. The hermit ate and drank with as much seeming satisfaction as he had done the evening before; and then addressing himself to the old servant, who watched them both, to prevent their stealing anything, and rudely pressed them to depart, he gave him the two pieces of gold he had received in the morning, and thanked him for his great civility.

"Pray," added he, "allow me to speak to thy master." The servant, filled with astonishment, introduced the two travelers. "Magnificent lord," said the hermit, "I cannot but return thee my most humble thanks for the noble manner in which thou hast entertained us. Be pleased to accept this golden basin as a small mark of my gratitude." The miser started, and was ready to fall backward; but the hermit, without giving him time to recover from his surprise, instantly departed with his young fellow traveler.

"Father," said Zadig, "what is the meaning of all this? Thou seemest to me to be entirely different from other men; thou stealest a golden basin adorned with precious stones from a lord who received thee magnificently, and givest it to a miser who treats thee with indignity."

"Son," replied the old man, "this magnificent lord, who receives strangers only from vanity and ostentation, will hereby be rendered more wise; and the miser will learn to practice the duties of hospitality. Be surprised at nothing, but follow me."

Zadig knew not as yet whether he was in company with the most foolish or the most prudent of mankind; but the hermit spoke with such an ascendancy, that Zadig, who was moreover bound by his oath, could not refuse to follow him.

In the evening they arrived at a house built with equal elegance and simplicity, where nothing favored either of prodigality or avarice. The master of it was a philosopher, who had retired from the world, and who cultivated in peace the study of virtue and wisdom, without any of that rigid and morose severity so commonly to be found in men of his character. He had chosen to build this country house, in which he received strangers with a generosity free from ostentation. He went himself to meet the two travelers, whom he led into a commodious apartment, where he desired them to repose themselves a little. Soon after he came and invited them to a decent and well-ordered repast during which he spoke with great judgment of the last revolutions in Babylon. He seemed to be strongly attached to the queen, and wished that Zadig had appeared in the lists to dispute the crown. "But the people," added he, "do not deserve to have such a king as Zadig."

Zadig blushed, and felt his griefs redoubled. They agreed, in the course of the conversation, that the things of this world did not always answer the wishes of the wise. The hermit still maintained that the ways of Providence were inscrutable; and that men were in the wrong to judge of a whole, of which they understood but the smallest part.

They talked of passions. "Ah," said Zadig, "how fatal are their effects!"

"They are in the winds," replied the hermit, "that swell the sails of the ship; it is true, they sometimes sink her, but without them she could not sail at all. The bile makes us sick and choleric; but without bile we could not live. Everything in this world is dangerous, and yet everything is necessary."

The conversation turned on pleasure; and the hermit proved that it was a present bestowed by the deity. "For," said he, "man cannot give himself either sensations or ideas;

he receives all; and pain and pleasure proceed from a foreign cause as well as his being."

Zadig was surprised to see a man, who had been guilty of such extravagant actions, capable of reasoning with so much judgment and propriety. At last, after a conversation equally entertaining and instructive, the host led back his two guests to their apartment, blessing Heaven for having sent him two men possessed of so much wisdom and virtue. He offered them money with such an easy and noble air as could not possibly give any offense. The hermit refused it, and said that he must now take his leave of him, as he set out for Babylon before it was light. Their parting was tender; Zadig especially felt himself filled with esteem and affection for a man of such an amiable character.

When he and the hermit were alone in their apartment, they spent a long time in praising their host. At break of day the old man awakened his companion. "We must now depart," said he, "but while all the family are still asleep, I will leave this man a mark of my esteem and affection." So saying, he took a candle and set fire to the house.

Zadig, struck with horror, cried aloud, and endeavored to hinder him from committing such a barbarous action; but the hermit drew him away by a superior force, and the house was soon in flames. The hermit, who, with his companion, was already at a considerable distance, looked back to the conflagration with great tranquillity.

"Thanks be to God," said he, "the house of my dear host is entirely destroyed! Happy man!"

At these words Zadig was at once tempted to burst out a-laughing, to reproach the reverend father, to beat him, and to run away. But he did none of all of these, for still subdued by the powerful ascendancy of the hermit, he followed him, in spite of himself, to the next stage.

This was at the house of a charitable and virtuous widow, who had a nephew fourteen years of age, a handsome and promising youth, and her only hope. She performed the honors of her house as well as she could. Next day, she ordered her nephew to accompany the strangers to a bridge, which being lately broken down, was become extremely dangerous in passing. The young man walked before them with

ZADIG THE BABYLONIAN

great alacrity. As they were crossing the bridge, "Come," said the hermit to the youth, "I must show my gratitude to thy aunt." He then took him by the hair and plunged him into the river. The boy sunk, apppeared again on the surface of the water, and was swallowed up by the current.

"O monster! O thou most wicked of mankind!" cried Zadig.

"Thou promisedst to behave with greater patience," said the hermit, interrupting him. "Know that under the ruins of that house which Providence hath set on fire the master hath found an immense treasure. Know that this young man, whose life Providence hath shortened, would have assassinated his aunt in the space of a year, and thee in that of two."

"Who told thee so, barbarian?" cried Zadig; "and though thou hadst read this event in thy Book of Destinies, art thou permitted to drown a youth who never did thee any harm?"

While the Babylonian was thus exclaiming, he observed that the old man had no longer a beard, and that his countenance assumed the features and complexion of youth. The hermit's habit disappeared, and four beautiful wings covered a majestic body resplendent with light.

"O sent of heaven! O divine angel!" cried Zadig, humbly prostrating himself on the ground, "hast thou then descended from the Empyrean to teach a weak mortal to submit to the eternal decrees of Providence?"

"Men," said the angel Jesrad, "judge of all without knowing anything; and, of all men, thou best deservest to be enlightened."

Zadig begged to be permitted to speak. "I distrust myself," said he, "but may I presume to ask the favor of thee to clear up one doubt that still remains in my mind? Would it not have been better to have corrected this youth, and made him virtuous, than to have drowned him?"

"Had he been virtuous," replied Jesrad, "and enjoyed a longer life, it would have been his fate to be assassinated himself, together with the wife he would have married, and the child he would have had by her."

"But why," said Zadig, "is it necessary that there should

be crimes and misfortunes, and that these misfortunes should fall on the good?"

"The wicked," replied Jesrad, "are always unhappy; they serve to prove and try the small number of the just that are scattered through the earth; and there is no evil that is not productive of some good."

"But," said Zadig, "suppose there were nothing but good and no evil at all."

"Then," replied Jesrad, "this earth would be another earth. The chain of events would be ranged in another order and directed by wisdom; but this other order, which would be perfect, can exist only in the eternal abode of the Supreme Being, to which no evil can approach. The Deity hath created millions of worlds, among which there is not one that resembles another. This immense variety is the effect of His immense power. There are not two leaves among the trees of the earth, nor two globes in the unlimited expanse of heaven that are exactly similar; and all that thou seest on the little atom in which thou art born, ought to be in its proper time and place, according to the immutable decree of Him who comprehends all. Men think that this child who hath just perished is fallen into the water by chance; and that it is by the same chance that this house is burned; but there is no such thing as chance; all is either a trial, or a punishment, or a reward, or a foresight. Remember the fisherman who thought himself the most wretched of mankind. Oromazes sent thee to change his fate. Cease, then, frail mortal, to dispute against what thou oughtest to adore."

"But," said Zadig—as he pronounced the word "But," the angel took his flight toward the tenth sphere. Zadig on his knees adored Providence, and submitted. The angel cried to him from on high, "Direct thy course toward Babylon."

The Enigmas

Zadig, entranced, as it were, and like a man about whose head the thunder had burst, walked at random. He entered Babylon on the very day when those who had fought at the tournaments were assembled in the grand vestibule of the

ZADIG THE BABYLONIAN

palace to explain the enigmas and to answer the questions of the grand magi. All the knights were already arrived, except the knight in green armor. As soon as Zadig appeared in the city the people crowded round him; every eye was fixed on him; every mouth blessed him, and every heart wished him the empire. The envious man saw him pass; he frowned and turned aside. The people conducted him to the place where the assembly was held. The queen, who was informed of his arrival, became a prey to the most violent agitations of hope and fear. She was filled with anxiety and apprehension. She could not comprehend why Zadig was without arms, nor why Itobad wore the white armor. A confused murmur arose at the sight of Zadig. They were equally surprised and charmed to see him; but none but the knights who had fought were permitted to appear in the assembly.

"I have fought as well as the other knights," said Zadig, "but another here wears my arms; and while I wait for the honor of proving the truth of my assertion, I demand the liberty of presenting myself to explain the enigmas." The question was put to the vote, and his reputation for probity was still so deeply impressed in their minds, that they admitted him without scruple.

The first question proposed by the grand magi was: "What, of all things in the world, is the longest and the shortest, the swiftest and the slowest, the most divisible and the most extended, the most neglected and the most regretted, without which nothing can be done, which devours all that is little, and enlivens all that is great?"

Itobad was to speak. He replied that so great a man as he did not understand enigmas, and that it was sufficient for him to have conquered by his strength and valor. Some said that the meaning of the enigma was Fortune; some, the Earth; and others the Light. Zadig said that it was Time. "Nothing," added he, "is longer, since it is the measure of eternity; nothing is shorter, since it is insufficient for the accomplishment of our projects; nothing more slow to him that expects, nothing more rapid to him that enjoys; in greatness, it extends to infinity; in smallness, it is infinitely divisible; all men neglect it; all regret the loss of it; nothing can be done without it; it consigns to oblivion whatever is unworthy of being transmitted to posterity, and it immortalizes such actions as are truly great." The assembly acknowledged that Zadig was in the right.

The next question was: "What is the thing which we receive without thanks, which we enjoy without knowing how, which we give to others when we know not where we are, and which we lose without perceiving it?"

Everyone gave his own explanation. Zadig alone guessed that it was Life, and explained all the other enigmas with the same facility. Itobad always said that nothing was more easy, and that he could have answered them with the same readiness had he chosen to have given himself the trouble. Questions were then proposed on justice, on the sovereign good, and on the art of government. Zadig's answers were judged to be the most solid. "What a pity is it," said they, "that such a great genius should be so bad a knight!"

"Illustrious lords," said Zadig, "I have had the honor of conquering in the tournaments. It is to me that the white armor belongs. Lord Itobad took possession of it during my sleep. He probably thought that it would fit him better than the green. I am now ready to prove in your presence, with my gown and sword, against all that beautiful white armor which he took from me, that it is I who have had the honor of conquering the brave Otamus."

Itobad accepted the challenge with the greatest confidence. He never doubted but what, armed as he was, with a helmet, a cuirass, and brassarts, he would obtain an easy victory over a champion in a cap and nightgown. Zadig drew his sword, saluting the queen, who looked at him with a mixture of fear and joy. Itobad drew his without saluting anyone. He rushed upon Zadig, like a man who had nothing to fear; he was ready to cleave him in two. Zadig knew how to ward off his blows, by opposing the strongest part of his sword to the weakest of that of his adversary, in such a manner that Itobad's sword was broken. Upon which Zadig, seizing his enemy by the waist, threw him on the ground; and fixing the point of

ZADIG THE BABYLONIAN

his sword at the breastplate, "Suffer thyself to be disarmed," said he, "or thou art a dead man."

Itobad, always surprised at the disgraces that happened to such a man as he, was obliged to yield to Zadig, who took from him with great composure his magnificent helmet, his superb cuirass, his fine brassarts, his shining cuishes; clothed himself with them, and in this dress ran to throw himself at the feet of Astarte. Cador easily proved that the armor belonged to Zadig. He was acknowledged king by the unanimous consent of the whole nation, and especially by that of Astarte, who, after so many calamities, now tasted the exquisite pleasure of seeing her lover worthy, in the eyes of all the world, to be her husband. Itobad went home to be called lord in his own house. Zadig was king, and was happy. The queen and Zadig adored Providence. He sent in search of the robber Arbogad, to whom he gave an honorable post in his army, promising to advance him to the first dignities if he behaved like a true warrior, and threatening to hang him if he followed the profession of a robber.

Setoc, with the fair Almona, was called from the heart of Arabia and placed at the head of the commerce of Babylon. Cador was preferred and distinguished according to his great services. He was the friend of the king; and the king was then the only monarch on earth that had a friend. The little mute was not forgotten.

But neither could the beautiful Semira be comforted for having believed that Zadig would be blind of an eye; nor did Azora cease to lament her having attempted to cut off his nose. Their griefs, however, he softened by his presents. The envious man died of rage and shame. The empire enjoyed peace, glory, and plenty. This was the happiest age of the earth; it was governed by love and justice. The people blessed Zadig, and Zadig blessed Heaven.

ABANDONED
BY GUY DE MAUPASSANT

ABANDONED

By GUY DE MAUPASSANT

"I REALLY think you must be mad, my dear, to go for a country walk in such weather as this. You have had some very strange notions for the last two months. You drag me to the seaside in spite of myself, when you have never once had such a whim during all the forty-four years that we have been married. You chose Fécamp, which is a very dull town, without consulting me in the matter, and now you are seized with such a rage for walking, you who hardly ever stir out on foot, that you want to take a country walk on the hottest day of the year. Ask d'Apreval to go with you, as he is ready to gratify all your whims. As for me, I am going back to have a nap."

Madame de Cadour turned to her old friend and said:

"Will you come with me, Monsieur d'Apreval?"

He bowed with a smile, and with all the gallantry of former years:

"I will go wherever you go," he replied.

"Very well, then, go and get a sunstroke," Monsieur de Cadour said: and he went back to the Hôtel des Bains to lie down for an hour or two.

As soon as they were alone, the old lady and her old companion set off, and she said to him in a low voice, squeezing his hand:

"At last! at last!"

"You are mad," he said in a whisper. "I assure you that you are mad. Think of the risk you are running. If that man——"

She started.

"Oh! Henri, do not say *that man*, when you are speaking of him."

"Very well," he said abruptly, "if our son guesses anything, if he has any suspicions, he will have you, he will have us both in his power. You have got on without seeing him for the last forty years. What is the matter with you to-day?"

They had been going up the long street that leads from the sea to the town, and now they turned to the right, to go to Etretat. The white road stretched in front of them under a blaze of brilliant sunshine, so they went on slowly in the burning heat. She had taken her old friend's arm, and was looking straight in front of her, with a fixed and haunted gaze, and at last she said:

"And so you have not seen him again, either?"

"No, never."

"Is it possible?"

"My dear friend, do not let us begin that discussion again. I have a wife and children and you have a husband, so we both of us have much to fear from other people's opinion."

She did not reply; she was thinking of her long past youth and of many sad things that had occurred. How well she recalled all the details of their early friendship, his smiles, the way he used to linger, in order to watch her until she was indoors. What happy days they were, the only really delicious days she had ever enjoyed, and how quickly they were over!

And then—her discovery—of the penalty she paid! What anguish!

Of that journey to the South, that long journey, her sufferings, her constant terror, that secluded life in the small, solitary house on the shores of the Mediterranean, at the bottom of a garden, which she did not venture to leave. How well she remembered those long days which she spent lying under an orange tree, looking up at the round, red fruit, amid the green leaves. How she used to long to go out, as far as the sea, whose fresh breezes came to her over the wall, and whose small waves she could hear lapping on the beach. She dreamed of its immense blue expanse sparkling under the sun, with the white sails of the small vessels, and a mountain on the horizon. But she did not dare to go outside the gate. Suppose anybody had recognized her!

And those days of waiting, those last days of misery and expectation! The impending suffering, and then that ter-

ABANDONED

rible night! What misery she had endured, and what a night it was! How she had groaned and screamed! She could still see the pale face of her lover, who kissed her hand every moment, and the clean-shaven face of the doctor and the nurse's white cap.

And what she felt when she heard the child's feeble cries, that wail, that first effort of a human's voice!

And the next day! the next day! the only day of her life on which she had seen and kissed her son; for, from that time, she had never even caught a glimpse of him.

And what a long, void existence hers had been since then, with the thought of that child always, always floating before her. She had never seen her son, that little creature that had been part of herself, even once since then; they had taken him from her, carried him away, and had hidden him. All she knew was that he had been brought up by some peasants in Normandy, that he had become a peasant himself, had married well, and that his father, whose name he did not know, had settled a handsome sum of money on him.

How often during the last forty years had she wished to go and see him and to embrace him! She could not imagine to herself that he had grown! She always thought of that small human atom which she had held in her arms and pressed to her bosom for a day.

How often she had said to M. d'Apreval: "I cannot bear it any longer; I must go and see him."

But he had always stopped her and kept her from going. She would be unable to restrain and to master herself; their son would guess it and take advantage of her, blackmail her; she would be lost.

"What is he like?" she said.

"I do not know. I have not seen him again, either."

"Is it possible? To have a son and not to know him; to be afraid of him and to reject him as if he were a disgrace! It is horrible."

They went along the dusty road, overcome by the scorching sun, and continually ascending that interminable hill.

"One might take it for a punishment," she continued; "I have never had another child, and I could no longer resist the longing to see him, which has possessed me for forty years. You men cannot understand that. You must remember that I shall not live much longer, and suppose I should never see him, never have seen him! ... Is it possible? How could I wait so long? I have thought about him every day since, and what a terrible existence mine has been! I have never awakened, never, do you understand, without my first thoughts being of him, of my child. How is he? Oh, how guilty I feel toward him! Ought one to fear what the world may say in a case like this? I ought to have left everything to go after him, to bring him up and to show my love for him. I should certainly have been much happier, but I did not dare, I was a coward. How I have suffered! Oh, how those poor, abandoned children must hate their mothers!"

She stopped suddenly, for she was choked by her sobs. The whole valley was deserted and silent in the dazzling light and the overwhelming heat, and only the grasshoppers uttered their shrill, continuous chirp among the sparse yellow grass on both sides of the road.

"Sit down a little," he said.

She allowed herself to be led to the side of the ditch and sank down with her face in her hands. Her white hair, which hung in curls on both sides of her face, had become tangled. She wept, overcome by profound grief, while he stood facing her, uneasy and not knowing what to say, and he merely murmured: "Come, take courage."

She got up.

"I will," she said, and wiping her eyes, she began to walk again with the uncertain step of an elderly woman.

A little farther on the road passed beneath a clump of trees, which hid a few houses, and they could distinguish the vibrating and regular blows of a blacksmith's hammer on the anvil; and presently they saw a wagon standing on the right side of the road in front of a low cottage, and two men shoeing a horse under a shed.

Monsieur d'Apreval went up to them.

"Where is Pierre Benedict's farm?" he asked.

"Take the road to the left, close to the inn, and then go straight on; it is the third house past Poret's. There is a small spruce fir close to the gate; you cannot make a mistake."

They turned to the left. She was walking very slowly now, her legs threatened to give way, and her heart was beating so violently that she felt as if she should suffocate, while at every step she murmured, as if in prayer:

"Oh! Heaven! Heaven!"

Monsieur d'Apreval, who was also nervous and rather pale, said to her somewhat gruffly:

"If you cannot manage to control your feelings, you will betray yourself at once. Do try and restrain yourself."

"How can I?" she replied. "My child! When I think that I am going to see my child."

They were going along one of those narrow country lanes between farmyards, that are concealed beneath a double row of beech trees at either side of the ditches, and suddenly they found themselves in front of a gate, beside which there was a young spruce fir.

"This is it," he said.

She stopped suddenly and looked about her. The courtyard, which was planted with apple trees, was large and extended as far as the small thatched dwelling house. On the opposite side were the stable, the barn, the cow house and the poultry house, while the gig, the wagon and the manure cart were under a slated outhouse. Four calves were grazing under the shade of the trees and black hens were wandering all about the enclosure.

All was perfectly still; the house door was open, but nobody was to be seen, and so they went in, when immediately a large black dog came out of a barrel that was standing under a pear tree, and began to bark furiously.

There were four bee-hives on boards against the wall of the house.

Monsieur d'Apreval stood outside and called out:

"Is anybody at home?"

Then a child appeared, a little girl of about ten, dressed in a chemise and a linen petticoat, with dirty, bare legs and a timid and cunning look. She remained standing in the doorway, as if to prevent any one going in.

"What do you want?" she asked.

"Is your father in?"
"No."
"Where is he?"
"I don't know."
"And your mother?"
"Gone after the cows."
"Will she be back soon?"
"I don't know."

Then suddenly the lady, as if she feared that her companion might force her to return, said quickly:

"I shall not go without having seen him."

"We will wait for him, my dear friend."

As they turned away, they saw a peasant woman coming toward the house, carrying two tin pails, which appeared to be heavy and which glistened brightly in the sunlight.

She limped with her right leg, and in her brown knitted jacket, that was faded by the sun and washed out by the rain, she looked like a poor, wretched, dirty servant.

"Here is mamma," the child said.

When she got close to the house, she looked at the strangers angrily and suspiciously, and then she went in, as if she had not seen them. She looked old and had a hard, yellow, wrinkled face, one of those wooden faces that country people so often have.

Monsieur d'Apreval called her back.

"I beg your pardon, madame, but we came in to know whether you could sell us two glasses of milk."

She was grumbling when she reappeared in the door, after putting down her pails.

"I don't sell milk," she replied.

"We are very thirsty," he said, "and madame is very tired. Can we not get something to drink?"

The peasant woman gave them an uneasy and cunning glance and then she made up her mind.

"As you are here, I will give you some," she said, going into the house, and almost immediately the child came out and brought two chairs, which she placed under an apple tree, and then the mother, in turn brought out two bowls of foaming milk, which she gave to the visitors. She did not return to the house, however, but remained standing near them, as if to watch them and to find out for what purpose they had come there.

"You have come from Fécamp?" she said.

"Yes," Monsieur d'Apreval replied, "we are staying at Fécamp for the summer."

And then, after a short silence, he continued:

"Have you any fowls you could sell us every week?"

The woman hesitated for a moment and then replied:

"Yes, I think I have. I suppose you want young ones?"

"Yes, of course."

"What do you pay for them in the market?"

D'Apreval, who had not the least idea, turned to his companion:

"What are you paying for poultry in Fécamp, my dear lady?"

"Four francs and four francs fifty centimes," she said, her eyes full of tears, while the farmer's wife, who was looking at her askance, asked in much surprise:

"Is the lady ill, as she is crying?"

He did not know what to say, and replied with some hesitation:

"No—no—but she lost her watch as we came along, a very handsome watch, and that troubles her. If anybody should find it, please let us know."

Mother Benedict did not reply, as she thought it a very equivocal sort of answer, but suddenly she exclaimed:

"Oh, here is my husband!"

She was the only one who had seen him, as she was facing the gate. D'Apreval started and Madame de Cadour nearly fell as she turned round suddenly on her chair.

A man bent nearly double, and out of breath, stood there, ten yards from them, dragging a cow at the end of a rope. Without taking any notice of the visitors, he said:

"Confound it! What a brute!"

And he went past them and disappeared in the cow house.

Her tears had dried quickly as she sat there startled, without a word and with the one thought in her mind, that this was her son, and D'Apreval, whom the same thought had struck very unpleasantly, said in an agitated voice:

"Is this Monsieur Benedict?"

ABANDONED

"Who told you his name?" the wife asked, still rather suspiciously.

"The blacksmith at the corner of the highroad," he replied, and then they were all silent, with their eyes fixed on the door of the cow house, which formed a sort of black hole in the wall of the building. Nothing could be seen inside, but they heard a vague noise, movements and footsteps and the sound of hoofs, which were deadened by the straw on the floor, and soon the man reappeared in the door, wiping his forehead, and came toward the house with long, slow strides. He passed the strangers without seeming to notice them and said to his wife:

"Go and draw me a jug of cider; I am very thirsty."

Then he went back into the house, while his wife went into the cellar and left the two Parisians alone.

"Let us go, let us go, Henri," Madame de Cadour said, nearly distracted with grief, and so d'Apreval took her by the arm, helped her to rise, and sustaining her with all his strength, for he felt that she was nearly fainting, he led her out, after throwing five francs on one of the chairs.

As soon as they were outside the gate, she began to sob and said, shaking with grief:

"Oh! oh! is that what you have made of him?"

He was very pale and replied coldly:

"I did what I could. His farm is worth eighty thousand francs, and that is more than most of the sons of the middle classes have."

They returned slowly, without speaking a word. She was still crying; the tears ran down her cheeks continually for a time, but by degrees they stopped, and they went back to Fécamp, where they found Monsieur de Cadour waiting dinner for them. As soon as he saw them, he began to laugh and exclaimed:

"So my wife has had a sunstroke, and I am very glad of it. I really think she has lost her head for some time past!"

Neither of them replied, and when the husband asked them, rubbing his hands:

"Well, I hope that, at least, you have had a pleasant walk?"

Monsieur d'Apreval replied:

"A delightful walk, I assure you; perfectly delightful."

THE GUILTY SECRET
BY PAUL DE KOCK

THE GUILTY SECRET

By PAUL DE KOCK

NATHALIE DE HAUTEVILLE was twenty-two years old, and had been a widow for three years. She was one of the prettiest women in Paris; her large dark eyes shone with remarkable brilliancy, and she united the sparkling vivacity of an Italian and the depth of feeling of a Spaniard to the grace which always distinguishes a Parisian born and bred. Considering herself too young to be entirely alone, she had long ago invited M. d'Ablaincourt, an old uncle of hers, to come and live with her.

M. d'Ablaincourt was an old bachelor; he had never loved anything in this world but himself. He was an egotist, too lazy to do any one an ill turn, but at the same time too selfish to do any one a kindness, unless it would tend directly to his own advantage. And yet, with an air of complaisance, as if he desired nothing so much as the comfort of those around him, he consented to his niece's proposal, in the hope that she would do many little kind offices for him, which would add materially to his comfort.

M. d'Ablaincourt accompanied his niece when she resumed her place in society; but sometimes, when he felt inclined to stay at home, he would say to her: "My dear Nathalie, I am afraid you will not be much amused this evening. They will only play cards; besides, I don't think any of your friends will be there. Of course, I am ready to take you, if you wish to go."

And Nathalie, who had great confidence in all her uncle said, would stay at home.

In the same manner, M. d'Ablaincourt, who was a great gourmand, said to his niece: "My dear, you know that I am not at all fond of eating, and am satisfied with the simplest fare; but I must tell you that your cook puts too much salt in everything! It is very unwholesome."

So they changed the cook.

Again, the garden was out of order; the trees before the old gentleman's window must be cut down, because their shade would doubtless cause a dampness in the house prejudicial to Nathalie's health; or the surrey was to be changed for a landau.

Nathalie was a coquette. Accustomed to charm, she listened with smiles to the numerous protestations of admiration which she received. She sent all who aspired to her hand to her uncle, saying: "Before I give you any hope, I must know my uncle's opinion."

It is likely that Nathalie would have answered differently if she had ever felt a real preference for any one; but heretofore she seemed to have preferred her liberty.

The old uncle, for his part, being now master in his niece's house, was very anxious for her to remain as she was. A nephew might be somewhat less submissive than Nathalie. Therefore, he never failed to discover some great fault in each of those who sought an alliance with the pretty widow.

Besides his egotism and his epicureanism, the dear uncle had another passion—to play backgammon. The game amused him very much; but the difficulty was to find any one to play with. If, by accident, any of Nathalie's visitors understood it, there was no escape from a long siege with the old gentleman; but most people preferred cards.

In order to please her uncle, Nathalie tried to learn this game; but it was almost impossible. She could not give her attention to one thing for so long a time. Her uncle scolded. Nathalie gave up in despair.

"It was only for your own amusement that I wished to teach it to you," said the good M. d'Ablaincourt.

Things were at this crisis when, at a ball one evening, Nathalie was introduced to a M. d'Apremont, a captain in the navy.

Nathalie raised her eyes, expecting to see a great sailor, with a wooden leg and a bandage over one eye; when to her great surprise, she beheld a man of about thirty, tall and finely formed, with two sound legs and two good eyes.

THE GUILTY SECRET

Armand d'Apremont had entered the navy at a very early age, and had arrived, although very young, to the dignity of a captain. He had amassed a large fortune, in addition to his patrimonial estates, and he had now come home to rest after his labors. As yet, however, he was a single man, and, moreover, had always laughed at love.

But when he saw Nathalie, his opinions underwent a change. For the first time in his life he regretted that he had never learned to dance, and he kept his eyes fixed on her constantly.

His attentions to the young widow soon became a subject of general conversation, and, at last, the report reached the ears of M. d'Ablaincourt. When Nathalie mentioned, one evening, that she expected the captain to spend the evening with her, the old man grew almost angry.

"Nathalie," said he, "you act entirely without consulting me. I have heard that the captain is very rude and unpolished in his manners. To be sure, I have only seen him standing behind your chair; but he has never even asked after my health. I only speak for your interest, as you are so giddy."

Nathalie begged her uncle's pardon, and even offered not to receive the captain's visit; but this he forbore to require—secretly resolving not to allow these visits to become too frequent.

But how frail are all human resolutions—overturned by the merest trifle! In this case, the game of backgammon was the unconscious cause of Nathalie's becoming Mme. d'Apremont. The captain was an excellent hand at backgammon. When the uncle heard this, he proposed a game; and the captain, who understood that it was important to gain the uncle's favor, readily acceded.

This did not please Nathalie. She preferred that he should be occupied with herself. When all the company were gone, she turned to her uncle, saying: "You were right, uncle, after all. I do not admire the captain's manners; I see now that I should not have invited him."

"On the contrary, niece, he is a very well-behaved man. I have invited him to come here very often, and play backgammon with me—that is, to pay his addresses to you."

Nathalie saw that the captain had gained her uncle's heart, and she forgave him for having been less attentive to her. He soon came again, and, thanks to the backgammon, increased in favor with the uncle.

He soon captivated the heart of the pretty widow, also. One morning, Nathalie came blushing to her uncle.

"The captain has asked me to marry him. What do you advise me to do?"

He reflected for a few moments. "If she refuses him, D'Apremont will come here no longer, and then no more backgammon. But if she marries him, he will be here always, and I shall have my games." And the answer was: "You had better marry him."

Nathalie loved Armand; but she would not yield too easily. She sent for the captain.

"If you really love me—"

"Ah, can you doubt it?"

"Hush! do not interrupt me. If you really love me, you will give me one proof of it."

"Anything you ask. I swear—"

"No, you must never swear any more; and, one thing more, you must never smoke. I detest the smell of tobacco, and I will not have a husband who smokes."

Armand sighed, and promised.

The first months of their marriage passed smoothly, but sometimes Armand became thoughtful, restless, and grave. After some time, these fits of sadness became more frequent.

"What is the matter?" asked Nathalie one day, on seeing him stamp with impatience. "Why are you so irritable?"

"Nothing—nothing at all!" replied the captain, as if ashamed of his ill humor.

"Tell me," Nathalie insisted, "have I displeased you in anything?"

The captain assured her that he had no reason to be anything but delighted with her conduct on all occasions, and for a time he was all right. Then soon he was worse than before.

Nathalie was distressed beyond measure. She imparted her anxiety to her uncle, who replied: "Yes, my dear, I know what you mean; I have often remarked it myself, at back-

THE GUILTY SECRET

gammon. He is very inattentive, and often passes his hand over his forehead, and starts up as if something agitated him."

And one day, when his old habits of impatience and irritability reappeared, more marked than ever, the captain said to his wife: "My dear, an evening walk will do me a world of good; an old sailor like myself cannot bear to sit around the house after dinner. Nevertheless, if you have any objection—"

"Oh, no! What objection can I have?"

He went out, and continued to do so, day after day, at the same hour. Invariably he returned in the best of good humor.

Nathalie was now unhappy indeed. "He loves some other woman, perhaps," she thought, "and he must see her every day. Oh, how wretched I am! But I must let him know that his perfidy is discovered. No, I will wait until I shall have some certain proof wherewith to confront him."

And she went to seek her uncle. "Ah, I am the most unhappy creature in the world!" she sobbed.

"What is the matter?" cried the old man, leaning back in his armchair.

"Armand leaves the house for two hours every evening, after dinner, and comes back in high spirits and as anxious to please me as on the day of our marriage. Oh, uncle, I cannot bear it any longer! If you do not assist me to discover where he goes, I will seek a separation."

"But, my dear niece—"

"My dear uncle, you who are so good and obliging, grant me this one favor. I am sure there is some woman in the secret."

M. d'Ablaincourt wished to prevent a rupture between his niece and nephew, which would interfere very much with the quiet, peaceable life which he led at their house. He pretended to follow Armand; but came back very soon, saying he had lost sight of him.

"But in what direction does he go?"

"Sometimes one way, and sometimes another, but always alone; so your suspicions are unfounded. Be assured, he only walks for exercise."

But Nathalie was not to be duped in this way. She sent for a little errand boy, of whose intelligence she had heard a great deal.

"M. d'Apremont goes out every evening."

"Yes, madame."

"To-morrow, you will follow him; observe where he goes, and come and tell me privately. Do you understand?"

"Yes, madame."

Nathalie waited impatiently for the next day, and for the hour of her husband's departure. At last, the time came—the pursuit is going on—Nathalie counted the moments. After three-quarters of an hour, the messenger arrived, covered with dust.

"Well," exclaimed Nathalie, "speak! Tell me everything that you have seen!"

"Madame, I followed M. d'Apremont, at a distance, as far as the Rue Vieille du Temple, where he entered a small house, in an alley. There was no servant to let him in."

"An alley! No servant! Dreadful!"

"I went in directly after him, and heard him go up-stairs and unlock a door."

"Open the door himself, without knocking! Are you sure of that?"

"Yes, madame."

"The wretch! So he has a key! But, go on."

"When the door shut after him, I stole softly up-stairs, and peeped through the keyhole."

"You shall have twenty francs more."

"I peeped through the keyhole, and saw him drag a trunk along the floor."

"A trunk?"

"Then he undressed himself, and—"

"Undressed himself!"

"Then, for a few seconds, I could not see him, and directly he appeared again, in a sort of gray blouse, and a cap on his head."

"A blouse! What in the world does he want with a blouse? What next?"

"I came away, then, madame, and made haste to tell you; but he is there still."

THE GUILTY SECRET

"Well, now run to the corner and get me a cab, and direct the coachman to the house where you have been."

While the messenger went for the cab, Nathalie hurried on her hat and cloak, and ran into her uncle's room.

"I have found him out—he loves another. He's at her house now, in a gray blouse. But I will go and confront him, and then you will see me no more."

The old man had no time to reply. She was gone, with her messenger, in the cab. They stopped at last.

"Here is the house."

Nathalie got out, pale and trembling.

"Shall I go up-stairs with you, madame?" asked the boy.

"No, I will go alone. The third story, isn't it?"

"Yes, madame; the left-hand door, at the head of the stairs."

It seemed that now, indeed, the end of all things was at hand.

Nathalie mounted the dark, narrow stairs, and arrived at the door, and, almost fainting, she cried: "Open the door, or I shall die!"

The door was opened, and Nathalie fell into her husband's arms. He was alone in the room, clad in a gray blouse, and—smoking a Turkish pipe.

"My wife!" exclaimed Armand, in surprise.

"Your wife—who, suspecting your perfidy, has followed you, to discover the cause of your mysterious conduct!"

"How, Nathalie, my mysterious conduct? Look, here it is!" (Showing his pipe.) "Before our marriage, you forbade me to smoke, and I promised to obey you. For some months I kept my promise; but you know what it cost me; you remember how irritable and sad I became. It was my pipe, my beloved pipe, that I regretted. One day, in the country, I discovered a little cottage, where a peasant was smoking. I asked him if he could lend me a blouse and cap; for I should like to smoke with him, but it was necessary to conceal it from you, as the smell of smoke, remaining in my clothes, would have betrayed me. It was soon settled between us. I returned thither every afternoon, to indulge in my favorite occupation; and, with the precaution of a cap to keep the smoke from remaining in my hair, I

THE GUILTY SECRET

contrived to deceive you. This is all the mystery. Forgive me."

Nathalie kissed him, crying: "I might have known it could not be! I am happy now, and you shall smoke as much as you please, at home."

And Nathalie returned to her uncle, saying: "Uncle, he loves me! He was only smoking, but hereafter he is to smoke at home."

"I can arrange it all," said D'Ablaincourt; "he shall smoke while he plays backgammon."

"In that way," thought the old man, "I shall be sure of my game."

JEAN MONETTE
BY EUGENE FRANCOIS VIDOCQ

JEAN MONETTE

By EUGENE FRANCOIS VIDOCQ

AT the time when I first became commissary of police, my arrondissement was in that part of Paris which includes the Rue St. Antoine—a street which has a great number of courts, alleys, and culs de sac, issuing from it in all directions. The houses in these alleys and courts are, for the most part, inhabited by wretches wavering betwixt the last shade of poverty and actual starvation, ready to take part in any disturbance, or assist in any act of rapine or violence.

In one of these alleys, there lived at that time a man named Jean Monette, who was tolerably well-stricken in years, but still a hearty man. He was a widower, and, with an only daughter, occupied a floor, au quatrième, in one of the courts; people said he had been in business and grown rich, but that he had not the heart to spend his money, which year after year accumulated, and would make a splendid fortune for his daughter, at his death. With this advantage, Emma, who was really a handsome girl, did not want for suitors, and thought that, being an heiress, she might wait till she really felt a reciprocal passion for some one, and not throw herself away upon the first tolerable match that presented itself. It was on a Sunday, the first in the month of June, that Emma had, as an especial treat, obtained sufficient money from her father for an excursion with some friends to see the fountains of Versailles.

It was a beautiful day, and the basin was thronged around with thousands and thousands of persons, looking, from the variety of their dresses, more like the colors of a splendid rainbow than aught besides; and when, at four o'clock, Triton and his satellites threw up their immense volumes of water, all was wonder, astonishment, and de-

EUGENE FRANCOIS VIDOCQ

light; but none were more delighted than Emma, to whom the scene was quite new.

And, then, it was so pleasant to have found a gentleman who could explain everything and everybody; point out the duke of this, and the count that, and the other lions of Paris; besides, such an agreeable and well-dressed man; it was really quite condescending in him to notice them! And then, toward evening, he would insist they should all go home together in a fiacre, and that he alone should pay all the expenses, and when, with a gentle pressure of the hand and a low whisper, he begged her to say where he might come and throw himself at her feet, she thought her feelings were different to what they had ever been before. But how could she give her address—tell so dashing a man that she lived in such a place? No, she could not do that, but she would meet him at the Jardin d'Eté next Sunday evening, and dance with no one else all night.

She met him on the Sunday, and again and again, until her father began to suspect, from her frequent absence of an evening—which was formerly an unusual circumstance with her—that something must be wrong. The old man loved his money, but he loved his daughter more. She was the only link in life that kept together the chain of his affections. He had been passionately fond of his wife, and when she died, Emma had filled up the void in his heart. They were all, save his money, that he had ever loved. The world had cried out against him as a hard-hearted, rapacious man, and he, in return, despised the world.

He was, therefore, much grieved at her conduct, and questioned Emma as to where her frequent visits led her, but could only obtain for answer that she was not aware she had been absent so much as to give him uneasiness. This was unsatisfactory, and so confirmed the old man in his suspicions that he determined to have his daughter watched.

This he effected through the means of an ancien ami, then in the profession of what he called an "inspector," though his enemies (and all men have such) called him a mouchard, or spy. However, by whatever name he called himself, or others called him, he understood his business, and so effectually watched the young lady, that he discovered her frequent absences to be for the purpose of meeting a man, who, after walking some distance with her, managed, despite the inspector's boasted abilities, to give him the slip.

This naturally puzzled him, and so it would any man in his situation. Fancy the feelings of one of the government's employees in the argus line of business, a man renowned for his success in almost all the arduous and intricate affairs that had been committed to his care, to find himself baffled in a paltry private intrigue, and one which he had merely undertaken for the sake of friendship!

For a second time, he tried the plan of fancying himself to be well paid, thinking this would stimulate his dormant energies, knowing well that a thing done for friendship's sake, is always badly done; but even here he failed. He watched them to a certain corner, but, before he could get around it, they were nowhere to be seen. This was not to be borne. It was setting him at defiance. Should he call in the assistance of a brother in the line? No, that would be to acknowledge himself beaten, and the disgrace he could not bear—his honor was concerned, and he would achieve it singlehanded; but, then, it was very perplexing.

The man, to his experienced eye, seemed not, as he had done to Emma, a dashing gentleman, but more like a foul bird in fine feathers. Something must be wrong, and he must find it out—but, then, again came that confounded question, how?

He would go and consult old Monette—he could, perhaps, suggest something; and, musing on the strangeness of the adventure, he walked slowly toward the house of the old man to hold a council with him on the situation.

On the road, his attention was attracted by a disturbance in the street, and mingling with the crowd, in hope of seizing some of his enemies exercising their illegal functions on whom the whole weight of his official vengeance might fall, he for the time forgot his adventure. The crowd had been drawn together by a difference of opinion between two gentlemen of the vehicular profession, respecting some right of way, and, after all the usual expressions of esteem common on such occasions had been exhausted, one of them drove off, leaving the other at least master of the field, if he had not got the expected job.

The crowd began to disperse, and with them also was going our friend, the detective, when, on turning round, he came in contact with Mlle. Monette, leaning on the arm of her mysterious lover. The light from a lamp above his head shone immediately on the face of Emma and her admirer, showing them both as clear as noonday, so that when his glance turned from the lady to the gentleman, and he obtained a full view of his face, he expressed his joy at the discovery by a loud "Whew!" which, though a short sound and soon pronounced, meant a great deal.

For first, it meant that he had made a great discovery; secondly, that he was not now astonished because he had not succeeded before in his watchfulness; thirdly—but perhaps the two mentioned may be sufficient; for, turning sharply round, he made the greatest haste to reach Monette and inform him, this time, of the result of his espionage.

After a long prelude, stating how fortunate Monette was to have such a friend as himself, a man who knew everybody and everything, he proceeded to inform him of the pleasing intelligence that his daughter was in the habit of meeting, and going to some place (he forgot to say where) with the most desperate and abandoned character in Paris—one who was so extremely dexterous in all his schemes, that the police, though perfectly aware of his intentions, had not been able to fix upon him the commission of any one of his criminal acts, for he changed his appearance so often as to set at naught all the assiduous exertions of the Corps des Espions.

The unhappy father received from his friend at parting the assurance that they would catch him yet, and give him an invitation to pass the rest of his days in the seclusion of a prison.

On Emma's return, he told her the information he had received, wisely withholding the means from which his knowledge came, saying that he knew she had that moment parted from a man who would lead her to the brink of destruction, and then cast her off like a child's broken plaything. He begged, nay, he besought her, with tears in his

JEAN MONETTE

eyes, to promise she would never again see him. Emma was thunderstruck, not only at the accuracy of her father's information, but at hearing such a character of one whom she had painted as perfection's self; and, calling to her aid those never-failing woman's arguments, a copious flood of tears, fell on her father's neck and promised never again to see her admirer and, if possible, to banish all thoughts of him from her mind.

"My child," said the old man, "I believe you from my heart—I believe you. I love you, but the world says I am rich—why, I know not. You know I live in a dangerous neighborhood, and all my care will be necessary to prevent my losing either my child or my reputed wealth; therefore, to avoid all accidents, I will take care you do not leave this house for the next six months to come, and in that time your lover will have forgotten you, or what will amount to the same thing, you will have forgotten him; but I am much mistaken if the man's intentions are not to rob me of my money, rather than my child."

The old man kept his word, and Emma was not allowed for several days to leave the rooms on the fourth floor.

She tried, during the time, if it were possible to forget the object of her affections, and thought if she could but see him once more, to bid him a long and last farewell, she might in time wear out his remembrance from her heart; but in order to do that, she must see him once more; and having made up her mind that this interview would be an essential requisite to the desired end, she took counsel with herself how it was to be accomplished. There was only one great obstacle presenting itself to her view, which was that "she couldn't get out."

Now women's invention never fails them, when they have set their hearts upon any desired object; and it occurred to her, that although she could not get out, yet it was not quite so apparent that he could not get in; and this point being settled, it was no very difficult matter to persuade the old woman who occasionally assisted her in the household arrangements, to be the bearer of a short note, purporting to say that her father having been unwell for the last few days, usually retired early to rest, and that if her dear

Despreau would come about eleven o'clock on the following evening, her father would be asleep, and she would be on the watch for a signal, which was to be three gentle taps on the door.

The old woman executed her commission so well, that she brought back an answer vowing eternal fidelity, and promising a punctual attendance at the rendezvous. Nor was it likely that he meant to fail—seeing it was the object he had had for months in view, and he reasoned with himself that if he once got there, he would make such good use of his time, as to render a second visit perfectly unnecessary.

Therefore, it would be a pity to disappoint any one, and he immediately communicated his plans to two of his confederates, promising them a good share of the booty, and also the girl herself, if either of them felt that way inclined, as a reward for their assistance.

His plans were very well managed, and would have gone on exceedingly well, but for one small accident which happened through the officious interference of the inspector, who, the moment he had discovered who the Lothario was, had taken all the steps he could to catch him, and gain the honor of having caught so accomplished a gentleman. He rightly judged that it would not be long before he would pay a visit to Monette's rooms, and the letters, before their delivery by the old woman, had been read by him, and met with his full approbation.

I was much pleased on being informed by the inspector that he wanted my assistance, one evening, to apprehend the celebrated Despreau, who had planned a robbery near the Rue St. Antoine, and make me acquainted with nearly all the circumstances. So, about half past ten o'clock, I posted myself with the inspector and four men where I could see Despreau pass, and at eleven o'clock, punctual to the moment, he and his two associates began to ascend the stairs.

The two confederates were to wait some time, when he was to come to the door on some pretext and let them in.

After the lapse of half an hour they were let in, when we ascended after them, and the inspector, having a duplicate key, we let ourselves gently in, standing in the passage, so

JEAN MONETTE

as to prevent our being seen; in a few minutes we heard a loud shriek from Emma, and old Monette's voice most vociferously crying "Murder!" and "Thieves!" On entering the rooms, we perceived that the poor girl was lying on the ground, while one of the men was endeavoring to stifle her cries by either gagging or suffocating her, though in the way he was doing it, the latter would have soon been the case.

The old man had been dragged from his bed, and Despreau stood over him with a knife, swearing that unless he showed him the place where his money and valuables were deposited, it should be the last hour of his existence.

Despreau, on seeing us, seemed inclined to make a most desperate resistance, but not being seconded by his associates, submitted to be pinioned, expressing his regret that we had not come half an hour later, when we might have been saved the trouble.

Despreau was shortly after tried for the offense, which was too clearly proved to admit of any doubt. He was sentenced to the galleys for life, and is now at Brest, undergoing his sentence. Emma, soon afterward, married a respectable man, and old Monette behaved on the occasion much more liberally than was expected.

SOLANGE
BY ALEXANDRE DUMAS

SOLANGE

Dr. Ledru's Story of the Reign of Terror

By ALEXANDRE DUMAS

LEAVING l'Abbaye, I walked straight across the Place Turenne to the Rue Tournon, where I had lodgings, when I heard a woman scream for help.

It could not be an assault to commit robbery, for it was hardly ten o'clock in the evening. I ran to the corner of the place whence the sounds proceeded, and by the light of the moon, just then breaking through the clouds, I beheld a woman in the midst of a patrol of sans-culottes.

The lady observed me at the same instant, and seeing, by the character of my dress, that I did not belong to the common order of people, she ran toward me, exclaiming:

"There is M. Albert! He knows me! He will tell you that I am the daughter of Mme. Ledieu, the laundress."

With these words the poor creature, pale and trembling with excitement, seized my arm and clung to me as a shipwrecked sailor to a spar.

"No matter whether you are the daughter of Mme. Ledieu or some one else, as you have no pass, you must go with us to the guard-house."

The young girl pressed my arm. I perceived in this pressure the expression of her great distress of mind. I understood it.

"So it is you, my poor Solange?" I said. "What are you doing here?"

"There, messieurs!" she exclaimed in tones of deep anxiety; "do you believe me now?"

"You might at least say 'citizens!'"

"Ah, sergeant, do not blame me for speaking that way," said the pretty young girl; "my mother has many customers among the great people, and taught me to be polite. That's

Copyrighted 1909 The Frank A. Munsey Company.

how I acquired this bad habit—the habit of the aristocrats; and, you know, sergeant, it's so hard to shake off old habits!"

This answer, delivered in trembling accents, concealed a delicate irony that was lost on all save me. I asked myself, who is this young woman? The mystery seemed complete. This alone was clear: she was not the daughter of a laundress.

"How did I come here, Citizen Albert?" she asked. "Well, I will tell you. I went to deliver some washing. The lady was not at home, and so I waited; for in these hard times every one needs what little money is coming to him. In that way it grew dark, and so I fell among these gentlemen —beg pardon, I would say citizens. They asked for my pass. As I did not have it with me, they were going to take me to the guard-house. I cried out in terror, which brought you to the scene; and as luck would have it, you are a friend. I said to myself, as M. Albert knows my name to be Solange Ledieu, he will vouch for me; and that you will, will you not, M. Albert?"

"Certainly, I will vouch for you."

"Very well," said the leader of the patrol; "and who, pray, will vouch for you, my friend?"

"Danton! Do you know him? Is he a good patriot?"

"Oh, if Danton will vouch for you, I have nothing to say."

"Well, there is a session of the Cordeliers to-day. Let us go there."

"Good," said the leader. "Citizens, let us go to the Cordeliers."

The club of the Cordeliers met at the old Cordelier monastery in the Rue l'Observance. We arrived there after scarce a minute's walk. At the door I tore a page from my note-book, wrote a few words upon it with a lead pencil, gave it to the sergeant, and requested him to hand it to Danton, while I waited outside with the men.

The sergeant entered the clubhouse and returned with Danton.

"What!" said he to me; "they have arrested you, my friend? You, the friend of Camilles—you, one of the most

SOLANGE

loyal republicans? Citizens," he continued, addressing the sergeant, "I vouch for him. Is that sufficient?"

"You vouch for him. Do you also vouch for her?" asked the stubborn sergeant.

"For her? To whom do you refer?"

"This girl."

"For everything; for everybody who may be in his company. Does that satisfy you?"

"Yes," said the man; "especially since I have had the privilege of seeing you."

With a cheer for Danton, the patrol marched away. I was about to thank Danton, when his name was called repeatedly within.

"Pardon me, my friend," he said; "you hear? There is my hand; I must leave you—the left. I gave my right to the sergeant. Who knows, the good patriot may have scrofula?"

"I'm coming!" he exclaimed, addressing those within in his mighty voice with which he could pacify or arouse the masses. He hastened into the house.

I remained standing at the door, alone with my unknown.

"And now, my lady," I said, "whither would you have me escort you? I am at your disposal."

"Why, to Mme. Ledieu," she said with a laugh. "I told you she was my mother."

"And where does Mme. Ledieu reside?"

"Rue Ferou, 24."

"Then, let us proceed to Rue Ferou, 24."

On the way neither of us spoke a word. But by the light of the moon, enthroned in serene glory in the sky, I was able to observe her at my leisure. She was a charming girl of twenty or twenty-two—brunette, with large blue eyes, more expressive of intelligence than melancholy—a finely chiseled nose, mocking lips, teeth of pearl, hands like a queen's, and feet like a child's; and all these, in spite of her costume of a laundress, betokened an aristocratic air that had aroused the sergeant's suspicions not without justice.

Arrived at the door of the house, we looked at each other a moment in silence.

"Well, my dear M. Albert, what do you wish?" my fair unknown asked with a smile.

"I was about to say, my dear Mlle. Solange, that it was hardly worth while to meet if we are to part so soon."

"Oh, I beg ten thousand pardons! I find it was well worth the while; for if I had not met you, I should have been dragged to the guard-house, and there it would have been discovered that I am not the daughter of Mme. Ledieu—in fact, it would have developed that I am an aristocrat, and in all likelihood they would have cut off my head."

"You admit, then, that you are an aristocrat?"

"I admit nothing."

"At least you might tell me your name."

"Solange."

"I know very well that this name, which I gave you on the inspiration of the moment, is not your right name."

"No matter; I like it, and I am going to keep it—at least for you."

"Why should you keep it for me, if we are not to meet again?"

"I did not say that. I only said that if we should meet again it will not be necessary for you to know my name any more than that I should know yours. To me you will be known as Albert, and to you I shall always be Solange."

"So be it, then; but I say, Solange," I began.

"I am listening, Albert," she replied.

"You are an aristocrat—that you admit."

"If I did not admit it, you would surmise it, and so my admission would be divested of half its merit."

"And you were pursued because you were suspected of being an aristocrat?"

"I fear so."

"And you are hiding to escape persecution?"

"In the Rue Ferou, No. 24, with Mme. Ledieu, whose husband was my father's coachman. You see, I have no secret from you."

"And your father?"

"I shall make no concealment, my dear Albert, of anything that relates to me. But my father's secrets are not my

SOLANGE

own. My father is in hiding, hoping to make his escape. That is all I can tell you."

"And what are you going to do?"

"Go with my father, if that be possible. If not, allow him to depart without me until the opportunity offers itself to me to join him."

"Were you coming from your father when the guard arrested you to-night?"

"Yes."

"Listen, dearest Solange."

"I am all attention."

"You observed all that took place to-night?"

"Yes. I saw that you had powerful influence."

"I regret my power is not very great. However, I have friends."

"I made the acquaintance of one of them."

"And you know he is not one of the least powerful men of the times."

"Do you intend to enlist his influence to enable my father to escape?"

"No, I reserve him for you."

"But my father?"

"I have other ways of helping your father."

"Other ways?" exclaimed Solange, seizing my hands and studying me with an anxious expression.

"If I serve your father, will you then sometimes think kindly of me?"

"Oh, I shall all my life hold you in grateful remembrance!"

She uttered these words with an enchanting expression of devotion. Then she looked at me beseechingly and said:

"But will that satisfy you?"

"Yes," I said.

"Ah, I was not mistaken. You are kind, generous. I thank you for my father and myself. Even if you should fail, I shall be grateful for what you have already done!"

"When shall we meet again, Solange?"

"When do you think it necessary to see me again?"

"To-morrow, when I hope to have good news for you."

"Well, then, to-morrow."

"Where?"

"Here."

"Here in the street?"

"Well, mon Dieu!" she exclaimed. "You see, it is the safest place. For thirty minutes, while we have been talking here, not a soul has passed."

"Why may I not go to you, or you come to me?"

"Because it would compromise the good people if you should come to me, and you would incur serious risk if I should go to you."

"Oh, I would give you the pass of one of my relatives."

"And send your relative to the guillotine if I should be accidentally arrested!"

"True. I will bring you a pass made out in the name of Solange."

"Charming! You observe Solange is my real name."

"And the hour?"

"The same at which we met to-night—ten o'clock, if you please."

"All right; ten o'clock. And how shall we meet?"

"That is very simple. Be at the door at five minutes of ten, and at ten I will come down."

"Then, at ten to-morrow, dear Solange."

"To-morrow at ten, dear Albert."

I wanted to kiss her hand; she offered me her brow.

The next day I was in the street at half past nine. At a quarter of ten Solange opened the door. We were both ahead of time.

With one leap I was by her side.

"I see you have good news," she said.

"Excellent! First, here is a pass for you."

"First my father!"

She repelled my hand.

"Your father is saved, if he wishes."

"Wishes, you say? What is required of him?"

"He must trust me."

"That is assured."

"Have you seen him?"

"Yes."

"You have discussed the situation with him?"

"It was unavoidable. Heaven will help us."

"Did you tell your father all?"

"I told him you had saved my life yesterday, and that you would perhaps save his to-morrow."

"To-morrow! Yes, quite right; to-morrow I shall save his life, if it is his will."

"How? What? Speak! Speak! If that were possible, how fortunately all things have come to pass!"

"However—" I began hesitatingly.

"Well?"

"It will be impossible for you to accompany him."

"I told you I was resolute."

"I am quite confident, however, that I shall be able later to procure a passport for you."

"First tell me about my father; my own distress is less important."

"Well, I told you I had friends, did I not?"

"Yes."

"To-day I sought out one of them."

"Proceed."

"A man whose name is familiar to you; whose name is a guarantee of courage and honor."

"And this man is?"

"Marceau."

"General Marceau?"

"Yes."

"True, he will keep a promise."

"Well, he has promised."

"Mon Dieu! How happy you make me! What has he promised? Tell me all."

"He has promised to help us."

"In what manner?"

"In a very simple manner. Kléber has just had him promoted to the command of the western army. He departs to-morrow night."

"To-morrow night! We shall have no time to make the smallest preparation."

"There are no preparations to make."

"I do not understand."

"He will take your father with him."

"My father?"

"Yes, as his secretary. Arrived in the Vendée, your father will pledge his word to the general to undertake nothing against France. From there he will escape to Brittany, and from Brittany to England. When he arrives in London, he will inform you; I shall obtain a passport for you, and you will join him in London."

"To-morrow," exclaimed Solange; "my father departs to-morrow!"

"There is no time to waste."

"My father has not been informed."

"Inform him."

"To-night?"

"To-night."

"But how, at this hour?"

"You have a pass and my arm."

"True. My pass."

I gave it to her. She thrust it into her bosom.

"Now, your arm."

I gave her my arm, and we walked away. When we arrived at the Place Turenne—that is, the spot where we had met the night before—she said: "Await me here."

I bowed and waited.

She disappeared around the corner of what was formerly the Hôtel Malignon. After a lapse of fifteen minutes she returned.

"Come," she said, "my father wishes to receive and thank you."

She took my arm and led me up to the Rue St. Guillaume, opposite the Hôtel Mortemart. Arrived here, she took a bunch of keys from her pocket, opened a small, concealed door, took me by the hand, conducted me up two flights of steps, and knocked in a peculiar manner.

A man of forty-eight or fifty years opened the door. He was dressed as a working man and appeared to be a bookbinder. But at the first utterance that burst from his lips, the evidence of the seigneur was unmistakable.

"Monsieur," he said, "Providence has sent you to us. I regard you an emissary of fate. Is it true that you can save me, or, what is more, that you wish to save me?"

SOLANGE

I admitted him completely to my confidence. I informed him that Marceau would take him as his secretary, and would exact no promise other than that he would not take up arms against France.

"I cheerfully promise it now, and will repeat it to him."

"I thank you in his name as well as in my own."

"But when does Marceau depart?"

"To-morrow."

"Shall I go to him to-night?"

"Whenever you please; he expects you."

Father and daughter looked at each other.

"I think it would be wise to go this very night," said Solange.

"I am ready; but if I should be arrested, seeing that I have no permit?"

"Here is mine."

"But you?"

"Oh, I am known."

"Where does Marceau reside?"

"Rue de l'Université, 40, with his sister, Mlle. Dégraviers-Marceau."

"Will you accompany me?"

"I shall follow you at a distance, to accompany mademoiselle home when you are gone."

"How will Marceau know that I am the man of whom you spoke to him?"

"You will hand him this tri-colored cockade; that is the sign of identification."

"And how shall I reward my liberator?"

"By allowing him to save your daughter also."

"Very well."

He put on his hat and extinguished the lights, and we descended by the gleam of the moon which penetrated the stair-windows.

At the foot of the steps he took his daughter's arm, and by way of the Rue des Saints Pères we reached Rue de l'Université. I followed them at a distance of ten paces. We arrived at No. 40 without having met any one. I rejoined them there.

"That is a good omen," I said; "do you wish me to go up with you?"

"No. Do not compromise yourself any further. Await my daughter here."

I bowed.

"And now, once more, thanks and farewell," he said, giving me his hand. "Language has no words to express my gratitude. I pray that heaven may some day grant me the opportunity of giving fuller expression to my feelings."

I answered him with a pressure of the hand.

He entered the house. Solange followed him; but she, too, pressed my hand before she entered.

In ten minutes the door was reopened.

"Well?" I asked.

"Your friend," she said, "is worthy of his name; he is as kind and considerate as yourself. He knows that it will contribute to my happiness to remain with my father until the moment of departure. His sister has ordered a bed placed in her room. To-morrow at three o'clock my father will be out of danger. To-morrow evening at ten I shall expect you in the Rue Ferou, if the gratitude of a daughter who owes her father's life to you is worth the trouble."

"Oh, be sure I shall come. Did your father charge you with any message for me?"

"He thanks you for your pass, which he returns to you, and begs you to join him as soon as possible."

"Whenever it may be your desire to go," I said, with a strange sensation at my heart.

"At least, I must know where I am to join him," she said. "Ah, you are not yet rid of me!"

I seized her hand and pressed it against my heart, but she offered me her brow, as on the previous evening, and said: "Until to-morrow."

I kissed her on the brow; but now I no longer strained her hand against my breast, but her heaving bosom, her throbbing heart.

I went home in a state of delirious ecstasy such as I had never experienced. Was it the consciousness of a generous action, or was it love for this adorable creature? I know not whether I slept or woke. I only know that all the

SOLANGE

harmonies of nature were singing within me; that the night seemed endless, and the day eternal; I know that though I wished to speed the time, I did not wish to lose a moment of the days still to come.

The next day I was in the Rue Ferou at nine o'clock. At half-past nine Solange made her appearance.

She approached me and threw her arms around my neck.

"Saved!" she said; "my father is saved! And this I owe you. Oh, how I love you!"

Two weeks later Solange received a letter announcing her father's safe arrival in England.

The next day I brought her a passport.

When Solange received it she burst into tears.

"You do not love me!" she exclaimed.

"I love you better than my life," I replied; "but I pledged your father my word, and I must keep it."

"Then, I will break mine," she said. "Yes, Albert; if you have the heart to let me go, I have not the courage to leave you."

Alas, she remained!

Three months had passed since that night on which we talked of her escape, and in all that time not a word of parting had passed her lips.

Solange had taken lodgings in the Rue Turenne. I had rented them in her name. I knew no other, while she always addressed me as Albert. I had found her a place as teacher in a young ladies' seminary solely to withdraw her from the espionage of the revolutionary police, which had become more scrutinizing than ever.

Sundays we passed together in the small dwelling, from the bedroom of which we could see the spot where we had first met. We exchanged letters daily, she writing to me under the name of Solange, and I to her under that of Albert.

Those three months were the happiest of my life.

In the meantime I was making some interesting experiments suggested by one of the guillotiniers. I had obtained permission to make certain scientific tests with the bodies and heads of those who perished on the scaffold. Sad to say, available subjects were not wanting. Not a day passed but thirty or forty persons were guillotined, and blood flowed so copiously on the Place de la Révolution that it became necessary to dig a trench three feet deep around the scaffolding. This trench was covered with deals. One of them loosened under the feet of an eight-year-old lad, who fell into the abominable pit and was drowned.

For self-evident reasons I said nothing to Solange of the studies that occupied my attention during the day. In the beginning my occupation had inspired me with pity and loathing, but as time wore on I said: "These studies are for the good of humanity," for I hoped to convince the lawmakers of the wisdom of abolishing capital punishment.

The Cemetery of Clamart had been assigned to me, and all the heads and trunks of the victims of the executioner had been placed at my disposal. A small chapel in one corner of the cemetery had been converted into a kind of laboratory for my benefit. You know, when the queens were driven from the palaces, God was banished from the churches.

Every day at six the horrible procession filed in. The bodies were heaped together in a wagon, the heads in a sack. I chose some bodies and heads in a haphazard fashion, while the remainder were thrown into a common grave.

In the midst of this occupation with the dead, my love for Solange increased from day to day; while the poor child reciprocated my affection with the whole power of her pure soul.

Often I had thought of making her my wife; often we had mutually pictured to ourselves the happiness of such a union. But in order to become my wife, it would be necessary for Solange to reveal her name; and this name, which was that of an emigrant, an aristocrat, meant death.

Her father had repeatedly urged her by letter to hasten her departure, but she had informed him of our engagement. She had requested his consent, and he had given it, so that all had gone well to this extent.

The trial and execution of the queen, Marie Antoinette, had plunged me, too, into deepest sadness. Solange was all tears, and we could not rid ourselves of a strange feeling of despondency, a presentiment of approaching danger, that compressed our hearts. In vain I tried to whisper courage

SOLANGE

to Solange. Weeping, she reclined in my arms, and I could not comfort her, because my own words lacked the ring of confidence.

We passed the night together as usual, but the night was even more depressing than the day. I recall now that a dog, locked up in a room below us, howled till two o'clock in the morning. The next day we were told that the dog's master had gone away with the key in his pocket, had been arrested on the way, tried at three, and executed at four.

The time had come for us to part. Solange's duties at the school began at nine o'clock in the morning. Her school was in the vicinity of the Botanic Gardens. I hesitated long to let her go; she, too, was loath to part from me. But it must be. Solange was prone to be an object of unpleasant inquiries.

I called a conveyance and accompanied her as far as the Rue des Fosses-Saint-Bernard, where I got out and left her to pursue her way alone. All the way we lay mutely wrapped in each other's arms, mingling tears with our kisses.

After leaving the carriage, I stood as if rooted to the ground. I heard Solange call me, but I dared not go to her, because her face, moist with tears, and her hysterical manner were calculated to attract attention.

Utterly wretched, I returned home, passing the entire day in writing to Solange. In the evening I sent her an entire volume of love-pledges.

My letter had hardly gone to the post when I received one from her.

She had been sharply reprimanded for coming late; had been subjected to a severe cross-examination, and threatened with forfeiture of her next holiday. But she vowed to join me even at the cost of her place. I thought I should go mad at the prospect of being parted from her a whole week. I was more depressed because a letter which had arrived from her father appeared to have been tampered with.

I passed a wretched night and a still more miserable day.

The next day the weather was appalling. Nature seemed to be dissolving in a cold, ceaseless rain—a rain like that which announces the approach of winter. All the way to the laboratory my ears were tortured with the criers announcing the names of the condemned, a large number of men, women, and children. The bloody harvest was over-rich. I should not lack subjects for my investigations that day.

The day ended early. At four o'clock I arrived at Clamart; it was almost night.

The view of the cemetery, with its large, new-made graves; the sparse, leafless trees that swayed in the wind, was desolate, almost appalling.

A large, open pit yawned before me. It was to receive to-day's harvest from the Place de la Révolution. An exceedingly large number of victims was expected, for the pit was deeper than usual.

Mechanically I approached the grave. At the bottom the water had gathered in a pool; my feet slipped; I came within an inch of falling in. My hair stood on end. The rain had drenched me to the skin. I shuddered and hastened into the laboratory.

It was, as I have said, an abandoned chapel. My eyes searched—I know not why—to discover if some traces of the holy purpose to which the edifice had once been devoted did not still adhere to the walls or to the altar; but the walls were bare, the altar empty.

I struck a light and deposited the candle on the operating-table on which lay scattered a miscellaneous assortment of the strange instruments I employed. I sat down and fell into a reverie. I thought of the poor queen, whom I had seen in her beauty, glory, and happiness, yesterday carted to the scaffold, pursued by the execrations of a people, to-day lying headless on the common sinners' bier—she who had slept beneath the gilded canopy of the throne of the Tuileries and St. Cloud.

As I sat thus, absorbed in gloomy meditation, wind and rain without redoubled in fury. The rain-drops dashed against the window-panes, the storm swept with melancholy moaning through the branches of the trees. Anon there mingled with the violence of the elements the sound of wheels.

It was the executioner's red hearse with its ghastly freight from the Place de la Révolution.

SOLANGE

The door of the little chapel was pushed ajar, and two men, drenched with rain, entered, carrying a sack between them.

"There, M. Ledru," said the guillotinier; "there is what your heart longs for! Be in no hurry this night! We'll leave you to enjoy their society alone. Orders are not to cover them up till to-morrow, and so they'll not take cold."

With a horrible laugh, the two executioners deposited the sack in a corner, near the former altar, right in front of me. Thereupon they sauntered out, leaving open the door, which swung furiously on its hinges till my candle flashed and flared in the fierce draft.

I heard them unharness the horse, lock the cemetery, and go away.

I was strangely impelled to go with them, but an indefinable power fettered me in my place. I could not repress a shudder. I had no fear; but the violence of the storm, the splashing of the rain, the whistling sounds of the lashing branches, the shrill vibration of the atmosphere, which made my candle tremble—all this filled me with a vague terror that began at the roots of my hair and communicated itself to every part of my body.

Suddenly I fancied I heard a voice! A voice at once soft and plaintive; a voice within the chapel, pronouncing the name of "Albert!"

I was startled.

"Albert!"

But one person in all the world addressed me by that name!

Slowly I directed my weeping eyes around the chapel, which, though small, was not completely lighted by the feeble rays of the candle, leaving the nooks and angles in darkness, and my look remained fixed on the blood-soaked sack near the altar with its hideous contents.

At this moment the same voice repeated the same name, only it sounded fainter and more plaintive.

"Albert!"

I bolted out of my chair, frozen with horror.

The voice seemed to proceed from the sack!

I touched myself to make sure that I was awake; then I

SOLANGE

walked toward the sack with my arms extended before me, but stark and staring with horror. I thrust my hand into it. Then it seemed to me as if two lips, still warm, pressed a kiss upon my fingers!

I had reached that stage of boundless terror where the excess of fear turns into the audacity of despair. I seized the head and, collapsing in my chair, placed it in front of me.

Then I gave vent to a fearful scream. This head, with its lips still warm, with eyes half closed, was the head of Solange!

I thought I should go mad.

Three times I called:

"Solange! Solange! Solange!"

At the third time she opened her eyes and looked at me. Tears trickled down her cheeks; then a moist glow darted from her eyes, as if the soul were passing, and the eyes closed, never to open again.

I sprang to my feet a raving maniac. I wanted to fly; I knocked against the table; it fell. The candle was extinguished; the head rolled upon the floor, and I fell prostrate, as if a terrible fever had stricken me down—an icy shudder convulsed me, and, with a deep sigh, I swooned.

The following morning at six the grave-diggers found me, cold as the flagstones on which I lay.

Solange, betrayed by her father's letter, had been arrested the same day, condemned, and executed.

The head that had called me, the eyes that had looked at me, were the head, the eyes, of Solange!

THE BIRDS IN THE LETTER-BOX
BY RENE BAZIN

THE BIRDS IN THE LETTER-BOX

By RENE BAZIN

NOTHING can describe the peace that surrounded the country parsonage. The parish was small, moderately honest, prosperous, and was used to the old priest, who had ruled it for thirty years. The town ended at the parsonage, and there began meadows which sloped down to the river and were filled in summer with the perfume of flowers and all the music of the earth. Behind the great house a kitchen-garden encroached on the meadow. The first ray of the sun was for it, and so was the last. Here the cherries ripened in May, and the currants often earlier, and a week before assumption, usually, you could not pass within a hundred feet without breathing among the hedges the heavy odor of the melons.

But you must not think that the abbé of St. Philémon was a gourmand. He had reached the age when appetite is only a memory. His shoulders were bent, his face was wrinkled, he had two little gray eyes, one of which could not see any longer, and he was so deaf in one ear that if you happened to be on that side you just had to get round on the other.

Mercy, no! he did not eat all the fruits in his orchard. The boys got their share—and a big share—but the biggest share, by all odds, was eaten by the birds—the blackbirds, who lived there comfortably all the year, and sang in return the best they could; the orioles, pretty birds of passage, who helped them in summer, and the sparrows, and the warblers of every variety; and the tomtits, swarms of them, with feathers as thick as your finger, and they hung on the branches and pecked at a grape or scratched a pear—veritable little beasts of prey, whose only "thank you" was a shrill cry like a saw.

Even to them, old age had made the abbé of St. Philémon indulgent. "The beasts cannot correct their faults," he used

THE BIRDS IN THE LETTER-BOX

to say; "if I got angry at them for not changing I'd have to get angry with a good many of my parishioners!"

And he contented himself with clapping his hands together loud when he went into his orchard, so he should not see too much stealing.

Then there was a spreading of wings, as if all the silly flowers cut off by a great wind were flying away; gray, and white, and yellow, and mottled, a short flight, a rustling of leaves, and then quiet for five minutes. But what minutes! Fancy, if you can, that there was not one factory in the village, not a weaver or a blacksmith, and that the noise of men with their horses and cattle, spreading over the wide, distant plains, melted into the whispering of the breeze and was lost. Mills were unknown, the roads were little frequented, the railroads were very far away. Indeed, if the ravagers of his garden had repented for long the abbé would have fallen asleep of the silence over his breviary.

Fortunately, their return was prompt; a sparrow led the way, a jay followed, and then the whole swarm was back at work. And the abbé could walk up and down, close his book or open it, and murmur: "They'll not leave me a berry this year!"

It made no difference; not a bird left his prey, any more than if the good abbé had been a cone-shaped pear-tree, with thick leaves, balancing himself on the gravel of the walk.

The birds know that those who complain take no action. Every year they built their nests around the parsonage of St. Philémon in greater numbers than anywhere else. The best places were quickly taken, the hollows in the trees, the holes in the walls, the forks of the apple-trees and the elms, and you could see a brown beak, like the point of a sword, sticking out of a whisp of straw between all the rafters of the roof. One year, when all the places were taken, I suppose, a tomtit, in her embarrassment, spied the slit of the letter-box protected by its little roof, at the right of the parsonage gate. She slipped in, was satisfied with the result of her explorations, and brought the materials to build a nest. There was nothing she neglected that would make it warm, neither the feathers, nor the horsehair, nor the wool, nor even the scales of lichens that cover old wood.

One morning the housekeeper came in perfectly furious, carrying a paper. She had found it under the laurel bush, at the foot of the garden.

"Look, sir, a paper, and dirty, too! They are up to fine doings!"

"Who, Philomène?"

"Your miserable birds; all the birds that you let stay here! Pretty soon they'll be building their nests in your soup-tureens!"

"I haven't but one."

"Haven't they got the idea of laying their eggs in your letter-box! I opened it because the postman rang and that doesn't happen every day. It was full of straw and horsehair and spiders' webs, with enough feathers to make a quilt, and, in the midst of all that, a beast that I didn't see hissed at me like a viper!"

The abbé of St. Philémon began to laugh like a grandfather when he hears of a baby's pranks.

"That must be a tomtit," said he, "they are the only birds clever enough to think of it. Be careful not to touch it, Philomène."

"No fear of that; it is not nice enough!"

The abbé went hastily through the garden, the house, the court planted with asparagus, till he came to the wall which separated the parsonage from the public road, and there he carefully opened the letter-box, in which there would have been room enough for all the mail received in a year by all the inhabitants of the village.

Sure enough, he was not mistaken. The shape of the nest, like a pine-cone, its color and texture, and the lining, which showed through, made him smile. He heard the hiss of the brooding bird inside and replied:

"Rest easy, little one, I know you. Twenty-one days to hatch your eggs and three weeks to raise your family; that is what you want? You shall have it. I'll take away the key."

He did take away the key, and when he had finished the morning's duties—visits to his parishioners who were ill or in trouble; instructions to a boy who was to pick him out some fruit at the village; a climb up the steeple because a storm had loosened some stones, he remembered the tomtit and began to be afraid she would be troubled by the arrival of a letter while she was hatching her eggs.

The fear was almost groundless, because the people of St. Philémon did not receive any more letters than they sent. The postman had little to do on his rounds but to eat soup at one house, to have a drink at another and, once in a long while, to leave a letter from some conscript, or a bill for taxes at some distant farm. Nevertheless, since St. Robert's Day was near, which, as you know, comes on the 29th of April, the abbé thought it wise to write to the only three friends worthy of that name, whom death had left him, a layman and two priests: "My friend, do not congratulate me on my saint's day this year, if you please. It would inconvenience me to receive a letter at this time. Later I shall explain, and you will appreciate my reasons."

They thought that his eye was worse and did not write.

The abbé of St. Philémon was delighted. For three weeks he never entered his gate one time without thinking of the eggs, speckled with pink, that were lying in the letter-box, and when the twenty-first day came round he bent down and listened with his ear close to the slit of the box. Then he stood up beaming:

"I hear them chirp, Philomène; I hear them chirp. They owe their lives to me, sure enough, and they'll not be the ones to regret it any more than I."

He had in his bosom the heart of a child that had never grown old.

Now, at the same time, in the green room of the palace, at the chief town of the department, the bishop was deliberating over the appointments to be made with his regular councilors, his two grand vicars, the dean of the chapter, the secretary-general of the palace, and the director of the great academy. After he had appointed several vicars and priests he made this suggestion:

"Gentlemen of the council, I have in mind a candidate suitable in all respects for the parish of X——; but I think it would be well, at least, to offer that charge and that honor to one of our oldest priests, the abbé of St. Philémon. He will undoubtedly refuse it, and his modesty, no less than his

THE BIRDS IN THE LETTER-BOX

age, will be the cause; but we shall have shown, as far as we could, our appreciation of his virtues."

The five councilors approved unanimously, and that very evening a letter was sent from the palace, signed by the bishop, and which contained in a postscript: "Answer at once, my dear abbé; or, better, come to see me, because I must submit my appointments to the government within three days."

The letter arrived at St. Philémon the very day the tomtits were hatched. The postman had difficulty in slipping it into the slit of the box, but it disappeared inside and lay, touching the base of the nest, like a white pavement at the bottom of the dark chamber.

The time came when the tiny points on the wings of the little tomtits began to be covered with down. There were fourteen of them, and they twittered and staggered on their little feet, with their beaks open up to their eyes, never ceasing, from morning till night, to wait for food, eat it, digest it, and demand more. That was the first period, when the baby birds hadn't any sense. But in birds it doesn't last long. Very soon they quarrelled in the nest, which began to break with the fluttering of their wings, then they tumbled out of it and walked along the side of the box, peeped through the slit at the big world outside, and at last they ventured out.

The abbé of St. Philémon, with a neighboring priest, attended this pleasant garden party. When the little ones appeared beneath the roof of the box—two, three—together and took their flight, came back, started again, like bees at the door of a hive, he said:

"Behold, a badyhood ended and a good work accomplished. They are hardy and strong, every one."

The next day, during his hour of leisure after dinner, the abbé came to the box with the key in his hand. "Tap, tap," he went. There was no answer. "I thought so," said he. Then he opened the box and, mingled with the débris of the nest, the letter fell into his hands.

"Good Heavens!" said he, recognizing the writing. "A letter from the bishop; and in what a state! How long has it been here?"

THE BIRDS IN THE LETTER-BOX

His cheek grew pale as he read.

"Philomène, harness Robin quickly."

She came to see what was the matter before obeying.

"What have you there, sir?"

"The bishop has been waiting for me three weeks!"

"You've missed your chance," said the old woman.

The abbé was away until the next evening. When he came back he had a peaceful air, but sometimes peace is not attained without effort and we have to struggle to keep it. When he had helped to unharness Robin and had given him some hay, had changed his cassock and unpacked his box, from which he took a dozen little packages of things bought on his visit to the city, it was the very time that the birds assembled in the branches to tell each other about the day. There had been a shower and the drops still fell from the leaves as they were shaken by these bohemian couples looking for a good place to spend the night.

Recognizing their friend and master as he walked up and down the gravel path, they came down, fluttered about him, making an unusually loud noise, and the tomtits, the fourteen of the nest, whose feathers were still not quite grown, essayed their first spirals about the pear-trees and their first cries in the open air.

The abbé of St. Philémon watched them with a fatherly eye, but his tenderness was sad, as we look at things that have cost us dear.

"Well, my little ones, without me you would not be here, and without you I would be dead. I do not regret it at all, but don't insist. Your thanks are too noisy."

He clapped his hands impatiently.

He had never been ambitious, that is very sure, and, even at that moment, he told the truth. Nevertheless, the next day, after a night spent in talking to Philomène, he said to her:

"Next year, Philomène, if the tomtit comes back, let me know. It is decidedly inconvenient."

But the tomtit never came again—and neither did the letter from the bishop!

JEAN GOURDON'S FOUR DAYS
BY EMILE ZOLA

JEAN GOURDON'S FOUR DAYS

By EMILE ZOLA

Spring

ON that particular day, at about five o'clock in the morning, the sun entered with delightful abruptness into the little room I occupied at the house of my uncle Lazare, parish priest of the hamlet of Dourgues. A broad yellow ray fell upon my closed eyelids, and I awoke in light.

My room, which was whitewashed, and had deal furniture, was full of attractive gaiety. I went to the window and gazed at the Durance, which traced its broad course amidst the dark green verdure of the valley. Fresh puffs of wind caressed my face, and the murmur of the trees and river seemed to call me to them.

I gently opened my door. To get out I had to pass through my uncle's room. I proceeded on tip-toe, fearing the creaking of my thick boots might awaken the worthy man, who was still slumbering with a smiling countenance. And I trembled at the sound of the church bell tolling the Angelus. For some days past my uncle Lazare had been following me about everywhere, looking sad and annoyed. He would perhaps have prevented me going over there to the edge of the river, and hiding myself among the willows on the bank, so as to watch for Babet passing, that tall dark girl who had come with the spring.

But my uncle was sleeping soundly. I felt something like remorse in deceiving him and running away in this manner. I stayed for an instant and gazed on his calm countenance, with its gentle expression enhanced by rest, and I recalled to mind with feeling the day when he had come to fetch me in the chilly and deserted home which my mother's funeral was leaving. Since that day, what tenderness, what devotedness, what good advice he had bestowed on me! He had given me his knowledge and his kindness, all his intelligence and all his heart.

I was tempted for a moment to cry out to him:

"Get up, uncle Lazare! let us go for a walk together along that path you are so fond of beside the Durance. You will enjoy the fresh air and morning sun. You will see what an appetite you will have on your return!"

And Babet, who was going down to the river in her light morning gown, and whom I should not be able to see! My uncle would be there, and I would have to lower my eyes. It must be so nice under the willows, lying flat on one's stomach, in the fine grass! I felt a languid feeling creeping over me, and, slowly, taking short steps, holding my breath, I reached the door. I went downstairs, and began running like a madcap in the delightful, warm May morning air.

The sky was quite white on the horizon, with exquisitely delicate blue and pink tints. The pale sun seemed like a great silver lamp, casting a shower of bright rays into the Durance. And the broad, sluggish river, expanding lazily over the red sand, extended from one end of the valley to the other, like a stream of liquid metal. To the west, a line of low rugged hills threw slight violet streaks on the pale sky.

I had been living in this out-of-the-way corner for ten years. How often had I kept my uncle Lazare waiting to give me my Latin lesson! The worthy man wanted to make me learned. But I was on the other side of the Durance, ferreting out magpies, discovering a hill which I had not yet climbed. Then, on my return, there were remonstrances: the Latin was forgotten, my poor uncle scolded me for having torn my trousers, and he shuddered when he noticed sometimes that the skin underneath was cut. The valley was mine, really mine; I had conquered it with my legs, and I was the real landlord by right of friendship. And that bit of river, those two leagues of the Durance, how I loved them, how well we understood one another when together! I knew all the whims of my dear stream, its anger, its charming ways, its different features at each hour of the day.

When I reached the water's edge on that particular morning, I felt something like giddiness at seeing it so gentle and

JEAN GOURDON'S FOUR DAYS

so white. It had never looked so gay. I slipped rapidly beneath the willows, to an open space where a broad patch of sunlight fell on the dark grass. There I laid me down on my stomach, listening, watching the pathway by which Babet would come, through the branches.

"Oh! how sound uncle Lazare must be sleeping!" I thought.

And I extended myself at full length on the moss. The sun struck gentle heat into my back, whilst my breast, buried in the grass, was quite cool.

Have you never examined the turf, at close quarters, with your eyes on the blades of grass? Whilst I was waiting for Babet, I pried indiscreetly into a tuft which was really a whole world. In my bunch of grass there were streets, cross roads, public squares, entire cities. At the bottom of it, I distinguished a great dark patch where the shoots of the previous spring were decaying sadly, then slender stalks were growing up, stretching out, bending into a multitude of elegant forms, and producing frail colonnades, churches, virgin forests. I saw two lean insects wandering in the midst of this immensity; the poor children were certainly lost, for they went from colonnade to colonnade, from street to street, in an affrighted, anxious way.

It was just at this moment that, on raising my eyes, I saw Babet's white skirts standing out against the dark ground at the top of the pathway. I recognised her printed calico gown, which was grey, with small blue flowers. I sunk down deeper in the grass, I heard my heart thumping against the earth and almost raising me with slight jerks. My breast was burning now, I no longer felt the freshness of the dew.

The young girl came nimbly down the pathway, her skirts skimming the ground with a swinging motion that charmed me. I saw her at full length, quite erect, in her proud and happy gracefulness. She had no idea I was there behind the willows; she walked with a light step, she ran without giving a thought to the wind, which slightly raised her gown. I could distinguish her feet, trotting along quickly, quickly, and a piece of her white stockings, which was perhaps as large as one's hand, and which made me blush in a manner that was alike sweet and painful.

Oh! then, I saw nothing else, neither the Durance, nor the willows, nor the whiteness of the sky. What cared I for the valley! It was no longer my sweetheart; I was quite indifferent to its joy and its sadness. What cared I for my friends, the stones, and the trees on the hills! The river could run away all at once if it liked; I would not have regretted it.

And the spring, I did not care a bit about the spring! Had it borne away the sun that warmed my back, its leaves, its rays, all its May morning, I should have remained there, in ecstasy, gazing at Babet, running along the pathway, and swinging her skirts deliciously. For Babet had taken the valley's place in my heart, Babet was the spring. I had never spoken to her. Both of us blushed when we met one another in my uncle Lazare's church. I could have vowed she detested me.

She talked on that particular day for a few minutes with the women who were washing. The sound of her pearly laughter reached as far as me, mingled with the loud voice of the Durance. Then she stooped down to take a little water in the hollow of her hand; but the bank was high, and Babet, who was on the point of slipping, saved herself by clutching the grass. I gave a frightful shudder, which made my blood run cold. I rose hastily, and, without feeling ashamed, without reddening, ran to the young girl. She cast a startled look at me; then she began to smile. I bent down, at the risk of falling. I succeeded in filling my right hand with water by keeping my fingers close together. And I presented this new sort of cup to Babet, asking her to drink.

The women who were washing laughed. Babet, confused, did not dare accept; she hesitated, and half turned her head away. At last she made up her mind, and delicately pressed her lips to the tips of my fingers; but she had waited too long, all the water had run away. Then she burst out laughing, she became a child again, and I saw very well that she was making fun of me.

I was very silly. I bent forward again. This time I took the water in both hands and hastened to put them to Babet's lips. She drank, and I felt the warm kiss from her mouth run up my arms to my breast, which it filled with heat.

"Oh! how my uncle must sleep!" I murmured to myself.

Just as I said that, I perceived a dark shadow beside me, and, having turned round, I saw my uncle Lazare, in person, a few paces away, watching Babet and me as if offended. His cassock appeared quite white in the sun; in his look I saw reproaches which made me feel inclined to cry.

Babet was very much afraid. She turned quite red, and hurried off stammering:

"Thanks, Monsieur Jean, I thank you very much."

As for me, wiping my wet hands, I stood motionless and confused before my uncle Lazare.

The worthy man, with folded arms, and bringing back a corner of his cassock, watched Babet, who was running up the pathway without turning her head. Then, when she had disappeared behind the hedges, he lowered his eyes to me, and I saw his pleasant countenance smile sadly.

"Jean," he said to me, "come into the broad walk. Breakfast is not ready. We have half an hour to spare."

He set out with his rather heavy tread, avoiding the tufts of grass wet with dew. A part of the bottom of his cassock that was dragging along the ground, made a dull crackling sound. He held his breviary under his arm; but he had forgotten his morning lecture, and he advanced dreamily, with bowed head, and without uttering a word.

His silence tormented me. He was generally so talkative. My anxiety increased at each step. He had certainly seen me giving Babet water to drink. What a sight, O Lord! The young girl, laughing and blushing, kissed the tips of my fingers, whilst I, standing on tip-toe, stretching out my arms, was leaning forward as if to kiss her. My action now seemed to me frightfully audacious. And all my timidity returned. I inquired of myself how I could have dared to have my fingers kissed so sweetly.

And my uncle Lazare, who said nothing, who continued walking with short steps in front of me, without giving a single glance at the old trees he loved! He was assuredly preparing a sermon. He was only taking me into the broad walk to scold me at his ease. It would occupy at least an hour: breakfast would get cold, and I would be unable to return to the water's edge and dream of the warm burns that Babet's lips had left on my hands.

We were in the broad walk. This walk, which was wide and short, ran beside the river; it was shaded by enormous oak trees, with trunks lacerated by seams, stretching out their great, tall branches. The fine grass spread like a carpet beneath the trees, and the sun, riddling the foliage, embroidered this carpet with a rosaceous pattern in gold. In the distance, all around, extended raw green meadows.

My uncle went to the bottom of the walk, without altering his step and without turning round. Once there, he stopped, and I kept beside him, understanding that the terrible moment had arrived.

The river made a sharp curve; a low parapet at the end of the walk formed a sort of terrace. This vault of shade opened on a valley of light. The country expanded wide before us, for several leagues. The sun was rising in the heavens, where the silvery rays of morning had become transformed into a stream of gold; blinding floods of light ran from the horizon, along the hills, and spread out into the plain with the glare of fire.

After a moment's silence, my uncle Lazare turned towards me.

"Good heavens, the sermon!" I thought, and I bowed my head. My uncle pointed out the valley to me, with an expansive gesture; then, drawing himself up, he said, slowly:

"Look, Jean, there is the spring. The earth is full of joy, my boy, and I have brought you here, opposite this plain of light, to show you the first smiles of the young season. Observe what brilliancy and sweetness! Warm perfumes rise from the country and pass across our faces like puffs of life."

He was silent and seemed dreaming. I had raised my head, astonished, breathing at ease. My uncle was not preaching.

"It is a beautiful morning," he continued, "a morning of youth. Your eighteen summers find full enjoyment amidst this verdure which is at most eighteen days old. All is great brightness and perfume, is it not? The broad valley seems to you a delightful place: the river is there to give you its

JEAN GOURDON'S FOUR DAYS

freshness, the trees to lend you their shade, the whole country to speak to you of tenderness, the heavens themselves to kiss those horizons that you are searching with hope and desire. The spring belongs to fellows of your age. It is it that teaches the boys how to give young girls to drink——"

I hung my head again. My uncle Lazare had certainly seen me.

"An old fellow like me," he continued, "unfortunately knows what trust to place in the charms of spring. I, my poor Jean, I love the Durance because it waters these meadows and gives life to all the valley; I love this young foliage because it proclaims to me the coming of the fruits of summer and autumn; I love this sky because it is good to us, because its warmth hastens the fecundity of the earth. I should have had to tell you this one day or other; I prefer telling it you now, at this early hour. It is spring itself that is giving you the lesson. The earth is a vast workshop wherein there is never a slack season. Observe this flower at our feet; to you it is perfume; to me it is labour, it accomplishes its task by producing its share of life, a little black seed which will work in its turn, next spring. And, now, search the vast horizon. All this joy is but the act of generation. If the country be smiling, it is because it is beginning the everlasting task again. Do you hear it now, breathing hard, full of activity and haste? The leaves sigh, the flowers are in a hurry, the corn grows without pausing; all the plants, all the herbs are quarrelling as to which shall spring up the quickest; and the running water, the river comes to assist in the common labour, and the young sun which rises in the heavens is entrusted with the duty of enlivening the everlasting task of the labourers."

At this point my uncle made me look him straight in the face. He concluded in these terms:

"Jean, you hear what your friend the spring says to you. He is youth, but he is preparing ripe age; his bright smile is but the gaiety of labour. Summer will be powerful, autumn bountiful, for the spring is singing at this moment, while courageously performing its work."

I looked very stupid. I understood my uncle Lazare. He

was positively preaching me a sermon, in which he told me I was an idle fellow and that the time had come to work.

My uncle appeared as much embarrassed as myself. After having hesitated for some instants he said, slightly stammering:

"Jean, you were wrong not to have come and told me all—as you love Babet and Babet loves you——"

"Babet loves me!" I exclaimed.

My uncle made me an ill-humoured gesture.

"Eh! allow me to speak. I don't want another avowal. She owned it to me herself."

"She owned that to you, she owned that to you!"

And I suddenly threw my arms round my uncle Lazare's neck.

"Oh! how nice that is!" I added. "I had never spoken to her, truly. She told you that at the confessional, didn't she? I would never have dared ask her if she loved me, and I would never have known anything. Oh! how I thank you!"

My uncle Lazare was quite red. He felt that he had just committed a blunder. He had imagined that this was not my first meeting with the young girl, and here he gave me a certainty, when as yet I only dared dream of a hope. He held his tongue now; it was I who spoke with volubility.

"I understand all," I continued. "You are right, I must work to win Babet. But you will see how courageous I shall be. Ah! how good you are, my uncle Lazare, and how well you speak! I understand what the spring says; I, also, will have a powerful summer and an autumn of abundance. One is well placed here, one sees all the valley; I am young like it, I feel youth within me demanding to accomplish its task——"

My uncle calmed me.

"Very good, Jean," he said to me. "I had long hoped to make a priest of you, and I imparted to you my knowledge with that sole aim. But what I saw this morning at the waterside, compels me to definitely give up my fondest hope. It is Heaven that disposes of us. You will love the Almighty in another way. You cannot now remain in this village, and

JEAN GOURDON'S FOUR DAYS

I only wish you to return when ripened by age and work, I have chosen the trade of printer for you; your education will serve you. One of my friends, who is a printer at Grenoble, is expecting you next Monday."

I felt anxious.

"And I shall come back and marry Babet?" I inquired.

My uncle smiled imperceptibly; and, without answering in a direct manner, said:

"The remainder is the will of Heaven."

"You are heaven, and I have faith in your kindness. Oh! uncle, see that Babet does not forget me. I will work for her."

Then my uncle Lazare again pointed out to me the valley which the warm golden light was overspreading more and more.

"There is hope," he said to me. "Do not be as old as I am, Jean. Forget my sermon, be as ignorant as this land. It does not trouble about the autumn; it is all engrossed with the joy of its smile; it labours, courageously and without a care. It hopes."

And we returned to the parsonage, strolling along slowly in the grass, which was scorched by the sun, and chatting with concern of our approaching separation.

Breakfast was cold, as I had foreseen; but that did not trouble me much. I had tears in my eyes each time I looked at my uncle Lazare. And, at the thought of Babet, my heart beat fit to choke me.

I do not remember what I did during the remainder of the day. I think I went and lay down under the willows at the riverside. My uncle was right, the earth was at work. On placing my ear to the grass I seemed to hear continual sounds. Then I dreamed of what my life would be. Buried in the grass until nightfall, I arranged an existence full of labour divided between Babet and my uncle Lazare. The energetic youthfulness of the soil had penetrated my breast, which I pressed with force against the common mother, and at times I imagined myself to be one of the strong willows that lived around me. In the evening I could not dine. My uncle, no doubt, understood the thoughts that were choking me, for he feigned not to notice my want of appetite. As soon as I was able to rise from table, I hastened to return and breathe the open air outside.

A fresh breeze rose from the river, the dull splashing of which I heard in the distance. A soft light fell from the sky. The valley expanded, peaceful and transparent, like a dark shoreless ocean. There were vague sounds in the air, a sort of impassioned tremor, like a great flapping of wings passing above my head. Penetrating perfumes rose with the cool air from the grass.

I had gone out to see Babet; I knew she came to the parsonage every night, and I went and placed myself in ambush behind a hedge. I had got rid of my timidity of the morning; I considered it quite natural to be waiting for her there, because she loved me and I had to tell her of my departure.

When I perceived her skirts in the limpid night, I advanced noiselessly. Then I murmured in a low voice:

"Babet, Babet, I am here."

She did not recognise me, at first, and started with fright. When she discovered who it was, she seemed still more frightened, which very much surprised me.

"It's you, Monsieur Jean," she said to me. "What are you doing there? What do you want?"

I was beside her and took her hand.

"You love me fondly, do you not?"

"I! who told you that?"

"My uncle Lazare."

She stood there in confusion. Her hand began to tremble in mine. As she was on the point of running away, I took her other hand. We were face to face, in a sort of hollow in the hedge, and I felt Babet's panting breath running all warm over my face. The freshness of the air, the rustling silence of the night, hung around us.

"I don't know," stammered the young girl, "I never said that—his reverence the curé misunderstood—For mercy's sake, let me be, I am in a hurry."

"No, no," I continued, "I want you to know that I am going away to-morrow, and to promise to love me always."

"You are leaving to-morrow!"

Oh! that sweet cry, and how tenderly Babet uttered it!

I seem still to hear her apprehensive voice full of affliction and love.

"You see," I exclaimed in my turn, "that my uncle Lazare said the truth. Besides, he never tells fibs. You love me, you love me, Babet! Your lips this morning confided the secret very softly to my fingers."

And I made her sit down at the foot of the hedge. My memory has retained my first chat of love in its absolute innocence. Babet listened to me like a little sister. She was no longer afraid, she told me the story of her love. And there were solemn sermons, ingenious avowals, projects without end. She vowed she would marry no one but me, I vowed to deserve her hand by labour and tenderness. There was a cricket behind the hedge, who accompanied our chat with his chaunt of hope, and all the valley, whispering in the dark, took pleasure in hearing us talk so softly.

On separating we forgot to kiss each other.

When I returned to my little room, it appeared to me that I had left it for at least a year. That day which was so short, seemed an eternity of happiness. It was the warmest and most sweetly-scented spring-day of my life, and the remembrance of it is now like the distant, faltering voice of my youth.

II

Summer

When I awoke at about three o'clock in the morning on that particular day, I was lying on the hard ground tired out, and with my face bathed in perspiration. The hot heavy atmosphere of a July night weighed me down.

My companions were sleeping around me, wrapped in their hooded cloaks; they speckled the grey ground with black, and the obscure plain panted; I fancied I heard the heavy breathing of a slumbering multitude. Indistinct sounds, the neighing of horses, the clash of arms rang out amidst the rustling silence.

The army had halted at about midnight, and we had received orders to lie down and sleep. We had been marching for three days, scorched by the sun and blinded by dust.

EMILE ZOLA

The enemy were at length in front of us, over there, on those hills on the horizon. At daybreak a decisive battle would be fought.

I had been a victim to despondency. For three days I had been as if trampled on, without energy and without thought for the future. It was the excessive fatigue, indeed, that had just awakened me. Now, lying on my back, with my eyes wide open, I was thinking whilst gazing into the night, I thought of this battle, this butchery, which the sun was about to light up. For more than six years, at the first shot in each fight, I had been saying good-bye to those I loved the most fondly, Babet and uncle Lazare. And now, barely a month before my discharge, I had to say good-bye again, and this time perhaps for ever.

Then my thoughts softened. With closed eyelids I saw Babet and my uncle Lazare. How long it was since I had kissed them! I remembered the day of our separation; my uncle weeping because he was poor, and allowing me to leave like that, and Babet, in the evening, had vowed she would wait for me, and that she would never love another. I had had to quit all, my master at Grenoble, my friends at Dourgues. A few letters had come from time to time to tell me they always loved me, and that happiness was awaiting me in my well-beloved valley. And I, I was going to fight, I was going to get killed.

I began dreaming of my return. I saw my poor old uncle on the threshold of the parsonage extending his trembling arms; and behind him was Babet, quite red, smiling through her tears. I fell into their arms and kissed them, seeking for expressions——

Suddenly the beating of drums recalled me to stern reality. Daybreak had come, the grey plain expanded in the morning mist. The ground became full of life, indistinct forms appeared on all sides; a sound that became louder and louder filled the air; it was the call of bugles, the galloping of horses, the rumble of artillery, the shouting out of orders. War came threatening, amidst my dream of tenderness. I rose with difficulty; it seemed to me that my bones were broken, and that my head was about to split. I hastily got my men together; for I must tell you that I had won the

JEAN GOURDON'S FOUR DAYS

rank of sergeant. We soon received orders to bear to the left and occupy a hillock above the plain.

As we were about to move, the sergeant-major came running along and shouting:

"A letter for Sergeant Gourdon!"

And he handed me a dirty crumpled letter, which had been lying perhaps for a week in the leather bags of the post-office. I had only just time to recognise the writing of my uncle Lazare.

"Forward, march!" shouted the major.

I had to march. For a few seconds I held the poor letter in my hand, devouring it with my eyes; it burnt my fingers; I would have given everything in the world to have sat down and wept at ease whilst reading it. I had to content myself with slipping it under my tunic against my heart.

I have never experienced such agony. By way of consolation I said to myself what my uncle had so often repeated to me: I was in the summer of my life, at the moment of the fierce struggle, and it was essential that I should perform my duty bravely, if I would have a peaceful and bountiful autumn. But these reasons exasperated me the more: this letter, which had come to speak to me of happiness, burnt my heart, which had revolted against the folly of war. And I could not even read it! I was perhaps going to die without knowing what it contained, without perusing my uncle Lazare's affectionate remarks for the last time.

We had reached the top of the hill. We were to await orders there to advance. The battle-field had been marvellously chosen to slaughter one another at ease. The immense plain expanded for several leagues, and was quite bare, without a house or tree. Hedges and bushes made slight spots on the whiteness of the ground. I have never since seen such a country, an ocean of dust, a chalky soil, bursting open here and there, and displaying its tawny bowels. And never either have I since witnessed a sky of such intense purity, a July day so lovely and so warm; at eight o'clock the sultry heat was already scorching our faces. O the splendid morning, and what a sterile plain to kill and die in!

Firing had broken out with irregular crackling sounds, a

long time since, supported by the solemn growl of the cannon. The enemy, Austrians dressed in white, had quitted the heights, and the plain was studded with long files of men, who looked to me about as big as insects. One might have thought it was an ant-hill in insurrection. Clouds of smoke hung over the battle-field. At times, when these clouds broke asunder, I perceived soldiers in flight, smitten with terrified panic. Thus there were currents of fright which bore men away, and outbursts of shame and courage which brought them back under fire.

I could neither hear the cries of the wounded, nor see the blood flow. I could only distinguish the dead which the battalions left behind them, and which resembled black patches. I began to watch the movements of the troops with curiosity, irritated at the smoke which hid a good half of the show, experiencing a sort of egotistic pleasure at the knowledge that I was in security, whilst others were dying.

At about nine o'clock we were ordered to advance. We went down the hill at the double and proceeded towards the centre which was giving way. The regular beat of our footsteps appeared to me funeral-like. The bravest among us panting, pale and with haggard features.

I have made up my mind to tell the truth. At the first whistle of the bullets, the battalion suddenly came to a halt, tempted to fly.

"Forward, forward!" shouted the chiefs.

But we were riveted to the ground, bowing our heads when a bullet whistled by our ears. This movement is instinctive; if shame had not restrained me, I would have thrown myself flat on my stomach in the dust.

Before us was a huge veil of smoke which we dared not penetrate. Red flashes passed through this smoke. And, shuddering, we still stood still. But the bullets reached us; soldiers fell with yells. The chiefs shouted louder:

"Forward, forward!"

The rear ranks, which they pushed on, compelled us to march. Then, closing our eyes, we made a fresh dash and entered the smoke.

We were seized with furious rage. When the cry of "Halt!" resounded, we experienced difficulty in coming to a standstill. As soon as one is motionless, fear returns and one feels a wish to run away. Firing commenced. We shot in front of us, without aiming, finding some relief in discharging bullets into the smoke. I remember I pulled my trigger mechanically, with lips firmly set together and eyes wide open; I was no longer afraid, for, to tell the truth, I no longer knew if I existed. The only idea I had in my head, was that I would continue firing until all was over. My companion on the left received a bullet full in the face and fell on me; I brutally pushed him away, wiping my cheek which he had drenched with blood. And I resumed firing.

I still remember having seen our colonel, M. de Montrevert, firm and erect upon his horse, gazing quietly towards the enemy. That man appeared to me immense. He had no rifle to amuse himself with, and his breast was expanded to its full breadth above us. From time to time, he looked down, and exclaimed in a dry voice:

"Close the ranks, close the ranks!"

We closed our ranks like sheep, treading on the dead, stupefied, and continuing firing. Until then, the enemy had only sent us bullets; a dull explosion was heard and a shell carried off five of our men. A battery which must have been opposite us and which we could not see, had just opened fire. The shells struck into the middle of us, almost at one spot, making a sanguinary gap which we closed unceasingly with the obstinacy of ferocious brutes.

"Close the ranks, close the ranks!" the colonel coldly repeated.

We were giving the cannon human flesh. Each time a soldier was struck down, I was taking a step nearer death, I was approaching the spot where the shells were falling heavily, crushing the men whose turn had come to die. The corpses were forming heaps in that place, and soon the shells would strike into nothing more than a mound of mangled flesh; shreds of limbs flew about at each fresh discharge. We could no longer close the ranks.

The soldiers yelled, the chiefs themselves were moved.

"With the bayonet, with the bayonet!"

And amidst a shower of bullets the battalion rushed in

fury towards the shells. The veil of smoke was torn asunder; we perceived the enemy's battery flaming red, which was firing at us from the mouths of all its pieces, on the summit of a hillock. But the dash forward had commenced, the shells stopped the dead only.

I ran beside Colonel Montrevert, whose horse had just been killed, and who was fighting like a simple soldier. Suddenly I was struck down; it seemed to me as if my breast opened and my shoulder was taken away. A frightful wind passed over my face.

And I fell. The colonel fell beside me. I felt myself dying. I thought of those I loved, and fainted whilst searching with a withering hand for my uncle Lazare's letter.

When I came to myself again I was lying on my side in the dust. I was annihilated by profound stupor. I gazed before me with my eyes wide open without seeing anything; it seemed to me that I had lost my limbs, and that my brain was empty. I did not suffer, for life seemed to have departed from my flesh.

The rays of a hot implacable sun fell upon my face like molten lead. I did not feel it. Life returned to me little by little; my limbs became lighter, my shoulder alone remained crushed beneath an enormous weight. Then, with the instinct of a wounded animal, I wanted to sit up. I uttered a cry of pain, and fell back upon the ground.

But I lived now, I saw, I understood. The plain spread out naked and deserted, all white in the broad sunlight. It exhibited its desolation beneath the intense serenity of heaven; heaps of corpses were sleeping in the warmth, and the trees that had been brought down, seemed to be other dead who were dying. There was not a breath of air. A frightful silence came from those piles of inanimate bodies; then, at times, there were dismal groans which broke this silence, and conveyed a long tremor to it. Slender clouds of grey smoke hanging over the low hills on the horizon, was all that broke the bright blue of the sky. The butchery was continuing on the heights.

I imagined we were conquerors, and I experienced selfish pleasure in thinking I could die in peace on this deserted plain. Around me the earth was black. On raising my head

JEAN GOURDON'S FOUR DAYS

I saw the enemy's battery on which we had charged, a few feet away from me. The struggle must have been horrible: the mound was covered with hacked and disfigured bodies; blood had flowed so abundantly that the dust seemed like a large red carpet. The cannon stretched out their dark muzzles above the corpses. I shuddered when I observed the silence of those guns.

Then gently, with a multitude of precautions, I succeeded in turning on my stomach. I rested my head on a large stone all splashed with gore, and drew my uncle Lazare's letter from my breast. I placed it before my eyes; but my tears prevented me reading it.

And whilst the sun was roasting me in the back, the acrid smells of blood were choking me. I could form an idea of the woeful plain around me, and was as if stiffened with the rigidness of the dead. My poor heart was weeping in the warm and loathsome silence of murder.

Uncle Lazare wrote to me:

"My Dear Boy,—I hear war has been declared; but I still hope you will get your discharge before the campaign opens. Every morning I beseech the Almighty to spare you new dangers; He will grant my prayer, He will, one of these days, let you close my eyes.

"Ah! my poor Jean, I am becoming old, I have great need of your arm. Since your departure I no more feel your youthfulness beside me, which gave me back my twenty summers. Do you remember our strolls in the morning along the oak-tree walk? Now I no longer dare to go beneath those trees; I am alone, I am afraid. The Durance weeps. Come quickly and console me, assuage my anxiety——"

The tears were choking me, I could not continue. At that moment a heartrending cry was uttered a few steps away from me; I saw a soldier suddenly rise, with the muscles of his face contracted; he extended his arms in agony, and fell to the ground, where he writhed in frightful convulsions; then he ceased moving.

"I have placed my hope in the Almighty," continued my uncle, "He will bring you back safe and sound to Dourgues, and we will resume our peaceful existence. Let me dream out loud, and tell you my plans for the future.

"You will go no more to Grenoble, you will remain with me; I will make my child a son of the soil, a peasant who shall live gaily whilst tilling the fields.

"And I will retire to your farm. In a short time my trembling hands will no longer be able to hold the Host. I only ask Heaven for two years of such an existence. That will be my reward for the few good deeds I may have done. Then you will sometimes lead me along the paths of our dear valley, where every rock, every hedge will remind me of your youth which I so greatly loved——"

I had to stop again. I felt such a sharp pain in my shoulder, that I almost fainted a second time. A terrible anxiety had just taken possession of me; it seemed as if the sound of the fusillade was approaching, and I thought with terror that our army was perhaps retreating, and that in its flight it would descend to the plain and pass over my body. But I still saw nothing but the slight clouds of smoke hanging over the low hills.

My uncle Lazare added:

"And we shall be three to love one another. Ah! my well-beloved Jean, how right you were to give her to drink that morning beside the Durance. I was afraid of Babet, I was ill-humoured, and now I am jealous, for I can see very well that I shall never be able to love you as much as she does. 'Tell him,' she repeated to me yesterday, blushing, 'that if he gets killed, I shall go and throw myself into the river at the spot where he gave me to drink.'

"For the love of God! be careful of your life. There are things that I cannot understand, but I feel that happiness awaits you here. I already call Babet my daughter; I can see her on your arm, in the church, when I shall bless your union. I wish that to be my last mass.

"Babet is a fine, tall girl now. She will assist you in your work——"

The sound of the fusillade had gone farther away. I was weeping sweet tears. There were dismal moans among soldiers who were in their last agonies between the cannon wheels. I perceived one who was endeavouring to get rid of a comrade, wounded as he was, whose body was crushing his chest; and, as this wounded man struggled and complained, the soldier pushed him brutally away, and made him roll down the slope of the mound, whilst the wretched creature yelled with pain. At that cry a murmur came from the heap of corpses. The sun, which was sinking, shed rays of a light fallow colour. The blue of the sky was softer.

I finished reading my uncle Lazare's letter.

"I simply wished," he continued, "to give you news of ourselves, and to beg you to come as soon as possible and make us happy. And here I am weeping and gossiping like an old child. Hope, my poor Jean, I pray, and God is good.

"Answer me quickly, and give me, if possible, the date of your return. Babet and I are counting the weeks. We trust to see you soon; be hopeful."

The date of my return!—I kissed the letter, sobbing, and fancied for a moment that I was kissing Babet and my uncle. No doubt I should never see them again. I would die like a dog in the dust, beneath the leaden sun. And it was on that desolated plain, amidst the death-rattle of the dying, that those whom I loved dearly were saying good-bye. A buzzing silence filled my ears; I gazed at the pale earth spotted with blood, which extended, deserted, to the grey lines of the horizon. I repeated: "I must die." Then, I closed my eyes, and thought of Babet and my uncle Lazare.

I know not how long I remained in a sort of painful drowsiness. My heart suffered as much as my flesh. Warm tears ran slowly down my cheeks. Amidst the nightmare that accompanied the fever, I heard a moan similar to the continuous plaintive cry of a child in suffering. At times, I awoke and stared at the sky in astonishment.

At last I understood that it was M. de Montrevert, lying a few paces off, who was moaning in this manner. I had thought him dead. He was stretched out with his face to the ground and his arms extended. This man had been good to me; I said to myself that I could not allow him to die thus, with his face to the ground, and I began crawling slowly towards him.

Two corpses separated us. For a moment I thought of passing over the stomachs of these dead men to shorten the distance; for, my shoulder made me suffer frightfully at every movement. But I did not dare. I proceeded on my knees, assisting myself with one hand. When I reached the colonel, I gave a sigh of relief; it seemed to me that I was less alone; we would die together, and this death shared by both of us no longer terrified me.

I wanted him to see the sun, and I turned him over as gently as possible. When the rays fell upon his face, he breathed hard; he opened his eyes. Leaning over his body, I tried to smile at him. He closed his eyelids again; I understood by his trembling lips that he was conscious of his sufferings.

"It's you, Gourdon," he said to me at last, in a feeble voice; "is the battle won?"

"I think so, colonel," I answered him.

There was a moment of silence. Then, opening his eyes and looking at me, he inquired—

"Where are you wounded?"

"In the shoulder—and you, colonel?"

"My elbow must be smashed. I remember; it was the same bullet that arranged us both like this, my boy."

He made an effort to sit up.

"But come," he said with sudden gaiety, "we are not going to sleep here?"

You cannot believe how much this courageous display of joviality contributed towards giving me strength and hope. I felt quite different since we were two to struggle against death.

"Wait," I exclaimed, "I will bandage up your arm with my handkerchief, and we will try and support one another as far as the nearest ambulance."

"That's it, my boy. Don't make it too tight. Now, let us take each other by the good hand and try to get up."

We rose staggering. We had lost a great deal of blood; our heads were swimming and our legs failed us. Any one would have mistaken us for drunkards, stumbling, supporting, pushing one another, and making zigzags to avoid the dead. The sun was setting with a rosy blush, and our gigantic shadows danced in a strange way over the field of battle. It was the end of a fine day.

The colonel joked; his lips were crisped by shudders, his laughter resembled sobs. I could see that we were going to

JEAN GOURDON'S FOUR DAYS

fall down in some corner never to rise again. At times we were seized with giddiness, and were obliged to stop and close our eyes. The ambulances formed small grey patches on the dark ground at the extremity of the plain.

We knocked up against a large stone, and were thrown down one on the other. The colonel swore like a pagan. We tried to walk on all-fours, catching hold of the briars. In this way we did a hundred yards on our knees. But our knees were bleeding.

"I have had enough of it," said the colonel, lying down; "they may come and fetch me if they will. Let us sleep."

I still had the strength to sit half up, and shout with all the breath that remained within me. Men were passing along in the distance picking up the wounded; they ran to us and placed us side by side on a stretcher.

"Comrade," the colonel said to me during the journey, "Death will not have us. I owe you my life, I will pay my debt, whenever you have need of me. Give me your hand."

I placed my hand in his, and it was thus that we reached the ambulances. They had lighted torches; the surgeons were cutting and sawing, amidst frightful yells; a sickly smell came from the blood-stained linen, whilst the torches cast dark rosy flakes into the basins.

The colonel bore the amputation of his arm with courage; I only saw his lips turn pale and a film come over his eyes. When it was my turn, a surgeon examined my shoulder.

"A shell did that for you," he said; "an inch lower and your shoulder would have been carried away. The flesh, only, has suffered."

And when I asked the assistant, who was dressing my wound, whether it was serious, he answered me with a laugh.

"Serious! you will have to keep to your bed for three weeks, and make new blood."

I turned my face to the wall, not wishing to show my tears. And with my heart's eyes I perceived Babet and my uncle Lazare stretching out their arms towards me. I had finished with the sanguinary struggles of my summer day.

III

Autumn

It was nearly fifteen years since I had married Babet in my uncle Lazare's little church. We had sought happiness in our dear valley. I had made myself a farmer; the Durance, my first sweetheart, was now a good mother to me, who seemed to take pleasure in making my fields rich and fertile. Little by little, by following the new methods of agriculture, I became one of the wealthiest landowners in the neighbourhood.

We had purchased the oak-tree walk and the meadows bordering on the river, at the death of my wife's parents. I had had a modest house built on this land, but we were soon obliged to enlarge it; each year I found a means of rounding off our property by the addition of some neighbouring field, and our granaries were too small for our harvests.

Those first fifteen years were uneventful and happy. They passed away in serene joy, and all they have left within me is the remembrance of calm and continued happiness. My uncle Lazare, on retiring to our home, had realised his dream; his advanced age did not permit of his reading his breviary of a morning; he sometimes regretted his dear church, but consoled himself by visiting the young vicar who had succeeded him. He came down from the little room he occupied at sunrise, and often accompanied me to the fields, enjoying himself in the open air, and finding a second youth amidst the healthy atmosphere of the country.

One sadness alone made us sometimes sigh. Amidst the fruitfulness by which we were surrounded, Babet remained childless. Although we were three to love one another we sometimes found ourselves too much alone: we would have liked to have had a little fair head running about amongst us, who would have tormented and caressed us.

Uncle Lazare had a frightful dread of dying before he was a great-uncle. He had become a child again, and felt sorrowful that Babet did not give him a comrade who would have played with him. On the day when my wife confided to us with hesitation, that we would no doubt soon be four, I saw my uncle turn quite pale, and make efforts not to cry. He kissed us, thinking already of the christening, and speaking of the child as if it were already three or four years old.

And the months passed in concentrated tenderness. We talked together in subdued voices, awaiting some one. I no longer loved Babet, I worshipped her with joined hands, I worshipped her for two, for herself and the little one.

The great day was drawing nigh. I had brought a midwife from Grenoble who never moved from the farm. My uncle was in a dreadful fright; he understood nothing about such things, he went so far as to tell me that he had done wrong in taking holy orders, and that he was very sorry he was not a doctor.

One morning in September, at about six o'clock, I went into the room of my dear Babet who was still asleep. Her smiling face was peaceful reposing on the white linen pillow-case. I bent over her holding my breath. Heaven had blessed me with the good things of this world. I all at once thought of that summer day when I was moaning in the dust, and at the same time I felt around me, the comfort due to labour and the quietude that comes from happiness. My good wife was asleep, all rosy, in the middle of her great bed; whilst the whole room recalled to me our fifteen years of tender affection.

I kissed Babet softly on the lips. She opened her eyes and smiled at me without speaking. I felt an almost uncontrollable desire to take her in my arms, and clasp her to my heart; but, latterly, I had hardly dared press her hand, she seemed so fragile and sacred to me.

I seated myself at the edge of the bed, and asked her in a low voice:

"Is it for to-day?"

"No, I don't think so," she replied. "I dreamt I had a boy: he was already very tall and wore adorable little black moustachios. Uncle Lazare told me yesterday that he also had seen him in a dream."

I acted very stupidly.

"I know the child better than you do," I said. "I see it every night. It's a girl——"

And as Babet turned her face to the wall, ready to cry, I realised how foolish I had been, and hastened to add:

"When I say a girl—I am not quite sure. I see a very small child with a long white gown—it's certainly a boy."

Babet kissed me for that pleasing remark.

"Go and look after the vintage," she continued, "I feel calm this morning."

"You will send for me if anything happens?"

"Yes, yes, I am very tired: I shall go to sleep again. You'll not be angry with me for my laziness?"

And Babet closed her eyes, looking languid and affected. I remained leaning over her, receiving the warm breath from her lips in my face. She gradually went off to sleep, without ceasing to smile. Then I disengaged my hand from hers with a multitude of precautions. I had to manœuvre for five minutes to bring this delicate task to a happy issue. After that I gave her a kiss on her forehead, which she did not feel, and withdrew with a palpitating heart, overflowing with love.

In the courtyard below, I found my uncle Lazare, who was gazing anxiously at the window of Babet's room. So soon as he perceived me he inquired:

"Well, is it for to-day?"

He had been putting this question to me regularly every morning for the past month.

"It appears not," I answered him. "Will you come with me and see them picking the grapes?"

He fetched his stick, and we went down the oak-tree walk. When we were at the end of it, on that terrace which overlooks the Durance, both of us stopped, gazing at the valley.

Small white clouds floated in the pale sky. The sun was shedding soft rays, which cast a sort of gold dust over the country, the yellow expanse of which spread out all ripe. One saw neither the brilliant light nor the dark shadows of summer. The foliage gilded the black earth in large patches. The river ran more slowly, weary at the task of having rendered the fields fruitful for a season. And the valley remained calm and strong. It already wore the first furrows of winter, but it preserved within it the warmth of its last labour, displaying its robust charms, free from the weeds of spring, more majestically beautiful, like that second youth of woman who has given birth to life.

My uncle Lazare remained silent; then, turning towards me, said:

"Do you remember, Jean? It is more than twenty years ago since I brought you here early one May morning. On that particular day I showed you the valley full of feverish activity, labouring for the fruits of autumn. Look: the valley has just performed its task again."

"I remember, dear uncle," I replied. "I was quaking with fear on that day; but you were good, and your lesson was convincing. I owe you all my happiness."

"Yes, you have reached the autumn. You have laboured and are gathering in the harvest. Man, my boy, was created after the way of the earth. And we, like the common mother, are eternal: the green leaves are born again each year from dry leaves; I am born again in you, and you will be born again in your children. I am telling you this so that old age may not alarm you, so that you may know how to die in peace, as dies this verdure, which will shoot out again from its own germs next spring."

I listened to my uncle and thought of Babet, who was sleeping in her great bed spread with white linen. The dear creature was about to give birth to a child after the manner of this fertile soil which had given us fortune. She also had reached the autumn: she had the beaming smile and serene robustness of the valley. I seemed to see her beneath the yellow sun, tired and happy, experiencing noble delight at being a mother. And I no longer knew whether my uncle Lazare was talking to me of my dear valley, or of my dear Babet.

We slowly ascended the hills. Below, along the Durance, were the meadows, broad, raw green swards; next came the yellow fields, intersected here and there by greyish olive and slender almond trees, planted wide apart in rows; then, right up above, were the vines, great stumps with shoots trailing along the ground.

The vine is treated in the south of France like a hardy housewife, and not like a delicate young lady, as in the north. It grows somewhat as it likes, according to the good will of rain and sun. The stumps, which are planted in double rows, and form long lines, throw sprays of dark verdure around them. Wheat or oats are sown between. A vineyard resembles an immense piece of striped material, made of the green bands formed by the vine leaves, and of yellow ribbon represented by the stubble.

Men and women stooping down among the vines, were cutting the bunches of grapes, which they then threw to the bottom of large baskets. My uncle and I walked slowly through the stubble. As we passed along, the vintagers turned their heads and greeted us. My uncle sometimes stopped to speak to some of the oldest of the labourers.

"Heh! Father André," he said, "are the grapes thoroughly ripe? Will the wine be good this year?"

And the countryfolk, raising their bare arms, displayed the long bunches, which were as black as ink, in the sun; and when the grapes were pressed they seemed to burst with abundance and strength.

"Look, Mr. Curé," they exclaimed, "these are small ones. There are some weighing several pounds. We have not had such a task these ten years."

Then they returned among the leaves. Their brown jackets formed patches in the verdure. And the women, bareheaded, with small blue handkerchiefs round their necks, were stooping down singing. There were children rolling in the sun, in the stubble, giving utterance to shrill laughter and enlivening this open-air workshop with their turbulency. Large carts remained motionless at the edge of the field waiting for the grapes; they stood out prominently against the clear sky, whilst men went and came unceasingly, carrying away full baskets, and bringing back empty ones.

I confess that in the centre of this field, I had feelings of pride. I heard the ground producing beneath my feet; ripe age ran all powerful in the veins of the vine, and loaded the air with great puffs of it. Hot blood coursed in my flesh, I was as if elevated by the fecundity overflowing from the soil and ascending within me. The labour of this swarm of work-people was my doing, these vines were my children; this entire farm became my large and obedient family. I

JEAN GOURDON'S FOUR DAYS

experienced pleasure in feeling my feet sink into the heavy land.

Then, at a glance, I took in the fields that sloped down to the Durance, and I was the possessor of those vines, those meadows, that stubble, those olive-trees. The house stood all white beside the oak-tree walk; the river seemed like a fringe of silver placed at the edge of the great green mantle of my pasture-land. I fancied, for a moment, that my frame was increasing in size, that by stretching out my arms, I would be able to embrace the entire property, and press it to my breast, trees, meadows, house, and ploughed land.

And as I looked, I saw one of our servant-girls racing, out of breath, up the narrow pathway that ascended the hill. Confused by the speed at which she was travelling, she stumbled over the stones, agitating both her arms, and hailing us with gestures of bewilderment. I felt choking with inexpressible emotion.

"Uncle, uncle," I shouted, "look how Marguerite's running. I think it must be for to-day."

My uncle Lazare turned quite pale. The servant had at length reached the plateau; she came towards us jumping over the vines. When she reached me, she was out of breath; she was stifling and pressing her hands to her bosom.

"Speak!" I said to her. "What has happened?"

She heaved a heavy sigh, agitated her hands, and finally was able to pronounce this single word:

"Madame——"

I waited for no more.

"Come! come quick, uncle Lazare! Ah! my poor dear Babet!"

And I bounded down the pathway at a pace fit to break my bones. The vintagers, who had stood up, smiled as they saw me running. Uncle Lazare, who could not overtake me, shook his walking stick in despair.

"Heh! Jean, the deuce!" he shouted, "wait for me. I don't want to be the last."

But I no longer heard uncle Lazare, and continued running.

I reached the farm panting for breath, full of hope and terror. I rushed upstairs and knocked with my fist at Babet's door, laughing, crying, and half crazy. The midwife set the door ajar, to tell me in an angry voice not to make so much noise. I stood there abashed and in despair.

"You can't come in," she added. "Go and wait in the courtyard."

And as I did not move, she continued: "All is going on very well. I will call you."

The door was closed. I remained standing before it, unable to make up my mind to go away. I heard Babet complaining in a broken voice. And, while I was there, she gave utterance to a heartrending scream that struck me right in the breast like a bullet. I felt an almost irresistible desire to break the door open with my shoulder. So as not to give way to it, I placed my hands to my ears, and dashed downstairs.

In the courtyard I found my uncle Lazare, who had just arrived out of breath. The worthy man was obliged to seat himself on the brink of the well.

"Hallo! where is the child?" he inquired of me.

"I don't know," I answered; "they shut the door in my face——Babet is in pain and in tears."

We gazed at one another, not daring to utter a word. We listened in agony, without taking our eyes off Babet's window, endeavouring to see through the little white curtains. My uncle, who was trembling, stood still, with both his hands resting heavily on his walking-stick; I, feeling very feverish, walked up and down before him, taking long strides. At times we exchanged anxious smiles.

The carts of the vintagers arrived one by one. The baskets of grapes were placed against a wall of the courtyard, and bare-legged men trampled the bunches under foot in wooden troughs. The mules neighed, the carters swore, whilst the wine fell with a dull sound to the bottom of the vat. Acrid smells pervaded the warm air.

And I continued pacing up and down, as if made tipsy by those perfumes. My poor head was breaking, and as I watched the red juice run from the grapes I thought of Babet. I said to myself with manly joy, that my child was

JEAN GOURDON'S FOUR DAYS

born at the prolific time of vintage, amidst the perfume of new wine.

I was tormented by impatience, I went upstairs again. But I did not dare knock, I pressed my ear against the door, and heard Babet's low moans and sobs. Then my heart failed me, and I cursed suffering. Uncle Lazare, who had crept up behind me, had to lead me back into the courtyard. He wished to divert me, and told me the wine would be excellent; but he spoke without attending to what he said. And at times we were both silent, listening anxiously to one of Babet's more prolonged moans.

Little by little the cries subsided, and became nothing more than a painful murmur, like the voice of a child falling off to sleep in tears. Then there was absolute silence. This soon caused me unutterable terror. The house seemed empty, now that Babet had ceased sobbing. I was just going upstairs, when the midwife opened the window noiselessly. She leant out and beckoned me with her hand:

"Come," she said to me.

I went slowly upstairs, feeling additional delight at each step I took. My uncle Lazare was already knocking at the door, whilst I was only half way up to the landing, experiencing a sort of strange delight in delaying the moment when I would kiss my wife.

I stopped on the threshold, my heart was beating double. My uncle had leant over the cradle. Babet, quite pale, with closed eyelids, seemed asleep. I forgot all about the child, and going straight to Babet, took her dear hand between mine. The tears had not dried on her cheeks, and her quivering lips were dripping with them. She raised her eyelids wearily. She did not speak to me, but I understood her to say: "I have suffered a great deal, my dear Jean, but I was so happy to suffer! I felt you within me."

Then, I bent down, I kissed Babet's eyes and drank her tears. She laughed with much sweetness; she resigned herself with caressing languidness. The fatigue had made her all aches and pains. She slowly moved her hands from the sheet, and taking me by the neck, placed her lips to my ear:

"It's a boy," she murmured in a weak voice, but with an air of triumph.

Those were the first words she uttered after the terrible shock she had undergone.

"I knew it would be a boy," she continued, "I saw the child every night. Give him me, put him beside me."

I turned round and saw the midwife and my uncle quarrelling.

The midwife had all the trouble in the world to prevent uncle Lazare taking the little one in his arms. He wanted to nurse it.

I looked at the child whom the mother had made me forget. He was all rosy. Babet said with conviction that he was like me; the midwife discovered that he had his mother's eyes; I, for my part, could not say, I was almost crying, I smothered the dear little thing with kisses, imagining I was still kissing Babet.

I placed the child on the bed. He kept on crying, but this sounded to us like celestial music. I sat on the edge of the bed, my uncle took a large arm-chair, and Babet, weary and serene, covered up to her chin, remained with open eyelids and smiling eyes.

The window was wide open. The smell of grapes came in along with the warmth of the mild autumn afternoon. One heard the trampling of the vintagers, the shocks of the carts, the cracking of whips; at times the shrill song of a servant working in the courtyard, reached us. All this noise was softened in the serenity of that room, which still resounded with Babet's sobs. And the window-frame enclosed a large strip of landscape, carved out of the heavens and open country. We could see the oak-tree walk in its entire length; then the Durance, looking like a white satin ribbon, passed amidst the gold and purple leaves; whilst above this square of ground were the limpid depths of a pale sky with blue and rosy tints.

It was amidst the calm of this horizon, amidst the exhalations of the vat and the joys attendant upon labour and reproduction, that we three talked together, Babet, uncle Lazare, and myself, whilst gazing at the dear little new-born babe.

JEAN GOURDON'S FOUR DAYS

"Uncle Lazare," said Babet, "what name will you give the child?"

"Jean's mother was named Jacqueline," answered my uncle. "I shall call the child Jacques."

"Jacques, Jacques," repeated Babet. "Yes, it's a pretty name. And, tell me, what shall we make the little man: parson or soldier, gentleman or peasant?"

I began to laugh.

"We shall have time to think of that," I said.

"But no," continued Babet almost angry, "he will grow rapidly. See how strong he is. He already speaks with his eyes."

My uncle Lazare was exactly of my wife's opinion. He answered in a very grave tone:

"Make him neither priest nor soldier, unless he have an irresistible inclination for one of those callings—to make him a gentleman would be a serious——"

Babet looked at me anxiously. The dear creature had not a bit of pride for herself; but like all mothers, she would have liked to be humble and proud before her son. I could have sworn that she already saw him a notary or a doctor. I kissed her and gently said to her:

"I wish our son to live in our dear valley. One day, he will find a Babet of sixteen, on the banks of the Durance, to whom he will give some water. Do you remember, my dear ——? The country has brought us peace: our son shall be a peasant as we are, and happy as we are."

Babet, who was quite touched, kissed me in her turn. She gazed at the foliage and the river, the meadows and the sky, through the window; then she said to me, smiling:

"You are right, Jean. This place has been good to us, it will be the same to our little Jacques. Uncle Lazare, you will be the godfather of a farmer."

Uncle Lazare made a languid, affectionate sign of approval with the head. I had been examining him for a moment, and saw his eyes becoming filmy, and his lips turning pale. Leaning back in the arm-chair, opposite the window, he had placed his white hands on his knees, and was watching the heavens fixedly with an expression of thoughtful ecstasy.

I felt very anxious.

"Are you in pain, uncle Lazare?" I inquired of him. "What is the matter with you? Answer, for mercy's sake."

He gently raised one of his hands, as if to beg me to speak lower; then he let it fall again, and said in a weak voice:

"I am broken down," he said. "Happiness, at my age, is mortal. Don't make a noise. It seems as if my flesh were becoming quite light: I can no longer feel my legs or arms."

Babet raised herself in alarm, with her eyes on uncle Lazare. I knelt down before him, watching him anxiously. He smiled.

"Don't be frightened," he resumed. "I am in no pain; a feeling of calmness is gaining possession of me; I believe I am going off into a good and just sleep. It came over me all at once, and I thank the Almighty. Ah! my poor Jean, I ran too fast down the pathway on the hillside; the child caused me too great joy."

And as we understood, we burst out into tears. Uncle Lazare continued, without ceasing to watch the sky:

"Do not spoil my joy, I beg of you. If you only knew how happy it makes me, to fall asleep for ever in this armchair! I have never dared expect such a consoling death. All I love is here, beside me—and see what a blue sky! The Almighty has sent a lovely evening."

The sun was sinking behind the oak-tree walk. Its slanting rays cast sheets of gold beneath the trees, which took the tones of old copper. The verdant fields melted into vague serenity in the distance. Uncle Lazare became weaker and weaker amidst the touching silence of this peaceful sunset, entering by the open window. He slowly passed away, like those slight gleams that were dying out on the lofty branches.

"Ah! my good valley," he murmured, "you are sending me a tender farewell. I was afraid of coming to my end in the winter, when you would be all black."

We restrained our tears, not wishing to trouble this saintly death. Babet prayed in an undertone. The child continued uttering smothered cries.

My uncle Lazare heard its wail in the dreaminess of his

agony. He endeavoured to turn towards Babet, and, still smiling, said:

"I have seen the child and die very happy."

Then he gazed at the pale sky and yellow fields, and, throwing back his head, heaved a gentle sigh.

No tremor agitated uncle Lazare's body; he died as one falls asleep.

We had become so calm that we remained silent and with dry eyes. In the presence of such great simplicity in death, all we experienced was a feeling of serene sadness. Twilight had set in, uncle Lazare's farewell had left us confident, like the farewell of the sun which dies at night to be born again in the morning.

Such was my autumn day, which gave me a son, and carried off my uncle Lazare in the peacefulness of the twilight.

IV

Winter

There are dreadful mornings in January that chill one's heart. I awoke on this particular day with a vague feeling of anxiety. It had thawed during the night, and when I cast my eyes over the country from the threshold, it looked to me like an immense dirty grey rag, soiled with mud and rent to tatters.

The horizon was shrouded in a curtain of fog, in which the oak-trees along the walk lugubriously extended their dark arms, like a row of spectres guarding the vast mass of vapour spreading out behind them. The fields had sunk, and were covered with great sheets of water, at the edge of which hung the remnants of dirty snow. The loud roar of the Durance was increasing in the distance.

Winter imparts health and strength to one's frame when the sun is clear and the ground dry. The air makes the tips of your ears tingle, you walk merrily along the frozen pathways, which ring with a silvery sound beneath your tread. But I know of nothing more saddening than dull, thawing weather: I hate the damp fogs which weigh one's shoulders down.

I shivered in the presence of that copper-like sky, and hastened to retire indoors, making up my mind that I would not go out into the fields that day. There was plenty of work in and around the farm-buildings.

Jacques had been up a long time. I heard him whistling in a shed, where he was helping some men remove sacks of corn. The boy was already eighteen years old; he was a tall fellow, with strong arms. He had not had an uncle Lazare to spoil him and teach him Latin, and he did not go and dream beneath the willows at the riverside. Jacques had become a real peasant, an untiring worker, who got angry when I touched anything, telling me I was getting old and ought to rest.

And as I was watching him from a distance, a sweet lithe creature, leaping on my shoulders, clapped her little hands to my eyes, inquiring:

"Who is it?"

I laughed and answered:

"It's little Marie, who has just been dressed by her mamma."

The dear little girl was completing her tenth year, and for ten years she had been the delight of the farm. Having come the last, at a time when we could no longer hope to have any more children, she was doubly loved. Her precarious health made her particularly dear to us. She was treated as a young lady; her mother absolutely wanted to make a lady of her, and I had not the heart to oppose her wish, so little Marie was a pet, in lovely silk skirts trimmed with ribbons.

Marie was still seated on my shoulders.

"Mamma, mamma," she cried, "come and look; I'm playing at horses."

Babet, who was entering, smiled. Ah! my poor Babet, how old we were! I remember we were shivering with weariness, on that day, gazing sadly at one another when alone.

Our children brought back our youth.

Lunch was eaten in silence. We had been compelled to light the lamp. The reddish glimmer that hung round the room was sad enough to drive one crazy.

JEAN GOURDON'S FOUR DAYS

"Bah!" said Jacques, "this tepid rainy weather is better than intense cold that would freeze our vines and olives."

And he tried to joke. But he was as anxious as we were, without knowing why. Babet had had bad dreams. We listened to the account of her nightmare, laughing with our lips but sad at heart.

"This weather quite upsets one," I said to cheer us all up.

"Yes, yes, it's the weather," Jacques hastened to add. "I'll put some vine branches on the fire."

There was a bright flame which cast large sheets of light upon the walls. The branches burnt with a cracking sound, leaving rosy ashes. We had seated ourselves in front of the chimney; the air, outside, was tepid; but great drops of icy cold damp fell from the ceilings inside the farmhouse. Babet had taken little Marie on her knees; she was talking to her in an undertone, amused at her childish chatter.

"Are you coming, father?" Jacques inquired of me. "We are going to look at the cellars and lofts."

I went out with him. The harvests had been getting bad for some years past. We were suffering great losses: our vines and trees were caught by frost, whilst hail had chopped up our wheat and oats. And I sometimes said that I was growing old, and that fortune, who is a woman, does not care for old men. Jacques laughed, answering that he was young, and was going to court fortune.

I had reached the winter, the cold season. I felt distinctly that all was withering around me. At each pleasure that departed, I thought of uncle Lazare, who had died so calmly; and with fond remembrances of him, asked for strength.

Daylight had completely disappeared at three o'clock. We went down into the common room. Babet was sewing in the chimney corner, with her head bent over her work; and little Marie was seated on the ground, in front of the fire, gravely dressing a doll. Jacques and I had placed ourselves at a mahogany writing-table, which had come to us from uncle Lazare, and were engaged in checking our accounts.

The window was as if blocked up; the fog, sticking to the panes of glass, formed a perfect wall of gloom. Behind this wall stretched emptiness, the unknown. A great noise, a loud roar, alone arose in the silence and spread through the obscurity.

We had dismissed the workpeople, keeping only our old woman-servant, Marguerite, with us. When I raised my head and listened, it seemed to me that the farmhouse hung suspended in the middle of a chasm. No human sound came from the outside, I heard naught but the riot of the abyss. Then I gazed at my wife and children, and experienced the cowardice of those old people who feel themselves too weak to protect those surrounding them against unknown peril.

The noise became harsher, and it seemed to us that there was a knocking at the door. At the same instant, the horses in the stable began to neigh furiously, whilst the cattle lowed as if choking. We had all risen, pale with anxiety. Jacques dashed to the door and threw it wide open.

A wave of muddy water burst into the room.

The Durance was overflowing. It was it that had been making the noise, that had been increasing in the distance since morning. The snow melting on the mountains had transformed each hillside into a torrent which had swelled the river. The curtain of fog had hidden from us this sudden rise of water.

It had often advanced thus to the gates of the farm, when the thaw came after severe winters. But the flood had never increased so rapidly. We could see through the open door that the courtyard was transformed into a lake. The water already reached our ankles.

Babet had caught up little Marie, who was crying and clasping her doll to her. Jacques wanted to run and open the doors of the stables and cowhouses; but his mother held him back by his clothes, begging him not to go out. The water continued rising. I pushed Babet towards the staircase.

"Quick, quick, let us go up into the bedrooms," I cried.

And I obliged Jacques to pass before me. I left the ground-floor the last.

Marguerite came down in terror from the loft where she happened to find herself. I made her sit down at the end of the room beside Babet, who remained silent, pale, and with beseeching eyes. We put little Marie into bed; she had insisted on keeping her doll, and went quietly to sleep pressing it in her arms. This child's sleep relieved me; when I turned round and saw Babet, listening to the little girl's regular breathing, I forgot the danger, all I heard was the water beating against the walls.

But Jacques and I could not help looking the peril in the face. Anxiety made us endeavour to discover the progress of the inundation. We had thrown the window wide open, we leant out at the risk of falling, searching into the darkness. The fog, which was thicker, hung above the flood, throwing out fine rain which gave us the shivers. Vague steel-like flashes were all that showed the moving sheet of water, amidst the profound obscurity. Below, it was splashing in the courtyard, rising along the walls in gentle undulations. And we still heard naught but the anger of the Durance, and the affrighted cattle and horses.

The neighing and lowing of these poor beasts pierced me to the heart. Jacques questioned me with his eyes; he would have liked to try and deliver them. Their agonising moans soon became lamentable, and a great cracking sound was heard. The oxen had just broken down the stable doors. We saw them pass before us, borne away by the flood, rolled over and over in the current. And they disappeared amid the roar of the river.

Then I felt choking with anger. I became as one possessed, I shook my fist at the Durance. Erect, facing the window, I insulted it.

"Wicked thing!" I shouted amidst the tumult of the waters, "I loved you fondly, you were my first sweetheart, and now you are plundering me. You come and disturb my farm, and carry off my cattle. Ah! cursed, cursed thing.—— Then you gave me Babet, you ran gently at the edge of my meadows. I took you for a good mother. I remembered uncle Lazare felt affection for your limpid stream, and I thought I owed you gratitude. You are a barbarous mother, I only owe you my hatred——"

But the Durance stifled my cries with its thundering voice; and, broad and indifferent, expanded and drove its flood onward with tranquil obstinacy.

I turned back to the room and went and kissed Babet, who was weeping. Little Marie was smiling in her sleep.

"Don't be afraid," I said to my wife. "The water cannot always rise. It will certainly go down. There is no danger."

"No, there is no danger," Jacques repeated feverishly. "The house is solid."

At that moment Marguerite, who had approached the window, tormented by that feeling of curiosity which is the outcome of fear, leant forward like a mad thing and fell, uttering a cry. I threw myself before the window, but could not prevent Jacques plunging into the water. Marguerite had nursed him, and he felt the tenderness of a son for the poor old woman. Babet had risen in terror, with joined hands, at the sound of the two splashes. She remained there, erect, with open mouth and distended eyes, watching the window.

I had seated myself on the wooden handrail, and my ears were ringing with the roar of the flood. I do not know how long it was that Babet and I were in this painful state of stupor, when a voice called to me. It was Jacques who was holding on to the wall beneath the window. I stretched out my hand to him, and he clambered up.

Babet clasped him in her arms. She could sob now; and she relieved herself.

No reference was made to Marguerite. Jacques did not dare say he had been unable to find her, and we did not dare question him anent his search.

He took me apart and brought me back to the window.

"Father," he said to me in an undertone, "there are more than seven feet of water in the courtyard, and the river is still rising. We cannot remain here any longer."

Jacques was right. The house was falling to pieces, the planks of the outbuildings were going away one by one. Then this death of Marguerite weighed upon us. Babet, bewildered, was beseeching us. Marie alone remained peaceful in the big bed, with her doll between her arms, and slumbering with the happy smile of an angel.

The peril increased at every minute. The water was on the point of reaching the handrail of the window and pouring into the room. Any one would have said that it was an engine of war making the farmhouse totter with regular, dull, hard blows. The current must be running right against the façade, and we could not hope for any human assistance.

"Every minute is precious," said Jacques in agony. "We shall be crushed beneath the ruins. Let us look for boards, let us make a raft."

He said that in his excitement. I would naturally have preferred a thousand times to be in the middle of the river, on a few beams lashed together, than beneath the roof of this house which was about to fall in. But where could we lay hands on the beams we required? In a rage I tore the planks from the cupboards, Jacques broke the furniture, we took away the shutters, every piece of wood we could reach. And feeling it was impossible to utilise these fragments, we cast them into the middle of the room in a fury, and continued searching.

Our last hope was departing, we understood our misery and want of power. The water was rising; the harsh voice of the Durance was calling to us in anger. Then, I burst out sobbing, I took Babet in my trembling arms, I begged Jacques to come near us. I wished us all to die in the same embrace.

Jacques had returned to the window. And, suddenly, he exclaimed:

"Father, we are saved!—Come and see."

The sky was clear. The roof of a shed, torn away by the current, had come to a standstill beneath our window. This roof, which was several yards broad, was formed of light beams and thatch; it floated, and would make a capital raft. I joined my hands together and would have worshipped this wood and straw.

Jacques jumped on the roof, after having firmly secured it. He walked on the thatch, making sure it was everywhere strong. The thatch resisted; therefore we could adventure on it without fear.

"Oh! it will carry us all very well," said Jacques joyfully. "See how little it sinks into the water! The difficulty will be to steer it."

He looked around him and seized two poles drifting along in the current, as they passed by.

"Ah! here are oars," he continued. "You will go to the stern, father, and I forward, and we will manœuvre the raft easily. There are not twelve feet of water. Quick, quick! get on board, we must not lose a minute."

My poor Babet tried to smile. She wrapped little Marie carefully up in her shawl; the child had just woke up, and, quite alarmed, maintained a silence which was broken by deep sobs. I placed a chair before the window and made Babet get on the raft. As I held her in my arms I kissed her with poignant emotion, feeling this kiss was the last.

The water was beginning to pour into the room. Our feet were soaking. I was the last to embark; then I undid the cord. The current hurled us against the wall; it required precautions and many efforts to quit the farmhouse.

The fog had little by little dispersed. It was about midnight when we left. The stars were still buried in mist; the moon which was almost at the edge of the horizon, lit up the night with a sort of wan daylight.

The inundation then appeared to us in all its grandiose horror. The valley had become a river. The Durance, swollen to enormous proportions and washing the two hillsides, passed between dark masses of cultivated land, and was the sole thing displaying life in the inanimate space bounded by the horizon. It thundered with a sovereign voice, maintaining in its anger the majesty of its colossal wave. Clumps of trees emerged in places, staining the sheet of pale water with black streaks. Opposite us I recognised the tops of the oaks along the walk; the current carried us towards these branches, which for us were so many reefs. Around the raft floated various kinds of remains, pieces of wood, empty barrels, bundles of grass; the river was bearing along the ruins it had made in its anger.

To the left we perceived the lights of Dourgues—flashes of lanterns moving about in the darkness. The water could not have risen as high as the village; only the low land had been submerged. No doubt assistance would come. We searched the patches of light hanging over the water; it seemed to us at every instant that we heard the sound of oars.

We had started at random. As soon as the raft was in

the middle of the current, lost amidst the whirlpools of the river, anguish of mind overtook us again; we almost regretted having left the farm. I sometimes turned round and gazed at the house, which still remained standing, presenting a grey aspect on the white water. Babet, crouching down in the centre of the raft, in the thatch of the roof, was holding little Marie on her knees, the child's head against her breast, to hide the horror of the river from her. Both were bent double, leaning forward in an embrace, as if reduced in stature by fear. Jacques, standing upright in the front, was leaning on his pole with all his weight; from time to time he cast a rapid glance towards us, and then silently resumed his task. I seconded him as well as I could, but our efforts to reach the bank remained fruitless. Little by little, notwithstanding our poles, which we buried into the mud until we nearly broke them, we drifted into the open; a force that seemed to come from the depths of the water drove us away. The Durance was slowly taking possession of us.

Struggling, bathed in perspiration, we had worked ourselves into a passion; we were fighting with the river as with a living being, seeking to vanquish, wound, kill it. It strained us in its giant-like arms, and our poles in our hands, became weapons which we thrust into its breast. It roared, flung its slaver into our faces, wriggled beneath our strokes. We resisted its victory with clenched teeth. We would not be conquered. And we had mad impulses to fell the monster, to calm it with blows from our fists.

We went slowly towards the offing. We were already at the entrance to the oak-tree walk. The dark branches pierced through the water, which they tore with a lamentable sound. Death, perhaps, awaited us there in a collision. I cried out to Jacques to follow the walk by clinging close to the branches. And it was thus that I passed for the last time in the middle of this oak-tree alley, where I had walked in my youth and ripe age. In the terrible darkness, above the howling depth, I thought of uncle Lazare, and saw the happy days of my youth smiling at me sadly.

The Durance triumphed at the end of the alley. Our poles no longer touched the bottom. The water bore us along in its impetuous bound of victory. And now it could do what it pleased with us. We gave ourselves up. We went downstream with frightful rapidity. Great clouds, dirty tattered rags hung about the sky; when the moon was hidden there came lugubrious obscurity. Then we rolled in chaos. Enormous billows as black as ink, resembling the backs of fish, bore us along, spinning us round. I could no longer see either Babet or the children. I already felt myself dying.

I know not how long this last run lasted. The moon was suddenly unveiled, and the horizon became clear. And in that light I perceived an immense black mass in front of us which blocked the way, and towards which we were being carried with all the violence of the current. We were lost, we would be broken there.

Babet had stood upright. She held out little Marie to me:

"Take the child," she exclaimed. "Leave me alone, leave me alone!"

Jacques had already caught Babet in his arms. In a loud voice he said:

"Father, save the little one—I will save mother."

We had come close to the black mass. I thought I recognised a tree. The shock was terrible, and the raft, split in two, scattered its straw and beams in the whirlpool of water.

I fell, clasping little Marie tightly to me. The icy cold water brought back all my courage. On rising to the surface of the river, I supported the child, I half laid her on my neck and began to swim laboriously. If the little creature had not lost consciousness but had struggled, we should both have remained at the bottom of the deep.

And, whilst I swam, I felt chocking with anxiety. I called Jacques, I tried to see in the distance; but I heard nothing save the roar of the waters, I saw naught but the pale sheet of the Durance. Jacques and Babet were at the bottom. She must have clung to him, dragged him down in a deadly strain of her arms. What frightful agony! I wanted to die; I sunk slowly, I was going to find them beneath the black water. And as soon as the flood touched little Marie's face, I struggled again with impetuous anguish to get near the waterside.

It was thus that I abandoned Babet and Jacques, in despair at having been unable to die with them, still calling out to them in a husky voice. The river cast me on the stones, like one of those bundles of grass it leaves on its way. When I came to myself again, I took my daughter, who was opening her eyes, in my arms. Day was breaking. My winter night was at an end, that terrible night which had been an accomplice in the murder of my wife and son.

At this moment, after years of regret, one last consolation remains to me. I am the icy winter, but I feel the approaching spring stirring within me. As my uncle Lazare said, we never die. I have had four seasons, and here I am returning to the spring, there is my dear Marie commencing the everlasting joys and sorrows over again.

BARON DE TRENCK
BY CLEMENCE ROBERT

BARON DE TRENCK

By CLEMENCE ROBERT

BARON DE TRENCK already had endured a year of arbitrary imprisonment in the fortress of Glatz, ignorant alike of the cause of his detention or the length of time which he was destined to spend in captivity.

During the early part of the month of September, Major Doo, aide to the governor of the prison of Glatz, entered the prisoner's apartment for a domiciliary visit, accompanied by an adjutant and the officer of the guard.

It was noon. The excessive heat of the dying summer had grown almost unsupportable in the tower chamber where Baron de Trenck was confined. Half empty flagons were scattered among the books which littered his table, but the repeated draughts in which the prisoner had sought refreshment had only served to add to his ever-increasing exasperation.

The major ransacked every nook and corner of the prisoner's chamber and the interior of such pieces of furniture as might afford a possible hiding-place. Remarking the annoyance which this investigation caused the Baron, Doo said arrogantly:

"The general has issued his orders, and it is a matter of little consequence to him whether or not they displease you. Your attempts to escape have greatly incensed him against you."

"And I," retorted Trenck, with like hauteur, "am equally indifferent to your general's displeasure. I shall continue to dispose of my time as may best please me."

"Good!" replied the major, "but in your own interests you would be wiser to philosophize with your books, and seek the key to the sciences, rather than that of the fortress."

"I do not need your advice, major," the baron observed, with sovereign disdain.

Copyrighted 1906 The Frank A. Munsey Company.

"You may perhaps repent later that you did not heed it. Your attempts to escape have angered even the king, and it is impossible to say just how far his severity toward you may go."

"But, great heavens! when I am deprived of my liberty without cause, have I not the right to endeavor to regain it?"

"They do not see the matter in that light in Berlin. As a matter of fact this spirit of revolt against your sovereign only serves to greatly aggravate your crime."

"My crime!" Trenck exclaimed, trembling with anger.

His glance fell upon the major's sword and the thought came to him to tear it from his side and pierce his throat with it. But in the same instant it occurred to him that he might rather profit by the situation. Pale and trembling as he was, he retained sufficient self-control to modify the expression of his countenance and the tone of his voice, though his glance remained fixed upon the sword.

"Major," he said, "no one can be called a criminal until he has been so adjudged by the courts. Happily a man's honor does not depend upon the inconsequent, malicious opinion of others. On the contrary blame should attach to him who condemns the accused without a hearing. No constituted power, whether that of king or judge, has yet convicted me of any culpable action. Apart from the courtesy which should be observed between officers of the same rank, you, out of simple justice, should refrain from such an accusation."

"Every one knows," retorted Doo, "that you entered into relations with the enemy."

"I? Great God!"

"Do you not consider the Pandours then, as such?"

"I visited their chief solely as a relative. A glass of wine shared with him in his tent can hardly be construed into a dangerous alliance!"

"But you hoped to inherit great riches from this relative. That hope might well impel you to cross the frontier of Bohemia for all time."

"Why, what egregious folly! What more could I hope for than that which I already possessed in Berlin? Was

BARON DE TRENCK

I a poor adventurer seeking his fortune by his sword? Rich in my own right; enjoying to the full the king's favor; attached to the court by all that satisfied pride could demand, as well as by ties of the tenderest sentiments. What more was there for me to covet or to seek elsewhere?"

The major turned his head aside with an air of indifference.

"One single fact suffices to discount everything you have said, Baron," he replied dryly. "You have twice attempted to escape from the fortress. An innocent man awaits his trial with confidence, knowing that it cannot be other than favorable. The culprit alone flees."

Trenck, though quivering with blind rage, continued to maintain his former attitude, his features composed, his eyes fixed upon the major's sword.

"Sir," he said, "in three weeks, on the twenty-fifth of September, I shall have been a prisoner for one year. You in your position may not have found the time long, but to me it has dragged interminably. And it has been still harder for me to bear because I have not been able to count the days or hours which still separate me from justice and liberty. If I knew the limit set to my captivity—no matter what it may be—I could surely find resignation and patience to await it."

"It is most unfortunate, then," said the major, "that no one could give you that information."

"Say rather, would not," replied Trenck. "Surely, something of the matter must be known here. You, for instance, major, might tell me frankly what you think to be the case."

"Ah!" said Doo, assuming the self-satisfied manner of a jailer; "it would not be proper for me to answer that."

"You would save me from despair and revolt," replied Trenck warmly. "For I give you my word of honor that from the moment I know when my captivity is to terminate —no matter when that may be, or what my subsequent fate —I will make no further attempts to evade it by flight."

"And you want me to tell you——"

"Yes," interrupted Trenck, with a shudder; "yes, once again I ask you."

Doo smiled maliciously as he answered:

"The end of your captivity? Why, a traitor can scarcely hope for release!"

The heat of the day, the wine he had drunk, overwhelming anger and his fiery blood, all mounted to Trenck's head. Incapable of further self-restraint, he flung himself upon the major, tore the coveted sword from his side, dashed out of the chamber, flung the two sentinels at the door down the stairs, took their entire length himself at a single bound and sprang into the midst of the assembled guards.

Trenck fell upon them with his sword, showering blows right and left. The blade flashed snakelike in his powerful grasp, the soldiers falling back before the fierce onslaught. Having disabled four of the men, the prisoner succeeded in forcing his way past the remainder and raced for the first rampart.

There he mounted the rampart and, never stopping to gauge its height, sprang down into the moat, landing upon his feet in the bottom of the dry ditch. Faster still, he flew to the second rampart and scaled it as he had done the first, clambering up by means of projecting stones and interstices.

It was just past noon; the sun blazed full upon the scene and every one within the prison stood astounded at the miraculous flight in which Trenck seemed to fairly soar through the air. Those of the soldiers whom Trenck had not overthrown pursued, but with little hope of overtaking him. Their guns were unloaded so that they were unable to shoot after him. Not a soldier dared to risk trying to follow him by the road he had taken, over the ramparts and moats; for, without that passion for liberty which lent wings to the prisoner there was no hope of any of them scaling the walls without killing himself a dozen times over.

They were, therefore, compelled to make use of the regular passages to the outer posterns and these latter being located at a considerable distance from the prisoner's avenue of escape, he was certain, at the pace he was maintaining, to gain at least a half-hour's start over his pursuers.

Once beyond the walls of the prison, with the woods close

BARON DE TRENCK

by, it seemed as if Trenck's escape was assured beyond doubt.

He had now come to a narrow passageway leading to the last of the inner posterns which pierced the walls. Here he found a sentinel on guard and the soldier sprang up to confront him. But a soldier to overcome was not an obstacle to stop the desperate flight of the baron. He struck the man heavily in the face with his sword, stunning him and sending him rolling in the dust.

Once through the postern there now remained only a single palisade or stockade—a great fence constructed of iron bars and iron trellis-work, which constituted the outermost barrier between the fleeing prisoner and liberty. Once over that iron palisade he had only to dash into the woods and disappear.

But it was ordained that Trenck was not to overcome this last obstacle, simple as it appeared. At a fatal moment, his foot was caught between two bars of the palisade and he was unable to free himself.

While he was engaged in superhuman but futile efforts to release his foot, the sentinel of the passage, who had picked himself up, ran through the postern toward the palisade, followed by another soldier from the garrison. Together they fell upon Trenck, overwhelming him with blows with the butts of their muskets and secured him.

Bruised and bleeding he was borne back to his cell.

Major Doo informed Trenck, after this abortive attempt to escape, that he had been condemned to one year's imprisonment only. That year was within three weeks of expiring when the infamous major, who was an Italian, goaded the unfortunate young man into open defiance of his sovereign's mandate. His pardon was at once annulled and his confinement now became most rigorous.

Another plot, headed by three officers and several soldiers of the guard, who were friendly to Trenck, was discovered at the last moment—in time for the conspirators themselves to escape to Bohemia, but under circumstances which prevented Baron de Trenck from accompanying them.

This also served to increase the hardships of the prisoner's lot, and he now found himself deprived of the former companionship of his friends and surrounded by strangers, the one familiar face remaining being that of Lieutenant Bach, a Danish officer, a braggart swordsman and ruffler, who had always been hostile to him.

But, despite his isolation, the energy and strength of Trenck's character were only augmented by his misfortunes, and he never ceased to plot for his deliverance. Weeks passed without any fruitful event occurring in the life of the prisoner, yet help was to come to him from a source from which he could never have expected it. But before that fortuitous result was destined to take place—in fact, as preliminary to its achievement—he was destined to be an actor in the most remarkable scene that ever has been recorded in the annals of prison life, and in one of the strangest duels of modern times.

One day Trenck had cast himself fully clothed upon his bed, in order to obtain a change of position in his cramped place of confinement. Lieutenant Bach was on duty as his guard.

The young baron had retained in prison the proud and haughty demeanor which had formerly brought upon him so much censure at court. Lieutenant Bach's countenance also bore the imprint of incarnate pride.

The two exchanged from time to time glances of insolence; for the rest, they remained silently smoking, side by side.

Trenck was the first to break the silence, for prisoners grasp every opportunity for conversation, and at any price.

"It appears to me your hand is wounded, lieutenant," Trenck said. "Have you found another opportunity to cross swords?"

"Lieutenant Schell, it seemed to me, looked somewhat obliquely at me," replied the Dane. "Therefore, I indulged him in a pass or two directed against his right arm."

"Such a delicate youth, and so mild-mannered! Are you not ashamed?"

"What could I do? There was no one else at hand."

"Nevertheless he seems to have wounded you?"

"Yes, accidentally though, without knowing what he did."

BARON DE TRENCK

"The fact, then, of having been expelled from two regiments for your highhanded acts, and finally transferred to the garrison of the fortress of Glatz as punishment, has not cured you of your fire-eating propensities?"

"When a man has the reputation of being the best swordsman in Prussia he values that title somewhat more than your military rank, which any clumsy fool can obtain."

"You, the best swordsman!" exclaimed Trenck, concluding his remark with an ironical puff of smoke.

"I flatter myself that such is the case," retorted Bach, emitting in turn a great cloud of tobacco-smoke.

"If I were free," said Trenck, "I might, perhaps, prove to you in short order that such is not the case."

"Do you claim to be my master at that art?"

"I flatter myself that such is the case."

"That we shall soon see," cried Bach, flushing with rage.

"How can we? I am disarmed and a prisoner."

"Ah, yes, you make your claim out of sheer boastfulness, because you think we cannot put it to the test!"

"Truly, lieutenant, set me at liberty and I swear to you that on the other side of the frontier we will put our skill to the test as freely as you like!"

"Well, I am unwilling to wait for that. We will fight here, Baron Trenck."

"In this room?"

"After your assertion, I must either humble your arrogance or lose my reputation."

"I shall be glad to know how you propose to do so?"

"Ah, you talk of Bohemia because that country is far away. As for me, I prefer this one, because it affords an immediate opportunity to put the matter to the test."

"I should ask nothing better if it were not impossible."

"Impossible! You shall see if it be."

Bach sprang up. An old door, supported by a couple of benches, had been placed in the chamber for a table. He hammered at the worm-eaten wood and knocked off a strip which he split in half. One of these substitutes for rapiers he gave to Trenck, retaining the other himself, and both placed themselves on guard.

After the first few passes, Trenck sent his adversary's make-shift sword flying through space, and with his own he met the lieutenant full in the chest.

"Touché!" he cried.

"Heavens! It is true!" growled Bach. "But I'll have my revenge!"

He went out hastily. Trenck watched him in utter amazement and he was even more astounded when, an instant later, he saw Bach return with a couple of swords, which he drew out from beneath his uniform.

"Now," he said to Trenck, "it is for you to show what you can do with good steel!"

"You risk," returned the baron, smiling calmly, "you risk, over and above the danger of being wounded, losing that absolute superiority in matters of the sword of which you are so proud."

"Defend yourself, braggart!" shouted Bach. "Show your skill instead of talking about it."

He flung himself furiously upon Trenck. The latter, seeming only to trifle lightly with his weapon at first, parried his thrusts, and then pressed the attack in turn, wounding Bach severely in the arm.

The lieutenant's weapon clattered upon the floor. For an instant he paused, immovable, overcome by amazement; then an irresistible admiration—a supreme tenderness, invaded his soul. He flung himself, weeping, in Trenck's arms, exclaiming:

"You are my master!"

Then, drawing away from the prisoner, he contemplated him with the same enthusiasm, but more reflectively, and observed:

"Yes, baron, you far exceed me in the use of the sword; you are the greatest duelist of the day, and a man of your caliber must not remain longer in prison."

The baron was somewhat taken by surprise at this, but, with his usual presence of mind, he immediately set himself to derive such profit as he might from his guardian's extravagant access of affection.

"Yes, my dear Bach," he replied, "yes, I should be free for the reason you mention, and by every right, but where is the man who will assist me to escape from these walls?"

"Here, baron!" said the lieutenant. "You shall regain your freedom as surely as my name is Bach."

"Oh, I believe in you, my worthy friend," cried Trenck; "you will keep your word."

"Wait," resumed Bach reflectively. "You cannot leave the citadel without the assistance of an officer. I should compromise you at every step. You have just seen what a hot-tempered scatterbrain I am. But I have in mind one who admires you profoundly. You shall know who he is to-night, and together we will set you at liberty."

Bach did, in fact, redeem his promise. He introduced Lieutenant Schell, who was to be Trenck's companion during their arduous flight into Bohemia, into the prisoner's cell, and himself obtained leave of absence for the purpose of securing funds for his fellow conspirators. The plot was discovered before his return and Schell, warned of this by one of the governor's adjutants, hastened the day of their flight.

In scaling the first rampart, Schell fell and sprained his ankle so severely that he could not use it. But Trenck was equal to all emergencies. He would not abandon his companion. He placed him across his shoulders, and, thus burdened, climbed the outer barriers and wandered all night in the bitter cold, fleeing through the snow to escape his pursuers. In the morning, by a clever ruse, he secured two horses and, thus mounted, he and his companion succeeded in reaching Bohemia.

Trenck directed his course toward Brandenburg where his sister dwelt, near the Prussian and Bohemian frontiers, in the Castle of Waldau, for he counted upon her assistance to enable him to settle in a foreign land where he would be safe.

The two friends, reduced shortly to the direst poverty, parted with their horses and all but the most necessary wearing apparel. Even now, though in Bohemia, they were not free from pursuit. Impelled one night, through hunger and cold, to throw themselves upon the bounty of an inn-keeper, they found in him a loyal and true friend.

The worthy host revealed to them the true identity of four supposed traveling merchants, who had that day accosted them on the road and followed them to the inn. These men were, in fact, emissaries from the fortress of Glatz who had attempted to bribe him to betray the fugitives into their hands, for they were sworn to capture Trenck and his companion and return them dead or alive to the enraged governor of the fortress.

In the morning the four Prussians, the carriage, the driver, and the horses set forth and soon disappeared in the distance.

Two hours later the fugitives, fortified by a good breakfast, took their departure from the Ezenstochow inn, leaving behind them a man whom they, at least, esteemed as the greatest honor to mankind.

The travelers hastened toward Dankow. They chose the most direct route and tramped along in the open without a thought of the infamous spies who might already be on their track.

They arrived at nightfall at their destination, however, without further hindrance.

The next day they set out for Parsemachi, in Bohemia.

They started early, and a day in the open, together with a night's sleep, had almost obliterated the memory of their adventure at the inn.

The cold was intense. The day was gray with heavy clouds that no longer promised rain, but which shrouded the country with a pall of gloom. The wind swirled and howled, and though the two friends struggled to keep their few thin garments drawn closely about them, they still searched the horizon hopefully, thinking of the journey's end and the peaceful existence which awaited them. To their right, the aspect of the countryside had altered somewhat. Great wooded stretches spread away into the distance, while to the left all was yet free and open.

They had gone about half a mile past the first clump of trees when they noticed, through the swaying branches by the roadside, a motionless object around which several men busied themselves. With every step they gained a clearer impression of the nature of this obstacle until, at last, an expression of half-mockery, half-anger overspread their features.

"Now God forgive me!" exclaimed Schell finally, "but that is the infernal brown traveling carriage from the inn!"

"May the devil take me!" rejoined Trenck, "if I delay or flee a step from those miserable rascals."

And they strode sturdily onward.

As soon as they were within speaking distance, one of the Prussians, a big man in a furred cap, believing them to be wholly unsuspicious, called to them:

"My dear sirs, in heaven's name come help us! Our carriage has been overturned and it is impossible to get it out of this rut."

The friends had reached an angle of the road where a few withered tree branches alone separated them from the others. They perceived the brown body of the carriage, half open like a huge rat-trap, and beside it the forbidding faces of their would-be captors. Trenck launched these words through the intervening screen of branches:

"Go to the devil, miserable scoundrels that you are, and may you remain there!"

Then, swift as an arrow, he sped toward the open fields to the left of the highroad, feigning flight. The carriage, which had been overturned solely for the purpose of misleading them, was soon righted and the driver lashed his horses forward in pursuit of the fugitives, the four Prussians accompanying him with drawn pistols.

When they were almost within reaching distance of their prey they raised their pistols and shouted:

"Surrender, rascals, or you are dead men!"

This was what Trenck desired. He wheeled about and discharged his pistol, sending a bullet through the first Prussian's breast, stretching him dead upon the spot.

At the same moment Schell fired, but his assailants returned the shot and wounded him.

Trenck again discharged his pistol twice in succession. Then, as one of the Prussians, who was apparently still uninjured, took to flight across the plain he sped furiously after him. The pursuit continued some two or three hundred paces. The Prussian, as if impelled by some irresistible force, whirled around and Trenck caught sight of his blanched countenance and blood-stained linen. One of the shots had struck him!

Instantly Trenck put an end to the half-finished task with a sword thrust. But the time wasted on the Prussian had cost him dear. Returning hastily to the field of action, he perceived Schell struggling in the grasp of the two remaining Prussians. Wounded as he was, he had been unable to cope single-handed with them, and was rapidly being borne toward the carriage.

"Courage, Schell!" Trenck shouted. "I am coming!"

At the sound of his friend's voice Schell felt himself saved. By a supreme effort he succeeded in releasing himself from his captors.

Frantic with rage and disappointment, the Prussians again advanced to the attack upon the two wretched fugitives, but Trenck's blood was up. He made a furious onslaught upon them with his sword, driving them back step by step to their carriage, into which they finally tumbled, shouting to the driver in frantic haste to whip up his horses.

As the carriage dashed away the friends drew long breaths of relief and wiped away the blood and powder stains from their heated brows. Careless of their sufferings, these ironhearted men merely congratulated each other upon their victory.

"Ah, it's well ended, Schell," exclaimed Trenck, "and I rejoice that we have had this opportunity to chastise the miserable traitors. But you are wounded, my poor Schell!"

"It is nothing," the lieutenant replied carelessly; "merely a wound in the throat, and, I think, another in the head."

This was the last attempt for a considerable time to regain possession of Trenck's person. But the two friends suffered greatly from hardships and were made to feel more than once the cruelty of Prussian oppression. Even Trenck's sister, instigated thereto by her husband, who feared to incur the displeasure of Frederick the Great, refused the poor fugitives shelter, money, or as much as a crust of bread, and this after Trenck had jeopardized his liberty by returning to Prussian soil in order to meet her.

BARON DE TRENCK

It was at this period, when starvation stared the exiles in the face, that Trenck met the Russian General Liewen, a relative of Trenck's mother, who offered the Baron a captaincy in the Tobolsk Dragoons, and furnished him with the money necessary for his equipment. Trenck and Schell were now compelled to part, the latter journeying to Italy to rejoin relatives there, the baron to go to Russia, where he was to attain the highest eminence of grandeur.

Baron de Trenck, on his journey to Russia, passed through Danzig, which was at that time neutral territory, bordering upon the confines of Prussia. Here he delayed for a time in the hope of meeting with his cousin the Pandour. During the interim he formed an intimacy with a young Prussian officer named Henry, whom he assisted lavishly with money. Almost daily they indulged in excursions in the environs, the Prussian acting as guide.

One morning, while at his toilet, Trenck's servant, Karl, who was devoted to him body and soul, observed:

"Lieutenant Henry will enjoy himself thoroughly on your excursion to-morrow."

"Why do you say that, Karl?" asked the baron.

"Because he has planned to take your honor to Langführ at ten o'clock."

"At ten or eleven—the hour is not of importance."

"No! You must be there on the stroke of ten by the village clock. Langführ is on the Prussian border and under Prussian rule."

"Prussia!" exclaimed Trenck, shaking his head, which Karl had not finished powdering. "Are you quite sure?"

"Perfectly. Eight Prussians—non-commissioned officers and soldiers—will be in the courtyard of the charming little inn that Lieutenant Henry described so well. As soon as your honor crosses the threshold they will fall upon you and bear you off to a carriage which will be in waiting."

"Finish dressing my hair, Karl," said Trenck, recovering his wonted impassibility.

"Oh, for that matter," continued the valet, "they will have neither muskets nor pistols. They will be armed with swords only. That will leave them free to fall bodily upon your honor and to prevent you using your weapons."

"Is that all, Karl?"

"No. There will be two soldiers detailed especially for my benefit, so that I can't get away to give the alarm."

"Well, is that all!"

"No. The carriage is to convey your honor to Lavenburg, in Pomerania, and you must cross a portion of the province of Danzig to get there. Besides the under officers at the inn who will travel with your honor, two others will accompany the carriage on horseback to prevent any outcry while you are on neutral ground."

"Famously planned!"

"M. Reimer, the Prussian resident here, outlined the plot and appointed Lieutenant Henry to carry it out."

"Afterward, Karl?"

"That's all—this time—and it's enough!"

"Yes, but I regret that it should end thus, for your account has greatly interested me."

"Your honor may take it that all I have said is absolutely correct."

"But when did you obtain this information?"

"Oh, just now!"

"And from whom?"

"Franz, Lieutenant Henry's valet, when we were watching the horses beneath the big pines, while your honors waited in that roadside pavilion for the shower to pass over."

"Is his information reliable?"

"Of course! As no one suspected him, the whole matter was discussed freely before him."

"And he betrayed the secret?"

"Yes, because he greatly admires your honor and wasn't willing to see you treated so."

"Karl, give him ten ducats from my purse and tell him I will take him in my own service, for he has afforded me great pleasure. The outing to-morrow will be a hundred times more amusing than I had hoped—indeed more amusing than any I have ever undertaken in my life."

"Your honor will go to Langführ, then!"

"Certainly, Karl. We will go together, and you shall

BARON DE TRENCK

see if I misled you when I promised you a delightful morning."

As soon as Baron de Trenck had completed his toilet, he visited M. Scherer, the Russian resident, spent a few moments in private with him and then returned to his apartments for dinner.

Lieutenant Henry arrived soon afterward. Trenck found delight in the course of dissimulation to which he stood committed. He overwhelmed his guest with courteous attentions, pressing upon him the finest wines and his favorite fruits, meanwhile beaming upon him with an affection that overspread his whole countenance, and expatiating freely upon the delights of the morrow's ride.

Henry accepted his attentions with his accustomed dreamy manner.

The next morning, at half past nine, when the lieutenant arrived, he found Trenck awaiting him.

The two officers rode off, followed by their servants, and took the road to Langführ. Trenck's audacity was terrifying. Even Karl, who was well aware of his master's great ability and cleverness, was nevertheless uneasy, and Franz, who was less familiar with the baron's character, was in a state of the greatest alarm.

The country, beautiful with its verdant grasslands, its budding bushes and flowers, its rich fields of wheat, dotted with spring blossoms, revealed itself to their delighted eyes. In the distance glistened the tavern of Langführ, with its broad red and blue stripes and its tempting signboard that displayed a well-appointed festive table.

The low door in the wall that enclosed the tavern courtyard was still closed. Inside, to the right of that door, was a little terrace, and against the wall was an arbor formed of running vines and ivy.

Lieutenant Henry, pausing near a clump of trees some two hundred paces from the tavern, said:

"Baron, our horses will be in the way in that little courtyard. I think it would be well to leave them here in the care of our servants until our return."

Trenck assented readily. He sprang from his horse and tossed his bridle to his valet and Henry did the same.

CLEMENCE ROBERT

The path leading to the tavern was enchanting, with its carpet of flowers and moss, and the two young men advanced arm in arm in the most affectionate manner. Karl and Franz watched them, overwhelmed with anxiety.

The door in the wall had been partly opened as they approached and the young men saw, within the arbor on the terrace, the resident, Herr Reimer—his three-cornered hat on his powdered wig, his arms crossed on the top of the adjacent wall, as he awaited their coming.

As soon as the officers were within ear-shot, he called out:

"Come on, Baron de Trenck, breakfast is ready."

The two officers were almost at the threshold. Trenck slackened his pace somewhat; then he felt Henry grip his arm more closely and forcibly drag him toward the doorway.

Trenck energetically freed his arm, upon observing this movement that spoke so eloquently of betrayal, and twice struck the lieutenant, with such violence that Henry was thrown to the ground.

Reimer, the resident, realizing that Trenck knew of the plot, saw that the time had come to resort to armed intervention.

"Soldiers, in the name of Prussia, I command you to arrest Baron de Trenck!" he shouted to the men who were posted in the courtyard.

"Soldiers, in the name of Russia!" Trenck shouted, brandishing his sword, "kill these brigands who are violating the rights of the country."

At these words, six Russian dragoons emerged suddenly from a field of wheat and, running up, fell upon the Prussians who had rushed from the courtyard at the resident's command.

This unexpected attack took the Prussians by surprise. They defended themselves only half-heartedly and finally they fled in disorder, throwing away their weapons, and followed by the shots of the Russians.

Lieutenant Henry and four soldiers remained in the custody of the victors. Trenck dashed into the arbor to seize Resident Reimer, but the only evidence of that personage was his wig, which remained caught in the foliage at an opening in the rear of the arbor through which the resident had made his escape. Trenck then returned to the prisoners.

As a fitting punishment for the Prussian soldiers, he commanded his dragoons to give each of them fifty blows, to turn their uniforms wrongside out, to decorate their helmets with straw cockades, and to drive them thus attired across the frontier.

While his men proceeded to execute his orders, Trenck drew his sword and turned to Lieutenant Henry.

"And now, for our affair, lieutenant!" he exclaimed.

The unfortunate Henry, under the disgrace of his position, lost his presence of mind. Hardly knowing what he did, he drew his sword, but dropped it almost immediately, begging for mercy.

Trenck endeavored to force him to fight, without avail, then, disgusted with the lieutenant's cowardice, he caught up a stick and belabored him heartily, crying:

"Rogue, go tell your fellows how Trenck deals with traitors!"

The people of the inn, attracted by the noise of the conflict, had gathered around the spot, and, as the baron administered the punishment, they added to the shame of the disgraced lieutenant by applauding the baron heartily.

The punishment over and the sentence of the Prussians having been carried out, Trenck returned to the city with his six dragoons and the two servants.

In this affair, as throughout his entire career, Trenck was simply faithful to the rule which he had adopted to guide him through life:

"Always face danger rather than avoid it."

THE PASSAGE OF THE RED SEA
BY HENRY MURGER

THE PASSAGE OF THE RED SEA

By HENRY MURGER

FOR five or six years Marcel had been engaged upon the famous painting which he said was meant to represent the Passage of the Red Sea; and for five or six years this masterpiece in color had been obstinately refused by the jury. Indeed, from its constant journeying back and forth, from the artist's studio to the Musée, and from the Musée to the studio, the painting knew the road so well that one needed only to set it on rollers and it would have been quite capable of reaching the Louvre alone. Marcel, who had repainted the picture ten times, and minutely gone over it from top to bottom, vowed that only a personal hostility on the part of the members of the jury could account for the ostracism which annually turned him away from the Salon, and in his idle moments he had composed, in honor of those watch-dogs of the Institute, a little dictionary of insults, with illustrations of a savage irony. This collection gained celebrity and enjoyed, among the studios and in the Ecole des Beaux-Arts, the same sort of popular success as that achieved by the immortal complaint of Giovanni Bellini, painter by appointment to the Grand Sultan of the Turks; every dauber in Paris had a copy stored away in his memory.

For a long time Marcel had not allowed himself to be discouraged by the emphatic refusal which greeted him at each exposition. He was comfortably settled in his opinion that his picture was, in a modest way, the companion piece long awaited by the "Wedding of Cana," that gigantic masterpiece whose dazzling splendor the dust of three centuries has not dimmed. Accordingly, each year, at the time of the Salon, Marcel sent his picture to be examined by the jury. Only, in order to throw the examiners off the track and if possible to make them abandon the policy of ex-

---

Copyrighted 1907 The Frank A. Munsey Company.

clusion which they seemed to have adopted toward the "Passage of the Red Sea," Marcel, without in any way disturbing the general scheme of his picture, modified certain details and changed its title.

For instance, on one occasion it arrived before the jury under the name of the "Passage of the Rubicon!" but Pharaoh, poorly disguised under Cæsar's mantle, was recognized and repulsed with all the honors that were his due.

The following year, Marcel spread over the level plane of his picture a layer of white representing snow, planted a pine-tree in one corner, and clothing an Egyptian as a grenadier of the Imperial Guard, rechristened the painting the "Passage of the Beresina."

The jury, which on that very day had polished its spectacles on the lining of its illustrious coat, was not in any way taken in by this new ruse. It recognized perfectly well the persistent painting, above all by a big brute of a horse of many colors, which was rearing out of one of the waves of the Red Sea. The coat of that horse had served Marcel for all his experiments in color, and in private conversation he called it his synoptic table of fine tones, because he had reproduced, in their play of light and shade, all possible combinations of color. But once again, insensible to this detail, the jury seemed scarcely able to find blackballs enough to emphasize their refusal of the "Passage of the Beresina."

"Very well," said Marcel; "no more than I expected. Next year I shall send it back under the title of 'Passage des Panoramas.'"

"That will be one on them—on them—on them, them, them," sang the musician, Schaunard, fitting the words to a new air he had been composing—a terrible air, noisy as a gamut of thunderclaps, and the accompaniment to which was a terror to every piano in the neighborhood.

"How could they refuse that picture without having every drop of the vermilion in my Red Sea rise up in their faces and cover them with shame?" murmured Marcel, as he gazed at the painting. "When one thinks that it contains a good hundred crowns' worth of paint, and a million of genius, not to speak of the fair days of my youth, fast growing bald as my hat! But they shall never have the last word; until my

THE PASSAGE OF THE RED SEA

dying breath I shall keep on sending them my painting. I want to have it engraved upon their memory."

"That is certainly the surest way of ever getting it engraved," said Gustave Colline, in a plaintive voice, adding to himself: "That was a good one, that was—really a good one; I must get that off the next time I am asked out."

Marcel continued his imprecations, which Schaunard continued to set to music.

"Oh, they won't accept me," said Marcel. "Ah! the government pays them, boards them, gives them the Cross, solely for the one purpose of refusing me once a year, on the 1st of March. I see their idea clearly now—I see it perfectly clearly; they are trying to drive me to break my brushes. They hope, perhaps, by refusing my Red Sea, to make me throw myself out of the window in despair. But they know very little of the human heart if they expect to catch me with such a clumsy trick. I shall no longer wait for the time of the annual Salon. Beginning with to-day, my work becomes the canvas of Damocles, eternally suspended over their existence. From now on, I am going to send it once a week to each one of them, at their homes, in the bosom of their families, in the full heart of their private life. It shall trouble their domestic joy, it shall make them think that their wine is sour, their dinner burned, their wives bad-tempered. They will very soon become insane, and will have to be put in strait-jackets when they go to the Institute, on the days when there are meetings. That idea pleases me."

A few days later, when Marcel had already forgotten his terrible plans for vengeance upon his persecutors, he received a visit from Father Medicis. For that was the name by which the brotherhood called a certain Jew, whose real name was Soloman, and who at that time was well known throughout the bohemia of art and literature, with which he constantly had dealings. Father Medicis dealt in all sorts of bric-à-brac. He sold complete house-furnishings for from twelve francs up to a thousand crowns. He would buy anything, and knew how to sell it again at a profit. His shop, situated in the Place du Carrousel, was a fairy spot where one could find everything that one might wish. All the products of nature, all the creations of art, all that comes forth from the bowels of the earth or from the genius of man, Medicis found it profitable to trade in. His dealings included everything, absolutely everything that exists; he even put a price upon the Ideal. Medicis would even buy ideas, to use himself or to sell again. Known to all writers and artists, intimate friend of the palette, familiar spirit of the writing-desk, he was the Asmodeus of the arts. He would sell you cigars in exchange for the plot of a dime novel, slippers for a sonnet, a fresh catch of fish for a paradox; he would talk at so much an hour with newspaper reporters whose duty was to record the lively capers of the smart set. He would get you passes to the parliament buildings, or invitations to private parties; he gave lodgings by the night, the week, or the month to homeless artists, who paid him by making copies of old masters in the Louvre. The greenroom had no secrets for him; he could place your plays for you with some manager; he could obtain for you all sorts of favors. He carried in his head a copy of the almanac of twenty-five thousand addresses, and knew the residence, the name, and the secrets of all the celebrities, even the obscure ones.

In entering the abode of the bohemians, with that knowing air which characterized him, the Jew divined that he had arrived at a propitious moment. As a matter of fact, the four friends were at that moment gathered in council, and under the domination of a ferocious appetite were discussing the grave question of bread and meat. It was Sunday, the last day of the month. Fatal day, sinister of date!

The entrance of Medicis was accordingly greeted with a joyous chorus, for they knew that the Jew was too avaricious of his time to waste it in mere visits of civility; accordingly his presence always announced that he was open to a bargain.

"Good evening, gentlemen," said the Jew; "how are you?"

"Colline," said Rodolphe from where he lay upon the bed, sunk in the delights of maintaining a horizontal line, "practise the duties of hospitality and offer our guest a chair; a guest is sacred. I salute you, Abraham," added the poet.

Colline drew forward a chair which had about as much elasticity as a piece of bronze and offered it to the Jew.

THE PASSAGE OF THE RED SEA

Medicis let himself fall into the chair, and started to complain of its hardness, when he remembered that he himself had once traded it off to Colline in exchange for a profession of faith which he afterward sold to a deputy. As he sat down the pockets of the Jew gave forth a silvery sound, and this melodious symphony threw the four bohemians into a reverie that was full of sweetness.

"Now," said Rodolphe, in a low tone, to Marcel, "let us hear the song. The accompaniment sounds all right."

"Monsieur Marcel," said Medicis, "I have simply come to make your fortune. That is to say, I have come to offer you a superb opportunity to enter into the world of art. Art, as you very well know, Monsieur Marcel, is an arid road, in which glory is the oasis."

"Father Medicis," said Marcel, who was on coals of impatience, "in the name of fifty per cent, your revered patron saint, be brief."

"Here is the offer," rejoined Medicis. "A wealthy amateur, who is collecting a picture-gallery destined to make the tour of Europe, has commissioned me to procude for him a series of remarkable works. I have come to give you a chance to be included in this collection. In one word, I have come to purchase your 'Passage of the Red Sea.'"

"Money down?" asked Marcel.

"Money down," answered the Jew, sounding forth the full orchestra of his pockets.

"Go on, Medicis," said Marcel, pointing to his painting. "I wish to leave to you the honor of fixing for yourself the price of that work of art which is priceless."

The Jew laid upon the table fifty crowns in bright new silver.

"Keep them going," said Marcel; "that is a good beginning."

"Monsieur Marcel," said Medicis, "you know very well that my first word is always my last word. I shall add nothing more. But think; fifty crowns; that makes one hundred and fifty francs. That is quite a sum."

"A paltry sum," answered the artist; "just in the robe of my Pharaoh there is fifty crowns' worth of cobalt. Pay me at least something for my work."

THE PASSAGE OF THE RED SEA

"Hear my last word," replied Medicis. "I will not add a penny more; but, I offer dinner for the crowd, wines included, and after dessert I will pay in gold."

"Do I hear any one object?" howled Colline, striking three blows of his fist upon the table. "It is a bargain."

"Come on," said Marcel. "I agree."

"I will send for the picture to-morrow," said the Jew. "Come, gentlemen, let us start. Your places are all set."

The four friends descended the stairs, singing the chorus from "The Huguenots," "to the table, to the table."

Medicis treated the bohemians in a fashion altogether sumptuous. He offered them a lot of things which up to now had remained for them a mystery. Dating from this dinner, lobster ceased to be a myth to Schaunard, and he acquired a passion for that amphibian which was destined to increase to the verge of delirium.

The four friends went forth from this splendid feast as intoxicated as on a day of vintage. Their inebriety came near bearing deplorable fruits for Marcel, because as he passed the shop of his tailor, at two o'clock in the morning, he absolutely insisted upon awakening his creditor in order to give him, on account, the one hundred and fifty francs that he had just received. But a gleam of reason still awake in the brain of Colline held back the artist from the brink of this precipice.

A week after this festivity Marcel learned in what gallery his picture had found a place. Passing along the Faubourg Saint-Honoré, he stopped in the midst of a crowd that seemed to be staring at a sign newly placed above a shop. This sign was none other than Marcel's painting, which had been sold by Medicis to a dealer in provisions. Only the "Passage of the Red Sea" had once again undergone a modification and bore a new title. A steamboat had been added to it, and it was now called "In the Port of Marseilles." A flattering ovation arose among the crowd when they discovered the picture. And Marcel turned away delighted with this triumph, and murmured softly: "The voice of the people is the voice of God!"

THE WOMAN AND THE CAT
BY MARCEL PREVOST

THE WOMAN AND THE CAT

By MARCEL PREVOST

"YES," said our old friend Tribourdeaux, a man of culture and a philosopher, which is a combination rarely found among army surgeons; "yes, the supernatural is everywhere; it surrounds us and hems us in and permeates us. If science pursues it, it takes flight and cannot be grasped. Our intellect resembles those ancestors of ours who cleared a few acres of forest; whenever they approached the limits of their clearing they heard low growls and saw gleaming eyes everywhere circling them about. I myself have had the sensation of having approached the limits of the unknown several times in my life, and on one occasion in particular."

A young lady present interrupted him:

"Doctor, you are evidently dying to tell us a story. Come now, begin!"

The doctor bowed.

"No, I am not in the least anxious, I assure you. I tell this story as seldom as possible, for it disturbs those who hear it, and it disturbs me also. However, if you wish it, here it is:

"In 1863 I was a young physician stationed at Orléans. In that patrician city, full of aristocratic old residences, it is difficult to find bachelor apartments; and, as I like both plenty of air and plenty of room, I took up my lodging on the first floor of a large building situated just outside the city, near Saint-Euverte. It had been originally constructed to serve as the warehouse and also as the dwelling of a manufacturer of rugs. In course of time the manufacturer had failed, and this big barrack that he had built, falling out of repair through lack of tenants, had been sold for a song with all its furnishings. The purchaser hoped to make a future profit out of his purchase, for the city was growing in that direction;

and, as a matter of fact, I believe that at the present time the house is included within the city limits. When I took up my quarters there, however, the mansion stood alone on the verge of the open country, at the end of a straggling street on which a few stray houses produced at dusk the impression of a jaw from which most of the teeth have fallen out.

"I leased one-half of the first floor, an apartment of four rooms. For my bedroom and my study I took the two that fronted on the street; in the third room I set up some shelves for my wardrobe, and the other room I left empty. This made a very comfortable lodging for me, and I had, for a sort of promenade, a broad balcony that ran along the entire front of the building, or rather one-half of the balcony, since it was divided into two parts (please note this carefully) by a fan of ironwork, over which, however, one could easily climb.

"I had been living there for about two months when, one night in July on returning to my rooms, I saw with a good deal of surprise a light shining through the windows of the other apartment on the same floor, which I had supposed to be uninhabited. The effect of this light was extraordinary. It lit up with a pale, yet perfectly distinct, reflection, parts of the balcony, the street below, and a bit of the neighboring fields.

"I thought to myself, 'Aha! I have a neighbor!'

"The idea indeed was not altogether agreeable, for I had been rather proud of my exclusive proprietorship. On reaching my bedroom I passed noiselessly out upon the balcony, but already the light had been extinguished. So I went back into my room, and sat down to read for an hour or two. From time to time I seemed to hear about me, as though within the walls, light footsteps; but after finishing my book I went to bed, and speedily fell asleep.

"About midnight I suddenly awoke with a curious feeling that something was standing beside me. I raised myself in bed, lit a candle, and this is what I saw. In the middle of the room stood an immense cat gazing upon me with phosphorescent eyes, and with its back slightly arched. It was a magnificent Angora, with long fur and a fluffy tail, and of a remarkable color—exactly like that of the yellow silk that one sees in cocoons—so that, as the light gleamed upon its coat, the animal seemed to be made of gold.

"It slowly moved toward me on its velvety paws, softly rubbing its sinuous body against my legs. I leaned over to stroke it, and it permitted my caress, purring, and finally leaping upon my knees. I noticed then that it was a female cat, quite young, and that she seemed disposed to permit me to pet her as long as ever I would. Finally, however, I put her down upon the floor, and tried to induce her to leave the room; but she leaped away from me and hid herself somewhere among the furniture, though as soon as I had blown out my candle, she jumped upon my bed. Being sleepy, however, I didn't molest her, but dropped off into a doze, and the next morning when I awoke in broad daylight I could find no sign of the animal at all.

"Truly, the human brain is a very delicate instrument, and one that is easily thrown out of gear. Before I proceed, just sum up for yourselves the facts that I have mentioned: a light seen and presently extinguished in an apartment supposed to be uninhabited; and a cat of a remarkable color, which appeared and disappeared in a way that was slightly mysterious. Now there isn't anything very strange about that, is there? Very well. Imagine, now, that these unimportant facts are repeated day after day and under the same conditions throughout a whole week, and then, believe me, they become of importance enough to impress the mind of a man who is living all alone, and to produce in him a slight disquietude such as I spoke of in commencing my story, and such as is always caused when one approaches the sphere of the unknown. The human mind is so formed that it always unconsciously applies the principle of the causa sufficiens. For every series of facts that are identical, it demands a cause, a law; and a vague dismay seizes upon it when it is unable to guess this cause and to trace out this law.

"I am no coward, but I have often studied the manifestation of fear in others, from its most puerile form in children up to its most tragic phase in madmen. I know that it is fed and nourished by uncertainties, although when one actually sets himself to investigate the cause, this fear is often transformed into simple curiosity.

"I made up my mind, therefore, to ferret out the truth. I questioned my caretaker, and found that he knew nothing about my neighbors. Every morning an old woman came to look after the neighboring apartment; my caretaker had tried to question her, but either she was completely deaf or else she was unwilling to give him any information, for she had refused to answer a single word. Nevertheless, I was able to explain satisfactorily the first thing that I had noted —that is to say, the sudden extinction of the light at the moment when I entered the house. I had observed that the windows next to mine were covered only by long lace curtains; and as the two balconies were connected, my neighbor, whether man or woman, had no doubt a wish to prevent any indiscreet inquisitiveness on my part, and therefore had always put out the light on hearing me come in. To verify this supposition, I tried a very simple experiment, which succeeded perfectly. I had a cold supper brought in one day about noon by my servant, and that evening I did not go out. When darkness came on, I took my station near the window. Presently I saw the balcony shining with the light that streamed through the windows of the neighboring apartment. At once I slipped quietly out upon my balcony, and stepped softly over the ironwork that separated the two parts. Although I knew that I was exposing myself to a positive danger, either of falling and breaking my neck, or of finding myself face to face with a man, I experienced no perturbation. Reaching the lighted window without having made the slightest noise, I found it partly open; its curtains, which for me were quite transparent since I was on the dark side of the window, made me wholly invisible to any one who should look toward the window from the interior of the room.

"I saw a vast chamber furnished quite elegantly, though it was obviously out of repair, and lighted by a lamp suspended from the ceiling. At the end of the room was a low sofa upon which was reclining a woman who seemed to me to be both young and pretty. Her loosened hair fell over her shoulders in a rain of gold. She was looking at herself

THE WOMAN AND THE CAT

in a hand mirror, patting herself, passing her arms over her lips, and twisting about her supple body with a curiously feline grace. Every movement that he made caused her long hair to ripple in glistening undulations.

"As I gazed upon her I confess that I felt a little troubled, especially when all of a sudden the young girl's eyes were fixed upon me—strange eyes, eyes of a phosphorescent green that gleamed like the flame of a lamp. I was sure that I was invisible, being on the dark side of a curtained window. That was simple enough, yet nevertheless I felt that I was seen. The girl, in fact, uttered a cry, and then turned and buried her face in the sofa-pillows.

"I raised the window, rushed into the room toward the sofa, and leaned over the face that she was hiding. As I did so, being really very remorseful, I began to excuse and to accuse myself, calling myself all sorts of names, and begging pardon for my indiscretion. I said that I deserved to be driven from her presence, but begged not to be sent away without at least a word of pardon. For a long time I pleaded thus without success, but at last she slowly turned, and I saw that her fair young face was stirred with just the faintest suggestion of a smile. When she caught a glimpse of me she murmured something of which I did not then quite get the meaning.

" 'It is you,' she cried out; 'it is you!'

"As she said this, and as I looked at her, not knowing yet exactly what to answer, I was harassed by the thought: Where on earth have I already seen this face, this look, this very gesture? Little by little, however, I found my tongue, and after saying a few more words in apology for my unpardonable curiosity, and getting brief but not offended answers, I took leave of her, and, retiring through the window by which I had come, went back to my own room. Arriving there, I sat a long time by the window in the darkness, charmed by the face that I had seen, and yet singularly disquieted. This woman so beautiful, so amiable, living so near to me, who said to me, 'It is you,' exactly as though she had already known me, who spoke so little, who answered all my questions with evasion, excited in me a feeling of fear. She had, indeed, told me her name—Linda—and that was all. I tried in vain to drive away the remembrance of her greenish eyes, which in the darkness seemed still to gleam upon me, and of those glints which, like electric sparks, shone in her long hair whenever she stroked it with her hand. Finally, however, I retired for the night; but scarcely was my head upon the pillow when I felt some moving body descend upon my feet. The cat had appeared again. I tried to chase her away, but she kept returning again and again, until I ended by resigning myself to her presence; and, just as before, I went to sleep with this strange companion near me. Yet my rest was this time a troubled one, and broken by strange and fitful dreams.

"Have you ever experienced the sort of mental obsession which gradually causes the brain to be mastered by some single absurd idea—an idea almost insane, and one which your reason and your will alike repel, but which nevertheless gradually blends itself with your thought, fastens itself upon your mind, and grows and grows? I suffered cruelly in this way on the days that followed my strange adventure. Nothing new occurred, but in the evening, going out upon the balcony, I found Linda standing upon her side of the iron fan. We chatted together for a while in the half darkness, and, as before, I returned to my room to find that in a few moments the golden cat appeared, leaped upon my bed, made a nest for herself there, and remained until the morning. I knew now to whom the cat belonged, for Linda had answered that very same evening, on my speaking of it, 'Oh, yes, my cat; doesn't she look exactly as though she were made of gold?' As I said, nothing new had occurred, yet nevertheless a vague sort of terror began little by little to master me and to develop itself in my mind, at first merely as a bit of foolish fancy, and then as a haunting belief that dominated my entire thought, so that I perpetually seemed to see a thing which it was in reality quite impossible to see."

"Why, it's easy enough to guess," interrupted the young lady who had spoken at the beginning of his story.

"Linda and the cat were the same thing."

Tribourdeaux smiled.

"I should not have been quite so positive as that," he said, "even then; but I cannot deny that this ridiculous fancy

THE WOMAN AND THE CAT

haunted me for many hours when I was endeavoring to snatch a little sleep amid the insomnia that a too active brain produced. Yes, there were moments when these two beings with greenish eyes, sinuous movements, golden hair, and mysterious ways, seemed to me to be blended into one, and to be merely the double manifestation of a single entity. As I said, I saw Linda again and again, but in spite of all my efforts to come upon her unexpectedly, I never was able to see them both at the same time. I tried to reason with myself, to convince myself that there was nothing really inexplicable in all of this, and I ridiculed myself for being afraid both of a woman and of a harmless cat. In truth, at the end of all my reasoning, I found that I was not so much afraid of the animal alone or of the woman alone, but rather of a sort of quality which existed in my fancy and inspired me with a fear of something that was incorporeal—fear of a manifestation of my own spirit, fear of a vague thought, which is, indeed, the very worst of fears.

"I began to be mentally disturbed. After long evenings spent in confidential and very unconventional chats with Linda, in which little by little my feelings took on the color of love, I passed long days of secret torment, such as incipient maniacs must experience. Gradually a resolve began to grow up in my mind, a desire that became more and more importunate in demanding a solution of this unceasing and tormenting doubt; and the more I cared for Linda, the more it seemed absolutely necessary to push this resolve to its fulfilment. I decided to kill the cat.

"One evening before meeting Linda on the balcony, I took out of my medical cabinet a jar of glycerin and a small bottle of hydrocyanic acid, together with one of those little pencils of glass which chemists use in mixing certain corrosive substances. That evening for the first time Linda allowed me to caress her. I held her in my arms and passed my hand over her long hair, which snapped and cracked under my touch in a succession of tiny sparks. As soon as I regained my room the golden cat, as usual, appeared before me. I called her to me; she rubbed herself against me with arched back and extended tail, purring the while with the greatest amiability. I took the glass pencil in my hand, moistened the point in the glycerin, and held it out to the animal, which licked it with her long red tongue. I did this three or four times, but at the fourth time I dipped the pencil in the acid. The cat unhesitatingly touched it with her tongue. In an instant she became rigid, and a moment after, a frightful tetanic convulsion caused her to leap thrice into the air, and then to fall upon the floor with a dreadful cry—a cry that was truly human. She was dead!

"With the perspiration starting from my forehead and with trembling hands I threw myself upon the floor beside the body that was not yet cold. The starting eyes had a look that froze me with horror. The blackened tongue was thrust out between the teeth; the limbs exhibited the most remarkable contortions. I mustered all my courage with a violent effort of will, took the animal by the paws, and left the house. Hurrying down the silent street, I proceeded to the quays along the banks of the Loire, and, on reaching them, threw my burden into the river. Until daylight I roamed around the city, just where I know not; and not until the sky began to grow pale and then to be flushed with light did I at last have the courage to return home. As I laid my hand upon the door, I shivered. I had a dread of finding there still living, as in the celebrated tale of Poe, the animal that I had so lately put to death. But no, my room was empty. I fell half-fainting upon my bed, and for the first time I slept, with a perfect sense of being all alone, a sleep like that of a beast or of an assassin, until evening came."

Some one here interrupted, breaking in upon the profound silence in which we had been listening.

"I can guess the end. Linda disappeared at the same time as the cat."

"You see perfectly well," replied Tribourdeaux, "that there exists between the facts of this story a curious coincidence, since you are able to guess so exactly their relation. Yes, Linda disappeared. They found in her apartment her dresses, her linen, all even to the night-robe that she was to have worn that night, but there was nothing that could give the slightest clue to her identity. The owner of the house had let the apartment to 'Mademoiselle Linda, concert-singer.' He knew nothing more. I was summoned before the police magis-

THE WOMAN AND THE CAT

trate. I had been seen on the night of her disappearance roaming about with a distracted air in the vicinity of the river. Luckily the judge knew me; luckily also, he was a man of no ordinary intelligence. I related to him privately the entire story, just as I have been telling it to you. He dismissed the inquiry; yet I may say that very few have ever had so narrow an escape as mine from a criminal trial."

For several moments the silence of the company was unbroken. Finally a gentleman, wishing to relieve the tension, cried out:

"Come now, doctor, confess that this is really all fiction; that you merely want to prevent these ladies from getting any sleep to-night."

Tribourdeaux bowed stiffly, his face unsmiling and a little pale.

"You may take it as you will," he said.

GIL BLAS AND DR. SANGRADO
BY ALAIN RENE LE SAGE

GIL BLAS AND DR. SANGRADO

By ALAIN RENE LE SAGE

AS I was on my way, who should come across me but Dr. Sangrado, whom I had not seen since the day of my master's death. I took the liberty of touching my hat. He knew me in a twinkling.

"Heyday!" said he, with as much warmth as his temperament would allow him, "the very lad I wanted to see; you have never been out of my thought. I have occasion for a clever fellow about me, and pitched upon you as the very thing, if you can read and write."

"Sir," replied I, "if that is all you require, I am your man."

"In that case," rejoined he, "we need look no further. Come home with me; you will be very comfortable; I shall behave to you like a brother. You will have no wages, but everything will be found you. You shall eat and drink according to the true scientific system, and be taught to cure all diseases. In a word, you shall rather be my young Sangrado than my footman."

I closed in with the doctor's proposal, in the hope of becoming an Esculapius under so inspired a master. He carried me home forthwith, to install me in my honorable employment; which honorable employment consisted in writing down the name and residence of the patients who sent for him in his absence. There had indeed been a register for this purpose, kept by an old domestic; but she had not the gift of spelling accurately, and wrote a most perplexing hand. This account I was to keep. It might truly be called a bill of mortality; for my members all went from bad to worse during the short time they continued in this system. I was a sort of bookkeeper for the other world, to take places in the stage, and to see that the first come were the first served. My pen was always in my hand, for Dr. San-

ALAIN RENE LE SAGE

grado had more practise than any physician of his time in Valladolid. He had got into reputation with the public by a certain professional slang, humored by a medical face, and some extraordinary cures more honored by implicit faith than scrupulous investigation.

He was in no want of patients, nor consequently of property. He did not keep the best house in the world; we lived with some little attention to economy. The usual bill of fare consisted of peas, beans, boiled apples, or cheese. He considered this food as best suited to the human stomach; that is to say, as most amenable to the grinders, whence it was to encounter the process of digestion. Nevertheless, easy as was their passage, he was not for stopping the way with too much of them; and, to be sure, he was in the right. But though he cautioned the maid and me against repletion in respect of solids, it was made up by free permission to drink as much water as we liked. Far from prescribing us any limits in that direction, he would tell us sometimes:

"Drink, my children; health consists in the pliability and moisture of the parts. Drink water by pailfuls; it is a universal dissolvent; water liquefies all the salts. Is the course of the blood a little sluggish? This grand principle sets it forward. Too rapid? Its career is checked."

Our doctor was so orthodox on this head that, though advanced in years, he drank nothing himself but water. He defined old age to be a natural consumption which dries us up and wastes us away; on this principle he deplored the ignorance of those who call wine "old men's milk." He maintained that wine wears them out and corrodes them; and pleaded with all the force of his eloquence against that liquor, fatal in common both to the young and old—that friend with a serpent in its bosom—that pleasure with a dagger under its girdle.

In spite of these fine arguments, at the end of a week I felt an ailment which I was blasphemous enough to saddle on the universal dissolvent and the new-fangled diet. I stated my symptoms to my master, in the hope that he would relax the rigor of his regimen and qualify my meals with a little wine; but his hostility to that liquor was inflexible.

GIL BLAS AND DR. SANGRADO

"If you have not philosophy enough," said he, "for pure water, there are innocent infusions to strengthen the stomach against the nausea of aqueous quaffings. Sage, for example, has a very pretty flavor; and if you wish to heighten it into a debauch, it is only mixing rosemary, wild poppy, and other simples with it—but no compounds!"

In vain did he sing the praise of water, and teach me the secret of composing delicious messes. I was so abstemious that, remarking my moderation, he said:

"In good sooth, Gil Blas, I marvel not that you are no better than you are; you do not drink enough, my friend. Water taken in a small quantity serves only to separate the particles of bile and set them in action; but our practise is to drown them in a copious drench. Fear not, my good lad, lest a superabundance of liquid should either weaken or chill your stomach; far from thy better judgment be that silly fear of unadulterated drink. I will insure you against all consequences; and if my authority will not serve your turn, read Celsus. That oracle of the ancients makes an admirable panegyric on water; in short, he says in plain terms that those who plead an inconstant stomach in favor of wine, publish a libel on their own viscera, and make their constitution a pretense for their sensuality."

As it would have been ungenteel in me to run riot on my entrance into the medical career, I pretended thorough conviction; indeed, I really thought there was something in it. I therefore went on drinking water on the authority of Celsus; or, to speak in scientific terms, I began to drown the bile in copious drenches of that unadulterated liquor; and though I felt myself more out of order from day to day, prejudice won the cause against experience. It is evident therefore that I was in the right road to the practise of physic.

Yet I could not always be insensible to the qualms which increased in my frame, to that degree as to determine me on quitting Dr. Sangrado. But he invested me with a new office which changed my tone.

"Hark you, my child," said he to me one day; "I am not one of those hard and ungrateful masters who leave their household to grow gray in service without a suitable reward.

ALAIN RENE LE SAGE

I am well pleased with you, I have a regard for you; and without waiting till you have served your time, I will make your fortune. Without more ado, I will initiate you in the healing art, of which I have for so many years been at the head. Other physicians make the science to consist of various unintelligible branches; but I will shorten the road for you, and dispense with the drudgery of studying natural philosophy, pharmacy, botany, and anatomy. Remember, my friend, that bleeding and drinking warm water are the two grand principles—the true secret of curing all the distempers incident to humanity.

"Yes, this marvelous secret which I reveal to you, and which nature, beyond the reach of my colleagues, has not been able to conceal from me, is comprehended in these two articles, namely, bleeding and drenching. Here you have the sum total of my philosophy; you are thoroughly bottomed in medicine, and may raise yourself to the summit of fame on the shoulders of my long experience. You may enter into partnership at once, by keeping the books in the morning and going out to visit patients in the afternoon. While I dose the nobility and clergy, you shall labor in your vocation among the lower orders; and when you have felt your ground a little, I will get you admitted into our body. You are a philosopher, Gil Blas, though you have never graduated; the common herd of them, though they have graduated in due form and order, are likely to run out the length of their tether without knowing their right hand from their left."

I thanked the doctor for having so speedily enabled me to serve as his deputy; and by way of acknowledging his goodness, promised to follow his system to the end of my career, with a magnanimous indifference about the aphorisms of Hippocrates. But that engagement was not to be taken to the letter. This tender attachment to water went against the grain, and I had a scheme for drinking wine every day snugly among the patients. I left off wearing my own suit a second time to take up one of my master's and look like an experienced practitioner. After which I brought my medical theories into play, leaving those it might concern to look to the event.

GIL BLAS AND DR. SANGRADO

I began on an alguazil (constable) in a pleurisy; he was condemned to be bled with the utmost rigor of the law, at the same time that the system was to be replenished copiously with water. Next I made a lodgment in the veins of a gouty pastry-cook, who roared like a lion by reason of gouty spasms. I stood on no more ceremony with his blood than with that of the alguazil, and laid no restriction on his taste for simple liquids. My prescriptions brought me in twelve reales (shillings)—an incident so auspicious in my professional career that I only wished for the plagues of Egypt on all the hale citizens of Valladolid.

I was no sooner at home than Dr. Sangrado came in. I talked to him about the patients I had seen, and paid into his hands eight reales of the twelve I had received for my prescriptions.

"Eight reales!" said he, as he counted them. "Mighty little for two visits! But we must take things as we find them." In the spirit of taking things as he found them, he laid violent hands on six of the coins, giving me the other two. "Here, Gil Blas," continued he, "see what a foundation to build upon. I make over to you the fourth of all you may bring me. You will soon feather your nest, my friend; for, by the blessing of Providence, there will be a great deal of ill-health this year."

I had reason to be content with my dividend; since, having determined to keep back the third part of what I recovered in my rounds, and afterward touching another fourth of the remainder, then half of the whole, if arithmetic is anything more than a deception, would become my perquisite. This inspired me with new zeal for my profession.

The next day, as soon as I had dined, I resumed my medical paraphernalia and took the field once more. I visited several patients on the list, and treated their several complaints in one invariable routine. Hitherto things had gone well, and no one, thank Heaven, had risen up in rebellion against my prescriptions. But let a physician's cures be as extraordinary as they will, some quack or other is always ready to rip up his reputation.

I was called in to a grocer's son in a dropsy. Whom should I find there before me but a little black-looking phy-

ALAIN RENE LE SAGE

sician, by name Dr. Cuchillo, introduced by a relation of the family. I bowed round most profoundly, but dipped lowest to the personage whom I took to have been invited to a consultation with me.

He returned my compliment with a distant air; then, having stared me in the face for a few seconds, "Sir," said he, "I beg pardon for being inquisitive; I thought I was acquainted with all my brethren in Valladolid, but I confess your physiognomy is altogether new. You must have been settled but a short time in town."

I avowed myself a young practitioner, acting as yet under direction of Dr. Sangrado.

"I wish you joy," replied he politely; "you are studying under a great man. You must doubtless have seen a vast deal of sound practise, young as you appear to be."

He spoke this with so easy an assurance that I was at a loss whether he meant it seriously, or was laughing at me. While I was conning over my reply, the grocer, seizing on the opportunity, said:

"Gentlemen, I am persuaded of your both being perfectly competent in your art; have the goodness without ado to take the case in hand, and devise some effectual means for the restoration of my son's health."

Thereupon the little pulse-counter set himself about reviewing the patient's situation; and after having dilated to me on all the symptoms, asked me what I thought the fittest method of treatment.

"I am of opinion," replied I, "that he should be bled once a day, and drink as much warm water as he can swallow."

At these words, our diminutive doctor said to me, with a malicious simper, "And so you think such a course will save the patient?"

"Not a doubt of it," exclaimed I in a confident tone; "it must produce that effect, because it is a certain method of cure for all distempers. Ask Señor Sangrado."

"At that rate," retorted he, "Celsus is altogether in the wrong; for he contends that the readiest way to cure a dropsical subject is to let him almost die of hunger and thirst."

"Oh, as for Celsus," interrupted I, "he is no oracle of

GIL BLAS AND DR. SANGRADO

mine; he is as fallible as the meanest of us; I often have occasion to bless myself for going contrary to his dogmas."

"I discover by your language," said Cuchillo, "the safe and sure method of practise Dr. Sangrado instils into his pupils! Bleeding and drenching are the extent of his resources. No wonder so many worthy people are cut off under his direction!"

"No defamation!" interrupted I, with some acrimony. "A member of the faculty had better not begin throwing stones. Come, come, my learned doctor, patients can get to the other world without bleeding and warm water; and I question whether the most deadly of us has ever signed more passports than yourself. If you have any crow to pluck with Señor Sangrado, publish an attack on him; he will answer you, and we shall soon see who will have the best of the battle."

"By all the saints in the calendar," swore he in a transport of passion, "you little know whom you are talking to! I have a tongue and a fist, my friend; and am not afraid of Sangrado, who with all his arrogance and affectation is but a ninny."

The size of the little death-dealer made me hold his anger cheap. I gave him a sharp retort; he sent back as good as I brought, till at last we came to fisticuffs. We had pulled a few handfuls of hair from each other's head before the grocer and his kinsman could part us. When they had brought this about, they feed me for my attendance, and retained my antagonist, whom they thought the more skilful of the two.

Another adventure succeeded close on the heels of this. I went to see a huge singer in a fever. As soon as he heard me talk of warm water, he showed himself so adverse to this specific as to fall into a fit of swearing. He abused me in all possible shapes, and threatened to throw me out of the window. I was in a greater hurry to get out of his house than to get in.

I did not choose to see any more patients that day, and repaired to the inn where I had agreed to meet Fabricio. He was there first. As we found ourselves in a tippling humor, we drank hard, and returned to our employers in a pretty pickle; that is to say, so-so in the upper story. Señor Sangrado was not aware of my being drunk, because he took the lively gestures which accompanied the relation of my quarrel with the little doctor for an effect of the agitation not yet subsided after the battle. Besides, he came in for his share in my report; and, feeling himself nettled by the insults of Cuchillo—

"You have done well, Gil Blas," said he, "to defend the character of our practise against this little abortion of the faculty. So he takes upon him to set his face against watery drenches in dropsical cases? An ignorant fellow! I maintain, I do, in my own person, that the use of them may be reconciled to the best theories. Yes, water is a cure for all sorts of dropsies, just as it is good for rheumatisms and the green sickness. It is excellent, too, in those fevers where the effect is at once to parch and to chill; and even miraculous in those disorders ascribed to cold, thin, phlegmatic, and pituitous humors. This opinion may appear strange to young practitioners like Cuchillo, but it is right orthodox in the best and soundest systems; so that if persons of that description were capable of taking a philosophical view, instead of crying me down, they would become my most zealous advocates."

In his rage, he never suspected me of drinking; for to exasperate him still more against the little doctor, I had thrown into my recital some circumstances of my own addition. Yet, engrossed as he was by what I had told him, he could not help taking notice that I drank more water than usual that evening.

In fact, the wine had made me very thirsty. Any one but Sangrado would have distrusted my being so very dry as to swallow down glass after glass; but, as for him, he took it for granted in the simplicity of his heart that I had begun to acquire a relish for aqueous potations.

"Apparently, Gil Blas," said he, with a gracious smile, "you have no longer such a dislike to water. As Heaven is my judge, you quaff it off like nectar! It is no wonder, my friend; I was certain you would before long take a liking to that liquor."

"Sir," replied I, "there is a tide in the affairs of men;

GIL BLAS AND DR. SANGRADO

with my present lights I would give all the wine in Valladolid for a pint of water."

This answer delighted the doctor, who would not lose so fine an opportunity of expatiating on the excellence of water. He undertook to ring the changes once more in its praise; not like a hireling pleader, but as an enthusiast in a most worthy cause.

"A thousand times," exclaimed he, "a thousand and a thousand times of greater value, as being more innocent than all our modern taverns, were those baths of ages past, whither the people went, not shamefully to squander their fortunes and expose their lives by swilling themselves with wine, but assembling there for the decent and economical amusement of drinking warm water. It is difficult to admire enough the patriotic forecast of those ancient politicians who established places of public resort where water was dealt out gratis to all comers, and who confined wine to the shops of the apothecaries, that its use might be prohibited save under the direction of physicians. What a stroke of wisdom! It is doubtless to preserve the seeds of that antique frugality, emblematic of the golden age, that persons are found to this day, like you and me, who drink nothing but water, and are persuaded they possess a prevention or a cure for every ailment, provided our warm water has never boiled; for I have observed that water when it is boiled is heavier, and sits less easily on the stomach."

While he was holding forth thus eloquently, I was in danger more than once of splitting my sides with laughing. But I contrived to keep my countenance; nay, more, to chime in with the doctor's theory. I found fault with the use of wine, and pitied mankind for having contracted an untoward relish for so pernicious a beverage. Then, finding my thirst not sufficiently allayed, I filled a large goblet with water, and, after having swilled it like a horse—

"Come, sir," said I to my master, "let us drink plentifully of this beneficial liquor. Let us make those early establishments of dilution you so much regret live again in your house."

He clapped his hands in ecstasy at these words, and preached to me for a whole hour about suffering no liquid but water to pass my lips. To confirm the habit, I promised to drink a large quantity every evening; and to keep my word with less violence to my private inclinations, I went to bed with a determined purpose of going to the tavern every day.

A FIGHT WITH A CANNON
BY VICTOR HUGO

A FIGHT WITH A CANNON

By VICTOR HUGO

LA VIEUVILLE was suddenly cut short by a cry of despair, and at the same time a noise was heard wholly unlike any other sound. The cry and sounds came from within the vessel.

The captain and lieutenant rushed toward the gun-deck, but could not get down. All the gunners were pouring up in dismay.

Something terrible had just happened.

One of the carronades of the battery, a twenty-four pounder, had broken loose.

This is the most dangerous accident that can possibly take place on shipboard. Nothing more terrible can happen to a sloop of war in open sea and under full sail.

A cannon that breaks its moorings suddenly becomes some strange, supernatural beast. It is a machine transformed into a monster. That short mass on wheels moves like a billiard-ball, rolls with the rolling of the ship, plunges with the pitching, goes, comes, stops, seems to meditate, starts on its course again, shoots like an arrow from one end of the vessel to the other, whirls around, slips away, dodges, rears, bangs, crashes, kills, exterminates. It is a battering ram capriciously assaulting a wall. Add to this, the fact that the ram is of metal, the wall of wood.

It is matter set free; one might say, this eternal slave was avenging itself; it seems as if the total depravity concealed in what we call inanimate things has escaped, and burst forth all of a sudden; it appears to lose patience, and to take a strange mysterious revenge; nothing more relentless than this wrath of the inanimate. This enraged lump leaps like a panther, it has the clumsiness of an elephant, the nimbleness of a mouse, the obstinacy of an axe, the uncertainty of the billows, the zigzag of the lightning, the deafness of the grave. It weighs ten thousand pounds, and it rebounds like a child's ball. It spins and then abruptly darts off at right angles.

And what is to be done? How put an end to it? A tempest ceases, a cyclone passes over, a wind dies down, a broken mast can be replaced, a leak can be stopped, a fire extinguished, but what will become of this enormous brute of bronze? How can it be captured? You can reason with a bulldog, astonish a bull, fascinate a boa, frighten a tiger, tame a lion; but you have no resource against this monster, a loose cannon. You can not kill it, it is dead; and at the same time it lives. It lives with a sinister life which comes to it from the infinite. The deck beneath it gives it full swing. It is moved by the ship, which is moved by the sea, which is moved by the wind. This destroyer is a toy. The ship, the waves, the winds, all play with it, hence its frightful animation. What is to be done with this apparatus? How fetter this stupendous engine of destruction? How anticipate its comings and goings, its returns, its stops, its shocks? Any one of its blows on the side of the ship may stave it in. How foretell its frightful meanderings? It is dealing with a projectile, which alters its mind, which seems to have ideas, and changes its direction every instant. How check the course of what must be avoided? The horrible cannon struggles, advances, backs, strikes right, strikes left, retreats, passes by, disconcerts expectation, grinds up obstacles, crushes men like flies. All the terror of the situation is in the fluctuations of the flooring. How fight an inclined plane subject to caprices? The ship has, so to speak, in its belly, an imprisoned thunderstorm, striving to escape; something like a thunderbolt rumbling above an earthquake.

In an instant the whole crew was on foot. It was the fault of the gun captain, who had neglected to fasten the screw-nut of the mooring-chain, and had insecurely clogged the four wheels of the gun carriage; this gave play to the sole and the framework, separated the two platforms, and the breeching. The tackle had given way, so that the cannon was no longer firm on its carriage. The stationary breeching, which prevents recoil, was not in use at this time. A heavy sea struck the port, the carronade, insecurely fastened,

A FIGHT WITH A CANNON

had recoiled and broken its chain, and began its terrible course over the deck.

To form an idea of this strange sliding, let one imagine a drop of water running over a glass.

At the moment when the fastenings gave way, the gunners were in the battery, some in groups, others scattered about, busied with the customary work among sailors getting ready for a signal for action. The carronade, hurled forward by the pitching of the vessel, made a gap in this crowd of men and crushed four at the first blow; then sliding back and shot out again as the ship rolled, it cut in two a fifth unfortunate, and knocked a piece of the battery against the larboard side with such force as to unship it. This caused the cry of distress just heard. All the men rushed to the companion-way. The gun-deck was vacated in a twinkling.

The enormous gun was left alone. It was given up to itself. It was its own master and master of the ship. It could do what it pleased. This whole crew, accustomed to laugh in time of battle, now trembled. To describe the terror is impossible.

Captain Boisberthelot and Lieutenant la Vieuville, although both dauntless men, stopped at the head of the companion-way and, dumb, pale, and hesitating, looked down on the deck below. Some one elbowed past and went down.

It was their passenger, the peasant, the man of whom they had just been speaking a moment before.

Reaching the foot of the companion-way, he stopped.

The cannon was rushing back and forth on the deck. One might have supposed it to be the living chariot of the Apocalypse. The marine lantern swinging overhead added a dizzy shifting of light and shade to the picture. The form of the cannon disappeared in the violence of its course, and it looked now black in the light, now mysteriously white in the darkness.

It went on in its destructive work. It had already shattered four other guns and made two gaps in the side of the ship, fortunately above the water-line, but where the water would come in, in case of heavy weather. It rushed frantically against the framework; the strong timbers withstood the shock; the curved shape of the wood gave them great power of resistance; but they creaked beneath the blows of this huge club, beating on all sides at once, with a strange sort of ubiquity. The percussions of a grain of shot shaken in a bottle are not swifter or more senseless. The four wheels passed back and forth over the dead men, cutting them, carving them, slashing them, till the five corpses were a score of stumps rolling across the deck; the heads of the dead men seemed to cry out; streams of blood curled over the deck with the rolling of the vessel; the planks, damaged in several places, began to gape open. The whole ship was filled with the horrid noise and confusion.

The captain promptly recovered his presence of mind and ordered everything that could check and impede the cannon's mad course to be thrown through the hatchway down on the gun-deck—mattresses, hammocks, spare sails, rolls of cordage, bags belonging to the crew, and bales of counterfeit assignats, of which the corvette carried a large quantity—a characteristic piece of English villainy regarded as legitimate warfare.

But what could these rags do? As nobody dared to go below to dispose of them properly, they were reduced to lint in a few minutes.

There was just sea enough to make the accident as bad as possible. A tempest would have been desirable, for it might have upset the cannon, and with its four wheels once in the air there would be some hope of getting it under control. Meanwhile, the havoc increased.

There were splits and fractures in the masts, which are set into the framework of the keel and rise above the decks of ships like great, round pillars. The convulsive blows of the cannon had cracked the mizzenmast, and had cut into the mainmast.

The battery was being ruined. Ten pieces out of thirty were disabled; the breaches in the side of the vessel were increasing, and the corvette was beginning to leak.

The old passenger having gone down to the gun-deck, stood like a man of stone at the foot of the steps. He

A FIGHT WITH A CANNON

cast a stern glance over this scene of devastation. He did not move. It seemed impossible to take a step forward. Every movement of the loose carronade threatened the ship's destruction. A few moments more and shipwreck would be inevitable.

They must perish or put a speedy end to the disaster; some course must be decided on; but what? What an opponent was this carronade! Something must be done to stop this terrible madness—to capture this lightning—to overthrow this thunderbolt.

Boisberthelot said to La Vieuville:

"Do you believe in God, chevalier?"

La Vieuville replied:

"Yes—no. Sometimes."

"During a tempest?"

"Yes, and in moments like this."

"God alone can save us from this," said Boisberthelot.

Everybody was silent, letting the carronade continue its horrible din.

Outside, the waves beating against the ship responded with their blows to the shocks of the cannon. It was like two hammers alternating.

Suddenly, in the midst of this inaccessible ring, where the escaped cannon was leaping, a man was seen to appear, with an iron bar in his hand. He was the author of the catastrophe, the captain of the gun, guilty of criminal carelessness, and the cause of the accident, the master of the carronade. Having done the mischief, he was anxious to repair it. He had seized the iron bar in one hand, a tiller-rope with a slip-noose in the other, and jumped down the hatchway to the gun-deck.

Then began an awful sight; a Titanic scene; the contest between gun and gunner; the battle of matter and intelligence; the duel between man and the inanimate.

The man stationed himself in a corner, and, with bar and rope in his two hands, he leaned against one of the riders, braced himself on his legs, which seemed two steel posts, and livid, calm, tragic, as if rooted to the deck, he waited.

He waited for the cannon to pass by him.

The gunner knew his gun, and it seemed to him as if the gun ought to know him. He had lived long with it. How many times he had thrust his hand into his mouth! It was his own familiar monster. He began to speak to it as if it were his dog.

"Come!" he said. Perhaps he loved it.

He seemed to wish it to come to him.

But to come to him was to come upon him. And then he would be lost. How could he avoid being crushed? That was the question. All looked on in terror.

Not a breast breathed freely, unless perhaps that of the old man, who was alone in the battery with the two contestants, a stern witness.

He might be crushed himself by the cannon. He did not stir.

Beneath them the sea blindly directed the contest.

At the moment when the gunner, accepting this frightful hand-to-hand conflict, challenged the cannon, some chance rocking of the sea caused the carronade to remain for an instant motionless and as if stupefied. "Come, now!" said the man.

It seemed to listen.

Suddenly it leaped toward him. The man dodged the blow.

The battle began. Battle unprecedented. Frailty struggling against the invulnerable. The gladiator of flesh attacking the beast of brass. On one side, brute force; on the other, a human soul.

All this was taking place in semi-darkness. It was like the shadowy vision of a miracle.

A soul—strange to say, one would have thought the cannon also had a soul; but a soul full of hatred and rage. This sightless thing seemed to have eyes. The monster appeared to lie in wait for the man. One would have at least believed that there was craft in this mass. It also chose its time. It was a strange, gigantic insect of metal, having or seeming to have the will of a demon. For a moment this colossal locust would beat against the low ceiling overhead, then it would come down on its four wheels like a tiger on its four paws, and begin to run at

A FIGHT WITH A CANNON

the man. He, supple, nimble, expert, writhed away like an adder from all these lightning movements. He avoided a collision, but the blows which he parried fell against the vessel, and continued their work of destruction.

An end of broken chain was left hanging to the carronade. This chain had in some strange way become twisted about the screw of the cascabel. One end of the chain was fastened to the gun-carriage. The other, left loose, whirled desperately about the cannon, making all its blows more dangerous.

The screw held it in a firm grip, adding a thong to a battering-ram, making a terrible whirlwind around the cannon, an iron lash in a brazen hand. This chain complicated the contest.

However, the man went on fighting. Occasionally, it was the man who attacked the cannon; he would creep along the side of the vessel, bar and rope in hand; and the cannon, as if it understood, and as though suspecting some snare, would flee away. The man, bent on victory, pursued it.

Such things can not long continue. The cannon seemed to say to itself, all of a sudden, "Come, now! Make an end of it!" and it stopped. One felt that the crisis was at hand. The cannon, as if in suspense, seemed to have, or really had—for to all it was a living being—a ferocious malice prepense. It made a sudden, quick dash at the gunner. The gunner sprang out of the way, let it pass by, and cried out to it with a laugh, "Try it again!" The cannon, as if enraged, smashed a carronade on the port side; then, again seized by the invisible sling which controlled it, it was hurled to the starboard side at the man, who made his escape. Three carronades gave way under the blows of the cannon; then, as if blind and not knowing what more to do, it turned its back on the man, rolled from stern to bow, injured the stern and made a breach in the planking of the prow. The man took refuge at the foot of the steps, not far from the old man who was looking on. The gunner held his iron bar in rest. The cannon seemed to notice it, and without taking the trouble to turn around, slid back on the man, swift as the blow of an axe. The man, driven against the side of the ship, was lost. The whole crew cried out with horror.

But the old passenger, till this moment motionless, darted forth more quickly than any of this wildly swift rapidity. He seized a package of counterfeit assignats, and, at the risk of being crushed, succeeded in throwing it between the wheels of the carronade. This decisive and perilous movement could not have been made with more exactness and precision by a man trained in all the exercises described in Durosel's "Manual of Gun Practice at Sea."

The package had the effect of a clog. A pebble may stop a log, the branch of a tree turn aside an avalanche. The carronade stumbled. The gunner, taking advantage of this critical opportunity, plunged his iron bar between the spokes of one of the hind wheels. The cannon stopped. It leaned forward. The man, using the bar as a lever, held it in equilibrium. The heavy mass was overthrown, with the crash of a falling bell, and the man, rushing with all his might, dripping with perspiration, passed the slipnoose around the bronze neck of the subdued monster.

It was ended. The man had conquered. The ant had control over the mastodon; the pygmy had taken the thunderbolt prisoner.

The mariners and sailors clapped their hands.

The whole crew rushed forward with cables and chains, and in an instant the cannon was secured.

The gunner saluted the passenger.

"Sir," he said, "you have saved my life."

The old man had resumed his impassive attitude, and made no reply.

The man had conquered, but the cannon might be said to have conquered as well. Immediate shipwreck had been avoided, but the corvette was not saved. The damage to the vessel seemed beyond repair. There were five breaches in her sides, one, very large, in the bow; twenty of the thirty carronades lay useless in their frames. The one which had just been captured and chained again was disabled; the screw of the cascabel was sprung, and consequently leveling the gun made impossible. The battery

A FIGHT WITH A CANNON

was reduced to nine pieces. The ship was leaking. It was necessary to repair the damages at once, and to work the pumps.

The gun-deck, now that one could look over it, was frightful to behold. The inside of an infuriated elephant's cage would not be more completely demolished.

However great might be the necessity of escaping observation, the necessity of immediate safety was still more imperative to the corvette. They had been obliged to light up the deck with lanterns hung here and there on the sides.

However, all the while this tragic play was going on, the crew were absorbed by a question of life and death, and they were wholly ignorant of what was taking place outside the vessel. The fog had grown thicker; the weather had changed; the wind had worked its pleasure with the ship; they were out of their course, with Jersey and Guernsey close at hand, further to the south than they ought to have been, and in the midst of a heavy sea. Great billows kissed the gaping wounds of the vessel—kisses full of danger. The rocking of the sea threatened destruction. The breeze had become a gale. A squall, a tempest, perhaps, was brewing. It was impossible to see four waves ahead.

While the crew were hastily repairing the damages to the gun-deck, stopping the leaks, and putting in place the guns which had been uninjured in the disaster, the old passenger had gone on deck again.

He stood with his back against the mainmast.

He had not noticed a proceeding which had taken place on the vessel. The Chevalier de la Vieuville had drawn up the marines in line on both sides of the mainmast, and at the sound of the boatswain's whistle the sailors formed in line, standing on the yards.

The Count de Boisberthelot approached the passenger.

Behind the captain walked a man, haggard, out of breath, his dress disordered, but still with a look of satisfaction on his face.

It was the gunner who had just shown himself so skilful in subduing monsters, and who had gained the mastery over the cannon.

The count gave the military salute to the old man in peasant's dress, and said to him:

"General, there is the man."

The gunner remained standing, with downcast eyes, in military attitude.

The Count de Boisberthelot continued:

"General, in consideration of what this man has done, do you not think there is something due him from his commander?"

"I think so," said the old man.

"Please give your orders," replied Boisberthelot.

"It is for you to give them, you are the captain."

"But you are the general," replied Boisberthelot.

The old man looked at the gunner.

"Come forward," he said.

The gunner approached.

The old man turned toward the Count de Boisberthelot, took off the cross of Saint-Louis from the captain's coat and fastened it on the gunner's jacket.

"Hurrah!" cried the sailors.

The mariners presented arms.

And the old passenger, pointing to the dazzled gunner, added:

"Now, have this man shot."

Dismay succeeded the cheering.

Then in the midst of the death-like stillness, the old man raised his voice and said:

"Carelessness has compromised this vessel. At this very hour it is perhaps lost. To be at sea is to be in front of the enemy. A ship making a voyage is an army waging war. The tempest is concealed, but it is at hand. The whole sea is an ambuscade. Death is the penalty of any misdemeanor committed in the face of the enemy. No fault is reparable. Courage should be rewarded, and negligence punished."

These words fell one after another, slowly, solemnly, in a sort of inexorable metre, like the blows of an axe upon an oak.

And the man, looking at the soldiers, added:

"Let it be done."

A FIGHT WITH A CANNON

The man on whose jacket hung the shining cross of Saint-Louis bowed his head.

At a signal from Count de Boisberthelot, two sailors went below and came back bringing the hammock-shroud; the chaplain, who since they sailed had been at prayer in the officers' quarters, accompanied the two sailors; a sergeant detached twelve marines from the line and arranged them in two files, six by six; the gunner, without uttering a word, placed himself between the two files. The chaplain, crucifix in hand, advanced and stood beside him. "March," said the sergeant. The platoon marched with slow steps to the bow of the vessel. The two sailors, carrying the shroud, followed. A gloomy silence fell over the vessel. A hurricane howled in the distance.

A few moments later, a light flashed, a report sounded through the darkness, then all was still, and the sound of a body falling into the sea was heard.

The old passenger, still leaning against the mainmast, had crossed his arms, and was buried in thought.

Boisberthelot pointed to him with the forefinger of his left hand, and said to La Vieuville in a low voice:

"La Vendée has a head."

TONTON
BY A. CHENEVIERE

TONTON

By A. CHENEVIERE

THERE are men who seem born to be soldiers. They have the face, the bearing, the gesture, the quality of mind. But there are others who have been forced to become so, in spite of themselves and of the rebellion of reason and the heart, through a rash deed, a disappointment in love, or simply because their destiny demanded it, being sons of soldiers and gentlemen. Such is the case of my friend Captain Robert de X——. And I said to him one summer evening, under the great trees of his terrace, which is washed by the green and sluggish Marne.

"Yes, old fellow, you are sensitive. What the deuce would you have done on a campaign where you were obliged to shoot, to strike down with a sabre and to kill? And then, too, you have never fought except against the Arabs, and that is quite another thing."

He smiled, a little sadly. His handsome mouth, with its blond mustache, was almost like that of a youth. His blue eyes were dreamy for an instant, then little by little he began to confide to me his thought, his recollections and all that was mystic and poetic in his soldier's heart.

"You know we are soldiers in my family. We have a marshal of France and two officers who died on the field of honor. I have perhaps obeyed a law of heredity. I believe rather that my imagination has carried me away. I saw war through my reveries of epic poetry. In my fancy I dwelt only upon the intoxication of victory, the triumphant flourish of trumpets and women throwing flowers to the victor. And then I loved the sonorous words of the great captains, the dramatic representations of martial glory. My father was in the third regiment of zouaves, the one which was hewn in pieces at Reichshofen, in the Niedervald, and

---
Copyrighted 1901 Current Literature Publishing Company.

which in 1859 at Palestro, made that famous charge against the Austrians and hurled them into the great canal. It was superb; without them the Italian divisions would have been lost. Victor Emmanuel marched with the zouaves. After this affair, while still deeply moved, not by fear but with admiration for this regiment of demons and heroes, he embraced their old colonel and declared that he would be proud, were he not a king, to join the regiment. Then the zouaves acclaimed him corporal of the Third. And for a long time on the anniversary festival of St. Palestro, when the roll was called, they shouted 'Corporal of the first squad, in the first company of the first battalion, Victor Emmanuel,' and a rough old sergeant solemnly responded: 'Sent as king into Italy.'

"That is the way my father talked to us, and by these recitals, a soldier was made of a dreamy child. But later, what a disillusion! Where is the poetry of battle? I have never made any campaign except in Africa, but that has been enough for me. And I believe the army surgeon is right, who said to me one day: 'If instantaneous photographs could be taken after a battle, and millions of copies made and scattered through the world, there would be no more war. The people would refuse to take part in it.'"

"Africa, yes, I have suffered there. On one occasion I was sent to the south, six hundred kilometres from Oran, beyond the oasis of Fignig, to destroy a tribe of rebels. . . . On this expedition we had a pretty serious affair with a military chief of the great desert, called Bon-Arredji. We killed nearly all of the tribe, and seized nearly fifteen hundred sheep; in short, it was a complete success. We also captured the wives and children of the chief. A dreadful thing happened at that time, under my very eyes! A woman was fleeing, pursued by a black mounted soldier. She turned around and shot at him with a revolver. The horse-soldier was furious, and struck her down with one stroke of his sabre. I did not have the time to interfere. I dismounted from my horse to take the woman up. She was dead, and almost decapitated. I uttered not one word of reproach to the Turkish soldier, who smiled fiercely, and turned back.

TONTON

"I placed the poor body sadly on the sand, and was going to remount my horse, when I perceived, a few steps back, behind a thicket, a little girl five or six years old. I recognized at once that she was a Touareg, of white race, notwithstanding her tawny color. I approached her. Perhaps she was not afraid of me, because I was white like herself. I took her on the saddle with me, without resistance on her part, and returned slowly to the place where we were to camp for the night. I expected to place her under the care of the women whom we had taken prisoners, and were carrying away with us. But all refused, saying that she was a vile little Touareg, belonging to a race which carries misfortune with it and brings forth only traitors.

"I was greatly embarrassed. I would not abandon the child.... I felt somewhat responsible for the crime, having been one of those who had directed the massacre. I had made an orphan! I must take her part. One of the prisoners of the band had said to me (I understood a little of the gibberish of these people) that if I left the little one to these women they would kill her because she was the daughter of a Touareg, whom the chief had preferred to them, and that they hated the petted, spoiled child, whom he had given rich clothes and jewels. What was to be done?

"I had a wide-awake orderly, a certain Michel of Batignolles. I called him and said to him: 'Take care of the little one.' 'Very well, Captain, I will take her in charge.' He then petted the child, made her sociable, and led her away with him, and two hours later he had manufactured a little cradle for her out of biscuit boxes which are used on the march for making coffins. In the evening Michel put her to bed in it. He had christened her 'Tonton,' an abbreviation of Touareg. In the morning the cradle was bound on an ass, and behold Tonton following the column with the baggage, in the convoy of the rear guard, under the indulgent eye of Michel.

"This lasted for days and weeks. In the evening at the halting place, Tonton was brought into my tent, with the goat, which furnished her the greater part of her meals, and her inseparable friend, a large chameleon, captured by

Michel, and responding or not responding to the name of Achilles.

"Ah, well! old fellow, you may believe me or not; but it gave me pleasure to see the little one sleeping in her cradle, during the short night full of alarm, when I felt the weariness of living, the dull sadness of seeing my companions dying, one by one, leaving the caravan; the enervation of the perpetual state of alertness, always attacking or being attacked, for weeks and months. I, with the gentle instincts of a civilized man, was forced to order the beheading of spies and traitors, the binding of women in chains and the kidnapping of children, to raid the herds, to make of myself an Attila. And this had to be done without a moment of wavering, and I the cold and gentle Celt, whom you know, remained there, under the scorching African sun. Then what repose of soul, what strange meditations were mine, when free at last, at night, in my sombre tent, around which death might be prowling, I could watch the little Touareg, saved by me, sleeping in her cradle by the side of her chameleon lizard. Ridiculous, is it not? But, go there and lead the life of a brute, of a plunderer and assassin, and you will see how at times your civilized imagination will wander away to take refuge from itself.

"I could have rid myself of Tonton. In an oasis we met some rebels, bearing a flag of truce, and exchanged the women for guns and ammunition. I kept the little one, notwithstanding the five months of march we must make, before returning to Tlemcen. She had grown gentle, was inclined to be mischievous, but was yielding and almost affectionate with me. She ate with the rest, never wanting to sit down, but running from one to another around the table. She had proud little manners, as if she knew herself to be a daughter of the chief's favorite, obeying only the officers and treating Michel with an amusing scorn. All this was to have a sad ending. One day I did not find the chameleon in the cradle, though I remembered to have seen it there the evening before. I had even taken it in my hands and caressed it before Tonton, who had just gone to bed. Then I had given it back to her and gone out. Accordingly I questioned her. She took me by the hand, and leading me

TONTON

to the camp fire, showed me the charred skeleton of the chameleon, explaining to me, as best she could, that she had thrown it in the fire, because I had petted it! Oh! women! women! And she gave a horrible imitation of the lizard, writhing in the midst of the flames, and she smiled with delighted eyes. I was indignant. I seized her by the arm, shook her a little, and finished by boxing her ears.

"My dear fellow, from that day she appeared not to know me. Tonton and I sulked; we were angry. However, one morning, as I felt the sun was going to be terrible, I went myself to the baggage before the loading for departure, and arranged a sheltering awning over the cradle. Then to make peace, I embraced my little friend. But as soon as we were on the march, she furiously tore off the canvas with which I had covered the cradle. Michel put it all in place again, and there was a new revolt. In short, it was necessary to yield because she wanted to be able to lean outside of her box, under the fiery sun, to look at the head of the column, of which I had the command. I saw this on arriving at the resting place. Then Michel brought her under my tent. She had not yet fallen asleep, but followed with her eyes all of my movements, with a grave air, without a smile, or gleam of mischief.

"She refused to eat and drink; the next day she was ill, with sunken eyes and body burning with fever. When the major wished to give her medicine she refused to take it and ground her teeth together to keep from swallowing.

"There remained still six days' march before arriving at Oran. I wanted to give her into the care of the nuns. She died before I could do so, very suddenly, with a severe attack of meningitis. She never wanted to see me again. She was buried under a clump of African shrubs near Géryville, in her little campaign cradle. And do you know what was found in her cradle? The charred skeleton of the poor chameleon, which had been the indirect cause of her death. Before leaving the bivouac, where she had committed her crime, she had picked it out of the glowing embers, and brought it into the cradle, and that is why her little fingers were burned. Since the beginning of the meningitis the major had never been able to explain the cause of these burns."

Robert was silent for an instant, then murmured: "Poor little one! I feel remorseful. If I had not given her that blow. . . . who knows? . . . she would perhaps be living still. . . .

"My story is sad, is it not? Ah, well, it is still the sweetest of my African memories. War is beautiful! Eh?"

And Robert shrugged his shoulders. . . .

THE LAST LESSON
BY ALPHONSE DAUDET

THE LAST LESSON

By ALPHONSE DAUDET

I STARTED for school very late that morning and was in great dread of a scolding, especially because M. Hamel had said that he would question us on participles, and I did not know the first word about them. For a moment I thought of running away and spending the day out of doors. It was so warm, so bright! The birds were chirping at the edge of the woods; and in the open field back of the saw-mill the Prussian soldiers were drilling. It was all much more tempting than the rule for participles, but I had the strength to resist, and hurried off to school.

When I passed the town hall there was a crowd in front of the bulletin-board. For the last two years all our bad news had come from there—the lost battles, the draft, the orders of the commanding officer—and I thought to myself, without stopping:

"What can be the matter now?"

Then, as I hurried by as fast as I could go, the blacksmith, Wachter, who was there, with his apprentice, reading the bulletin, called after me:

"Don't go so fast, bub; you'll get to your school in plenty of time!"

I thought he was making fun of me, and reached M. Hamel's little garden all out of breath.

Usually, when school began, there was a great bustle, which could be heard out in the street, the opening and closing of desks, lessons repeated in unison, very loud, with our hands over our ears to understand better, and the teacher's great ruler rapping on the table. But now it was all so still! I had counted on the commotion to get to my desk without being seen; but, of course, that day everything had to be as quiet as Sunday morning. Through the

Copyrighted 1909 The Frank A. Munsey Company.

ALPHONSE DAUDET

window I saw my classmates, already in their places, and M. Hamel walking up and down with his terrible iron ruler under his arm. I had to open the door and go in before everybody. You can imagine how I blushed and how frightened I was.

But nothing happened. M. Hamel saw me and said very kindly:

"Go to your place quickly, little Franz. We were beginning without you."

I jumped over the bench and sat down at my desk. Not till then, when I had got a little over my fright, did I see that our teacher had on his beautiful green coat, his frilled shirt, and the little black silk cap, all embroidered, that he never wore except on inspection and prize days. Besides, the whole school seemed so strange and solemn. But the thing that surprised me most was to see, on the back benches that were always empty, the village people sitting quietly like ourselves; old Hauser, with his three-cornered hat, the former mayor, the former postmaster, and several others besides. Everybody looked sad; and Hauser had brought an old primer, thumbed at the edges, and he held it open on his knees with his great spectacles lying across the pages.

While I was wondering about it all, M. Hamel mounted his chair, and, in the same grave and gentle tone which he had used to me, he said:

"My children, this is the last lesson I shall give you. The order has come from Berlin to teach only German in the schools of Alsace and Lorraine. The new master comes to-morrow. This is your last French lesson. I want you to be very attentive."

What a thunder-clap these words were to me!

Oh, the wretches; that was what they had put up at the town-hall!

My last French lesson! Why, I hardly knew how to write! I should never learn any more! I must stop there, then! Oh, how sorry I was for not learning my lessons, for seeking birds' eggs, or going sliding on the Soar! My books, that had seemed such a nuisance a while ago, so heavy to carry, my grammar, and my history of the saints, were old friends now that I couldn't give up. And M.

THE LAST LESSON

Hamel, too; the idea that he was going away, that I should never see him again, made me forget all about his ruler and how cranky he was.

Poor man! It was in honor of this last lesson that he had put on his fine Sunday-clothes, and now I understood why the old men of the village were sitting there in the back of the room. It was because they were sorry, too, that they had not gone to school more. It was their way of thanking our master for his forty years of faithful service and of showing their respect for the country that was theirs no more.

While I was thinking of all this, I heard my name called. It was my turn to recite. What would I not have given to be able to say that dreadful rule for the participle all through, very loud and clear, and without one mistake? But I got mixed up on the first words and stood there, holding on to my desk, my heart beating, and not daring to look up. I heard M. Hamel say to me:

"I won't scold you, little Franz; you must feel bad enough. See how it is! Every day we have said to ourselves: 'Bah! I've plenty of time. I'll learn it to-morrow.' And now you see where we've come out. Ah, that's the great trouble with Alsace; she puts off learning till to-morrow. Now those fellows out there will have the right to say to you: 'How is it; you pretend to be Frenchmen, and yet you can neither speak nor write your own language?' But you are not the worst, poor little Franz. We've all a great deal to reproach ourselves with.

"Your parents were not anxious enough to have you learn. They preferred to put you to work on a farm or at the mills, so as to have a little more money. And I? I've been to blame also. Have I not often sent you to water my flowers instead of learning your lessons? And when I wanted to go fishing, did I not just give you a holiday?"

Then, from one thing to another, M. Hamel went on to talk of the French language, saying that it was the most beautiful language in the world—the clearest, the most logical; that we must guard it among us and never forget it, because when a people are enslaved, as long as they hold fast to their language it is as if they had the key to their prison. Then he opened a grammar and read us our lesson. I was amazed to see how well I understood it. All he said seemed so easy, so easy! I think, too, that I had never listened so carefully, and that he had never explained everything with so much patience. It seemed almost as if the poor man wanted to give us all he knew before going away, and to put it all into our heads at one stroke.

After the grammar, we had a lesson in writing. That day M. Hamel had new copies for us, written in a beautiful round hand: France, Alsace, France, Alsace. They looked like little flags floating everywhere in the school-room, hung from the rod at the top of our desks. You ought to have seen how every one set to work, and how quiet it was! The only sound was the scratching of the pens over the paper. Once some beetles flew in; but nobody paid any attention to them, not even the littlest ones, who worked right on tracing their fish-hooks, as if that was French, too. On the roof the pigeons cooed very low, and I thought to myself:

"Will they make them sing in German, even the pigeons?"

Whenever I looked up from my writing I saw M. Hamel sitting motionless in his chair and gazing first at one thing, then at another, as if he wanted to fix in his mind just how everything looked in that little school-room. Fancy! For forty years he had been there in the same place, with his garden outside the window and his class in front of him, just like that. Only the desks and benches had been worn smooth; the walnut-trees in the garden were taller, and the hop-vine that he had planted himself twined about the windows to the roof. How it must have broken his heart to leave it all, poor man; to hear his sister moving about in the room above, packing their trunks! For they must leave the country next day.

But he had the courage to hear every lesson to the very last. After the writing, we had a lesson in history, and then the babies chanted their ba, be, bi, bo, bu. Down there at the back of the room old Hauser had put on his spectacles and, holding his primer in both hands, spelled the letters with them. You could see that he, too, was crying; his voice trembled with emotion, and it was so funny to

THE LAST LESSON

hear him that we all wanted to laugh and cry. Ah, how well I remember it, that last lesson!

All at once the church-clock struck twelve. Then the Angelus. At the same moment the trumpets of the Prussians, returning from drill, sounded under our windows. M. Hamel stood up, very pale, in his chair. I never saw him look so tall.

"My friends," said he, "I—I—" But something choked him. He could not go on.

Then he turned to the blackboard, took a piece of chalk, and, bearing on with all his might, he wrote as large as he could:

"Vive La France!"

Then he stopped and leaned his head against the wall, and, without a word, he made a gesture to us with his hand:

"School is dismissed—you may go."

CROISILLES
BY ALFRED DE MUSSET

CROISILLES

By ALFRED DE MUSSET

I

AT the beginning of the reign of Louis XV., a young man named Croisilles, son of a goldsmith, was returning from Paris to Havre, his native town. He had been intrusted by his father with the transaction of some business, and his trip to the great city having turned out satisfactorily, the joy of bringing good news caused him to walk the sixty leagues more gaily and briskly than was his wont; for, though he had a rather large sum of money in his pocket, he travelled on foot for pleasure. He was a good-tempered fellow, and not without wit, but so very thoughtless and flighty that people looked upon him as being rather weak-minded. His doublet buttoned awry, his periwig flying to the wind, his hat under his arm, he followed the banks of the Seine, at times finding enjoyment in his own thoughts and again indulging in snatches of song; up at daybreak, supping at wayside inns, and always charmed with this stroll of his through one of the most beautiful regions of France. Plundering the apple-trees of Normandy on his way, he puzzled his brain to find rhymes (for all these rattlepates are more or less poets), and tried hard to turn out a madrigal for a certain fair damsel of his native place. She was no less than a daughter of a fermier-général, Mademoiselle Godeau, the pearl of Havre, a rich heiress, and much courted. Croisilles was not received at M. Godeau's otherwise than in a casual sort of way, that is to say, he had sometimes himself taken there articles of jewelry purchased at his father's. M. Godeau, whose somewhat vulgar surname ill-fitted his immense fortune, avenged himself by his arrogance for the stigma of his birth, and showed himself on all occasions

Copyrighted 1888 Brentano.

enormously and pitilessly rich. He certainly was not the man to allow the son of a goldsmith to enter his drawing-room; but, as Mademoiselle Godeau had the most beautiful eyes in the world, and Croisilles was not ill-favored; and as nothing can prevent a fine fellow from falling in love with a pretty girl, Croisilles adored Mademoiselle Godeau, who did not seem vexed thereat. Thus was he thinking of her as he turned his steps toward Havre; and, as he had never reflected seriously upon anything, instead of thinking of the invincible obstacles which separated him from his lady-love, he busied himself only with finding a rhyme for the Christian name she bore. Mademoiselle Godeau was called Julie, and the rhyme was found easily enough. So Croisilles, having reached Honfleur, embarked with a satisfied heart, his money and his madrigal in his pocket, and as soon as he jumped ashore ran to the paternal house.

He found the shop closed, and knocked again and again, not without astonishment and apprehension, for it was not a holiday; but nobody came. He called his father, but in vain. He went to a neighbor's to ask what had happened; instead of replying, the neighbor turned away, as though not wishing to recognize him. Croisilles repeated his questions; he learned that his father, his affairs having long been in an embarrassed condition, had just become bankrupt, and had fled to America, abandoning to his creditors all that he possessed.

Not realizing as yet the extent of his misfortune, Croisilles felt overwhelmed by the thought that he might never again see his father. It seemed to him incredible that he should be thus suddenly abandoned; he tried to force an entrance into the store; but was given to understand that the official seals had been affixed; so he sat down on a stone, and giving way to his grief, began to weep piteously, deaf to the consolations of those around him, never ceasing to call his father's name, though he knew him to be already far away. At last he rose, ashamed at seeing a crowd about him, and, in the most profound despair, turned his steps towards the harbor.

On reaching the pier, he walked straight before him like

CROISILLES

a man in a trance, who knows neither where he is going, nor what is to become of him. He saw himself irretrievably lost, possessing no longer a shelter, no means of rescue and, of course, no longer any friends. Alone, wandering on the sea-shore, he felt tempted to drown himself, then and there. Just at the moment when, yielding to this thought, he was advancing to the edge of a high cliff, an old servant named Jean, who had served his family for a number of years, arrived on the scene.

"Ah! my poor Jean!" he exclaimed, "you know all that has happened since I went away. Is it possible that my father could leave us without warning, without farewell?"

"He is gone," answered Jean, "but indeed not without saying good-bye to you."

At the same time he drew from his pocket a letter, which he gave to his young master. Croisilles recognized the handwriting of his father, and, before opening the letter, kissed it rapturously; but it contained only a few words. Instead of feeling his trouble softened, it seemed to the young man still harder to bear. Honorable until then, and known as such, the old gentleman, ruined by an unforeseen disaster (the bankruptcy of a partner), had left for his son nothing but a few commonplace words of consolation, and no hope, except, perhaps, that vague hope without aim or reason, which constitutes, it is said, the last possession one loses.

"Jean, my friend, you carried me in your arms," said Croisilles, when he had read the letter, "and you certainly are to-day the only being who loves me at all; it is a very sweet thing to me, but a very sad one for you; for, as sure as my father embarked there, I will throw myself into the same sea which is bearing him away; not before you nor at once, but some day I will do it, for I am lost."

"What can you do?" replied Jean, not seeming to have understood, but holding fast to the skirt of Croisilles' coat; "What can you do, my dear master? Your father was deceived; he was expecting money which did not come, and it was no small amount either. Could he stay here? I have seen him, sir, as he made his fortune, during the thirty years that I served him; I have seen him working, attending to his business, the crown-pieces coming in one by one. He was an honorable man, and skilful; they took a cruel advantage of him. Within the last few days, I was still there, and as fast as the crowns came in, I saw them go out of the shop again. Your father paid all he could, for a whole day, and, when his desk was empty, he could not help telling me, pointing to a drawer where but six francs remained: 'There were a hundred thousand francs there this morning!' That does not look like a rascally failure, sir? There is nothing in it that can dishonor you."

"I have no more doubt of my father's integrity," answered Croisilles, "than I have of his misfortune. Neither do I doubt his affection. But I wish I could have kissed him, for what is to become of me? I am not accustomed to poverty, I have not the necessary cleverness to build up my fortune. And, if I had it, my father is gone. It took him thirty years, how long would it take me to repair this disaster? Much longer. And will he be living then? Certainly not; he will die over there, and I cannot even go and find him; I can join him only by dying."

Utterly distressed as Croisilles was, he possessed much religious feeling. Although his despondency made him wish for death, he hesitated to take his life. At the first words of this interview, he had taken hold of old Jean's arm, and thus both returned to the town. When they had entered the streets and the sea was no longer so near:

"It seems to me, sir," said Jean, "that a good man has a right to live and that a misfortune proves nothing. Since your father has not killed himself, thank God, how can you think of dying? Since there is no dishonor in his case, and all the town knows it is so, what would they think of you? That you felt unable to endure poverty. It would be neither brave nor Christian; for, at the very worst, what is there to frighten you? There are plenty of people born poor, and who have never had either mother or father to help them on. I know that we are not all alike, but, after all, nothing is impossible to God. What would you do in such a case? Your father was not born rich, far from it,— meaning no offence—and that is perhaps what consoles him now. If you had been here, this last month, it would have given you courage. Yes, sir, a man may be ruined, nobody is secure from bankruptcy; but your father, I make bold to say, has borne himself, through it all, like a man, though he did leave us so hastily. But what could he do? It is not every day that a vessel starts for America. I accompanied him to the wharf, and if you had seen how sad he was! How he charged me to take care of you; to send him news from you!—Sir, it is a right poor idea you have, that throwing the helve after the hatchet. Every one has his time of trial in this world, and I was a soldier before I was a servant. I suffered severely at the time, but I was young; I was of your age, sir, and it seemed to me that Providence could not have spoken His last word to a young man of twenty-five. Why do you wish to prevent the kind God from repairing the evil that has befallen you? Give Him time, and all will come right. If I might advise you, I would say, just wait two or three years, and I will answer for it, you will come out all right. It is always easy to go out of this world. Why will you seize an unlucky moment?"

While Jean was thus exerting himself to persuade his master, the latter walked in silence, and, as those who suffer often do, was looking this way and that as though seeking for something which might bind him to life. As chance would have it, at this juncture, Mademoiselle Godeau, the daughter of the fermier-général, happened to pass with her governess. The mansion in which she lived was not far distant; Croisilles saw her enter it. This meeting produced on him more effect than all the reasonings in the world. I have said that he was rather erratic, and nearly always yielded to the first impulse. Without hesitating an instant, and without explanation, he suddenly left the arm of his old servant, and crossing the street, knocked at Monsieur Godeau's door.

II

When we try to picture to ourselves, nowadays, what was called a "financier" in times gone by, we invariably imagine enormous corpulence, short legs, a gigantic wig, and a broad face with a triple chin,—and it is not without reason that we have become accustomed to form such a picture of such a personage. Everyone knows to what great abuses the royal tax-farming led, and it seems as though there were a law of nature which renders fatter than the rest of mankind those who fatten, not only upon their own laziness, but also upon the work of others.

Monsieur Godeau, among financiers, was one of the most classical to be found,—that is to say, one of the fattest. At the present time he had the gout, which was nearly as fashionable in his day as the nervous headache is in ours. Stretched upon a lounge, his eyes half-closed, he was coddling himself in the coziest corner of a dainty boudoir. The panel-mirrors which surrounded him, majestically duplicated on every side his enormous person; bags filled with gold covered the table; around him, the furniture, the wainscot, the doors, the locks, the mantel-piece, the ceiling were gilded; so was his coat. I do not know but that his brain was gilded too. He was calculating the issue of a little business affair which could not fail to bring him a few thousand louis; and was even deigning to smile over it to himself when Croisilles was announced. The young man entered with an humble, but resolute air, and with every outward manifestation of that inward tumult with which we find no difficulty in crediting a man who is longing to drown himself. Monsieur Godeau was a little surprised at this unexpected visit; then he thought his daughter had been buying some trifle, and was confirmed in that thought by seeing her appear almost at the same time with the young man. He made a sign to Croisilles not to sit down but to speak. The young lady seated herself on a sofa, and Croisilles, remaining standing, expressed himself in these terms:

"Sir, my father has failed. The bankruptcy of a partner has forced him to suspend his payments, and unable to witness his own shame, he has fled to America, after having paid his last sou to his creditors. I was absent when all this happened; I have just come back and have known of these events only two hours. I am absolutely without resources, and determined to die. It is very probable that, on leaving your house, I shall throw myself into the water. In all probability, I would already have done so, if I had not chanced to meet, at the very moment, this young lady, your daughter. I love her, sir, from the very depths of my heart; for two years I have been in love with her, and my silence, until now, proves better than anything else the respect I feel for her; but to-day, in declaring my passion to you, I fulfill an imperative duty, and I would think I was offending God, if, before giving myself over to death, I did not come to ask you Mademoiselle Julie in marriage. I have not the slightest hope that you will grant this request; but I have to make it, nevertheless, for I am a good Christian, sir, and when a good Christian sees himself come to such a point of misery that he can no longer suffer life, he must at least, to extenuate his crime, exhaust all the chances which remain to him before taking the final and fatal step."

At the beginning of this speech, Monsieur Godeau had supposed that the young man came to borrow money, and so he prudently threw his handkerchief over the bags that were lying around him, preparing in advance a refusal, and a polite one, for he always felt some good-will toward the father of Croisilles. But when he had heard the young man to the end, and understood the purport of his visit, he never doubted one moment but that the poor fellow had gone completely mad. He was at first tempted to ring the bell and have him put out; but, noticing his firm demeanor, his determined look, the fermier-général took pity on so inoffensive a case of insanity. He merely told his daughter to retire, so that she might be no longer exposed to hearing such improprieties.

While Croisilles was speaking, Mademoiselle Godeau had blushed as a peach in the month of August. At her father's bidding, she retired, the young man making her a profound bow, which she did not seem to notice. Left alone with Croisilles, Monsieur Godeau coughed, rose, then dropped again upon the cushions, and, trying to assume a paternal air, delivered himself to the following effect:

"My boy," said he, "I am willing to believe that you are not poking fun at me, but you have really lost your head. I not only excuse this proceeding, but I consent not to punish you for it. I am sorry that your poor devil of a father has become bankrupt and has skipped. It is indeed very sad, and I quite understand that such a misfortune should affect your brain. Besides, I wish to do something for you; so take this stool and sit down there."

"It is useless, sir," answered Croisilles; "If you refuse me, as I see you do, I have nothing left but to take my leave. I wish you every good fortune."

"And where are you going?"

"To write to my father and say good-bye to him."

"Eh! the devil! Any one would swear you were speaking the truth. I'll be damned if I don't think you are going to drown yourself."

"Yes, sir; at least I think so, if my courage does not forsake me."

"That's a bright idea! Fie on you! How can you be such a fool? Sit down, sir, I tell you, and listen to me."

Monsieur Godeau had just made a very wise reflection, which was that it is never agreeable to have it said that a man, whoever he may be, threw himself into the water on leaving your house. He therefore coughed once more, took his snuff-box, cast a careless glance upon his shirt-frill, and continued:

"It is evident that you are nothing but a simpleton, a fool, a regular baby. You do not know what you are saying. You are ruined, that's what has happened to you. But, my dear friend, all that is not enough; one must reflect upon the things of this world. If you came to ask me—well, good advice, for instance,—I might give it to you; but what is it you are after? You are in love with my daughter?"

"Yes, sir, and I repeat to you, that I am far from supposing that you can give her to me in marriage; but as there is nothing in the world but that, which could prevent me from dying, if you believe in God, as I do not doubt you do, you will understand the reason that brings me here."

"Whether I believe in God or not, is no business of yours. I do not intend to be questioned. Answer me first: where have you seen my daughter?"

"In my father's shop, and in this house, when I brought jewelry for Mademoiselle Julie."

"Who told you her name was Julie? What are we com-

CROISILLES

ing to, great heavens! But be her name Julie or Javotte, do you know what is wanted in any one who aspires to the hand of the daughter of a fermier-général?"

"No, I am completely ignorant of it, unless it is to be as rich as she."

"Something more is necessary, my boy; you must have a name."

"Well! my name is Croisilles."

"Your name is Croisilles, poor wretch! Do you call that a name?"

"Upon my soul and conscience, sir, it seems to me to be as good a name as Godeau."

"You are very impertinent, sir, and you shall rue it."

"Indeed, sir, do not be angry; I had not the least idea of offending you. If you see in what I said anything to wound you, and wish to punish me for it, there is no need to get angry. Have I not told you that on leaving here I am going straight to drown myself?"

Although M. Godeau had promised himself to send Croisilles away as gently as possible, in order to avoid all scandal, his prudence could not resist the vexation of his wounded pride. The interview to which he had to resign himself was monstrous enough in itself; it may be imagined then, what he felt at hearing himself spoken to in such terms.

"Listen," he said, almost beside himself, and determined to close the matter at any cost. "You are not such a fool that you cannot understand a word of common sense. Are you rich? No. Are you noble? Still less so. What is this frenzy that brings you here? You come to worry me; you think you are doing something clever; you know perfectly well that it is useless; you wish to make me responsible for your death. Have you any right to complain of me? Do I owe a sou to your father? Is it my fault that you have come to this? Mon Dieu! When a man is going to drown himself, he keeps quiet about it—"

"That is what I am going to do now. I am your very humble servant."

"One moment! It shall not be said that you had recourse to me in vain. There, my boy, here are three louis d'or; go and have dinner in the kitchen, and let me hear no more about you."

"Much obliged; I am not hungry, and I have no use for your money."

So Croisilles left the room, and the financier, having set his conscience at rest by the offer he had just made, settled himself more comfortably in his chair, and resumed his meditations.

Mademoiselle Godeau, during this time, was not so far away as one might suppose; she had, it is true, withdrawn in obedience to her father; but, instead of going to her room, she had remained listening behind the door. If the extravagance of Croisilles seemed incredible to her, still she found nothing to offend her in it; for love, since the world has existed, has never passed as an insult. On the other hand, as it was not possible to doubt the despair of the young man, Mademoiselle Godeau found herself a victim, at one and the same time, to the two sentiments most dangerous to women —compassion and curiosity. When she saw the interview at an end, and Croisilles ready to come out, she rapidly crossed the drawing-room where she stood, not wishing to be surprised eavesdropping, and hurried towards her apartment; but she almost immediately retraced her steps. The idea that perhaps Croisilles was really going to put an end to his life troubled her in spite of herself. Scarcely aware of what she was doing, she walked to meet him; the drawing-room was large, and the two young people came slowly towards each other. Croisilles was as pale as death, and Mademoiselle Godeau vainly sought words to express her feelings. In passing beside him, she let fall on the floor a bunch of violets which she held in her hand. He at once bent down and picked up the bouquet in order to give it back to her, but instead of taking it, she passed on without uttering a word, and entered her father's room. Croisilles, alone again, put the flowers in his breast, and left the house with a troubled heart, not knowing what to think of his adventure.

CROISILLES

III

Scarcely had he taken a few steps in the street, when he saw his faithful friend Jean running towards him with a joyful face.

"What has happened?" he asked; "have you news to tell me?"

"Yes," replied Jean; "I have to tell you that the seals have been officially broken and that you can enter your home. All your father's debts being paid, you remain the owner of the house. It is true that all the money and all the jewels have been taken away; but at least the house belongs to you, and you have not lost everything. I have been running about for an hour, not knowing what had become of you, and I hope, my dear master, that you will now be wise enough to take a reasonable course."

"What course do you wish me to take?"

"Sell this house, sir, it is all your fortune. It will bring you about thirty thousand francs. With that at any rate you will not die of hunger; and what is to prevent you from buying a little stock in trade, and starting business for yourself? You would surely prosper."

"We shall see about this," answered Croisilles, as he hurried to the street where his home was. He was eager to see the paternal roof again. But when he arrived there so sad a spectacle met his gaze, that he had scarcely the courage to enter. The shop was in utter disorder, the rooms deserted, his father's alcove empty. Everything presented to his eyes the wretchedness of utter ruin. Not a chair remained; all the drawers had been ransacked, the till broken open, the chest taken away; nothing had escaped the greedy search of creditors and lawyers; who, after having pillaged the house, had gone, leaving the doors open, as though to testify to all passers-by how neatly their work was done.

"This, then," exclaimed Croisilles, "is all that remains after thirty years of work and a respectable life,—and all through the failure to have ready, on a given day, money enough to honor a signature imprudently given!"

While the young man walked up and down given over

to the saddest thoughts, Jean seemed very much embarrassed. He supposed that his master was without ready money, and that he might perhaps not even have dined. He was therefore trying to think of some way to question him on the subject, and to offer him, in case of need, some part of his savings. After having tortured his mind for a quarter of an hour to try and hit upon some way of leading up to the subject, he could find nothing better than to come up to Croisilles, and ask him, in a kindly voice:

"Sir, do you still like roast partridges?"

The poor man uttered this question in a tone at once so comical and so touching, that Croisilles, in spite of his sadness, could not refrain from laughing.

"And why do you ask me that?" said he.

"My wife," replied Jean, "is cooking me some for dinner, sir, and if by chance you still liked them—"

Croisilles had completely forgotten till now the money which he was bringing back to his father. Jean's proposal reminded him that his pockets were full of gold.

"I thank you with all my heart," said he to the old man, "and I accept your dinner with pleasure; but, if you are anxious about my fortune, be reassured. I have more money than I need to have a good supper this evening, which you, in your turn, will share with me."

Saying this, he laid upon the mantel four well-filled purses, which he emptied, each containing fifty louis.

"Although this sum does not belong to me," he added, "I can use it for a day or two. To whom must I go to have it forwarded to my father?"

"Sir," replied Jean, eagerly, "your father especially charged me to tell you that this money belongs to you, and, if I did not speak of it before, it was because I did not know how your affairs in Paris had turned out. Where he has gone your father will want for nothing; he will lodge with one of your correspondents, who will receive him most gladly; he has moreover taken with him enough for his immediate needs, for he was quite sure of still leaving behind more than was necessary to pay all his just debts. All that he has left, sir, is yours; he says so himself in his letter, and I am especially charged to repeat it to you. That gold is,

CROISILLES

therefore, legitimately your property, as this house in which we are now. I can repeat to you the very words your father said to me on embarking: 'May my son forgive me for leaving him; may he remember that I am still in the world only to love me, and let him use what remains after my debts are paid as though it were his inheritance.' Those, sir, are his own expressions; so put this back in your pocket, and, since you accept my dinner, pray let us go home."

The honest joy which shone in Jean's eyes, left no doubt in the mind of Croisilles. The words of his father had moved him to such a point that he could not restrain his tears; on the other hand, at such a moment, four thousand francs were no bagatelle. As to the house, it was not an available resource, for one could realize on it only by selling it, and that was both difficult and slow. All this, however, could not but make a considerable change in the situation the young man found himself in; so he felt suddenly moved— shaken in his dismal resolution, and, so to speak, both sad and, at the same time, relieved of much of his distress. After having closed the shutters of the shop, he left the house with Jean, and as he once more crossed the town, could not help thinking how small a thing our affections are, since they sometimes serve to make us find an unforeseen joy in the faintest ray of hope. It was with this thought that he sat down to dinner beside his old servant, who did not fail, during the repast, to make every effort to cheer him.

Heedless people have a happy fault. They are easily cast down, but they have not even the trouble to console themselves, so changeable is their mind. It would be a mistake to think them, on that account, insensible or selfish; on the contrary they perhaps feel more keenly than others and are but too prone to blow their brains out in a moment of despair; but, this moment once passed, if they are still alive, they must dine, they must eat, they must drink, as usual; only to melt into tears again, at bed-time. Joy and pain do not glide over them but pierce them through like arrows. Kind, hot-headed natures which know how to suffer, but not how to lie, through which one can clearly read,—not fragile and empty like glass, but solid and transparent like rock crystal.

ALFRED DE MUSSET

After having clinked glasses with Jean, Croisilles, instead of drowning himself, went to the play. Standing at the back of the pit, he drew from his bosom Mademoiselle Godeau's bouquet, and, as he breathed the perfume in deep meditation, he began to think in a calmer spirit about his adventure of the morning. As soon as he had pondered over it for awhile, he saw clearly the truth; that is to say, that the young lady, in leaving the bouquet in his hands, and in refusing to take it back, had wished to give him a mark of interest; for otherwise this refusal and this silence could only have been marks of contempt, and such a supposition was not possible. Croisilles, therefore, judged that Mademoiselle Godeau's heart was of a softer grain than her father's and he remembered distinctly that the young lady's face, when she crossed the drawing-room, had expressed an emotion the more true that it seemed involuntary. But was this emotion one of love, or only of sympathy? Or was it perhaps something of still less importance,—mere commonplace pity? Had Mademoiselle Godeau feared to see him die—him, Croisilles—or merely to be the cause of the death of a man, no matter what man? Although withered and almost leafless, the bouquet still retained so exquisite an odor and so brave a look, that in breathing it and looking at it, Croisilles could not help hoping. It was a thin garland of roses round a bunch of violets. What mysterious depths of sentiment an Oriental might have read in these flowers, by interpreting their language! But after all, he need not be an Oriental in this case. The flowers which fall from the breast of a pretty woman, in Europe, as in the East, are never mute; were they but to tell what they have seen while reposing in that lovely bosom, it would be enough for a lover, and this, in fact, they do. Perfumes have more than one resemblance to love, and there are even people who think love to be but a sort of perfume; it is true the flowers which exhale it are the most beautiful in creation.

While Croisilles mused thus, paying very little attention to the tragedy that was being acted at the time, Mademoiselle Godeau herself appeared in a box opposite.

The idea did not occur to the young man that, if she should notice him, she might think it very strange to find the would-be suicide there after what had transpired in the morning. He, on the contrary, bent all his efforts towards getting nearer to her; but he could not succeed. A fifth-rate actress from Paris had come to play Mérope, and the crowd was so dense that one could not move. For lack of anything better, Croisilles had to content himself with fixing his gaze upon his lady-love, not lifting his eyes from her for a moment. He noticed that she seemed pre-occupied and moody, and that she spoke to every one with a sort of repugnance. Her box was surrounded, as may be imagined, by all the fops of the neighborhood, each of whom passed several times before her in the gallery, totally unable to enter the box, of which her father filled more than three-fourths. Croisilles noticed further that she was not using her opera-glasses, nor was she listening to the play. Her elbows resting on the balustrade, her chin in her hand, with her far-away look, she seemed, in all her sumptuous apparel, like some statue of Venus disguised en marquise. The display of her dress and her hair, her rouge, beneath which one could guess her paleness, all the splendor of her toilet, did but the more distinctly bring out the immobility of her countenance. Never had Croisilles seen her so beautiful. Having found means, between the acts, to escape from the crush, he hurried off to look at her from the passage leading to her box, and, strange to say, scarcely had he reached it, when Mademoiselle Godeau, who had not stirred for the last hour, turned round. She started slightly as she noticed him and only cast a glance at him; then she resumed her former attitude. Whether that glance expressed surprise, anxiety, pleasure or love; whether it meant "What, not dead!" or "God be praised! There you are, living!"—I do not pretend to explain. Be that as it may; at that glance, Croisilles inwardly swore to himself to die or gain her love.

IV

Of all the obstacles which hinder the smooth course of love, the greatest is, without doubt, what is called false shame, which is indeed a very potent obstacle.

Croisilles was not troubled with this unhappy failing.

which both pride and timidity combine to produce; he was not one of those who, for whole months, hover round the woman they love, like a cat round a caged bird. As soon as he had given up the idea of drowning himself, he thought only of letting his dear Julie know that he lived solely for her. But how could he tell her so? Should he present himself a second time at the mansion of the fermier-général, it was but too certain that M. Godeau would have him ejected. Julie, when she happened to take a walk, never went without her maid; it was therefore useless to undertake to follow her. To pass the nights under the windows of one's beloved is a folly dear to lovers, but, in the present case, it would certainly prove vain. I said before that Croisilles was very religious; it therefore never entered his mind to seek to meet his lady-love at church. As the best way, though the most dangerous, is to write to people when one cannot speak to them in person, he decided on the very next day to write to the young lady.

His letter possessed, naturally, neither order nor reason. It read somewhat as follows:

"Mademoiselle,—Tell me exactly, I beg of you, what fortune one must possess to be able to pretend to your hand. I am asking you a strange question; but I love you so desperately, that it is impossible for me not to ask it, and you are the only person in the world to whom I can address it. It seemed to me, last evening, that you looked at me at the play. I had wished to die; would to God I were indeed dead, if I am mistaken, and if that look was not meant for me. Tell me if Fate can be so cruel as to let a man deceive himself in a manner at once so sad and so sweet. I believe that you commanded me to live. You are rich, beautiful. I know it. Your father is arrogant and miserly, and you have a right to be proud; but I love you, and the rest is a dream. Fix your charming eyes on me; think of what love can do, when I who suffer so cruelly, who must stand in fear of every thing, feel, nevertheless, an inexpressible joy in writing you this mad letter, which will perhaps bring down your anger upon me. But think also, mademoiselle, that you are a little to blame for this, my folly. Why did you drop that bouquet? Put yourself for an instant, if possible, in my place; I dare think that you love me, and I dare ask you to tell me so. Forgive me, I beseech you. I would give my life's blood to be sure of not offending you, and to see you listening to my love with that angel smile which belongs only to you.

"Whatever you may do, your image remains mine; you can remove it only by tearing out my heart. As long as your look lives in my remembrance, as long as the bouquet keeps a trace of its perfume, as long as a word will tell of love, I will cherish hope."

Having sealed his letter, Croisilles went out and walked up and down the street opposite the Godeau mansion, waiting for a servant to come out. Chance, which always serves mysterious loves, when it can do so without compromising itself, willed it that Mademoiselle Julie's maid should have arranged to purchase a cap on that day. She was going to the milliner's when Croisilles accosted her, slipped a louis into her hand, and asked her to take charge of his letter. The bargain was soon struck; the servant took the money to pay for her cap and promised to do the errand out of gratitude. Croisilles, full of joy, went home and sat at his door awaiting an answer.

Before speaking of this answer, a word must be said about Mademoiselle Godeau. She was not quite free from the vanity of her father, but her good nature was ever uppermost. She was, in the full meaning of the term, a spoilt child. She habitually spoke very little, and never was she seen with a needle in her hand; she spent her days at her toilet, and her evenings on the sofa, not seeming to hear the conversation going on around her. As regards her dress, she was prodigiously coquettish, and her own face was surely what she thought most of on earth. A wrinkle in her collarette, an ink-spot on her finger, would have distressed her; and, when her dress pleased her, nothing can describe the last look which she cast at her mirror before leaving the room. She showed neither taste nor aversion for the pleasures in which young ladies usually delight. She went to balls willingly enough, and renounced going to them without a show of temper, sometimes without motive. The play wearied her, and she was in the constant habit of falling asleep there. When her father, who worshipped her, proposed to make her some present of her own choice, she took an hour to decide, not being able to think of anything she cared for. When M. Godeau gave a reception or a dinner, it often happened that Julie would not appear in the drawing-room, and at such times she passed the evening alone in her own room, in full dress, walking up and down, her fan in her hand. If a compliment was addressed to her, she turned away her head, and if any one attempted to pay court to her, she responded only by a look at once so dazzling and so serious as to disconcert even the boldest. Never had a sally made her laugh; never had an air in an opera, a flight of tragedy, moved her; indeed, never had her heart given a sign of life; and, on seeing her pass in all the splendor of her nonchalant loveliness one might have taken her for a beautiful somnambulist, walking through the world as in a trance.

So much indifference and coquetry did not seem easy to understand. Some said she loved nothing, others that she loved nothing but herself. A single word, however, suffices to explain her character,—she was waiting. From the age of fourteen she had heard it ceaselessly repeated that nothing was so charming as she. She was convinced of this, and that was why she paid so much attention to dress. In failing to do honor to her own person, she would have thought herself guilty of sacrilege. She walked, in her beauty, so to speak, like a child in its holiday dress; but she was very far from thinking that her beauty was to remain useless. Beneath her apparent unconcern she had a will, secret, inflexible, and the more potent the better it was concealed. The coquetry of ordinary women, which spends itself in ogling, in simpering, and in smiling, seemed to her a childish, vain, almost contemptible way of fighting with shadows. She felt herself in possession of a treasure, and she disdained to stake it piece by piece; she needed an adversary worthy of herself; but, too accustomed to see her wishes anticipated, she did not seek that adversary; it may even be said that she felt astonished at his failing to present himself. For the four or five years that she had been out in society and had conscientiously displayed her flowers, her furbelows, and her beautiful shoulders, it seemed to her inconceivable that she had not yet inspired some great passion. Had she said what was really behind her thoughts, she certainly would have replied to her many flatterers: "Well! if it is true that I am so beautiful, why do you not blow your brains out for me?" An answer which many other young girls might make, and which more than one who says nothing hides away in a corner of her heart, not far perhaps from the tip of her tongue.

What is there, indeed, in the world, more tantalizing for a woman than to be young, rich, beautiful, to look at herself in her mirror and see herself charmingly dressed, worthy in every way to please, fully disposed to allow herself to be loved, and to have to say to herself: "I am admired, I am praised, all the world thinks me charming, but nobody loves me. My gown is by the best maker, my laces are superb, my coiffure is irreproachable, my face the most beautiful on earth, my figure slender, my foot prettily turned, and all this helps me to nothing but to go and yawn in the corner of some drawing-room! If a young man speaks to me he treats me as a child; if I am asked in marriage, it is for my dowry; if somebody presses my hand in a dance, it is sure to be some provincial fop; as soon as I appear anywhere, I excite a murmur of admiration; but nobody speaks low, in my ear, a word that makes my heart beat. I hear impertinent men praising me in loud tones, a couple of feet away, and never a look of humbly sincere adoration meets mine. Still I have an ardent soul full of life, and I am not, by any means, only a pretty doll to be shown about, to be made to dance at a ball, to be dressed by a maid in the morning and undressed at night—beginning the whole thing over again the next day."

That is what Mademoiselle Godeau had many times said to herself; and there were hours when that thought inspired her with so gloomy a feeling that she remained mute and almost motionless for a whole day. When Croisilles wrote her, she was in just such a fit of ill-humor. She had just been taking her chocolate and was deep in meditation, stretched upon a lounge, when her maid entered and handed her the letter with a mysterious air. She looked at the address, and not recognizing the handwriting, fell again to musing. The maid then saw herself forced to explain what it was, which she did with a rather disconcerted air, not being at all sure how the young lady would take the matter. Mademoiselle Godeau listened without moving, then opened the letter, and cast only a glance at it; she at once asked for a sheet of paper, and nonchalantly wrote these few words:

"No, sir, I assure you I am not proud. If you had only a hundred thousand crowns, I would willingly marry you."

Such was the reply which the maid at once took to Croisilles, who gave her another louis for her trouble.

V

A hundred thousand crowns are not found "in a donkey's hoof-print," and if Croisilles had been suspicious he might have thought in reading Mademoiselle Godeau's letter that she was either crazy or laughing at him. He thought neither, for he only saw in it that his darling Julie loved him, and that he must have a hundred thousand crowns, and he dreamed from that moment of nothing but trying to secure them.

He possessed two hundred louis in cash, plus a house which, as I have said, might be worth about thirty thousand francs. What was to be done? How was he to go about transfiguring these thirty-four thousand francs, at a jump, into three hundred thousand. The first idea which came into the mind of the young man was to find some way of staking his whole fortune on the toss-up of a coin, but for that he must sell the house. Croisilles therefore began by putting a notice upon the door, stating that his house was for sale; then, while dreaming what he would do with the money that he would get for it, he awaited a purchaser.

A week went by, then another; not a single purchaser applied. More and more distressed, Croisilles spent these days with Jean, and despair was taking possession of him once more, when a Jewish broker rang at the door.

CROISILLES

"This house is for sale, sir, is it not? Are you the owner of it?"

"Yes, sir."

"And how much is it worth?"

"Thirty thousand francs, I believe; at least I have heard my father say so."

The Jew visited all the rooms, went upstairs and down into the cellar, knocking on the walls, counting the steps of the staircase, turning the doors on their hinges and the keys in their locks, opening and closing the windows; then, at last, after having thoroughly examined everything, without saying a word and without making the slightest proposal, he bowed to Croisilles and retired.

Croisilles, who for a whole hour had followed him with a palpitating heart, as may be imagined, was not a little disappointed at this silent retreat. He thought that perhaps the Jew had wished to give himself time to reflect and that he would return presently. He waited a week for him, not daring to go out for fear of missing his visit, and looking out of the windows from morning till night. But it was in vain; the Jew did not reappear. Jean, true to his unpleasant rôle of adviser, brought moral pressure to bear to dissuade his master from selling his house in so hasty a manner and for so extravagant a purpose. Dying of impatience, ennui, and love, Croisilles one morning took his two hundred louis and went out, determined to tempt fortune with this sum, since he could not have more.

The gaming-houses at that time were not public, and that refinement of civilization which enables the first comer to ruin himself at all hours, as soon as the wish enters his mind, had not yet been invented.

Scarcely was Croisilles in the street before he stopped, not knowing where to go to stake his money. He looked at the houses of the neighborhood, and eyed them, one after the other, striving to discover suspicious appearances that might point out to him the object of his search. A good-looking young man, splendidly dressed, happened to pass. Judging from his mien, he was certainly a young man of gentle blood and ample leisure, so Croisilles politely accosted him.

"Sir," he said, "I beg your pardon for the liberty I take.

I have two hundred louis in my pocket and I am dying either to lose them or win more. Could you not point out to me some respectable place where such things are done?"

At this rather strange speech the young man burst out laughing.

"Upon my word, sir!" answered he, "if you are seeking any such wicked place you have but to follow me, for that is just where I am going."

Croisilles followed him, and a few steps farther they both entered a house of very attractive appearance, where they were received hospitably by an old gentleman of the highest breeding. Several young men were already seated round a green cloth. Croisilles modestly took a place there, and in less than an hour his two hundred louis were gone.

He came out as sad as a lover can be who thinks himself beloved. He had not enough to dine with, but that did not cause him any anxiety.

"What can I do now," he asked himself, "to get money? To whom shall I address myself in this town? Who will lend me even a hundred louis on this house that I can not sell?"

While he was in this quandary, he met his Jewish broker. He did not hesitate to address him, and, featherhead as he was, did not fail to tell him the plight he was in.

The Jew did not much want to buy the house; he had come to see it only through curiosity, or, to speak more exactly, for the satisfaction of his own conscience, as a passing dog goes into a kitchen, the door of which stands open, to see if there is nothing to steal. But when he saw Croisilles so despondent, so sad, so bereft of all resources, he could not resist the temptation to put himself to some inconvenience, even, in order to pay for the house. He therefore offered him about one-fourth of its value. Croisilles fell upon his neck, called him his friend and saviour, blindly signed a bargain that would have made one's hair stand on end, and, on the very next day, the possessor of four hundred new louis, he once more turned his steps toward the gambling-house where he had been so politely and speedily ruined the night before.

On his way, he passed by the wharf. A vessel was about leaving; the wind was gentle, the ocean tranquil. On all

CROISILLES

sides, merchants, sailors, officers in uniform were coming and going. Porters were carrying enormous bales of merchandise. Passengers and their friends were exchanging farewells, small boats were rowing about in all directions; on every face could be read fear, impatience, or hope; and, amidst all the agitation which surrounded it, the majestic vessel swayed gently to and fro under the wind that swelled her proud sails.

"What a grand thing it is," thought Croisilles, "to risk all one possesses and go beyond the sea, in perilous search of fortune! How it fills me with emotion to look at this vessel setting out on her voyage, loaded with so much wealth, with the welfare of so many families! What joy to see her come back again, bringing twice as much as was intrusted to her, returning so much prouder and richer than she went away! Why am I not one of those merchants? Why could I not stake my four hundred louis in this way? This immense sea! What a green cloth, on which to boldly tempt fortune! Why should I not myself buy a few bales of cloth or silk? What is to prevent my doing so, since I have gold? Why should this captain refuse to take charge of my merchandise? And who knows? Instead of going and throwing away this—my little all—in a gambling-house, I might double it, I might triple it, perhaps, by honest industry. If Julie truly loves me, she will wait a few years, she will remain true to me until I am able to marry her. Commerce sometimes yields greater profits than one thinks; examples are not wanting in this world of wealth gained with astonishing rapidity in this way on the changing waves —why should Providence not bless an endeavor made for a purpose so laudable, so worthy of His assistance? Among these merchants who have accumulated so much and who send their vessels to the ends of the world, more than one has begun with a smaller sum than I have now. They have prospered with the help of God; why should I not prosper in my turn? It seems to me as though a good wind were filling these sails, and this vessel inspires confidence. Come! the die is cast; I will speak to the captain, who seems to be a good fellow; I will then write to Julie, and set out to become a clever and successful trader."

The greatest danger incurred by those who are habitually but half crazy, is that of becoming, at times, altogether so. The poor fellow, without further deliberation, put his whim into execution. To find goods to buy, when one has money and knows nothing about the goods, is the easiest thing in the world. The captain, to oblige Croisilles, took him to one of his friends, a manufacturer, who sold him as much cloth and silk as he could pay for. The whole of it, loaded upon a cart, was promptly taken on board. Croisilles, delighted and full of hope, had himself written in large letters his name upon the bales. He watched them being put on board with inexpressible joy; the hour of departure soon came, and the vessel weighed anchor.

VI

I need not say that in this transaction, Croisilles had kept no money in hand. His house was sold; and there remained to him, for his sole fortune, the clothes he had on his back;— no home, and not a sou. With the best will possible, Jean could not suppose that his master was reduced to such an extremity; Croisilles was not two proud, but too thoughtless to tell him of it. So he determined to sleep under the starry vault, and as for his meals, he made the following calculation: he presumed that the vessel which bore his fortune would be six months before coming back to Havre; Croisilles, therefore, not without regret, sold a gold watch his father had given him, and which he had fortunately kept; he got thirty-six livres for it. That was sufficient to live on for about six months, at the rate of four sous a day. He did not doubt that it would be enough, and, reassured for the present, he wrote to Mademoiselle Godeau to inform her of what he had done. He was very careful in his letter not to speak of his distress; he announced to her, on the contrary, that he had undertaken a magnificent commercial enterprise, of the speedy and fortunate issue of which there could be no doubt; he explained to her that La Fleurette, a merchant-vessel of one hundred and fifty tons, was carrying to the Baltic his cloths and his silks, and implored her to remain faithful to him for a year, reserving to himself the right of

CROISILLES

asking, later on, for a further delay, while, for his part, he swore eternal love to her.

When Mademoiselle Godeau received this letter, she was sitting before the fire, and had in her hand, using it as a screen, one of those bulletins which are printed in seaports, announcing the arrival and departure of vessels, and which also report disasters at sea. It had never occurred to her, as one can well imagine, to take an interest in this sort of thing; she had in fact never glanced at any of these sheets. The perusal of Croisilles' letter prompted her to read the bulletin she had been holding in her hand; the first word that caught her eye was no other than the name of La Fleurette.—The vessel had been wrecked on the coast of France, on the very night following its departure. The crew had barely escaped, but all the cargo was lost.

Mademoiselle Godeau, at this news, no longer remembered that Croisilles had made to her an avowal of his poverty; she was as heartbroken as though a million had been at stake. In an instant, the horrors of the tempest, the fury of the winds, the cries of the drowning, the ruin of the man who loved her, presented themselves to her mind like a scene in a romance. The bulletin and the letter fell from her hands. She rose in great agitation, and, with heaving breast and eyes brimming with tears, paced up and down, determined to act, and asking herself how she should act.

There is one thing that must be said in justice to love; it is that the stronger, the clearer, the simpler the considerations opposed to it, in a word, the less common sense there is in the matter, the wilder does the passion become and the more does the lover love. It is one of the most beautiful things under heaven, this irrationality of the heart. We should not be worth much without it. After having walked about the room (without forgetting either her dear fan or the passing glance at the mirror), Julie allowed herself to sink once more upon her lounge. Whoever had seen her at this moment would have looked upon a lovely sight; her eyes sparkled, her cheeks were on fire; she sighed deeply, and murmured in a delicious transport of joy and pain:

"Poor fellow! He has ruined himself for me!"

Independently of the fortune which she could expect from

her father, Mademoiselle Godeau had in her own right the property her mother had left her. She had never thought of it. At this moment, for the first time in her life, she remembered that she could dispose of five hundred thousand francs. This thought brought a smile to her lips; a project, strange, bold, wholly feminine, almost as mad as Croisilles himself, entered her head;—she weighed the idea in her mind for some time, then decided to act upon it at once.

She began by inquiring whether Croisilles had any relatives or friends; the maid was sent out in all directions to find out. Having made minute inquiries in all quarters, she discovered, on the fourth floor of an old rickety house, a half-crippled aunt, who never stirred from her arm-chair, and had not been out for four or five years. This poor woman, very old, seemed to have been left in the world expressly as a specimen of hungry misery. Blind, gouty, almost deaf, she lived alone in a garret; but a gayety, stronger than misfortune and illness, sustained her at eighty years of age, and made her still love life. Her neighbors never passed her door without going in to see her, and the antiquated tunes she hummed enlivened all the girls of the neighborhood. She possessed a little annuity which sufficed to maintain her; as long as day lasted, she knitted. She did not know what had happened since the death of Louis XIV.

It was to this worthy person that Julie had herself privately conducted. She donned for the occasion all her finery; feathers, laces, ribbons, diamonds, nothing was spared. She wanted to be fascinating; but the real secret of her beauty, in this case, was the whim that was carrying her away. She went up the steep, dark staircase which led to the good lady's chamber, and, after the most graceful bow, spoke somewhat as follows:

"You have, madame, a nephew, called Croisilles, who loves me and has asked for my hand; I love him too and wish to marry him; but my father, Monsieur Godeau, fermier-général of this town, refuses his consent, because your nephew is not rich. I would not, for the world, give occasion to scandal, nor cause trouble to anybody; I would therefore never think of disposing of myself without the consent of my family. I come to ask you a favor, which I beseech you

CROISILLES

to grant me. You must come yourself and propose this marriage to my father. I have, thank God, a little fortune which is quite at your disposal; you may take possession, whenever you see fit, of five hundred thousand francs at my notary's. You will say that this sum belongs to your nephew, which in fact it does. It is not a present that I am making him, it is a debt which I am paying, for I am the cause of the ruin of Croisilles, and it is but just that I should repair it. My father will not easily give in; you will be obliged to insist and you must have a little courage; I, for my part, will not fail. As nobody on earth excepting myself has any right to the sum of which I am speaking to you, nobody will ever know in what way this amount will have passed into your hands. You are not very rich yourself, I know, and you may fear that people will be astonished to see you thus endowing your nephew; but remember that my father does not know you, that you show yourself very little in town, and that, consequently, it will be easy for you to pretend that you have just arrived from some journey. This step will doubtless be some exertion to you; you will have to leave your arm-chair and take a little trouble; but you will make two people happy, madame, and if you have ever known love, I hope you will not refuse me."

The old lady, during this discourse, had been in turn surprised, anxious, touched, and delighted. The last words persuaded her.

"Yes, my child," she repeated several times, "I know what it is,—I know what it is."

As she said this she made an effort to rise; her feeble limbs could barely support her; Julie quickly advanced and put out her hand to help her; by an almost involuntary movement they found themselves, in an instant, in each other's arms. A treaty was at once concluded; a warm kiss sealed it in advance, and the necessary and confidential consultation followed without further trouble.

All the explanations having been made, the good lady drew from her wardrobe a venerable gown of taffeta, which had been her wedding-dress. This antique piece of property was not less than fifty years old; but not a spot, not a grain of dust had disfigured it; Julie was in ecstasies over it. A coach was sent for, the handsomest in the town. The good lady prepared the speech she was going to make to Monsieur Godeau; Julie tried to teach her how she was to touch the heart of her father, and did not hesitate to confess that love of rank was his vulnerable point.

"If you could imagine," said she, "a means of flattering this weakness, you will have won our cause."

The good lady pondered deeply, finished her toilet without another word, clasped the hands of her future niece, and entered the carriage. She soon arrived at the Godeau mansion; there, she braced herself up so gallantly for her entrance that she seemed ten years younger. She majestically crossed the drawing-room where Julie's bouquet had fallen, and when the door of the boudoir opened, said in a firm voice to the lackey who preceded her:

"Announce the dowager Baroness de Croisilles."

These words settled the happiness of the two lovers. Monsieur Godeau was bewildered by them. Although five hundred thousand francs seemed little to him, he consented to everything, in order to make his daughter a baroness, and such she became;—who would dare contest her title? For my part, I think she had thoroughly earned it.

THE VASE OF CLAY
BY JEAN AICARD

THE VASE OF CLAY
A STORY
By JEAN AICARD

I

JEAN had inherited from his father a little field close beside the sea. Round this field the branches of the pine trees murmured a response to the plashing of the waves. Beneath the pines the soil was red, and the crimson shade of the earth mingling with the blue waves of the bay gave them a pensive violet hue, most of all in the quiet evening hours dear to reveries and dreams.

In this field grew roses and raspberries. The pretty girls of the neighborhood came to Jean's home to buy these fruits and flowers, so like their own lips and cheeks. The roses, the lips, and the berries had all the same youth, had all the same beauty.

Jean lived happily beside the sea, at the foot of the hills, beneath an olive tree planted near his door, which in all seasons threw a lance-like blue shadow upon his white wall.

Near the olive tree was a well, the water of which was so cold and pure that the girls of the region, with their cheeks like roses and their lips like raspberries, came thither night and morning with their jugs. Upon their heads, covered with pads, they carried their jugs, round and slender as themselves, supporting them with their beautiful bare arms, raised aloft like living handles.

Copyrighted 1909 Current Literature Publishing Company.

JEAN AICARD

Jean observed all these things, and admired them, and blessed his life.

As he was only twenty years old, he fondly loved one of the charming girls who drew water from his well, who ate his raspberries and breathed the fragrance of his roses.

He told this younger girl that she was as pure and fresh as the water, as delicious as the raspberries and as sweet as the roses.

Then the young girl smiled.

He told it her again, and she made a face at him.

He sang her the same song, and she married a sailor who carried her far away beyond the sea.

Jean wept bitterly, but he still admired beautiful things, and still blessed his life. Sometimes he thought that the frailty of what is beautiful and the brevity of what is good adds value to the beauty and goodness of all things.

II

One day he learned by chance that the red earth of his field was an excellent clay. He took a little of it in his hand, moistened it with water from his well, and fashioned a simple vase, while he thought of those beautiful girls who are like the ancient Greek jars, at once round and slender.

The earth in his field was, indeed, excellent clay.

He built himself a potter's wheel. With his own hands, and with his clay, he built a furnace against the wall of his house, and he set himself to making little pots to hold raspberries.

He became skilful at this work, and all the gardeners round about came to him to provide themselves with these light, porous pots, of a beautiful red hue, round and slender, wherein the raspberries could be heaped without crushing them, and where they slept under the shelter of a green leaf.

THE VASE OF CLAY

The leaf, the pot, the raspberries, these enchanted everybody by their form and color; and the buyers in the city market would have no berries save those which were sold in Jean the potter's round and slender pots.

Now more than ever the beautiful girls visited Jean's field.

Now they brought baskets of woven reeds in which they piled the empty pots, red and fresh. But now Jean observed them without desire. His heart was forevermore far away beyond the sea.

Still, as he deepened and broadened the ditch in his field, from which he took the clay, he saw that his pots to hold the raspberries were variously colored, tinted sometimes with rose, sometimes with blue or violet, sometimes with black or green.

These shades of the clay reminded him of the loveliest things which had gladdened his eyes: plants, flowers, ocean, sky.

Then he set himself to choose, in making his vases, shades of clay, which he mingled delicately. And these colors, produced by centuries of alternating lights and shadows, obeyed his will, changed in a moment according to his desire.

Each day he modelled hundreds of these raspberry pots, moulding them upon the wheel which turned like a sun beneath the pressure of his agile foot. The mass of shapeless clay, turning on the center of the disk, under the touch of his finger, suddenly raised itself like the petals of a lily, lengthened, broadened, swelled or shrank, submissive to his will.

The creative potter loved the clay.

III

As he still dreamed of the things which he had most admired, his thought, his remembrance, his will, descended into his fingers, where—without his knowing how—they communicated to the clay that mysterious principle of life which the

JEAN AICARD

wisest man is unable to define. The humble works of Jean the potter had marvellous graces. In such a curve, in such a tint, he put some memory of youth, or of an opening blossom, or the very color of the weather, and of joy or sorrow.

In his hours of repose he walked with his eyes fixed upon the ground, studying the variations in the color of the soil on the cliffs, on the plains, on the sides of the hills.

And the wish came to him to model a unique vase, a marvellous vase, in which should live through all eternity something of all the fragile beauties which his eyes had gazed upon; something even of all the brief joys which his heart had known, and even a little of his divine sorrows of hope, regret and love.

He was then in the full strength and vigor of manhood.

Yet, that he might the better meditate upon his desire he forsook the well-paid work, which, it is true, had allowed him to lay aside a little hoard. No longer, as of old, his wheel turned from morning until night. He permitted other potters to manufacture raspberry pots by the thousand. The merchants forgot the way to Jean's field.

The young girls still came there for pleasure, because of the cold water, the roses, and the raspberries; but the ill-cultivated raspberries perished, the rose-vines ran wild, climbed to the tops of the high walls, and offered their dusty blossoms to the travellers on the road.

The water in the well alone remained the same, cold and plenteous, and that sufficed to draw about Jean eternal youth and eternal gaiety.

Only youth had grown mocking for Jean. For him gaiety had now become scoffing.

"Ah, Master Jean! Does not your furnace burn any more? Your wheel, Master Jean, does it scarcely ever turn? When shall we see your amazing pot which will be as beautiful as everything which is beautiful, blooming like the rose, beaded like the raspberry, and speak-

THE VASE OF CLAY

ing—if we must believe what you say about it—like our lips?"

Now Jean is ageing; Jean is old. He sits upon his stone seat beside the well, under the lace-like shade of the olive tree, in front of his empty field, all the soil of which is good clay but which no longer produces either raspberries or roses.

Jean said formerly: "There are three things: roses, raspberries, lips."

All the three have forsaken him.

The lips of the young girls, and even those of the children, have become scoffing.

"Ah, Father Jean! Do you live like the grasshoppers? Nobody ever sees you eat, Father Jean! Father Jean lives on cold water. The man who grows old becomes a child again!

"What will you put into your beautiful vase, if you ever make it, silly old fellow? It will not hold even a drop of water from your well. Go and paint the hen-coops and make water-jugs!"

Jean silently shakes his head, and only replies to all these railleries by a kindly smile.

He is good to animals, and he shares his dry bread with the poor.

It is true that he eats scarcely anything, but he does not suffer in consequence. He is very thin, but his flesh is all the more sound and wholesome. Under the arch of his eyebrows his old eyes, heedful of the world, continue to sparkle with the clearness of the spring which reflects the light.

IV

One bright morning, upon his wheel, which turns to the rhythmic motion of his foot, Jean sets himself to model a vase, the vase which he has long seen with his mind's eye.

The horizontal wheel turns like a sun to the rhythmic

beating of his foot. The wheel turns. The clay vase rises, falls, swells, becomes crushed into a shapeless mass, to be born again under Jean's hand. At last, with one single burst, it springs forth like an unlooked-for flower from an invisible stem.

It blooms triumphantly, and the old man bears it in his trembling hands to the carefully prepared furnace where fire must add to its beauty of form the illusive, decisive beauty of color.

All through the night Jean has kept up and carefully regulated the furnace-fire, that artisan of delicate gradations of color.

At dawn the work must be finished.

And the potter, old and dying, in his deserted field, raises toward the light of the rising sun the dainty form, born of himself, in which he longs to find, in perfect harmony, the dream of his long life.

In the form and tint of the frail little vase he has wished to fix for all time the ephemeral forms and colors of all the most beautiful things.

Oh, god of day! The miracle is accomplished. The sun lights the round and slender curves, the colorations infinitely refined, which blend harmoniously, and bring back to the soul of the aged man, by the pathway of his eyes, the sweetest joys of his youth, the skies of daybreak and the mournful violet waves of the sea beneath the setting sun.

Oh, miracle of art, in which life is thus epitomized to make joy eternal!

The humble artist raises toward the sun his fragile masterpiece, the flower of his simple heart; he raises it in his trembling hands as though to offer it to the unknown divinities who created primeval beauty.

But his hands, too weak and trembling, let it escape from them suddenly, even as his tottering body lets his soul escape—and the potter's dream, fallen with him to the ground, breaks and scatters into fragments.

THE VASE OF CLAY

Where is it now, the form of that vase brought to the light for an instant, and seen only by the sun and the humble artist? Surely, it must be somewhere, that pure and happy form of the divine dream, made real for an instant!